Kudos for The Heartland File

In his second novel, *The Heartland File*, Bill Charland combines outrageous humor and keen insight into the flaws in academia with down-to-earth, good writing. He starts the book with the hero, Matt, and his wife, Cynthia, driving a rented truck across the country, headed for a new life with Matt as dean at his alma mater, Hopewell College, in Mayflower, Kansas. From Matt and Cynthia's arrival on campus to an amazing, totally unexpected climax, Charland skillfully builds his plot from one revelation to the next, never allowing his characters—or his readers—a moment's rest. Be warned from the outset: you won't want to put this book down until you have read the last page.

Linda Jo Scott , PhD

A young academic leaves his eastern university to return to the midwestern college where he earned his BA and played basketball. You might think that sounds like a rather low-keyed affair, but you would be wrong. The young narrator and protagonist, Matt Bradshaw, finds himself at a campus under siege by known and unknown forces and must, like some Harrison Ford character, somehow rise to meet one challenge after another.

The challenges he faces are not just those of academia. Major social forces and daunting personalities conspire against the existence of the little liberal arts college and its ideals. As the novel rushes to its conclusion in a series of intrigues and revelations, Bradshaw is at the center of a maelstrom involving the college, the town, a religious cult, and a voracious corporation in the mounting information age. Like every good novel, *The Heartland File* will grip you and make you wonder and think.

Paul Heffron, PhD

Bill Charland's wit and acuity are at their wickedest as he gives us a look inside the bubbling cauldron of a small college in crisis. The takeaway for readers is an increased understanding of how things work—and a lingering aura of delight.

Rick Stansberger, MFA, author of *Expelling Trelnitz*

The
Heartland File

The
Heartland File

William Charland

The Heartland File

Cover art: Catherine J. Lee, www.catherinejlee.com

Published by Wheatmark®
610 East Delano Street, Suite 104
Tucson, Arizona 85705 U.S.A.
www.wheatmark.com

International Standard Book Number: 978-1-60494-055-8
Library of Congress Control Number: 2008923114

for Phoebe

"If a college did nothing else in this Western land than, by its sharp contrast with eager haste for wealth and power, to show by its quiet, patient, long continuous following of something that did not immediately pay, that life had another and possibly a wiser interpretation, this result alone would justify all that is done to build it up...

"What can be nobler than to found an institution that, by the simple force of its daily life, shall go out among the young and call each one to a higher life than he could have found without it!"

Joseph Ward,
Founder of Yankton College

1

*T*here was no shade.

Cynthia saw that first, about twenty miles west of Topeka. "Jesus, Matt. You can count the trees out here!"

It was true. A couple of hours into Kansas, the wooded hills that had lined the Kansas River had gone bare. Now the earth rose in groundswells, undulating into the distance like an endless, enveloping sea. I suppose I'd driven this way any number of times as a kid, but I'd never really noticed the landscape; when you grow up in Wichita, there's a lot about the plains you take for granted. But today the terrain looked different through the eyes of my East Coast wife. It was August, 1995.

"My God, this place is barren. And it's hot as hell. What do you suppose the temperature is?"

"You got me, Cyn. As far as I remember, August is the worst of it." (Although the humidity is nothing like back East.) "Look at those heat waves up on the highway, against the horizon."

"I guess I might as well," Cynthia muttered. "From where I sit, there's not a whole hell of a lot else to see."

Actually, there were road signs.

"Matt, look up ahead. Is that picture what I think it is?"

I glanced at the billboard: a crude drawing of a gangly plant. "Turn in marijuana growers. Call 1-800-KS-CRIME!" This was followed by a full-blown photo of a red-faced fetus every five or ten miles: "Abortion stops a beating heart."

In addition to the weather and the scenery and the moral admonitions, our Ryder rental truck was no walk in the park. Neither of us had ever driven anything this size, and a 1500-mile trip is a tough apprenticeship. Especially in Kansas, in August.

Late morning, we'd had a reprieve. Cyn had pulled off the interstate at a cafe outside Lawrence to get some coffee. She was backing up to the diner when we heard a shimmering sound, like the tinkling of sleigh bells. But it wasn't bells.

I gaped in the mirror—glass all over the parking lot—and tried to recall if I'd taken out truck rental insurance. She'd backed into the sign outside the restaurant and sliced off two feet of neon tubing.

"Jesus! What do you think we should do?" I stammered.

"Well, how 'bout this for starters," she muttered, as she shifted from reverse into first gear, grinding the gears and spinning the wheels. "Maybe they didn't hear anything in there."

"Cynthia!" I hollered. "Stop the truck. Right now. Just stop it." She shifted into neutral and pulled the emergency brake.

"Listen, Cynthia. Think a minute, will you? We just shattered somebody's sign. Now, who do you suppose owns that restaurant? Do you think they're any better fixed than we are? I mean, just think about it."

If there was one thing I'd got from my PhD in history, I guess it was an involuntary habit of stopping and thinking. That and a convoluted conscience. Along with an inability to act on impulse. I was trained like a dog who stops at every intersection—conditioned to consider two or three sides of every issue, to reinvent every possible moral wheel.

But Cyn was something else, although exactly what or who, I still could not precisely say. But I sensed she seemed to feel her way through the world as I struggled to comprehend it.

"Okay, Matt. How long do you want to sit here? If you really think somebody's going to be hurt by what I did—and I mean some individual, not some fucking franchise—we'll go in and ask. Since you're the one who's so frazzled, why don't you go?"

I trudged across the parking lot, scuffling through the shards of glass and pondering the cost of neon. Do they sell it by the foot or do you have to buy the whole sign? Should I ask if they're locally owned before I tell 'em what happened?

Inside, I found the manager: a thick, ruddy-faced fellow with a shock of white hair and a streak of cream gravy down his apron. "Ya hit what?" he asked me, slowly.

I pointed to the sign.

As he squinted through the window, first he frowned and then he sighed. And then his face crumpled into a wry grin. He gave the counter a whack with his bar towel.

"Hell, son, that sign's been out more'n two years. Now, tell me a real-life problem...Say, you look kinda wrung out. Cup o' coffee?"

I told him my wife was in the truck.

"Well, bring 'er in! If I'm good fer one cup, I reckon I can rustle up another."

We sat there swilling coffee and scarfing down the remnants of the morning's pastries for the next half-hour. The fellow said this was the slack part of his day. "So, where ya headed?" he asked us.

We told him about the move from Eastbourne University to Hopewell College, in Mayflower out in the prairies of west Kansas. Just two months after our marriage. (And six months after our first date.) A scant two weeks after I'd turned in my dissertation. And thirty days before the start of the fall semester out at Hopewell.

"He's the new dean of students," Cynthia announced. "And, as it happens, he went to school there. The man's going back to the scene of the crime. He'll nab all the kids trying to get away with the same stuff he did. I tell him he has an unfair advantage."

The fat man laughed, his apron jiggling, and launched into a few prolonged stories of his own. As we climbed back in the truck, Cynthia was grumbling, "Nothing like a keg of local history to go with your coffee." And then she smiled. "But I'd have to say it feels ten degrees more livable out here right now."

An hour later, however, as the sun climbed toward noon, the heat stoked up and the interstate threatened to stretch on forever. The highway rose and fell over swells the size of the Sahara.

Cynthia had been sketching odd barns and abandoned farmhouses that poked up from the countryside. But suddenly she clamped her sketch pad shut and slung it to the dashboard. She drew her knees up under her chin and stared vacantly at the horizon, then nodded off to sleep not long after that.

I scanned her from the corner of my eye, her billowing, dark red hair. Her chest slowly rose and fell in her slumber. My God, that body! What a creature. What an enigma. And my wife! As the road droned on, I tried to remember just how all of this had happened. I poked a rewind button in the recesses of my memory, and replayed my final months at Eastbourne. I remembered all the times I'd berated myself: "Come on, Bradshaw—get a life!" And then, suddenly, mysteriously, one day I had one.

✖

I remember the day my road turned home. The gray day in Boston. That February afternoon with the low-hanging clouds and the dank, freezing drizzle. I was huddled in the lobby of the Marriott Hotel on Copley Square, peering out at the historic Victorian church I'd been told lay just across the street. But it was hard to see through the frozen rain. The drizzle was turning to sleet and splattering against the windows like spittle.

The East Coast was like that, I'd been thinking. The climate was nothing like the high plains of west Kansas. Back there, the weather could be brutal. There were tornados that could funnel you into the next county. Blizzards that could bury you. But the weather was definitive in Kansas. You could see what you were in for as it swept across the prairie.

Here, almost everything seemed indefinite, indecisive. If not inscrutable. That was my mood as I sat scrunched up against the arm of a Naugahyde couch. My neck was getting stiff as I arched back, trying to get some distance from the guy who'd driven down to this conference with me. His name was Channing Coe; he taught in the religion department.

I didn't see him that often, for I was in history. Chan was more a colleague than a friend. Beyond that, he had academic rank as an assistant professor; I was still a teaching assistant.

I liked him, in a way, but found him a textbook pedant. With his bow tie and wire-rimmed glasses, he had all the accouterments of a college prof—save one. All that Channing lacked was tenure. But if he could squeeze a juried journal article out of this symposium, maybe get on the docket for next year's program, that just might put him over the top with the tenure review committee. The prospect had him salivating. This guy was in professional heat.

"Can you believe that last panelist?" Channing sputtered, waving his granny-glasses, nose in my face. He'd written his dissertation on the subject of the conference, so he thought he had a leg up on some of the other stuffed shirts on the program.

"Believe what?" I muttered. Craning backward, I smacked my head into a potted palm.

"Well, talk about unexamined assumptions. I mean, that man goes on and on about career paths and the value of career progression and the like. But he doesn't grasp the evolution of the concept, 'career.' You know, the etymology of it."

"Wha's that," I mumbled, ratcheting my neck for a look at the old, rococo church on the square.

"Why, look at it in historical context. I'm sure you know what I mean. 'Career': progress through life; a chosen path. You know the derivation of the term, don't you?"

"Can't say that I recall," I acknowledged, wriggling on the couch. I seemed to be getting a cramp in my left buttock.

"Well, it's 'carrus': the Latin word for a two-wheeled cart. That's where we get 'career.' Also 'car,' of course. You know, the proximate derivation is 'cararria.' Literally, the way of the cart. Now, then, isn't that significant? How we've come to conceive our careers in straight lines: like tracks in the mud, ruts from a cart.

"It's that unfortunate presumption of linear progress: career paths, and all that. What a reductionist image! Say, Matthew, I've been thinking. What about proposing a paper for next year's conference: 'Linearity and the Loss of Meaning in the Contemporary Workplace.' What would you say to that?"

I was plumbing the numb tissue in my brain for some sort of response when a flurry of color outside caught my eye. It wasn't the church; it was moving. There was a flicker of light and then an explosion—purple and teal, purple and teal. The garish colors flashed like a kaleidoscope in the plate glass window of the hotel, over and over and over.

As I sat up to look, the revolving door spun into motion. Whirling like a turbine, it began to deliver to the lobby a long line of tall black men. In an instant there was a whole troupe of them, in striped rep-ties and blazers with suit bags of bright teal and purple slung over their shoulders. As they strode into the glass and chrome lobby, it sparkled with their sheen.

I recognized them at once. There was Robert Parrish, Dell Curry, Hersey Hawkins, and Kenny Gattison ambling along in an easy but elegant procession. Then Kendall Gill, Larry Johnson, and Alonzo Mourning: one big, sleek black guy after another. It was the Charlotte Hornets, come to take on the Celtics in the Boston Garden. Tall as Watusis, they walked proud as though they'd come straight from a parade.

One look at those super jocks and my heart sank. Oh, Lord. And to think I might've gone in the first few rounds of the NBA draft! For a moment I just sat there on the plastic couch and quivered.

Then I remembered Channing. He was still peering at me expectantly. "Now wouldn't that be a fascinating paper? Look, we could co-author it. I'll bet there's an extensive literature on linearity. We'd each get a publication and a citation for our CVs. And we'd have a whole year to prepare before the next ..."

I glanced past Channing as the last of the Hornets stepped into the elevator, listened to their easy laughter. A couple of them slapped hands over a joke. Then the door closed, and there I was left in the lobby. Immured in my academic world once more.

Now my butt ached bad and my head hurt, too. "Oh, Jesus," I cried silently, glancing at my lanky legs. The long, strong fingers that could still palm a ball. "Just look at what I lost!"

⚜

The land leveled out around Salida and now and then we caught a cooling breeze. Off to the northwest, I saw a long, serried row of cotton clouds scudding along on the horizon. Maybe some moisture moving in, but the clouds didn't look nearly dark enough. A tumbleweed came bouncing across a dusty field and ricocheted off my windshield. Hm, pretty far east for that... I looked closely at the field. A month ahead of harvest, it had been plowed under. It was sweltering still, the wind not much more than a zephyr.

I remembered something the cafe owner had said, wiping his brow with a bar towel. "You think it's hot here, wait till you get down the road a piece, out by Hayes. They's rationin' water. First thing to go was the flower gardens. Then the lawns. Now the trees in town are dyin'. Folks can't sprinkle, and it don't rain. They say there's only one good thing about it."

"What's that?" Cynthia asked.

"The town folks have been findin' out what it feels like to be a farmer."

I glanced over at Cynthia, still asleep. Cynthia, the sociology major. Well, she'd need those analytic skills out in these parts. Mayflower was nothing like Greenwich, Connecticut, her upscale home town.

She shoved at her seat belt, stirred and mumbled something.

"Damned fat man."

"What's that? Hey, I was just thinking you liked that guy in the restaurant."

Her eyelids flickered and she muttered, "Damned flatland—goes on forever." Then she gave a shudder and nodded off again.

Soon I was back in reverie.

Yup, I'd gone on to study history and given up the NBA draft. Set out to earn a PhD. But five years into grad school, the consequences of my choice had begun to rankle. There was the dismal job market for one thing. In a way I was fortunate, for I had a job. But I found myself employed cramming data in the craws of reluctant underclassmen at Eastbourne University. It was like the sign someone put up in the faculty lounge, beneath the drawing of an angry hog:

NEVER TRY TO TEACH A PIG TO SING.
IT WASTES YOUR TIME, AND IT ANNOYS THE PIG.

History of Western Civilization 101. Required course—four enormous sections of it. The classes were clustered three days a week—8:00, 10:00, 2:00, and 4:00—like those old "Drink Dr Pepper 10-2-and-4" ads. By 5:00 p.m., my voice croaked and my brain was jelly. The job was not only tedious but exhausting.

But then one morning, several months after the conference in Boston, something flushed me out of my career rut. And then a series of events sent me catapulting back to a place I'd almost forgotten, to a time in my life I'd loved more than any other. It was subtle, the way it started.

There was a certain student in the first row of my 10:00 class that morning. She was swinging her foot back and forth in a kind of primal rhythm, the way some girls do in class. Are they ruminating or masturbating? I've never decided.

Anyway, I'd become half conscious of the foot that morning as I tried to prepare my cast-of-thousands class for a tedious test in a subject they'd forget as soon as they fulfilled the course requirement. It was the final exam at the end of spring term, and all of us wanted to get this academic ritual over fast. "Now, these are some of the dates you'll need to pass this test," I reminded them, and on the eve of an exam they wrote down everything I said. "You'll need to remember the dates of the Hebrew prophets and the Greek philosophers. Let's go through a few. Socrates, 470-399 BC; Plato, 427-347 BC; Aristotle, … "

I found myself tracking the rhythmic foot up the undulating leg of its owner: a slim coed in Levis and a tattered, black turtleneck sweater. I noticed there was a hole in the sweater, strategically worn at the upper edge of her left breast. At first glance, she looked like a 1950s Greenwich Village beatnik out of season. But there was something incongruous about her, and it was her hair. While her clothes were almost slovenly, this girl had long, radiant, chestnut hair like an ad for Breck Shampoo.

I saw that she was drawing something on a sketch pad, as the others took notes. It was an abstract design—somewhat sexual. Undeterred, I kept focused on the dates of the dead Greeks.

Presently, she raised her hand.

"Yes, you had a question?"

"Mr. Bradshaw, you know there's something I've been wondering all term. Why did the Hebrews hate themselves so when it seems like the Greeks could accept everything they found in their psyches? I mean, look at this stuff we've been reading: Socrates, Plato, Sophocles. Those dudes were into homosexuality, pedophilia, incest: everything the Bible calls 'sin.'

"It's like the National Enquirer in togas. But the Greeks saw all those sides of themselves, and they didn't seem to panic. Sometimes I think that's the way we should be. We should learn to accept all the fascinating instincts that swim around inside us. At least I'd like to learn that."

Then she looked up coyly. "Wouldn't you?"

There was a tittering along the front row, and I glanced down at the promontory swelling behind the zipper of my pants. Taking a quick step closer to the lectern, I mumbled something about conferring after class and fled back to my lecture notes.

We met a couple of weeks later, after final exams, up in the garret of an old Victorian mansion just off campus where I had my office. As offices for junior faculty go, these were not bad digs. The mansion that housed the Religion and Philosophy Department had been put up by an industrial tycoon back at the turn of the century, then willed to his widow who'd deeded the relic to the university just before she died. "The relic from the relict," the faculty called it.

It was a big, musty place that had a nice design and might even have qualified for a spot on the National Historic Register had anyone at Eastbourne ever come up with the cash to refurbish it. But donors don't pay big bucks to patch up other people's bequests, so the mansion sat in a constant state of deferred maintenance. The roof leaked and the floors creaked, and the windows let in drafts of winter air. The Rel/Phil Building was a classic white elephant.

My office was a four-story walk-up—a small room with a slanted ceiling that originally had been designed as a live-in maid's quarters. It offered a half-moon window with a good view of a tree-lined street, plus one other amenity. The industrialist had provided a separate bathroom for his maid. That was a real convenience—were it not for the fact that every prof who had an office on the floor below me came up to use the can.

Since it was built as a private bath, the industrialist had foregone insulation. As a result, you could hear everything that went on next door—from the opening zip to the final flush of every visitation.

I arrived about a half-hour early on the afternoon of my appointment, to see if I could straighten the place up a little. There were stacks of blue exam booklets all over the floor—a pile for each section of my course—plus mounds of books that I used for my lecture notes and research for my dissertation. I scanned the books for some study of the Greek psyche that I could set casually on the corner of my desk.

"Ah yes. Now, what were we meeting to discuss?" That might make a good opening gambit, if I could keep my eyes off the swelling turtleneck. "Oh, of course: the spirit of the Hellenic psyche. Well, it so happens that I have a volume on that subject right here on my desk."

Actually, I didn't speak that way, but some of my older colleagues did and if I wanted my academic career to go anywhere I thought it might not hurt to practice. At Eastbourne, it was the fashion to be formal. I knew of one prof who unfailingly called all his students by their last names—even, it was said, in bed.

Sex with undergrads was something I didn't do. I wasn't sure I could justify the act, given the inequalities of faculty and students. Besides, there was little need to hit on my students, given the kind of sexual generosity my fellow grad students displayed. But something about this young woman had made me uneasy.

I was just finishing my arrangements and adjusting the cover of the book I'd chosen for my desk prop, Edith Hamilton's *The Greek Way*, when there was a soft knock on the door. My heart stepped up a beat as I negotiated the piles of paper on the floor to answer it. It raced a bit faster as I opened the door. She stood there with a backpack in one hand and a notebook pressed against the same tight turtleneck with the same strategically worn hole at her chest.

"Hi," she said, as she looked up, smiling shyly.

"Ah ye…" I began, scrambling to duck down behind my defenses. But before I could get three words into my script, my heart fell as I heard the unmistakable sound of a toilet paper roll unraveling. I'd forgot about the bathroom next door. Why hadn't I arranged this assignation at a coffee house or a bar? Well, it was too late now. To make matters worse, whoever was settling in next door was here for something far more serious than a tinkle.

She caught my hesitation. "Hey, Mr. Bradshaw, is this an inconvenient time for you? I'll just stay a few minutes."

"Why don't you call me 'Matt'?"

"Why, I think I'd like that," she said softly, flashing the same winsome smile. "I'm Cynthia. My friends call me, 'Cyn.'" As she sat down in the chair next to my desk, she leaned toward me, obliterating the head of Zeus on the cover of The Greek Way.

"You know, I've had lots of instructors here at Eastbourne," she began, very slowly. "I don't know if you're aware that I'm older than all those freshmen in the class. I took your course in my last semester; I just graduated."

"So you're not a student here anymore," I said with enthusiasm, if somewhat redundantly.

"No, I'm not." She smiled again. "I put that course off as long as I could because it didn't seem to have anything to do with my major in sociology. But now I'm glad I did. I'm not just saying this, uh, Matt, but you were one of the most stimulating professors I had here. It almost makes me sorry I'll be graduating.

"So, um, I thought maybe you could suggest some other readings—some way I could continue to pursue the ideas we began to explore. I seemed to experience a, well, um, a sense of release in your class that I haven't really known before."

At this point I found myself forgetting all the lines I'd rehearsed for this conference, not to mention the reference book beneath my now ex-student's turtlenecked chest. My mind was racing several millennia ahead of Homer, at a pace with my pulse, and my phallus was arcing toward the Parthenon.

I sat for a moment to take stock of my thoughts, and considered my next line in this script. Not for the first time in my life, I found myself mired in the paralysis of analysis. Part of my problem was that I hadn't been prepared to see this person as anything but a student. What did she want from me?

I was about to move ahead with a safely provocative line such as: "Well, Cynthia, what did you have in mind?" but the words caught in my throat.

"Well, Cynth…" I took a deep breath and cleared my throat when an echoing cough came from the next room. This was followed by an earnest grunt, a resounding fart, and the clanging of a toilet seat on a porcelain commode. Then the unmistakable rumble of a long-overdue defecation.

Cynthia and I looked down at our shoes. Then we glanced at each other simultaneously and broke up in snickers.

Suddenly she stopped laughing, stared at me for a moment and dabbed at her eyes. Then she opened her backpack and groped around inside. "Now what the hell is she after?" I wondered. "Her class notes? A condom?" She pulled out a sketchpad and opened it on her lap. She took out a pencil and, staring at the head of Zeus on the book cover, began to draw a sketch of it.

"Ah yes, ol' Zeus," she murmured. "The god-king. Maybe there's the dude can help me find what I'm looking for. Whatever it is that I seem to have lost." She peered at the hoary-headed statue on the book cover and sketched for a few minutes more.

When she looked up again, I saw that her eyes were moist with tears. "You know, Mr. Bradshaw," she began. "This isn't the first time I've pulled this stunt: set up some bogus, half-assed academic conference."

She took out a Kleenex and dabbed at her eyes. "I dunno, Matt. What am I looking for? And why have I done this with you?"

She sat and smiled wistfully, gazing out the window, as I tried to think of something to say. Then she slowly folded her sketch pad and got up from her chair. Her smile froze into a grimace as she picked up her backpack and turned on her heel. In an instant, she was out the door.

I sat there stunned for a moment and wondered what all that had been about. What the hell had she come by for—enlightenment about the ancient Greeks, or a workout in the attic? Presently, I got up and reshelved the Zeus book. As I stumbled among the stacks of books and piles of exam papers that littered my floor, I considered how dumb and clumsy I must have looked with that prop on my desk—ruddy as a piece of raw meat.

I snapped off the light and stormed out of the office, pausing just long enough to grab my gym bag by the door. Taking the stairs two at a time and slamming the door of the Rel/Phil House, I lit out down the street, heading for the old brick field house around the corner.

I trotted up the stairs to the gym, almost lunging through the door, and slipped into another world that had often been my refuge. Once inside, I stopped for a moment and took a deep breath as my bag fell to the floor. Closing my eyes, I savored all the odd aromas of the human body in exertion: stale sweat, oil of wintergreen, and excrement.

In ten minutes' time I was immersed in this world, out on the court shooting hoops. My routine never varied. I'd start out with a few layups, in a rhythm I'd picked up like a virus before high school and absorbed into my bloodstream over the years.

"Bend your knees like a spring. Get up on the balls of your feet. Find your balance," a voice once had spoken. "Lean into your dribble; don't slap at the ball. Let it meet your hand as it comes up off the floor. Then push it back down about two feet in front of your shoulder."

I heard the voice as though it were yesterday. It was Jeb Collard, my crusty old coach at Hopewell College. The guy who'd taught me how to dribble a basketball and shoot layups back in junior high school. For he'd been my coach back then, as well. By now, the rhythm he'd taught me was autonomic. And it was a hell of a gift. Whatever else might bollix up my life, I could always float off to another plane and take comfort in that cadence. Dribbling a basketball was like a second heartbeat.

After maybe five minutes of layups, I'd move out to the foul line: shoot free throws, then soft jumpers before heading out to the top of the key. Out here the rhythms were more complex and the balance more refined. Everything had to work in synchrony at the top of the key, if you hoped to hit even half your shots. But, mostly, I still could.

Some days I'd find myself drifting out to certain spots on the floor without thinking, and before long I'd be recreating all the clutch shots in the critical games of my career. In my mind, I'd watch the clock ticking down. Hear the maniacal crowd. Feel the adrenalin pump as I set up for my game-winning jumper.

Only as the ball clanged off the rim or swished through the net would I come to earth and find myself alone in the gym. That's when I'd notice the time and head for the locker room, always with a sigh for the life I'd left behind.

On this particular afternoon, however, my fantasies mostly bounced off the backboard or evaporated into air balls. I was so off-stride from my meeting with that student, I couldn't hit a third of my shots. So after about fifteen minutes of frustration, I showered and dressed and trudged back over to my office.

I pulled out a book on English land reformers, trying to transport myself back to the seventeenth century. But I couldn't get into my dissertation. So I imagined I was back at Hopewell, my little college in west Kansas. Tried to recreate a certain spring morning when something struck me in the light on the green fields, and I first took an interest in the history of land reform. But still I couldn't concentrate. Damn! Something about that Cynthia still nettled me. Here, she'd strode in here so super cool and played me like a cello.

And every time the stairs creaked, I hoped and feared she might be coming back for more.

2

C ynthia woke with a curse as a gust of wind rocked the truck and slammed her head against the side window. She slumped in silence for a time, and I let her be. Then I heard a rustling.

"Yo, Dean!"

I glanced over. Good, she was sitting up and smiling.

"You with us, dude?"

"I don't know. I've just been driving along thinking about old times. And what's ahead. After five years, it feels strange coming back here. You know, I almost said, 'Coming home—home to Hopewell.' Dunno. I just hope this is the right thing to do."

"Well, it's a crap shoot," she conceded. "From what you've said about the financial condition of this place, they don't call it 'Hopewell' for nothing. I just hope you get paid, before…"

We rode along in silence.

"But what were you getting at Eastbourne? Besides, the job has a neat title. 'Dean Bradshaw.' Certain ring to it. And from what I hear, you were a major stud out in these parts."

"Well, don't believe every…"

"Hey, it's not every day a guy from a hick college like that gets drafted by the N.B. of A."

I ruminated. "Cyn, I only hope it isn't too weird for you."

"I'm up for it, at least for a while. You know, I put out a few feelers back at the soc department at Eastbourne for some research projects—something I can do on my own. Hey, get me a computer and a modem, and I can entertain myself. Just as long as *you* know why *you're* coming back here. But every time you space out and those eyes glaze over, I'm afraid you're still trying to dope that out."

"Well, there are some people I'd like to see again. Some of the guys on the team, my old profs, and…"

I fell silent as old memories began to stir. Those roadhouses out in Milo County. The tranquility of a Saturday morning in the college library. The NAIA playoffs in Kansas City. My last-second shot at the buzzer. The last time I saw Sarah . . .

As the hot wind whipped across my face, I felt a chill in my chest. My college days were five years older than anything I'd known back East. Or anyone. And many times more real.

We drove another couple of hours in the heartland heat, as the afternoon wore on and the sun slowly settled into the plains. About three o'clock, the sun became blinding and the cab of the truck felt like a sauna. Cynthia was awake, and restless. It was past time to think of pulling off the highway, but I saw no signs of an oasis. Then I spotted a turnoff to the town of Ellsworth.

"Hey, Cyn, here's a place you might like. Just your classic Kansas town. I remember coming up here one time in ninth grade. Our jayvees played their varsity."

"I'll take anything for a little local color," Cynthia muttered, "including a tree."

She was in luck. The exit to Ellsworth turned into a two-lane highway that dipped down into a long, low hollow of hills with a bright green field in the center. It was a rambling road with cottonwoods the color of parchment, clumps of burgundy salt cedar alongside a quiet stream. In five minutes' time, the temperature fell fifteen degrees and the interstate was nothing more than a bad memory.

The hills were still tan and taupe and tawny, like the land that lined the interstate. But now furrows of black soil fed out from the riverbanks below them. Ribbons of green wheat shimmered like banners against the ebony farmland. Ah, the wonders of irrigation. It was a silent, peaceful setting, broken only by the mist of irrigators and an occasional droning tractor.

I pulled off the road and drank it all in. Took a good, deep, belt-level breath for the first time in five years.

"Come on, Cyn. Let's turn in here."

We found a motel, the Garden Prairie Inn, and the Country Corner Co-op convenience store where we picked up some beer. (Thank God it wasn't Sunday.) There was a Pizza Hut next door, which didn't excite me. After the deep dish delights of the East Coast, it was hard to face that franchise from Wichita with their bland pizza, flat as the landscape. But we took a pepperoni back to our room and after the first few beers the pizza didn't matter.

Cynthia seemed to take to Ellsworth. She snickered at a sign on the wall, from hunting season: "No dogs in rooms. Please clean pheasants outside." Then I heard a squeal as she cracked a door at the far end of the room and swung it open wide. "A swimming pool! Hey, Matt, God is good."

The door led into a two-story atrium with a small pool, maybe ten strokes to the lap. It was enough to loosen up and the cool water was refreshing. Afterward we shed our suits and flopped down on the bed, exhausted. The room was still strewn with pizza crusts and beer cans.

As I dozed off, I remember casting a few admiring glances at my helpmate's unclothed body. But I was too tired to do anything more. I drifted into a bleary trance, and before long I was back at Blotto's.

I'd dated in graduate school, if you could call it that. For I had very few formal engagements. Some fem from a seminar would phone up in the late afternoon. "Oh, Matt, I see you have *Technology in the Middle Ages* checked out. Could I borrow it?"

One learned to listen for code words in these conversations. "Matt, I hate to impose but do you suppose you could bring it by? I'm home now." (That was an open invitation.) "Say, if you don't have plans, we could eat in here." (The gates just opened wider.)

Or sometimes we'd just bump into one another at the local beer hall.

"Tanya, I didn't know you worked at Blotto's."

She was a chunky, dark-haired girl from my seminar on the history of labor unions. Tanya always had a well-constructed look about her. Tonight she was sporting a tight tee shirt under a waitress apron. I saw her smirking as I perused her chest.

"It's my internship. You got a minute, I'll tell you all about it. Slavic girl wins scholarship to grad school, right? Family owned a roadhouse back in Utica, okay? Looks for marketable field, and guess what? Say, Matt, what beer you drinking? Genessee? I'm off in a few minutes. I'll draw one for myself."

I learned that she was doing her dissertation on trends in dinner wines. Trading on her bar skills if the job market didn't pan out. Swigging her beer, she told me her story, belched into the back of her hand. Then she looked up and smiled demurely. "Look here, you wanta decent meal?" She swept up some crumbs of fried zucchini. "I mean, a guy can't live on bar food. Come on up to my place and I'll fix something Slavic. We can eat in, right?"

The rest was destiny.

A cabbage dish larded with sausage and paprika. More beers on her hideabed couch. Our butts brushed, then our tongues touched in a spice-laden kiss. I watched her stolid breasts unfold from the broad bra underneath her tee shirt.

Crouching naked, wrestling cushions from the couch we'd hauled out the bed frame. As we'd climbed on the mattress, we had turned to one another expectantly. "Got one?" Shook our heads in synchrony.

"Well, hell, the night's not lost," Tanya snickered as she nuzzled against my chest. "Who needs a condom? We can do ourselves."

And so we did, in tandem. I remembered how her face flushed and her spine arched as she clutched her crotch at the climax. Finally she let out a lowing groan and hoisted herself up on one elbow. "Your turn, Tiger. Show time!" And as she shifted her weight for a better view, she farted.

As I slogged home through the gray streets of Tanya's ethnic neighborhood—the endless row houses, asbestos siding, asphalt shingles—I thought of how seamless and meaningless my life had become. My sex life was a flush of fluids, which was par for the course in grad school. We were all in limbo here, marking time toward a future none of us could grasp.

It was the next day that I phoned the dean's office in desperation. Maybe he'd heard some rumor of a job opening—anything but what I had.

His secretary said that actually there was a new opening at

Eastbourne in arts and sciences, and my spirits rose, if only for an instant.

"Although it's not in history," she added. "In the religion department. Besides," (she lowered her voice) "there's a rumor they may freeze the position. We have problems in retention, you know."

Down at Blotto's, another rumor was making the rounds. It was said the dean had come up with a new language requirement for PhDs in history. In addition to the standard French and German exams, they'd added one in English, a useful, six-word phrase:

"Would you like fries with that?"

I shuddered—still at Eastbourne, half dozing. But no! It was twilight and I was in Kansas. I reached across the wide bed for my wife. Empty sheets! And then I heard a rustling sound. She was tidying up the motel room, cleaning up from supper. Still half dozing, I watched as she walked over to the wastebasket by the window and then back to the washbasin. Cynthia was still nude. I saw her rinse her hands and reach for a towel.

But she paused as though to survey herself in the mirror, moist hands sliding slowly down her body. Her nipples rose as she touched herself. Then down along her stomach to the tufted triangle where her legs met. She clasped herself there as in prayer.

I watched her lift her hands high in a votive sort of gesture, toward the ceiling. As her long breasts rose, silhouetted in the twilight, a part of me also began rising.

"I say, Cynthia, does all this come with room service?" She turned to me, half smiling, and her breasts swayed.

"Wait and see, sodbuster." As she settled her soft lips down on me, around me, I felt myself filling and rising, rising... till she stopped short for a moment and lifted her head. "Say, you think this is legal in Kansas?"

At dusk, we took a walk through Ellsworth, down Kunkel Drive over to Lincoln Avenue, then Sixth Street to Washington Avenue. The streets with their Middle American monikers felt as placid as the neighborhoods I remembered from Wichita. They were lined with big frame houses, three stories high, with broad porches. They all had double lots with elm trees, and a big wooden swing on iron hooks hung in every other veranda.

The trees were so old they arched over the streets. It was the kind of corn-fed neighborhood you wished everyone could live in: a place where you could grow up like Dwight Eisenhower from over in Abilene, with a good Midwestern grin. As the sun went down, we heard the first, sonorous chirping of cicadas.

Then other lights began to come on in cadence. As we walked along, spotlights flashed over the garages. And porch lights, one after the next. Every house in sequence.

"Did you see that?" I asked Cynthia. "These lights come on just a step ahead of us. They seem to be on timers."

"Right," she said. "It's a motion sensor: some kind of home security system. We're triggering a photo cell when we get within ten feet. That's weird. So, why would they need this in Kansas?"

"You got me. And look over there." It was a tall phalanx of amber lights on the north edge of town. Too muted for a football field, and twice as high as streetlights. There must have been at least two dozen of these light towers, and they cast their eerie glow along a vast tract of ground like enormous praying mantises.

The next morning, we hiked downtown for breakfast at the Cozy Cupboard. It seemed to be the only cafe of any size in town and it was clearly the morning watering hole. The place was a maze of cross-hatched booths, each holding four or five farmers and storekeepers. Most of them were talking in low tones, heads down, mopping up egg yolks and syrup with enormous biscuits.

At the back of the cafe there was a fill-your-own Long John bar where three or four customers kibitzed as they crammed their pastries full of fillings: butterscotch, maple, and vanilla.

Now and then, the murmuring coffee talk would break into a shout as a popular figure local walked through the door: "Hey, Arnie! Wife let you out today?"

I settled into a scene that so felt familiar it seemed I'd never left the Heartland. For the second time in two days, I took a deep breath at belt level. As we sat eating, I felt a heavy hand on my shoulder and turned to see a red-faced farmer in the next booth. "Hey, big fella," he said with a grin, and proffered a coffee pot in a great, gnarled hand. "You drink this stuff?"

But over in a corner of the cafe, there was a scene that didn't fit. It was a table full of women, listening earnestly to one another. Young women, mostly in their twenties, they seemed serious as a support group. I watched as they spoke in turn. Now and then, one of the women would dab at her eyes as she listened to the others or told her own story. Several of the women were black. That, too, seemed unusual, in Ellsworth.

Leaving town, we picked up Highway 140 and headed up through Black Wolf toward the Interstate. Just north of town, I saw a sign to an industrial park, then a big green factory where they appeared to be making some sort of farm equipment.

"Well, at least they've landed an employer," I told Cynthia. "Out here, some of these industrial parks are nothing but a cornfield and a billboard."

I noticed there was one other outfit in the industrial park, and it looked like a large farm. There were three big buildings in the compound, each a couple of stories tall and painted barn red. At the base of each building was a low, tan, one-story structure. About the height of a chicken coop, but much wider.

As we drew closer, I saw what a large farm this was. Hundreds of acres, with a row of high hedges all around it. "I never saw a spread this size, right at the edge of town," I exclaimed. "Why would they ... "

Suddenly a spark shot up from one of the hedges, then spurted from another. The bushes seemed to be catching fire, but the flames flashed and gleamed like metal.

Then, slowly, I began to see the border of hedges for what it was. It was a chain link fence circling the compound, about twelve feet high, with a three-foot coil of razor wire all around the top of it. The sharp wire glistened menacingly in the sun. And I saw a road around the fence, with two patrol cars circling it slowly. The long light poles stood like sentries, speechlessly surveying the scene.

"Well, it looks like Ellsworth found an industry for the industrial park," I muttered. "They got themselves a prison."

"Wan-ted, one good hearted wo-man
Who'll forgive imperfections
In the man that she loves..."

I couldn't remember the last time I'd listened to a country music station, but I'd had one tuned in for the past couple of hours. Maybe ever since we crossed the 100th meridian: that cartographic boundary where precipitation drops below twenty inches a year. That's the break point at which you need to give some good second thoughts to pursuing a career in agriculture.

"Hey, Matt. Why don't they ever say 'woman' in these country songs? It's always 'woe-man.' Do you think they're trying to tell us something?"

I slapped her thigh. Cynthia had stayed awake, even alert, all morning. Her eyes were bright and I could see the sociologist part of her clicking in. Ah, those powers of trained observation.

For my part, I was still mulling over that prison. And one of the stories we'd heard from the restaurateur back in Lawrence.

"College folks, huh? Well, that ain't me. I been slingin' hash so long it's ruined me for anything else. But lemme tell ya a story 'bout this town right here: 'bout Lawrence. Place is a-boomin', ya know. I could have me three, four cafes like this one if I wanted the aggravation of findin' help."

"It looked pretty busy on the main street," I acknowledged. "Why's that?"

"Well, it started 'bout a hundred years ago when they got them the university in here," he continued. "Thirty miles up the road there's another town called Leavenworth. Ya heard of that one, haven't ya? When I say 'Leavenworth,' whadda ya think of?"

"Why..."

"Ya, I know. Ya gonna say ya think of the prison. Well, that's fair enough 'cause that's all they got up there, and I say let 'em have it. Ya drive up past the prison and take a look at the town of Leavenworth there, and you'll see it's stone cold.

"Nothin' like this here Lawrence. Hey, this place is humming:

computer companies, boutiques that sell stuff to the students. No comparison 'tween what people can spend if they're students at a university or locked up in a prison.

"Well, now, I'm gettin' round to my point. Ya see, there was a big hoo-haw in the legislature 'bout the time Kansas got the university and the federal penitentiary. Both of 'em was startin' up at once. Leavenworth had the most clout in the state back then, and they got the first call. So, which one'd they want, the university or the prison? An' ya know which one those jackasses chose, now, don't ya?"

"Well, I guess they got the ... "

"Thas' right, big fella, they picked the prison. And why d'ya suppose they took that over the school? Huh, why ya think they did that?"

"Well, it could be ... "

"I'll tell ya why. It was all about employment. Them jokers in Leavenworth, they looked at the kindsa jobs that's in jails and in universities and they says, 'Hey, one a them's got jobs we ain't qualified for. They gonna bring in perfessors from the East with them fancy diplomas.' (Ya know what I mean, and no offense: folks like you.) 'But, hey, a lockup,' they says, 'now we can work that fine. Don't take nothin' but two feet and a key.

"Point is, any them farmers in Mayflower give ya grief 'cause you workin' at a college, tell 'em to have a look at Leavenworth and Lawrence. Tell 'em they better appreciate what you're doin'. You folks gonna do 'em some good!"

But I didn't appreciate the look of the landscape I was seeing as we drove west toward Mayflower. I knew a lot of farmers out here were beginning to reconsider some traditions. Their grandfathers had bought land in west Kansas when the nineteenth-century East Coast real estate developers and railroaders had sold them on the notion this was farmland. It wasn't, not west Kansas. Not three years out of ten.

Back then, those Eastern toadies had touted a slogan: "Rain follows the plow." And the settlers had bought it. They'd actually believed that if you burned down the grassland and turned up the soil, rainfall would follow. But it hadn't. And so the fathers of these farmers had come up with the technology of irrigation, siphoning water from the Oglala Aquifer.

For a while they made this damn-near desert bloom.

But not for much longer. There were serious signs the underground water was being depleted. The aquifer was drying up, although no one knew how fast. That's why they'd been rationing water in Hays.

I wondered what shape Mayflower was in. A good part of me was reluctant to see, but another part felt drawn like a magnet. I was making record time until... "Matt, Jesus Christ!"

As we crested a hill, a wallop of wind hit the top of our truck and took it like a sail. I clutched the wheel, wrestling frantically as the truck careened out in the far lane.

"What the fuck, Matt—you trying to get us killed?"

I slowed down to seventy-five. Thank God there'd been no one coming. Had we enough possessions to fill up the van, I'd have some decent ballast. But when you've only been married two months...

"Sorry, Cynthia. I guess I was deep in thought."

"So where have I heard that line before! I'm telling you, I fear for my life when those eyes glaze over. Here, here's a rest stop. Pull over."

I shut off the engine and forked over the keys. My eyelids were sagging.

"About four hours to go," I said. "I think I'll try to get some sleep. Besides, I need to take a break. A lot of what I see feels so familiar, and then something'll come along that doesn't quite fit, like that prison."

She moved the seat forward, adjusted the mirror. Her frown was fading. "Well, I had an odd thought a few miles back, before you almost offed us."

"And what was that?"

"I remembered something from your class. About the early Christians and the mystery cults. You know, the origins of Communion. Eating the god and all those cool, dark rites. Stuff they picked up from the ancient nature cults. That was one thing I wrote down in my notes: 'the underside of life; the forces we can only half see.' That's the way you put it. That was hip."

"Uh huh?"

"Well, it came to me, staring out over the next five counties. If you grew up around here, it'd be tough to work up a sense of mystery. I mean, wouldn't you assume that the whole world was like this landscape? Just laid out there for you, plain as day. As though this were all there was to see."

I sat up and took that in. "You know, Cynthia, in all the years I taught that course, you were the best student I had. It was eerie, almost as though you'd ... "

"As thought I'd what?"

"Maybe already been through the material."

I glanced at her under the bill of my cap as I pulled it down over my eyes. Now her hair was flowing in the wind, glowing in the sunlight as the truck picked up speed. She looked like a young diva or a goddess, even in her jeans and tee shirt. Except for a hint of a grin.

"I mean, Cyn, you were brighter than most of my colleagues."

I saw her arch her brow. "Cooh-wal," was all she said.

As I dozed off, I found myself drifting back in time. Back to Eastbourne. Probing the past. Turning it over, one more time.

I was on a high place, looking down on some trees. They had dark green, shiny leaves and they were potted. I was watching my colleague, Channing Coe. He was staring at the trees. Standing in the middle of a walkway that hung suspended in space, four stories up, in the vast student union at Eastbourne. The bridge overlooked a grove of giant ficus trees on the main floor of the atrium.

Chan was leaning forward with his hands on the rail. I noticed he'd set down his satchel and lined up a stack of books in a definitive pile. Something about this scene made me uneasy.

"Hey Channing, whatcha doing: contemplating the career paths of potted plants?" It was a weak joke, but it caught his attention. I looked at him closely as he slowly turned to face me.

"Oh, hello, Matthew," he said in his normal formal manner, but an unusually somber tone. As I drew nearer, I saw his eyes were wide and glassy.

I took a step closer and put a hand on his shoulder. His hands were trembling as he leaned against the ledge. "Channing, you okay?"

As it turned out, he wasn't, although it took some time to get it out.

"You remember how I always said it is vital we find some way of conceiving our careers other than straight lines?"

I told him I remembered a conversation like that one afternoon in Boston. "I think it was something about 'linearity.'"

"Well said." He smiled, then sputtered, "W-well … it's not what one might call an 'academic question' any longer." He gave a dark laugh. "At least not for me. Not in my case. Not any more."

"Whadda ya mean, Chan?"

"Well, you see, in … in my case, Matthew … " He gasped and his shoulder shuddered in my hand. "I can scarcely bring myself to say it. Oh, my God, I'm leaving Eastbourne. Losing my career!"

He stood that way for a couple of minutes, staring into space. Then he gathered himself, snatched up his books and satchel, and bolted toward the exit from the bridge. He turned and gave me a sad smile from the door. "Thank you for listening, Matthew. We'll be in touch," he said.

But I never saw him again at Eastbourne. When I passed by his office a few days later, his final exams sat piled on a chair outside the door. A note on the door said simply that he was gone.

I worried about Channing for a few days, not to mention my own career in academe.

But what could I do? At this point, I knew I was so far into my fate there was no turning back. So I buried myself in my dissertation, researched it to death. And taught my course till I could deliver my lectures by rote, hear my students in my sleep…

Oh God, here comes another one. Bitching again. What is it, her grade on an exam? What's that she said?

"… damned flatland—can't believe that sign. Fifty miles to May-flower. Another fifty fucking miles of vacant plains."

Pushing up my cap, I squinted off into the distance. Then I rubbed my eyes and stared again. "Cyn, you must have read that sign wrong. It's only five miles. Look, there it is. I see it!"

"Look at what?"

"Those hills up on the horizon. Trace the ridge, out to the west. There's the farmers co-op grain elevator. That church spire. That's Mayflower! Cyn, look over there!"

"Look where?"

I said, "Cynthia, we're home!"

3

I t was some time before I could step back and take a good look at Mayflower, my once and future home. Cynthia and I put in full days finding a place to live, buying a car, returning the rental truck.

We lucked out in the housing department, and Cynthia was amazed at the local real estate values. For the price of a walkup apartment back East, we were able to rent a whole house. It was a one-story, two-bedroom bungalow on a hilltop just north of downtown. Corner of Winthrop Avenue and Fifth Street, to be exact.

Sure, it was a small house and 70 years old, so the window sills sagged and the floors creaked. But it was a neat little place with mahogany paneling and floor-to-ceiling bookshelves in the living room. Outside, a low veranda ran across the front of the house and rounded a corner all the way to the back yard. At the far end of the veranda, a high trellis sat laden with blue morning glories. The flowers were thriving and the lawn freshly cut, so it seemed the place hadn't been vacant long. Somebody had been watering, somewhat. All in all, Mayflower looked dusty but not bad.

As I sat with a beer on the veranda, having lugged a dozen boxes of furnishings from the truck, it occurred to me that I must have walked past this house many times. The campus was just a half mile north of here. Winthrop was a broad, brick-paved boulevard that bisected the town south to north. Beginning at the railroad yards down near the river, it climbed a long incline through the business section. At the hillcrest near our house, Winthrop subdivided into an avenue with a median of elm trees.

There was a forty-foot flag pole at the base of the boulevard, with an outsized American flag. In the next block there was a funeral parlor, an old Grange Hall, and another big frame building that looked like a rooming house. Across the street was a large park with a bandstand, all shaded and sheltered by elms. Any stock, red-blooded American might get a rush of serenity just walking through this neighborhood, although till now I never had. A sojourn in the East will change your perspective.

Cynthia saw Mayflower with a sharp, fresh eye and she was full of questions. "Why are there so many empty storefronts in the business district?" she'd asked me. And, "If they had to bring in a fucking Wal-Mart, why not stick it in one of those vacant buildings downtown? Does somebody think it's hip to have a strip mall on the edge of a hick town like this?"

There was more. "Did you ever notice the industries in this place? You've got your banks, churches, nursing homes, and funeral parlors. And that's about it. Everything you could ask for, if you're a fossil."

She set up a bedroom as an electronic office and art studio and before long was zapping into data bases and cranking out maps of the local economy. I liked her energy, but it concerned me.

"Look, Cynthia, when we go over to the Collards' tomorrow night, cut back on the social commentary, will you? I mean, this guy's a coach who's never lived any place but Kansas. And I'm not sure his wife has even been anywhere else."

But my hope was in vain. Before the first course of dinner was half done, Emily Collard had asked Cyn her impressions of the town. Cynthia grabbed the opening like a baton in a relay race and took off from a running start. I had a pretty good idea what was coming, and I shuddered.

"Here's another thing that gets me," she concluded fifteen minutes later. "You've got this old movie theater downtown and that's totally cool. Inside, I hear it's awesome. But it sits vacant. Next door is a huge hotel that seems to be a retirement home. Meanwhile, some dude's putting up this three-screen, Brand-X movie theater out at the edge of town, across from the Wal-Mart. Now, why'd they close up the downtown theater? Because the old folks liked to go to the picture show and the young kids didn't want to hang with them?"

There was a long silence, then Jeb Collard muttered dully. "We got a lot to answer for, all right."

Emily stepped in. "Why, Cynthia, Jeb and I may be able to answer some of your questions about Mayflower. But you know we're so close to this town there's a lot we've never paid any mind."

"Yuh, it's like they say," Jeb observed. "Whoever it was discovered water, you can bet it warn't a fish."

Cynthia smiled and I relaxed a bit. For a moment I felt a twinge of hope. For all the difference in their worlds, maybe he and my wife would get along. I wondered how she saw Jeb after all I'd said about him.

With his steel-gray hair and clear blue eyes, fifty-five-year-old Jeb Collard was your classic, robust, ex-athlete. At 6-2 and maybe 200 pounds, he was housed in the kind of constitution that never seemed to age. Emily was not so fortunate. She'd aged a good deal in the five years I'd been gone. White hair, wide haunches: she looked like a typical west Kansas housewife. In fact, I thought (and then I winced) if you didn't know she was Jeb Collard's wife, she might well have passed for his mother.

I steered the conversation to the upcoming school year and then back to old basketball seasons. I was pleased to see Cynthia respond as Jeb and I began reminiscing. She took off her car-window sociology face and seemed to lighten up.

"So, tell me about my husband as a ballplayer, Coach Collard. By the way, is that what you'd like me to call you? I don't think Matt knows either, now that the two of you are colleagues."

He looked at her quizzically. Then, for a moment, he sat still, and I remembered Collard's trademark silences. For a stranger, they could go on just long enough to verge on the uncomfortable.

"Friends all call me 'Jeb,'" he said, and glanced my way.

"What kinda ballplayer was he? You're asking me, Ma'm? Hey, you could be lettin' yourself in for a long evening. Ask any coach 'bout the best player he's ever had, and he could carry on for some time."

From past experience, I knew that Jeb could do just that, when he found a listener who cared to hear him expound on a subject he cared about.

"Jeb, you'll embarrass the boy!" Emily interjected.

"Pshaw, I'm 'bout like a parent to him. You know that, Em. Coached him since he was thirteen, in junior high school. Saw him through his growing pains. I gotta right to take pride in him. Besides, he's no boy. The man's my colleague, just like his wife here says. He's dean of students.

"Anyway, Ma'm." (I saw Cynthia cringe.) "I've known coaches stay on two, three years past when they shoulda retired just to follow a player through his high school or college career. See if he could go on to the next level. Now, was this guy any good?"

"Look, I don't know if you're athletically inclined, Ma'm, but did you ever try dunking a basketball? I mean, on the top women's college teams these days you got some gals can do it. A league like we're in here, maybe half the guys can slam it with a running start. But now and then you got a guy with leg spring. Nobody knows where that comes from; it's like velocity in a baseball pitcher's arm. But this guy here, even at six feet tall he had leg spring. And then the kid shoots up to six-foot-seven. Why, he could slam 'er from a standing jump. Why, Ma'm … "

Cynthia suddenly scraped her chair back. "Look, make that 'Cynthia.' Or 'Cyn.'" Her eyes were blazing. Collard sat up stiffly, unsettled.

"It's okay," I intervened. "Why don't we just make it a rule. We'll call each other by our first names." I paused and looked over at Collard. And thought to myself, "Even in the case of a guy who's basically my stepfather."

"Hey, no problemo," Cynthia sat back down and smiled. "Anyway, I just picked up some useful information. You know, Jeb, Matt's too modest to talk about himself, but you've confirmed what I suspected. I know parts of him are pretty good-sized and he's a hell of an athlete in certain positions. But leg spring? Hey, that's a bonus! Can't wait to get home and try him out."

Jeb blinked as Emily bustled up to clear the table, her face flushing under her silver hair.

"Here, let me help you," Cyn said, as she picked up a stack of plates and took off for the kitchen through the swinging door. It was perhaps the most domestic act I'd seen Cynthia perform in the eight weeks of our marriage. For a moment, Jeb sat and said nothing.

"I 'spect it's cooler on the porch," he finally said, and he led me outside through the front parlor.

I found a lounge chair and settled in for the quietude to follow. As I sat there listening to the night, I remembered Jeb as a coach and his silences. I could recall entire timeouts when he never said a word to his players. The opposing coach would be hollering the whole time, screaming himself hoarse and Jeb would just stand there staring off in space, pondering his strategy.

Sometimes he'd break the silence with a kind of Socratic dialogue. He'd pose a question at the beginning of the time out, and then he'd go off and stand by himself to ruminate. We'd mull it over while we caught our wind.

"Never foul a jump shooter," he'd admonish a guy who had just done so. Then he'd ask, "Why's that, Cal?" and leave him alone on the bench with his thoughts. At the tag end of the time out, Collard would come back to the player. He'd give him a nod and a smile: "Now, whaddaya say to that, Cal?"

"No point fouling. You're playing him tight, you've already got him out of his rhythm. Odds are he'll miss the shot anyway."

"Well put!" Jeb would commend him. "Now, guys, on defense let's drop back in zone and, Cal, you front that number 55 in the low post. Eddie, keep feeding Bradshaw. Let him try posting up on that small forward. Matt, I'm pretty sure you can back him in for a six-foot turnaround. Okay now? Let's go get 'em!"

We'd huddle up and clasp hands. "One, two, three, HOPE!"

If Collard's Socratic silence was his strength, it was also his notable flaw. Some said it was the reason his career had stalled at Hopewell. His press conferences were as loquacious as his time outs. He answered questions in monosyllables. Needless to say, he was never in demand as a motivational speaker on the banquet circuit. While he had a phenomenal winning record, the big-time schools saw Collard as a taciturn misfit in coaching.

But anyone who'd played for Jeb knew better. After all the years I'd logged as a professional student, I suspected he was the best teacher I'd ever had. So I sat on the porch and waited Jeb Collard out. I could imagine what he was thinking. Sooner or later, I expected he'd have something to say about my wife—although I wasn't so sure I wanted to hear it.

But his first comment wasn't about Cynthia. He cleared his throat. "Matt, what brings you back?"

I sat for a few minutes and tried to gather my thoughts. The quiet had begun to feel comfortable—like a familiar language I hadn't spoken for a time. I sat and watched the last faint trace of sunlight touch the treetops as the sky faded black.

Finally, I said, "Maybe that's a question for me, too, Jeb. I'm sure it has a lot to do with life on the East Coast, for one thing. The quality of my other options."

And, with a deep breath, I tried to recount that strange, synchronous series of events that had transpired not more than six months ago. It was slow going, like driving a pickup truck in March mud, spinning my wheels in a morass of memories I hadn't begun to negotiate. My last half year at Eastbourne still left me mystified and rankled.

After a couple of stumbling attempts, I gave up and retreated to the safe ground of abstract analysis. "Jeb, it was a lot like the ancient Greek concept of seasonal time. You know, they measured time in a couple of ways. There was chronos, the kind of quantitative time we keep track of with clocks and calendars."

I saw his face begin to crinkle in a billious grimace. Philosophical speculation didn't rank high among his favorite sports. But I pressed on. "Then, you see, they had another conception of time..."

"Kairos," came a voice from the doorway. "I've got it in my notes. Means seasonal time. Fullness of time. Opportune time. The right time. Did I get that right, prof?"

"You pass the exam. Well, that's part of the answer to another question that I expect is coming: how'd I meet Cynthia."

"My, yes, we'd like to hear about that," chirped Emily as she passed around giant slabs of rhubarb pie slathered with ice cream. "Just everything. Now, wouldn't we, Jeb."

There was a long pause, and I thought I heard him start to clear his throat. But suddenly the silence of the night was shattered by a deep, croaking sound like a thousand buzz saws. Cynthia yelped and jumped a foot. The cicadas were in full voice late in August, first from one side of the house, then the other. Soloists and antiphonal chorus—their droning drowned out any prospect of conversation.

Emily got up and went back to the kitchen. She returned with a pot of coffee. And then as she sat down again, as if on cue, the cicadas fell silent. We were enveloped in the quiet of the night.

"Matt, of course all that's of interest to me," Jeb remarked. I sensed he was getting ready to wrap up the evening. "Wouldn't you say so, Em? What you got to hear of Matt's story? I can fill you in on the rest of what he told me."

"An education's what I'd call it," Emily affirmed. "That and an adventure. But, now, tell us more about you and Cynthia."

"One more question, if you can answer it," Jeb interjected. Cynthia looked miffed but he ignored her. He took a deep breath, expelling it slowly. "Matt, do you have any idea what's been going on around here? I mean, it's great to have you back and all. But how much do you know about the condition of the college?"

"Not a lot," I admitted. "I've driven around the campus, and I did notice some crumbling sidewalks, peeling paint on a couple of the buildings."

"'Deferred maintenance,' is what you call it," Jeb sneered, sardonically. That's what we're taught to say 'round here. Our peerless president has his own way of puttin' things."

"Now Jeb, don't you get started in on Julian Reid," Emily broke in. "You promised you wouldn't say anything disheartening this evening. Remember, young Matt just got here."

"That's okay, Emily," I told her. "I lost my innocence some time ago."

Cynthia snorted.

"Actually, I have an appointment with the president in the morning," I continued. "To lay out my duties, and all. I guess I also need to figure out what to call him."

"Talk with folks on the faculty, and you'll get a passel of suggestions," Collard offered.

Emily cautioned, "Jeb..."

"'The Greased Beast from the East.' That's the formal title," Jeb went on in one breath, before she could stop him. "You knew old Jules when you were a student here, didn't you?"

"Yeah, he came from Boston, my sophomore year."

"Well, you're sure to recognize him. Still wears his hair in that black pompadour, propped up with all that pomade. Shorthand 'round here they call him 'The Greaser.' Or just 'Slick.' He was a pig outta shit when he got here, and from what I can tell he still ain't caught sight o' the barnyard."

"Jeb, just stop!" said Emily, her voice a couple of decibels louder.

"Well, only one more thing, Matthew. Whatever old Julie tells you, I'd advise you to get it in writing. Otherwise you're gonna find yourself dean of students and chairman of two academic departments. Faculty been droppin' like rats from the Titanic. Ya know who lived in that place you all are rentin'?"

I was about to tell him I didn't when the droning started up again. But this time it came from a distance: low and sonorous, far down the street from the edge of town. As the hum grew louder, it seemed more strident than the cicadas. There was an edge to the sound, and it mounted to a roar.

And then a couple of Harley Davidsons rounded the corner. I watched the riders pass beneath the streetlight: just your basic bikers in their black leather jackets and indigo bandanas, going slow for show through the neighborhood. But then I noticed their hair and their beards. These guys were grizzled gray, grandfather color, wiry with age.

"Bikers?" I muttered, as the noise of the engines subsided. "Can't say I remember anything like that out here in Mayflower."

"Up from the Bottoms," Jeb responded. "Whole colony of 'em down there, what I hear. Just one more feature of the changing landscape ... Well, Matthew, *tempus fugit.* Welcome home to Mayflower. That's for starters. And I'd say you got a whole lot more to discover."

The red digits read 2:08 as I raised my head groggily from the pillow and peered at the clock face on the bed stand. I'd been restless and writhing all night. Something in my stomach felt like molten lead. That second helping of Emily's rhubarb pie!

But there was more. My mind was grappling with another conundrum. Why couldn't I explain to Jeb how I got out here? As I lay there wrestling with the covers, I tried to make sense of my meeting with Harold Alabaster.

⚜

He had a killer office, as academic quarters go. It was a corner suite on the third floor of the biggest brick building on campus. Alabaster was dean of arts and sciences, and an awesome figure: an in-your-face administrator who'd gut the budget of another department as readily as he'd sign a diploma. Some said he had designs on the presidency of Eastbourne.

As I sat in his waiting room, it seemed hard to bet against him. The pine-paneled walls were plastered with Alabaster's diplomas in sociology, plus photos of him conferring honorary degrees on some portly guys who looked suspiciously like donors.

I remembered watching His Deanship in action at faculty meetings. He was a big man, maybe 6-6, and he tipped the scales at a good 250. Alabaster had a powerful mystique about him. He was a racial enigma—a mulatto with wide nostrils and the sculpted lips of a Bantu—and he knew how to play that card. Eastbourne counted him in its slim store of minority faculty members. But his skin was so light, it was almost olive-like. In truth, the man looked mostly Italian. He billed himself as a "multicultural specialist."

Now he was twenty minutes late for my 3:00 appointment. Finally, the intercom phone buzzed, and his austere secretary answered. She sat nodding and murmuring, taking notes. Then she carefully replaced the receiver and stepped over to where I stood before a photo of Alabaster passing a plaque to the leader of a West African coup.

"Mister Bradshaw," she pronounced in clipped syllables. "Dr. Alabaster has asked me to convey his apologies. He indicates that he is occupied with a difficult question of academic rank, but that the discussion is close to consummation. He appreciates your forbearance.

"In addition, he wished me to convey..." She peered at her notebook. "'Chill out, dude, and grab some pine. Take five, and we be jammin'!'"

"And now then," she concluded, smiling faintly. "May I offer you some tea?"

It was another twenty minutes before Alabaster came lumbering through the door. He turned to me with a weary sigh. Motioned me into his office. "There are some days, Bradshaw, when I wish I had chosen another line of work... Did you know that I played college ball?"

"Might have guessed it, sir," I responded, somewhat cautiously. "What are you: about six-six?"

He smiled. "An inch less than you: correct? In fact, I know it."

He opened a sunflower-yellow folder and consulted a computer printout.

"Hm: it's an interesting story you have there, Bradshaw. Entered college as a six-foot point guard and graduated as a six-seven forward. I've heard of cases like that: Jack Sikma at Illinois Wesleyan; Jerome Kersey, Longwood College in Virginia. Classic case of a kid with good tools, but too small to make it at a major university. Till he goes through a late growth spurt. By then, he's enrolled in a little school and it's too late to transfer.

"From what my sources tell me, you kept all your backcourt skills: quickness, shooting range. 'Exceptional peripheral vision and court-sense; plays forward like a point guard. Potential point forward a la Chris Mullin,'" he read. It sounded like an NBA scouting report.

Looking back, it's easy to see that I might have offered a rejoinder. Such as, "How do you know that?" Or, "Who the hell are your sources?" Or maybe, "Cut the crap. Can't you see this is serious? I'm here to talk about a job!"

But in fact I lacked that kind of chutzpa just then. I'd heard stories of the dean drawing out a switchblade knife in faculty meetings—to make a point, so to speak, in the discussion.

So I wound up listening to a chronicle of his exploits as the first black basketball player to don the colors of the Fighting Quakers at the University of Pennsylvania. As he got rolling, he took on the argot of the streets: "Hey, man, we come up on Princeton next year, and here be that same dude threw down thirty, year befo'! No shit: I see that mo-fo, I be pumped, man—no jivin!'"

I sat there and took all this in—uncertain how much of his rambling tale to believe. Did the dean really have another life where he spoke like this, or had he completed a course in conversational street talk? Maybe they required that in multicultural studies.

But he made one comment I was inclined to believe. "I'd had a lot more press except for my Sicilian mother," he noted, his dialect fading. He gazed out the window with a sigh. "Was I black or was I white? 'The Great Gray Hope'—that's what they called me."

There was a knock on the door and his secretary timorously stepped in. "Will that be all, sir?"

"Why yes, of course, Edna. Have a splendid evening." He turned to me: "Now then, Bradshaw, about your interest in employment..."

Alabaster took three minutes to review a three-page summary of my doctoral dissertation on seventeenth-century English land reform: a study it had taken me three years to complete. Then he peered at me over his half-moon reading glasses and slowly shook his head.

"How the hell'd you come up with a subject like this: Gerrard Winstanley, leader of the Diggers. Never heard of the dude. You think this is gonna make him a household word? And you along with him?"

I gulped and took a deep breath, my academic career swaying on the high wire. Then I launched into a long account of the enclosure movement in seventeenth-century England, the loss of the commons. And of family farms in Kansas. I went on to describe that Saturday morning in the library of Hopewell College when I caught sight of the glowing sun on the wheat fields, and recognized how someone in another time could have had the same vision. Saw the value of the commons, how the past and the present were intertwined like the roots in a grove of cottonwoods—I believe that's how I put it.

"And from that time on, I knew I had to..."

"CLICK!" An echo through the office. I turned to see Alabaster attending to his fingernails with a six-inch switchblade knife. I couldn't tell if he'd stopped listening to me entirely, but it was evident that a clot of dirt under his left index fingernail now occupied a good part of his attention.

"Well I guess that's a long enough answer to your question."

For a time, Alabaster continued his manicure. Then he said, "Bradshaw," very slowly, with the 'D' as a separate syllable. He smiled faintly. "Let me lay this out to you as artfully as I can.

"I like you. First time I read your folder, I kinda took a shine to you. Maybe it's 'cause you played some ball. Maybe 'cause you come here for a reason. I get so fuckin' fed up with these fatuous faggots don't know jackshit 'bout anything outside a school. Most of 'em never caught on how to piss straight— but that ain't you. You coulda done somethin' else with your life. But, hey, you chose to go on to school.

"So now you pumpin' you brains out tryin' to get through to them jag-offs gotta take your class."

He set down his knife and leafed through the yellow folder. "The Boston Celtics and ancient Greek philosophy. The point guard as prime mover. Hee-hee! Cain't say you ain't tryin to get it up and take it to the hole. And the evaluations show it. 'Course, most those kids got no clue what the fuck you talkin' 'bout. But they like it that you tryin' to make contact.

"An' so now whadda we got you doin' here but stoop labor… But, Bradshaw, how the hell are you intendin' to make a living with a doctorate in history and a specialty like that? Look here, it's getting late and my third wife is home, waiting dinner." He tossed my folder aside.

I watched him pick up his knife and balance the slender tip against the middle finger of his left hand. Then he laid it down carefully. Almost involuntarily, I followed the long blade back to the notch at the shank. I noticed the handle. It was mother-of-pearl.

Suddenly, I caught sight of myself in my mind's eye, and I shuddered. Saw myself lined up with all those other limp dicks at the faculty meetings, taking our cues from a weird dean with an upscale, switchblade knife.

"All right, then," I heard myself say as I rose to my feet. He was leaning down to stuff some papers in a satchel. "I know you have to leave. We've had a lot to talk about: seventeenth-century history, college ball. But I need to get on with my life. What I mean to say is: are there any other jobs around here?"

When he looked up I was leaning on his desk, standing over him.

Alabaster peered at me a moment, eyes slitted. "Never can tell," he muttered. Then he took out a business card and wrote on the back. He handed it to me. "Might pay to get you more involved. Enrollment management committee—be at this meeting."

"An' get the lights as you go out." He shrugged on his trench coat, brushing by me out the door.

※

Swinging my feet slowly to the floor, I took care not to wake Cynthia. Drowsily, I exulted in one of the great features of married life—the assurance of another warm body in bed. There was something downright Middle American and comforting about it. I glanced toward the soft, rounded hillock of my wife.

But the bed covers lay flat! She wasn't there. It was just about then that I heard the first, low, humming sound coming from outdoors. It was regular and rhythmic. Guttural, like a chant.

I stumbled from the bedroom into the living room toward the front door, and as the floor board creaked the humming stopped abruptly. For a moment, I stood still, listening to the silence of the night. Then I opened the door to find Cynthia. She was sitting in a folding chair on the veranda.

"God, you scared me," I told her. "I woke up and you were nowhere in sight. Then I heard some weird kind of singing—some sort of chanting. Was that you?"

She didn't look up. "Just practicing for the cicada chorus," she mumbled. "Heard they're having open tryouts tomorrow night."

I noticed that she was sitting cross-legged, drawing on her sketchpad. Cynthia was leaning to one side, and she seemed to be peering at something down south on Winthrop, toward the town flag. She still hadn't looked up at me.

"May I see what you're drawing?"

"Sure. But just don't ask me to explain it. I'm afraid it's somewhat unconventional. Might not find a market around here."

I ignored the rancor in her voice and leaned over her shoulder to look at the sketchpad, pausing to peruse her flowing hair and the fullness of her breasts beneath her nightgown. As I focused on the drawing, I tried to make it out. The sketch was elaborate and she must have been at it for a while.

It was centered in a long, vertical shaft—like a flag pole or even a phallus. At the top of the shaft, a thick, oblong object hung limply from a single tendril on one side. There was something streaming from the object, like tattered fabric or maybe a liquid substance like blood. It might have been a flag unfurled, or a horrible dismemberment—a patriotic emblem or a symbol for castration. Whatever the drawing represented, it was dark and grotesquely energetic.

I knew better than to press for an explanation. "Been out here long?" I asked.

She was silent for a moment, staring down the street, still sketching. "Maybe a half-hour."

"Did I wake you? I've got this major indigestion. I know I've been tossing around. Seems I'm going to have to get back in practice for the cuisine out here."

"I wish *I* knew what to practice," Cynthia said, softly. She returned to her drawing.

"Meaning?"

"Oh, I dunno." She set down her pad and moved to face me. As she turned around, Cynthia shook her head and let her hair tumble down toward the floor of the veranda. Then she tossed her head back and smoothed her hair with spread fingers. It was a gesture that always presaged some serious statement.

"Look, Matt, I know we haven't been here all that long. But something about this town is starting to give me the creeps."

"Such as?"

"Last night: Jeb Collard. I don't know what I expected to find in him. Maybe a Buddha-like guy: what you told me about his silences and all. Some kind of heartland Siddhartha. But once he opened up … Christ, that sexist 'Ma'm' shit! And talk about your regional bias: slamming the college president just because he came from the East. As it happens, that's the direction I rode in from … Matt, I just don't know about all this."

I stood there and felt my heart sink down into the pit of my upset stomach. Now my insides ached as one.

"Cynthia, believe me, I know exactly what it's like to feel like an alien. But give this place a chance. Give these people a chance. I know they're not saints, and I may have oversold them. But I know you'll find some people you like out here."

"Sure, if I keep my mouth shut and my thoughts to myself. But you know I'm interested in new places. Here I am, a soc major. I'm psyched, excited to be seeing this place. But from what I can tell, these folks don't exactly wanta be seen."

"Well, I'll bet you'll find some way of making contact. At the college, say. Maybe some kind of research. With everything they need, there are bound to be some openings."

At that, she slowly rose to her feet and set her sketch pad aside. She snuggled against me, then looked up slyly. "Uh, speaking of openings, wanta give that leg spring a try?"

4

Julian Reid wore a smile. That's all I could remember as I left my house the next morning and hiked up the hill to meet with him. My appointment was at ten, and I left myself some time to stroll and savor the sights of my neighborhood.

Crossing Winthrop, I cut through the park past a playground where a couple of towhead moms were out with their kids. The morning sun was streaming through the elm trees, and it sparkled on their flaxen hair. Chatting as they rocked two toddlers back and forth on creaking, chain-link swings, they looked up and smiled as I came by.

I thought some more about Julian Reid's smile. It was an extraordinary expression: a broad, expansive grin that lit up his face like a nickelodeon. As I recalled, the smile was damned near perpetual. Unremitting. Reid would grin, whatever the occasion. I remembered him as minister of the Mayflower Congregational Church, before they'd made him president of the college.

It was a cold, cloudy day in March. A dismal day and, to top it off, Good Friday. Reid had got up in the pulpit and described the crucifixion of Jesus in some detail—all the blood and gore and horror of it—and he did it with a smile. People were shaking their heads in the pews all the while.

His smile was a trait that might have served him well in some other profession. But in Mayflower, Kansas it didn't play well. That grin had a way of making you wonder what he was up to.

I wondered just what Julian Reid might have in mind for me this morning, how he viewed my role as dean of students. It was only two weeks till the beginning of the school year, so we didn't have a lot of time to negotiate. I'd brought along a legal pad to keep notes and planned to ask him for a written job description. I remembered Jeb's advice.

But as I sauntered along this morning, I knew I was in no mood to dicker over my duties. For the time being, I was just so damn glad to be back in High Plains Kansas that I'd have doubled as dean of students and dorm mother, had anyone asked.

Turning up Salem Street, four blocks from campus, I gazed at all the great frame houses surrounded by shade trees. Three stories tall with thirty-foot front porches. One of the largest homes sat at an angle, on a corner across from the park, and I could imagine the view from the veranda: the expanse of elm trees, the playground, and the bandstand in the shadow of that looming flag.

I noticed there were smaller homes on every block with signs of younger families: bikes and basketballs scattered across the yards. No concern for security around here. In one house, a kid of eight or nine dashed out the front door, screen door slamming. Then he jumped on his bike and took off down the street with a holler to a friend across the way. It was the first loud noise I'd heard all morning.

But not for long.

I became aware of a strange, grating sound swelling up from the north end of town, toward the campus. It was oddly irritating and it got louder as I neared the college dorms. Pretty soon it permeated the whole neighborhood, polluting the morning. A crass, metallic beat. And I recognized the genre.

Gangsta rap.

As I walked on toward the noise, I surveyed the college grounds. In the last weeks before school, clusters of work-study students were sprucing the place up. They were digging weeds, mowing grass, and painting trim on the dormitories. Several of the painters were black students, and one of them had brought a portable CD player on the job.

A lanky painter in a Crips-blue bandana was rocking to the rhythm as he leaned from a ladder to touch up trim around a dorm window on the third floor. I walked over to the base of the ladder and hollered up at him, "Hey there."

He looked down. "Yo."

"Mind turning that down? Still pretty early in the morning."

He set down his brush on the window sill and stared at me. "Who you?" he sneered.

"I'm Matt Bradshaw. New dean of students. Now, would you mind turning that down?"

He turned away, took up his brush and resumed painting. I watched him for a moment, then reached down and found the volume dial on a two-foot long black plastic box that sat at the foot of the ladder. I turned it down by half, then resumed my trek toward Old Main and the president's office. It occurred to me that the students of Hopewell College might not be overawed by my title. Not if the rapster were any indication.

I watched another group of students mount a large sign in front of another dormitory, and noticed there were new signs on most of the other buildings as well. Even the park benches. There was a new brass plaque on the drinking fountain in front of Old Main. And then I saw that the big old limestone building had a new sign, too. It had been designated "Cleaver Hall."

I peered at the sign for a minute and thought of my classmate, Rollie Cleaver. Then I shook my head. Naw, it couldn't be.

The admin building was always cool. I remembered that. Even on the hottest days, the stone walls created a climate of their own, and no one ever gave a thought to air conditioning. There was a rock-solid aura about the building: thick stone walls and shade trees. As I mounted the stairs, I picked up the familiar scent of pine tar disinfectant. Old Main even smelled the same.

The president's office was up four flights of stairs, in a cupola off the top floor surrounded by elm trees. I noticed the waiting room had been freshly carpeted. No one at the reception desk, so I took a seat in a lime green divan. It, too, looked new. I glanced at my watch; I was ten minutes early.

The door to Reid's office was shut, but not tight, and there were sounds of voices from behind it. At first the conversation was merely a murmur, but I soon recognized the president's voice. It had a smooth, oleaginous tone with the cadence of a career diplomat. That was Julian Reid, all right. No mistaking it.

The other speaker was a woman and her voice seemed familiar, too—a bright, strident sound. Now the voice was rising.

In a moment, I placed it: Hazel Gottschalk, head of the math department. She must have been here twenty years by now. Bright woman: single, maybe forty. Pretty well preserved, last I saw her. She was one of the first people I'd seen use a computer around here. "Hey!" I thought, "I should try to get to know her better. There's somebody Cynthia might take to."

But on this morning Hazel was in no mood for kibitzing. I could tell that by the way her voice continued to escalate as she carried on, faster and faster. It was a four-star diatribe. As I listened more closely, I could make out snatches.

"Head of the math department? Chair of the math department? Think... titles matter? Julian, I am the math department!"

"... tenure, Julian? ... offer me tenure? What good ... suffer a stroke? Part-time faculty, Julian? I've already ... every banker and accountant in town."

She opened the door a crack but postponed her exit, hand on the knob, to rail at him some more.

"My Lord, Julian, almost everyone in this town who can turn on a calculator is already serving on the math faculty. What I need is somebody who can teach upper division courses. Somebody other than yours truly. That, and a living wage. Aren't you embarrassed when you meet me in my other job? Doesn't it bother you to see me moonlighting like that?"

"Hazel, of course it's difficult for you." Reid could lather on the unction. (Cruise escort, TV game show host: there were other fields where he might have missed his calling. Not to mention fur salesman, funeral director.)

"But, Hazel, please consider this. I'm asking all my dear friends on the faculty to do so. We can raise more revenue: even in time for the new academic year. We can hire more faculty. God knows I'm still getting resumes. Even reinstate those poor souls we've had to let go. But you know what that means ... Don't you?"

There was a very long pause.

"Category Three," she said slowly, her voice subdued.

"That's right," Reid replied. "Now, do we want to repeat the events of last spring? Another round of expulsions? The police? The lawyers? That is what we must decide. You know, it's not so easy to find good student personnel people. Not when the entire staff resigns in midterm.

"Oh, yes, and that reminds me. It's ten o'clock and I need to see if Matt Bradshaw is here. You know he's come back as dean of students, don't you?"

Hazel Gottschalk swung the door open and strode into the anteroom. She wore the same, strong visage I remembered from my student days. But now I remembered how her dark eyes sparkled. Not a bad looking woman. I got up and smiled as she extended her hand.

"Hello there, Matt," she said, surprisingly warmly.

I said, "Hi, Ms. Gottsch..."

She cut me off: "How's that again?"

"Hazel," I said, with a smile.

Then I turned to greet Julian Reid who was grinning from ear to ear. He must have known I'd heard at least the last part of his conversation, but if it fazed him he didn't show it.

I told Hazel a bit about what I'd done at Eastbourne. About Cynthia and her career with computers. "Sometime I'll have to introduce the two of you."

"What's wrong with tonight? Bring her on out to the Hoof'n Horn. Friday night's Rib Night."

"What time?" I asked.

"Any time, five o'clock to midnight," she reported somewhat glumly. "You can bet I'll be there." She turned to Julian Reid and studied him a moment. And with that, she was out the door.

Julian shook his head wearily as he ushered me into his office. As I took a seat, I remembered the comforting feel of the place. Four stories up, sheltered by elm trees. Today it smelled of fresh paint. The turreted walls had been done up in a soft green that melded with the leaves outside the leaded windows. I'd always enjoyed visiting the president's office. It was a cross between an executive suite and a tree house.

"My, but we're delighted you've come back here!" Reid began, and I felt a rush of warmth, although I suspected he'd have said the same to the Unabomber.

"I do wish I had more time this morning—and we'll have many more occasions to visit—but I have an important meeting with one of our fine supporters at eleven. So I've made up a packet of materials for you, and I thought we'd spend some time in orientation. By the way, that will be one of your first responsibilities, you know. Freshman orientation comes up in two weeks. Of course, having been a student here should give you a good head start." He smiled even more broadly.

Julian spent the rest of the hour running through the prime events of the academic year. By the time we arrived at June commencement, he must have offered me a half dozen additional assignments, each with an impressive title but no pay. Everything from teaching a required freshman religion and philosophy course (I muttered, "No thanks." He said, "Well, there's a new minister in town.") to assisting Jeb with the basketball squad (I told him I wasn't sure).

He had nothing at all to say about the condition of the college, and seemed caught up in the rites of academe. ("Shall we have a full academic procession for the fall convocation?") We might have been talking about some smug, svelte, Eastern institution that didn't have to sweat its next payroll. Maybe Oberlin or Swarthmore: not this beleaguered little college in Kansas.

Then, close to 11:00, he glanced at his watch and began looking out the window for his guest. He explained that, with budget constraints, he'd been unable to hire a replacement for his secretary, Mavis Lindholm. She was on vacation.

I spoke up, "Julian, I have one other question. I'm sure you know how glad I am to be back at Hopewell; it's about like home to me. But there's one thing I need to know." I paused and looked him in the eye.

"Just how bad is it?"

He looked thoughtful for a moment, then offered a quizzical smile. For an instant, I thought I saw a glint of recognition in his eye and a hint of substance: some sort of substratum to the man. It was as though a curtain briefly parted.

But just that fast the curtain closed and Julian took his familiar stance above the footlights. "Matthew, sometimes I have asked myself: what is life without a challenge? Adversity enriches life. After all, what would an athletic contest be without the opposition? Nietzsche put it so well: 'That which does not destroy me, makes me stronger.'

"Ah, my young friend, you are about to embark on an altogether fortifying venture!" He gazed off into the elm trees with an enigmatic smile.

Suddenly, there was a cacophony out on the stairwell. Whoever it was sounded like a member of the Budweiser team of Clydesdales as he clambered up the steps, two or three at a time. Then a loud pounding on the outer door.

"Ah, my next appointment," Reid announced with an eager, almost salivating smile. "I'll be back in a moment. In fact, I'll likely bring this person in. It might be he's someone you know."

He closed the door as he left, but I could still pick up the tone of his voice. It rose like a jet at takeoff as he greeted his visitor. Something about this guest was animating.

Meanwhile, I sat and mused over whatever the hell it was I'd just been told. "Fortifying venture" sounded politely ominous. I found myself pondering other careers for the president: ballet dancer, competitive figure skater. No one could pirouette around a tough question quite like Julian Reid.

In a few minutes, he charged back into the office with a sandy-haired, broadheaded fellow in a purple plaid suit. Julian held him by a coat sleeve with one hand. In his other hand he clutched a pale green bank draft, waving it as the ink dried.

"Matt!" Rollie Cleaver thundered as he lurched into the office. He had a big, hoarse voice that always seemed on the verge of breaking into a full-blown holler. As Rollie freed his sleeve from the president's grip, he gave me a hearty handshake.

"Well, hi, Rollie. Geez, has it really been five years?"

Julian Reid quickly recounted the career exploits of my fellow classmate and former basketball teammate. As he rattled on, I remembered Rollie's history. His family had owned a large feed lot just over the hill, north of town. The operation sat well out of sight from the college, but when the north wind blew it was never out of mind. They must have had several thousand cattle on the grounds out there, and they all smelled awful. Rollie had taken a ragging for it on campus.

"So after Pa died," Rollie said, picking up his own story, "I went an' expanded. Seemed there was lots of folks come down the highway had never seen themselves a feed lot. Not one big as ours anyway. So we put in a scenic overlook.

"Then, pretty soon I saw so many folks was comin' by to take a gander at the cattle, I thought to myself: why not put in a steak house? Well, now, just wait until you see it. I bet you've heard about it already, now, haven't you? The Hoof'n Horn!"

"As a matter of fact I have, Rollie. I may even see you out there tonight."

He glowed with pride.

"Well, there is so much more to tell about Rollie's accomplishments," Reid exuded, "and his generosity. Especially when it comes to the college. I'm sure you saw the sign out front: Cleaver Hall. And then, of course, there's the Steer A Year Club."

"Right," Rollie added. "In fact, we have our monthly breakfast meeting next Tuesday, and I still haven't found a speaker." He looked at me, knowingly. "But I believe I might have got one now!"

Julian chuckled and walked around his desk to pull something from the top drawer. It was a plaque: mahogany with a brass plate. Then he drew out a Polaroid camera and handed it to me.

"Matt, please take a snapshot of our newest adjunct faculty member." He read from the plaque as he handed it to Rollie and clasped his hand: "To Rowland Cleaver, Marketing Instructor in the Business Department, Hopewell College. In recognition of your esteemed and faithful service. August, 1995."

I clicked the shutter and caught them in a toothsome grin. And then I took off, with a promise to look up Rollie at the steak house that evening. "An' don't forget the speech now. Steer A Year Club!" Rollie hollered.

As I ushered myself out through the anteroom, I noticed a column of dark, flat objects teetering next to the secretary's desk. It was a stack of mahogany plaques, same as Rollie's.

I must have an office here, somewhere, I thought, as I made my way downstairs. I tried to recall where the dean of students had been when I was a student here, and vaguely remembered a cubbyhole somewhere in the basement. I asked a clerk in the business office and, sure enough, she pointed down a flight of stairs. Then she rustled around in a cabinet and found a key.

The stairwell outside the basement smelled a bit dank and musty, but that was nothing compared to what I found inside my office door. As I flicked the light switch, something black and fast and furry skittered from under a desk and darted behind a file cabinet in the far corner.

I took a sidestep and stumbled over a pile of mail in the middle of the floor. Leaning down to pick it up, I shook off a layer of dried rodent turds. About then, I took my first deep breath in my new quarters. I almost passed out. The smell was acrid and fetid, overpowering—mildew and rat shit. I cut the lights and slammed the door.

Upstairs, I asked the business office clerk if she'd find a custodian to clean up my garden-level quarters. She nodded, with a sympathetic smile. Then she found me a packet for my pile of mail and I headed back across campus toward home.

Now the campus felt different. The freshness of the morning had dissipated, and the air was merely Midwest hot and humid. Hopewell College looked like Kansas in August: more barren than I'd remembered. I wondered how the place would seem when the students arrived to repopulate it and tried to envision them buzzing around campus. Then I found myself wondering whether they'd show up at all.

As I shambled down the long, sloping hill toward the south end of campus, I heard at least one sound of life. It was a familiar, gritty sound: sort of like sand in a meat grinder.

"Baby, come on down,
Gonna show you around!"

"Hey, you up there on the ladder … Hey, Picasso!"
This time, the kid simply shook his butt to the beat and carried on with his touch-up work on the third floor of the dorm. He ignored me.

I walked over to the ladder and set my notepad and mail on the ground. Then I grabbed the squawk box by its handle and started up the ladder, very slowly.

As I was halfway up the first story, he must have felt the ladder jar and it seemed I had his attention. He looked down and then drew back involuntarily as he saw me ascending, rung by rung. As I neared the second story, he dropped his brush in the paint can and stuck out an arm to probe the nearest window. But the window was closed. He saw that he was stuck there on the ladder as I continued my climb. Now I was only a half dozen steps below him.

"Hey you—Ofay! Who the fuck you think you are, man?"

"Why, I'm the dean of students. I thought I'd mentioned that last time I was by here. And I believe I also said that I'd be mighty grateful if you turned this thing down." I lifted the black box toward him.

"Fuck you, muthafucka! Get your ass off this fuckin' ladder or I'm comin' down … "

His eyes were wide, and I could see his knees tremble beneath his Levis. He was a tall kid, close to my height but thin as a rail. I mounted the last few rungs until I stood next to him on the last, slim segment of the ladder. It was shuddering with the flutter of his knees—more or less in synch with the rap tune, still blaring.

"Baby, come back soon,
Ya know, I need some poon!"

"I'll give you one more chance to turn this thing down," I told him, as I crowded in on his rung of the ladder. I held the boom box in front of his face, a foot out in space. Now the young man looked at me closely, noted the size of his vertical visitor. I saw sweat begin to drip from beneath his blue bandana.

"Gimme that!" he squawked, and clutched at the CD player. But as he grabbed the ghetto blaster, he glanced at the ground three stories down. And he froze. For an instant, it seemed he might lose his balance. He'd leaned out a half inch too far.

As he quavered on the rung, I held the ladder tight with one hand and clutched him with the other. He caught his balance and steadied himself. But as he leaned back on the ladder, the plastic CD player slowly slid from his perspiring hand.

Together, we stood and watched it catapult, end over end. It smashed in several pieces on the sidewalk.

Not much was said as we climbed back down the ladder. The kid picked up the remnants of his sound box and extricated the rap disk from the ruins. He stuck it in its case and tossed the player back on the ground.

"Shee-it," he declared, and looked away. "Be some shit to pay for this. Call the brothers!" I saw he was still shaking.

"You mean you're gonna call out the Crips on me, right here in Mayflower, Kansas? Whoa!" Then I remembered my role on campus.

"Look, it's too bad about what happened up there. But it was either you or the boomer. Geez, I cannot believe you're the first student I met, my first day on this job. So, what's your name?"

"Simpkins. Ja-mal Simp-kins."

"You're tall. Play some ball?"

"Better believe it. An' Coach gonna hear 'bout this," he muttered darkly as he strode away.

"First the Crips and now Coach Collard," I called after him. "Now I know I'm in trouble!"

It was a glib line and I laughed for a while, but it didn't sit well. As I hiked on home, the incident still rankled. When I got to the park, I sat down on a tree-shaded bench for a time. When I closed my eyes, a scene came on in the back of my mind.

I showed up for my regular workout at the Eastbourne gym and there was a sign on the door. "OPEN TRYOUT. Connecticut Pride, CBA." A locker room full of big black guys. Changing clothes, slapping hands, bantering in sound bites. "Hey, Zeke. Yo, whazzup, bro?" An invasion by the Continental Basketball Association—the major minor league in pro basketball and, for these guys, their only shot at the NBA.

I started to turn around and leave but a guy named Cleanthe— "Call me Cle"—grabbed my hand and welcomed me into the mix. "You tall 'nuff, got your gym bag. Lesse if you can play some." And before I knew it, I was on the court in a shiny blue jersey with silver letters: "Connecticut Pride."

The game that ensued was not really a game. Most times up and down the court, the only guys who touched the ball were the one who brought it up and fired a three-pointer and the one who snared the rebound. But Cle and I got into a rhythm, passing and cutting and dishing to the one who was free. He hit a short jumper, curling off my screen. I buried a shot from the top of the key and he applauded, "You got it, Baby."

One of the coaches began to take notice. I considered I should advise him, "I'm not really here for a tryout. You see, I'm a college professor. I give boring lectures … "

But I was into it, with Cle. I took his pass at the foul line, faked my defender, and with two steps soared to the hole and slammed it. There was a shout from some of the players. And then crunch and a rip and a scream, from me, as I came down hard and my ankle gave way.

They carried me out of the gym.

I opened my eyes. How long had I been sitting here? Must be time for lunch. But how clearly I could see it all, hear the voices. And feel the warm support of my teammate. There was Cleanthe, hoisting me into the van that took me to the emergency room. *"One thing 'bout you, man. You had one fine game, in you' time."*

5

The music was blaring as I came in the door: vintage Cheryl Crow, full volume. But I could hear Cynthia rustling around up in the second floor bedroom. We had a half attic with a slanted ceiling and a single window—a little dormer that looked out on the park. A snug space, carpeted, with burlap on the walls. I'd had my eye on it for a home office, but Cyn had claimed it first. I was sure to have a nice office at the college, she'd said.

I trotted up the half flight of stairs and found her sitting lotus-style in the center of the room, surrounded by packing boxes and bubble wrap. She was poking at the keyboard of a sleek, black laptop computer with a bright, colored screen.

"Look here, Matt. Can you believe this?" She was grinning like a kid at Toys R Us as I bent over to give her a kiss. "It showed up this morning: UPS, from Intelcor."

"Who's that?"

"Oh, some outfit that's offered me a job. Online social research. They're some kind of spinoff from the soc department at Eastbourne. But look at all this! There's a shitload of instructions I have to get through to go online. But I'm having a blast just messing with the programs on the hard drive. This thing's fast as a frat brother."

We set out looking for a phone jack to hook up the modem and found one just behind the door.

I told Cynthia about my encounters with Julian, Hazel, Rollie, and Jamal, and we made plans for a late dinner at the Hoof 'n Horn. Then I took a lawn chair out back to sift through my mail as Cynthia continued her high-tech excursions. Every now and then I heard her squeal, and she'd come running downstairs to show me some other hot button on the computer.

"I had no idea they'd ship me this kind of hardware," she exclaimed at the end of the day, as we cracked a couple of beers and lounged out on our lawn chairs. "Sort of makes me wonder what they have in mind."

We sat out back for about an hour as the sun slowly set and the stars came up. "My God, will you look at 'em all!" she sighed with genuine wonder.

"There's a lot to see when you turn off the city lights," I told her. "And the sounds and the smells—God's country."

But by suppertime I wished to retract that last line. As we drove up Winthrop, past the college to the highway intersection north of town, Cynthia started to furrow her brow. Then she grabbed her nose and made a gagging sound. "Shit, what is that smell?"

"Hate to tell you, Cyn, but you just said it. Rollie's feed lot sits next door to our destination. Eau du Manure. That's what they always called that fragrance on campus."

Once in the parking lot, the smell of methane was even more over-powering. That concentrated cow shit caught in your throat: a thousand bovine bowels, all moving in synchrony. Still, you couldn't fault the steak house for authenticity. From the pungency of cow dung to the braying of the steers, Rollie's restaurant was genuine Americana. It was the real deal for anyone who liked to eat his steak up close to the source. A tour bus with Pennsylvania plates sat idling in the parking lot.

There was a big, gold medallion with an etching of a longhorn steer hanging from a timber at the entrance to the Hoof'n Horn Steak House. The place was log-covered and inside it had a warm, rustic look. The walls were dark barn wood, laden with colorful license plates from all around the States.

As we walked in, George Jones was wailing on the juke box.

We ordered beers at the bar while we waited for a table, and it wasn't long till Rollie came rushing by. The place was jammed and he appeared to be filling three or four job functions at the same time, from cleaning tables to cashiering. I grabbed his shoulder next time he ran by, and he turned around and grinned.

"You'd think he could hire help for what he's doing, if this place is so successful," Cynthia remarked as we sat down and dug into our first plate of ribs. If Rib Night meant all-you-can-eat, this platter was nothing more than a warm-up.

"Not Rollie, Cyn. This guy's wired. He's no Rhodes scholar, and I can't believe they have him teaching at the college, but I don't know anybody with more drive. If he weren't chasing around here, he'd be knocking himself out for somebody else."

On her second plate of ribs, Cynthia began bobbing her head to the beat of the juke box, and it occurred to me she might not have paid any attention to country music till we left the East Coast two weeks ago. Rollie's juke box offered decades of country classics, and she began quizzing me about the artists. I envied her, discovering George Jones and Vince Gill. The Oak Ridge Boys, the Statlers…

A clarion voice rang out from the barroom. "So the student asked me, 'Why is it you always refer to your computer as *he*'? And do you know what I told her?"

"Wha's that, Hazel?" from a loud, liquored patron.

"Because they're obviously male. First you have to turn them on, and show them what to do—and then they're done before you know it!"

There was a chorus of guffaws from the bar as she swept in carrying a tray of cocktails. An echo of appreciative comments. "Hey, Hazel, I never had a math teacher like you!"

She looked chic tonight in a black cocktail dress that matched her hair, and her dark eyes sparkled. This was a side of her I'd never seen on campus. As she came up to our table, a big ruddy fellow in a string tie and business suit stuck his head around the corner. "What time you gettin' off, Hazel?" he inquired with some feeling.

I introduced her to Cynthia, who flashed an admiring smile. "Hazel," I said, "Do you ever get a break?"

She said she'd take one. "I have a thing or two to say to you, Matt. You know, news travels fast around here and we haven't had much good news for a while." She whirled around to pick up another order.

"So what was that about, Your Deanship?" Cynthia inquired.

"I have no idea … But, God, I'm stuffed. Hey, you want to dance?" A half-hour later we collapsed in a booth, after stumbling through a line dance to "Achy, Breaky Heart."

We were still catching our breath when Rollie appeared. He slid in, butt-up next to Cynthia. "I must say, the scenery 'round here's improved quite a bit." He proffered a beefy hand.

"I guess I'll take that as a compliment," Cyn said. "Hey, Bro, glad to know you. I like your place a lot."

He grinned and stuck his hand straight up, three fingers in the air. "Hazel! Round o' Coors!" I thought I saw her middle finger waggle as she flashed the sign on toward the bar. Cynthia was smirking.

"Ya know, last time you lived out here, I was raisin' my hand like that in her math class. Huh, Matt?"

"Must be an adjustment, Rollie. For both of you. Well, from what I can tell, you've done all right for yourself."

"An' then some." He went on to recount all the businesses he had an interest in around town. To hear him tell it, it seemed he was a partner in half the economy of Mayflower and Milo County.

"Started a couple years ago, when we had to bail out the college, refinance the debt. That's when we come up with the Steer A Year Club. Then we got this idea of sellin' names to the buildings, and the agent-faculty program after that. Hey, we been movin'. There's a lot I got to catch you up on, Matt!"

But I saw that we were losing Cynthia. She was staring off in space. Then Hazel came by. "Another round of ribs?"

Cyn shook her head. "No thanks. Rollie's been filling us up with his exploits." Then she turned to him with a winsome smile. "But you know, there's one line of business I'm surprised you haven't considered."

"Yuh?" he looked up, with a smug grin.

"Gas masks. Ever think of that, Rollie? Hey, you could rent 'em at the door." His smile slowly faded to a muddled frown. We sat in silence.

"Break time!" Hazel declared. She tossed a bar towel in the general vicinity of Rollie and he caught it in midair. As he lumbered to his feet, he laid a large hand on my shoulder.

"Look here, Matt, seven o'clock in the morning, okay? Don't much matter what you say. Folks'll show up for the steak and egg boo-fay. That an' word's been gettin' 'round you're back here."

He picked up Hazel's beer tray on his way back to the bar.

"Well, I was gonna add that he could keep those respirators in a bucket by the door," Cyn said, "like the restaurants back East do with umbrellas. But that might not have been diplomatic."

Hazel scooted into the booth, laughing silently.

"So, tell me. Do you like doing this?" I asked.

She sat quietly for a moment.

"I guess you mean: do I have to. Well, I'm sure you've found out about the salaries at the college. But there are a few other advantages, such as getting away from that place for a few hours."

I asked her about the debt on the school and she us told that two years before Hopewell had almost gone under. "We had to persuade the vocal locals—the creditors—to take payment of ten cents on the dollar. Of course, by that time we were so short of staff that half of them were teaching part time. So they had a vested interest refinancing the place. As adjunct faculty."

"Must be what Rollie means by 'agent faculty,'" Cyn said.

Hazel shook her head and said nothing.

"Hey, Hazel!"

It was the red-faced fellow, at the door to the barroom. She got up, untying her apron. Then turned back to me. "One more thing— it's what I'd come over to tell you. I just wanted to thank you, Matt. Everybody around the college knows what went on between you and that Category Three kid this morning. You gave us all a lift. Congratulations."

"So, what'd she mean by 'Category Three?'" I wondered aloud as we were driving home. "You ever hear that term, Cyn?"

No sound but the wheels whirring.

"Well, I can speculate," I said. "I'll bet it's code for 'black kids.' But what'd she mean by 'side benefits,' working out there at the steak house?"

"You didn't get that? Jesus, Matt, we soc majors might not have any job skills, but at least we're trained observers."

"So what'd you observe?"

"I saw a nice-looking single woman in a pretty small town."

"And?"

"If you're unhitched and want a sex life in an outpost like this, maybe you'd better find a way to run into travelers."

"Huh, I guess that's right. And if you're not single?"

She unclipped her seatbelt and sidled over next to me, set a hand inside my thigh. Instinctively, I drove past our house and took a right turn on Main Street toward the river.

"Hey, Bradshaw, where you taking me? Where are we going?"

It was an old abandoned quarry, high on the bluffs, pretty well filled in now and overgrown with scrub oak and vines. As I turned off on the winding gravel road that led uphill, I had a passionate flash of déjà vu—another partner. This was a popular spot among the local undergrads. Given the undergrowth, you could be qualifying for a paternity suit ten yards from the next couple and no one was the wiser.

"Hm, I wonder what you used to do up here," Cyn sniffed as we spread a blanket at the edge of a clearing. You don't put much past a trained observer.

Afterward, we were quiet for a long time. I lay and gazed at the sky. The stars were out in profusion. Perhaps I'd been too busy up here on the bluff to notice before.

Finally, she went back to the car for her pad and started sketching.

🏵

There was a time, not too many months before, when I'd learned a bit about Cynthia, the artist. We were in a place called Zach's, up the hill from Eastbourne, on a Sunday morning. It was a new fern bar in an old brownstone and the place sparkled with ficus trees, the autumn sun streaming in through skylights.

She was radiant in a casually classy outfit: pink cashmere sweater, gold earrings, and faded blue jeans. I'd been surprised when she called me up one night after we'd run into one another at a meeting of the enrollment management committee, the one Alabaster had sent me to. She was there to show some charts and maps of high schools that fed students to Eastbourne. The computer graphics were stunning and I'd taken time to tell her so. Now she'd called and asked me out for brunch.

I followed her up the stairs to the table she'd reserved on a balcony that overlooked the main floor. I remembered the awkwardness of her visit to my office. Today, something was different about her. Maybe just that she'd graduated. Was that it?

We sat up on there on the mezzanine and had a good, long small talk. She was explaining her apparently conflicting interests in sociology and art, and how it seemed they'd begun to intersect.

"I wanted to tell you about that this morning," she explained. "But ... well, I'd just like you to know a bit more about me, so you won't think I'm totally home alone."

She described having gone to Eastbourne for their art department, then ending up minoring in it. But she couldn't find a career where anyone would let her draw. Every art-related field she looked at—fashion merchandising was one of them—had high-tech CAD programs. Computer aided design did all the drawing.

"I remember how you like to draw. You were always doing sketches in my class," I responded.

"I still do. All my life. I have to."

As it happened, in sociology they had a required course in computer graphics—layouts, charts, data mapping. And it turned out she was pretty good at designing maps. Even if no one would let her draw for a living, she said, she understood design.

"As an artist, I knew what looked good."

I might have wondered where all of this was leading, but found myself enjoying just looking at her. After a steady diet of grungy graduate school women, this girl was ...

"And that just might be my ticket to the real world," she was saying. "I learned how to link up data bases with the maps, all kinds of cool patterns and colors. And now, hey, even with my degree in sociology—my B.S. in B.S— I think I might have some marketable skills."

Then she looked at me, expectantly. "So, does that make sense, Matt?"

I hesitated. What was this, a back flip into our old roles as student and prof? "Sounds reasonable to me," I mumbled. I took a deep breath. "But let's go back to that business about knowing what looks good."

She looked puzzled.

The waiter came by with more coffee and I stared at her as I took a swallow. My stomach was churning. "Cynthia, you look fabulous this morning. I'd like to say that, now that I'm permitted. Now that you're no longer my student. You look absolutely great."

She flashed a smile. And I watched her eyes shift down toward the main floor. Behind a row of ficus trees, a group of male diners were falling into an impromptu line dance, to the hot, throbbing beat of Queen: "Somebody to Love."

The line was growing as some waiters joined in. Pushing back tables, poking, giggling, grabbing shoulders. I saw one guy skip in line with a fellow who might have been his twin. Matching perms and pastel sweaters.

Then I saw him at the head of the line. Head-bopping, grooving moves even the pale-faced could follow. Dr. Harold Alabaster. Cool dude. Dean of arts and sciences. He looked up as the line dance snaked our way and didn't seem to notice me. But I saw him glance at Cynthia and she nodded.

It was five days later that I found a notice shoved under my office door. Position Vacancy: Dean of Students, Hopewell College.

"Matt, look there," Cyn nudged me at the edge of the bluff, as we gathered up our things to go home. "Down there along the river." I stared at the dusky, tangled thickets of cottonwood trees that lined the riverbank. It was land that the Indians had never settled. Because of the threat of floods, they'd camped up on the bluffs well above the alluvial plain.

But when the white settlers arrived, they'd built down on the fertile farmland of the Bottoms and had struck it rich for a year or so, only to be flooded out every few decades. In time the river would change its course, engulfing every trace of civilization. Leaving it all to the gnarled trunks of cottonwoods, the russet stalks of salt cedar. It was said there were remnants of old, abandoned settlements all up and down the river.

"Matt, is that a town down there?"

I peered down from the bluff toward the dark floodplain they now called the Bottoms. Then I saw where she was pointing. Way back in the cottonwood groves, deep in the thickets, a dozen lights were flickering like candles at a midnight rite. I recalled Jeb's comment. Someone was living down there in the Bottoms.

We drove back by way of the campus, and I pulled in behind Old Main to see if the janitors had left a fan on to air out my office. Cyn waited in the car while I hiked around to the front of the building. As I rounded the corner, I was relieved to see the windows raised and hear a big fan whirring in the basement.

And then I heard another sound, from somewhere far off—overhead. It was a low murmur, sort of sporadic. I listened closely, but it stopped. Then it started up again—a kind of muffled moaning. I walked out on the lawn and looked up at Old Main. There was only one light in the building. It was glowing like a coal, from a turret on the fourth floor. And that's when I saw Julian Reid. He sat slumped before a small desk lamp, his head in his hands.

As I watched, he got up slowly and walked over to the window. He leaned out, with his hands propped on the sill, and looked all around. It seemed he gave a tremor. He groaned as he scanned the campus, from the north end to the south. I stepped back in the shadows of an elm tree, not sure he'd want to be seen in this state. There was no sign of his trademark smile.

As I stood and debated whether to call out to Reid or go up the stairs, he slowly drew in his head. And then the light went out in his office.

First thing in the morning, the Hoof'n Horn was a different world. Rollie's dance floor was filled with long folding tables, covered with red-checkered cloths and even small bouquets of flowers. Along the back wall, another row of tables held steaming plates of scrambled eggs and sirloin tips, Danish sweet rolls, and another high-cholesterol concoction I remembered from my student days. They called them "clams"—Bismarck sweet rolls sliced in two and stuffed with a half inch thick layer of white cream frosting. I made the mistake of scarfing one down before I had any nourishing food and felt my head buzz like a crop duster.

Whatever accounted for the crowd—whether it was me or, more likely, the boo-fay—the Hoof'n Horn was clearly the place to be in Mayflower on this Tuesday morning. Someone had got up in the middle of the night to fix this spread, and I suspected it was Rollie himself.

As I swilled a glass of orange juice, I tried to shake my head clear from the killer clam and recalled something Cynthia had said on our way home: "Man's got shit for brains, but you can tell he has ambition. That guy's juiced like a guava."

Rollie greeted all the Steer A Year Clubbers as they rounded the buffet table. There was some mumbling about the lack of rain. But the men seemed to brighten up as Rollie passed out buttons of black and gold: "Hopewell College. Harvard of the High Plains."

I found my place and got to visiting with a couple of others at the speakers' table. They were older fellows I'd never met but remembered having seen around town. One was a physician who told me he now doubled as county coroner. On my other side was the chief of police: a former basketball player who was a regular at the college games. Said he remembered my exploits: "Six-foot-seven, with a twenty-foot jump shot and a crossover dribble. How in the hell did you ever get permission not to play in the pros!"

After a time, Rollie got up and conducted a raffle. Then he displayed the plaque that would be awarded to every club member who donated a steer that year. It was a mahogany plaque, with a brass plate. Vaguely familiar.

"I'd expected President Reid would be here to introduce our speaker," Rollie noted, "but I don't see him, so I reckon I'll do the honors myself." He then spent most of the intro recounting how he'd been the one who'd snared the rebound and fed me the ball for my last-second shot to win the NAIA championship in Kansas City. I saw Jeb Collard squirm.

When he finally turned the microphone over to me, I rose to a warm round of applause. It felt good to be home again, and I told them so. But I thought I'd test the waters.

"What kind of town have I come back to? I'm not sure it's the same place I left. I believe I see Mayflower in a different light. Let me tell you what I mean."

I spoke about the bikers on the Bottoms, black students at the college. Some middle-aged burghers in blue suits at the front tables exchanged somber glances.

"Now, that's not the kind of community I remember," I told them, and the blue suits nodded gravely. "But I don't find that so bad. I believe the Mayflower of today is more vibrant, more alive, more open to new possibilities than the place I left five years ago. You know, I wonder if we're not learning to celebrate diversity."

There was a polite smattering of applause, and I looked up expectantly. But the front row fellows had folded their hands. They were staring at their shoes. I glanced back at my notes, for another foray. But just then a beeper went off and there was a flurry at the speakers' table. The police chief threw down his napkin and got up, scraping his chair. The crowd gave a murmur.

I waited till they'd settled down: "Hope it wasn't something I said." A ripple of laughter. "Now, the question is this. How do we deal with diversity, not just in our community but all across our nation?

"I've been thinking about that a lot these past few weeks—about a lesson I've learned from the game of basketball. A lesson from a man I consider the best teacher I've had, and I don't want to embarrass him because he's here with us this morning. But you all know who I mean: Jeb Collard!"

Now the applause was vigorous, and a number of men turned in their chairs to give Jeb a wave and nod at him. At the far end of the speakers' table, Rollie leaped from his chair, applauding, and a few others in the crowd stood up as well.

"Basketball is a deceptive sport," I went on. "I know a number of you have played the game—let me see your hands, all you ex-varsity players. High school or college. Well, that's most of the room. So I'll bet you know the great irony in the sport. And that is that very often the teams with the best players aren't winners. Am I right, those of you who've played ball?" Heads nodded.

"No, the winning teams have a special skill—like a sixth player—that goes beyond the abilities of individuals: shooting, passing, rebounding, defending. It's a skill that no one player has alone. A kind of sixth sense that the team must find together. We call it 'court sense.' It's the ability to see the other players—to be aware of everybody else on the floor."

Now I put my notes down and set sail toward my conclusion. "Court sense is a skill for life. It has everything to do with how we see others around us—whether, in fact, we can see them at all. Whether we can acknowledge other people as different from ourselves. Whether we can appreciate diversity.

"So that's the message I have to share with you this morning. It's court sense. Whatever our backgrounds, whether or not we've played ball, it seems to me we all can … "

Now the beeper on my left shrieked, loud as the first, and the coroner pushed back his chair. He gave me a pat on the back as he left the table hurriedly. The murmur of the crowd was mounting, and I found myself shouting over them. I could see I'd better wrap this up.

"So, we all can learn to see the whole court and acknowledge all the players in it. Accept others for who they are. Celebrate their diversity. All right?" I shouted, "Court sense!"

As I sat down, the audience broke into polite applause. Rollie got up and headed toward the podium, toting a bronze-plated mahogany plaque. He motioned me back to the mike, and I cringed. But before he reached me, someone burst through the back door and ran to the podium. He handed Rollie a note.

Rollie read it over, wide-eyed. Then he turned to face the microphone, haltingly. I'd never seen him move so slow. He set the plaque down. He cleared his throat once, then again. "It's from the po-lice," he said hoarsely. "It's President Reid. He's passed on."

There was an exhalation in the audience like a rush of wind, then a rising murmur that mounted to a question. Finally "shh, shh, shh," from all around the room and they fell silent.

"Says here they found him this morning," Rollie went on. "On the sidewalk outside his office. Four stories down … "

He stared at the note, red-faced, and started crying.

6

I t took me two days to come out with my revelation.

"Jeb, I saw him."

He sat there for a minute. "Saw who? Whom? I guess that's how you say it. Saw whom?"

"Julian Reid. I saw him, not too long before he died!"

Collard took a long draft of his coffee and chomped down on the remnants of a sweet roll. "So, tell me. No, wait. Stow it—here comes Mavis—unless you want the whole town to know."

The midmorning coffee break on the second floor of the admin building was a ritual at Hopewell College. It was hosted by Mavis Lindholm, a buxom matron in her mid-fifties who'd served as secretary to Julian Reid. She was one of those hot-wired, middle-aged women who seem to thrive on hot flashes—not the menopausal but the unpublished-news variety. In another day, she'd have made a great town crier.

"You knew he was a preacher when he came here, didn't you?" Jeb quickly changed the course of our conversation. I said I did.

"I 'spect that's how he came by all that charm. Man was a glad hander by vocation. Professional pleaser. Minister of the Congregational Church. Then, about ten years ago, college got itself in a mess."

Mavis leaned in, with a fresh plate of sweet rolls. "Oh my, yes, just ask my husband. Ask Gus about that. We own Mayflower Office Supply, you know. The college owed him $25,000 and he didn't think he'd ever see a dime of it. Not a dime. It was the same all over town. That's when we brought in Julian."

Jeb took up the story, as Mavis moved on. "They canned the president and gave the job to the minister of the church where the biggest creditors belonged. Figured they could trust the preacher to look out for their interests, even if he didn't know squat about running a college. Then they settled all those bills for ten cents on the dollar.

Saved the place from bankruptcy." His gaze sank into his coffee cup. "Least for a while."

"Okay, Jeb, so here's what I was saying." I described the scene outside the admin building late the other night. And confessed I sure as hell ought to have gone up the stairs to see if I could help him. But Jeb did not appear overly impressed. Around town, the speculation seemed to be that Reid been despondent over something or other—say, the college's financial condition—and taken a swan dive out his office window.

"But don't you think I ought to go by and see the chief of police? About what I saw. That might have a bearing on his investigation."

"Chief of police? That ol' codger couldn't find his ass with both hands. Investigation! Look here, Matt, I know you're long past seekin' my advice. But if you're gonna live here long-term—not just four years o' college, but really put down roots and stick around a spell—you gonna have ta learn one thing. In a town like this, you don't try to dope out everything 'bout everybody. In a small town, there's stuff you let go by."

The funeral was Saturday morning and we walked over. Cynthia put on a sleek, black power/business dress she'd brought from the East. I wore my one presentable suit. As we rounded the corner to the Mayflower Congregational Church, she pulled up short. It was the Collards.

Jeb was in high gear, one of his loquacious phases. "Now you think Reid was some kinda crowd pleaser, wait'll you see this new guy they got at the Congo Church. Talk about a grip-'n-grinner!"

"Jeb!" hissed Emily. "On the day of a funeral!"

But Collard ran on as we climbed the long flight of steps into the church, his head crooked in my ear. "One-time TV newscaster. Seems he threw it all over, enrolled in seminary once his kids were grown. Could be his ratings were down. Anyhow, he turns up in town this past summer, couple months before you folks. Name's Roger Squire—'nother East Coast Toady, can't you tell?"

Cynthia took my arm as Jeb swung open the big oak door into the vestibule. "Mighty nice get-up, Ma-am," he offered. "You can always spot a well-bred lady—touch o' class."

Cyn smiled demurely as she passed by into the sanctuary. Then she leaned over to Collard and belched in his ear.

I clutched her elbow and steered her down a side aisle, glancing back at Collard. He was staring at the two of us with a look of some sorrow. And then he lowered one eyelid very slowly.

A wink?

I plopped into a back pew and settled down into all the old familiar smells of the Mayflower Congregational Church. Pine tar varnish, musty seat cushions. Hymnals with the scent of aging pages. The place was redolent with tradition, like the archives of an old library. I saw Cynthia pull a pad out of her purse. She set to sketching something with a sharp, agitated motion.

I took in the scene: what a store of memories. Sarah had grown up in this church, and she'd introduced me to the Congregationalists. It was about the same time I'd got interested in seventeenth-century history, and I'd relished the Pilgrims: their venturesome spirit, non-conformist theology.

For a time, I'd even given thought to enrolling in seminary and becoming a Congregational minister, an ambition that scored points with Sarah. But as I saw what these guys actually did all week—praying over Ladies' Aid luncheons—I decided the word "minister" worked better as a verb than a noun. So I settled on teaching about the history of people like the Pilgrims.

What I couldn't foretell was that grad school would cost me my girlfriend. Sarah trusted her experience in this church and town, but she didn't care to venture past the city limits. So she'd wed my rival, a clod named Walt Wagstaff.

Now the organ stirred and rumbled into a Bach prelude. "Come Sweetest Death; Come Blessed Rest," according to the bulletin. I strained to hear the resonant chords beneath the rustling of bulletins and the whispering of parishioners. "Such a fine man ... Such a loss ... Who'd have thought ... "

As the organ grumbled, vying with the susurration, suddenly the sanctuary came to life. The morning sun broke through the clouds and lit up a vast, stained glass window on the east side. And there stood a familiar figure, backlit in his pastel garden. White-frocked, he leaned on a shepherd's crook. Surrounded by a flock of shampooed sheep and garlands of well-tended flowers.

Jesus gazed across the congregation with an abstracted stare as he lifted one languid hand toward a lamb that had struck his fancy. Same old gentle Jesus with his yen for sheep: our Lord in his Victorian garden.

For all my cynicism, I had to admit that it felt pretty good to be back in this place. The sanctuary seemed locked in time, like Jesus in his window. I glanced at Cynthia to see what she was drawing. It was Jesus, I could tell by his robes and flowing hair. But she had him hunkered down, hunched over one of the larger ewes, and I didn't like the looks of what he was doing. On the other side of Cynthia, a matron had turned her back.

"Cyn!" But then the prelude ended and a resonant voice rang out from the pulpit. "Our help is in the name of the Lord!" Roger Squire declared. I saw he was a trim, tall man with an aquiline nose and an abundance of silver hair. Handsome as a news anchor.

He raised his arms to hoist us from the pews, and as I stumbled to my feet something caught my eye. I looked up and stopped cold, staring across the chancel. A trim brunette in a black robe sat behind the lectern. Her deep brown hair hugged her oval cheeks, set off her dark eyes. She looked every bit the same.

"Seek ye the Lord while he may be found," Squire went on in his big, broadcast baritone. "Call ye upon him while he is near."

The next line was our turn. "Let the wicked forsake his way, and the unrighteous man his thoughts." Then back to the liturgist: "And let him return unto the Lord."

I lapsed into the rhythm of the responsive reading, lulled down into the mantra. But I kept watching Sarah, walleyed. What the hell was she doing up there, officiating at a funeral? I scanned the program, found a note down at the bottom.

Mrs. Sarah Wagstaff, President of the Hopewell College Alumni Association and Deaconess of the Church, is assisting in the service today.

A pillar of the town and gown. And just five years out of college! Ah, but brethren, I could tell you all some stories...

The responsive reading wrapped up:

"And let him return unto the Lord, and he will have mercy upon him; And to our God, for he will abundantly pardon."

Pardon what? I wondered as they broke into the Gloria Patri. Have mercy on whom, and for what? For giving up on his life? For failing the college?

"Glory be to the Father, and to the Son and to the Holy..."

Roger Squire held his hands outstretched, palms up like a liturgical deodorant ad, and the congregation remained standing as the organist launched into a traditional funereal hymn.

" For all the saints who from their labors rest,
Who thee by faith before the world confessed.
Thy name, O Jesus, be forever blessed.
Ah-hah-leh-heh-loo-yah!"

When we were reseated, Squire spent five minutes thanking everybody who'd had any kind of hand in staging the service. He said there'd be no graveside rite, but invited everyone to a reception downstairs in the fellowship hall. All this info was delivered in a crisp, upbeat manner not unlike the evening news.

Squire gave a brief obituary: just the names and dates and places of Julian Reid's journey. Nothing so personal as a eulogy. Then he took in a deep breath and let loose with a flood of Biblical passages: the kind everyone expects to hear at funerals.

"In my Father's house are many mansions. If it were not so, would I have told you that I go to prepare a place for you? And when I go and prepare a place for you, I will come again..."

I glanced at Cynthia, saw her eyes glaze. Nodding off.

"The souls of the righteous are in the hand of God, and no torment will ever ... "

Now my own eyelids were drooping, until Squire got to the end of his script and plunked down in his chair. I watched Sarah slowly step up to the lectern. For a moment, she just stood there. And then, in a clear and ringing voice: "I was an exile long before I went away."

Was that from James Baldwin? I wasn't sure. But I remembered the voice, the timbre and the offbeat cadence. Sarah read with a rhythm that kept you off stride, like a lyric phrased by Frank Sinatra. I'd forgot about her talent as an actress.

"A voice says, 'Cry!' And I said, what shall I cry? All flesh is grass, and all its beauty is like the flower of the field. The grass withers, the flower fades ...

"And there are some who have no memorial, who have perished as though they had not lived; they have become as though they had not been born, and so have their children ... "

I noticed that the Biblical passages had been edited, with all the pie-in-the-sky parts purged out of them. All that remained were these plain, dark images: on the limitations and the loneliness of life. It was the most candid funereal commentary I'd ever heard. Just an honest lamentation for all the losses in mortality.

Then the readings turned to pilgrims—wandering, lost in strange lands. But with a sense of destination. Like the Pilgrim forebears of these Congregationalists. I noticed there were footnotes in the bulletin. The next line was from one William Erbury, a leader of the Seekers in the seventeenth century.

"To be solitary and walk alone is a wilderness condition, which with God is the most comfortable state."

And then more Biblical passages on pilgrimage, wandering.

"A wandering Aramean was my father, and he went down into Egypt and sojourned there ... "

"Not having received what was promised, but having seen it and greeted it from afar ... having acknowledged that they were strangers and exiles."

At the end of it, Sarah stood silent at the lectern for a few seconds. Then she picked up her script, for a last quotation.

" ... and happy they whose hearts are set upon the Pilgrim quest."

I flipped back to the bulletin. That was from The Psalms of David in Meeter, 1650. So, who'd assembled this stuff? Someone who'd not only read about the Pilgrims but understood their faith firsthand. Someone who knew what this church was all about, this tradition. At the base of my spine I felt a chill ripple.

Sarah turned around and walked slowly back to her chair.

I glanced at Cynthia. She was staring at Sarah intently. I tried to think—how much had I told her?

In a moment, Mavis's husband Gus Lindholm, the office supply guy, got up to give a kind of eulogy. He told how bad things had got in Mayflower when the college had almost gone under. Said they'd scoured the town to find anyone they could have confidence in as a leader. Couldn't find a candidate at the college.

I watched Jeb Collard and his cronies from the faculty, down in the front pews. There was some serious squirming.

In the end, noted Gus, it was their own minister, Julian Reid, who had come to the fore and taken the helm at Hopewell. And that had given folks in town confidence to continue supporting the college by writing off all the bad debts. "But of course it cost Julian the career he'd trained for, when he answered that call," Gus said sadly. "And maybe it cost him more than that."

As Gus sat down, Roger Squire re-emerged in the pulpit. But he looked like another man. His face was flushed and his voice faltered as he entreated us to join him in prayer. He kept stopping and starting as he prayed, evidently without a script.

"O Thou who art the end of life for all who truly seek Thee, open Thou our hearts to the testimonies of faith we have heard today. Grant us ears to heed the needs of this world and feet to follow where'er Thy calling leads us. So, too, may we tread in the steps of our Lord and of Thy faithful servant, Julian Reid."

Squire pronounced a barely audible "Amen" and stood propped against the pulpit for several seconds. Then he roused us for another rollicking hymn.

> "We've a story to tell to the nations
> That will turn their hearts to the right
> (to the right).
> A story of love and mercy,
> A story that God is li-i-ight,
> A story that God is Light!
>
> "For the darkness shall turn to dawning,
> And the dawning to noonday bright!
> And Christ's great kingdom shall come on earth,
> The kingdom of love and light,
> The kingdom of love and light!"

The parishioners seemed to know this hymn and they belted it out like a Congregational fight song. The church reverberated as Squire marched down the aisle on the final stanza, Reid's widow at his side.

From the back of the sanctuary, Squire bellowed the benediction: "Go forth into the world as the people of God, in the power of God, to follow in His service. Go forth to serve, as did our brother. For people need the Lord, and the Lord needs people!"

Two beats after, the organist broke into a baroque fugue. At that, the worshipers sprang up to mass in the aisles where they took up conversations they'd postponed for the past hour.

As we moved up the aisle, 50 percent of me felt like taking off out the door for my back yard, to crack a beer and digest what had just transpired. Or maybe head for the gym to shoot baskets. But instead I found myself trailing Cynthia, caught up in one of the slow-moving streams that wound into two narrow aisles down to Fellowship Hall in the church basement.

It was a huge room that could be carved up into Sunday school classrooms with room dividers or used as open space. As we wormed our way down the stairs, the place was packed. A line was forming in the center for those who would console Mrs. Reid. As I stood there pondering what I might say, I felt a prod in my ribs. "So how about it, Matt? You have a story to tell the Great Unwashed? Can you take up the White Man's Burden?"

"Oh, hi there, Hazel." I shook my head. "Try my wife, here."

Cynthia snorted. Then she looked up with a puzzled frown. "But, seriously, did you get the impression that minister might see himself as the next president of the college?"

"Wouldn't surprise me to find him standing in line next to the widow, passing out his resume," snapped the math professor.

"Speaking of lines, I'm not sure I belong in this one," Cynthia continued. "Having never met Julian Reid, I'm clueless what to say to his widow."

"Well, if you don't stay here," Hazel advised, "I'd say you have two choices. See that well-heeled coffee klatch over in the corner? Those are the same folks who talked Julian into taking over the college: Gus Lindholm and his ilk."

I saw Rollie Cleaver in the center of the group, talking animatedly with Roger Squire. The minister still appeared ashen, as though he were recovering from a vision he hadn't planned on when he'd plotted the funeral service. Cleaver had a beefy hand clamped on his shoulder.

"And my other option?" asked Cynthia.

"All the way over on the other side, near the exit."

"You mean that gaggle of guys in bad suits?"

"Those men are the remnant of what once was a real college faculty. Before the blood began to flow from the budget," Hazel sighed.

"There's your buddy, Jeb," I told Cynthia. "Why don't you go turn his darkness to dawning?" She winced, but when Hazel moved to join the group, she followed along. I said I'd stay in line and have a word with Mrs. Reid.

She was a thin, sparrowlike creature in a dark blue dress that looked a size and a half too big for her. As I drew closer, I wasn't sure we'd ever met. Standing beside a guest registry, she looked sleepless and shaken.

A heavy-set lady in a flowered dress lurched toward the widow and embraced her. She toddled off, and I was next in line. I extended my hand and framed an empathic smile, waiting for whatever inspiration might come to me. But just then a dark-robed man came rushing up and bulled in front of me.

"More coffee, Mabel? May I fill your cup?"

"Oh, yes, Mr. Squire. Thank you so much. I'm afraid I've been living on caffeine these past few days."

Mabel Reid reached behind the guest book for a white china cup. But as she passed it to Squire, her hand gave a tremor and the cup slipped from her grasp.

In the instant that I saw it fall, I swooped down with my outstretched hand and batted it toward the ceiling. Then I caught it in midair with the other hand.

"Jesus, what reflexes!" the Reverend Squire swore, before he could catch himself.

"Fastest hands in the High Plains Conference," came a clear, bell-like voice behind me.

"Fastest hands in some folks' memory—am I right, Sarah?" As I turned to her, she smiled and blushed and looked down at the floor. I gave her the cup for a refill and, as she took it with one hand, she brushed the inside of my wrist with the other.

I saw Roger Squire watch us. Then I returned to Mrs. Reid: "No one gave more of his life to our college than your husband." It was all I could think of to say.

I left her to the next in line and looked at Squire. He regarded me with a curious smile, like a reporter on the trail of a lead story. His color and his confidence seemed to be returning. He scanned me to the top of my head, took my full measure.

"I say, you're pretty tall. Ever play ball?"

"Yeah, some. I'm Matt Bradshaw. Went to college here. Moved back a few weeks ago. And I understand you're a newcomer, too."

"Matt Bradshaw. Of course!" He grasped my hand. "I've heard your name a number of times."

"Well, don't believe it all," I said, glancing past his shoulder. I felt a little rattled, seeing Sarah. There she was, coming back this way. "Time to look up my wife," I stuttered. "I'm sure we'll meet again."

I tossed a wave at Sarah, and took off to look for my wife. I saw that Squire was still studying me closely.

Cynthia was leaning against a chalk board papered with crude drawings of bearded men in bathrobes. A sign at the top read, "Mrs. Abbott's Third Grade Class. Vacation Bible School." She was listening to Hazel who was holding court with a dozen male colleagues from the faculty.

"I'm telling you, there's no time for that," the math prof/waitress admonished. Several of the academics nodded as others stroked their beards in contemplation.

"You mean they'll rush into a search?" asked Collard. "I doubt that. Ol' J.R.'s not half cold yet."

"Jeb, you are in a church!" hissed Emily. I saw Cynthia crack a smile.

"It's more serious than that," Hazel countered. "What I'm saying is we can't count on a formal search of any kind. I overheard a couple of the parishioners out at the steak house last night. They want another of their own in that president's slot."

"Have they someone in mind?" one of the professors inquired. "Perhaps a tenured member of our faculty?"

Hazel huffed, "Pemberton, only in the kind of world you love would anyone even conceive that question. Now, consider the precedent. How did they recruit the last president? Where'd they find him?"

Jeb's eyes expanded. "I guess I'm catching on. People need the Lord."

The others echoed, "And the Lord needs people."

"Correct," commended Hazel. "But the next question is more difficult."

"And that's what the hell we can do about it," Jeb offered.

"Now then," Hazel continued, "I'm working late tonight at the steak house; maybe I'll hear some more scuttlebutt. But I can get up for a breakfast meeting, if you can. How about my house, 8:00 in the morning?"

They all nodded agreement.

"And one more thing," she added. "I believe we should be thinking in very practical, political terms. If the Reverend Newsreader heeds the call, who could represent our interests? Is there anyone with both town and gown supporters?"

"Athletic supporters?" Cynthia whispered a bit loud.

Hazel didn't blush, but flinched a little. She glanced at Jeb. And then I thought I saw her head half turn in my direction.

7

Three o'clock, and my world was turning sea green. I sat slumped at the desk in my office, awash in a tide of pale green computer printouts. Midafternoon was always a challenging hour in the groves of academe, in an industry where the greatest occupational hazard was falling asleep.

But I needed to plow through this printout. A ton of data on the incoming freshman class, compiled by some outfit called "The Gray Group," according to a footnote on the first page.

Gazing out my window, even the plot outside my basement office looked green. The rest of the campus was the color of sand in these last, desperate weeks of summer. The wheat crop had been a total loss and the corn had not got thigh high. Farmers were no longer praying for rain but for hail, to collect on their insurance.

But "Cleaver Hall" was framed by a patch of green grass and verdant shrubbery. I could see the rainbow mist from an underground sprinkler, glistening in the sun. The sprinklers must have been part of Rollie's gift when they put up the sign with his name on it. I wondered if he'd provided for fertilizer.

Back on task! I stood up and shook my head, fighting off my stupor. It was a list of some 300 names. I'd set out to scan it for an overview: in-state, out-of-state. That sort of thing. But as I peered at the printout, I saw that someone at the Gray Group had beat me to it. In addition to the usual name, rank, and social security number, they'd tacked on another few columns. One of them classified each student as Category One, Two, or Three.

So, what was that about? I remembered Hazel referring to Jamal Simpkins as a Category Three. A black kid with a boom box. Was it simply a race code? That seemed a bit crass. In another column, a few of the males were marked: JUCO. I tried cross-referencing that group. The JUCOS were Category Threes, to a man.

Before long, the figures fuzzed over, then started bobbing like flotsam on the pale green page. My mind was adrift. So, how does a college get along without a president? And how long would it take to name a new one? Squire? I found myself missing Julian, even though I'd hardly known him. His name was the only one above mine in the administrative flow chart. And now he was gone.

I sank back into my swivel chair and thought about that odd, haunting scene outside this building. That night I'd backed off, let Julian down. I closed my eyes and tried to remember.

⚜

The light glowing from his desk lamp, steady as a coal. The profile shrouded in darkness. Not his full face, just skull-like ridges and shadows. Stripped of the smile.

Were there sounds in the night? The cry of an owl. Some croaking cicadas. A whirring hum from the fan in the basement. And another sound. I remembered it now, in the distance—a faint sort of thrumming. Somewhere past the town, down toward the river. Almost the sound of a drum.

⚜

All right. Get with it, Bradshaw! I stuffed the printout in my gym bag and headed out. But I paused as I stepped out in the stairwell. There was a big manila envelope lying just outside my office. Hmm. I never knew them to deliver campus mail. Someone had written my name on the envelope, in block letters.

I stopped to open it. Inside, there was a thin black folder.

AGENDA

HOPEWELL COLLEGE

BOARD OF TRUSTEES

The folder was dated last April. Oh, terrific—more administrivia to go through. I crammed it in my gym bag next to the printout and took off out the door.

Hopewell had one of those small college gyms that echoes like a subterranean cavern. I'd never forget the clamor of a close game—cheers bouncing off the bleachers, ricocheting up to the rafters. The squeak of sneakers, honking horns from the scorers' table. I'd been looking forward to a workout ever since we'd been back here. Maybe fire up a few game-winning fantasies. Relive the most electrifying buckets of my career, and from the very spots where I had shot them. Even if I couldn't go full speed anymore, I could still take a good ego trip in this building.

But as I swung open the door, I pulled back. The noise was deafening, although it wasn't the sound of a crowd. Someone was blasting rap music over the loudspeaker.

"I got a Jones for ya, mama,
Got me some gas.
Down in my bones, for ya, mama,
Show me some ass."

The lyric was set against a cacophony of orgasmic grunts—Ugh! Ugh! Whoo!—with assorted moans and heavy breathing. And with that, another antiphonal beat: the slap, slap, slap of a basketball on the hard court. Plus a cheer now and then for an exceptional shot, or a curse for a disputed foul.

"Hey, Dude, you lightin' it up today. You be smokin'!"

Then slap, slap, slap. A tumble to the floor, and a shout.

"Don' you be hackin' my man like that, muthafucka!"

"I ain't doin' shit, Cuz. That mutha takin' steps. You know that be naggin'! He be walkin' on y'all, you be buggin'."

"Hey, chill out, Bro. Jes' take the ball out—it's cool."

Five years out of college ball, I still could decode the violent vocabulary of the street game. And marvel at the ability of inner city kids to spew out energy and work out conflicts on the court that might well have led to mayhem. There was a reason to their rhetoric—all that hyperbolic trash talk—much as it might unsettle folks in white-bred places like Mayflower.

As I walked down to the locker room, I saw they were playing four on three. I gave a nod and called over, "Join you?"

That got me a glare from Jamal—the tall, skinny kid I'd met on the ladder. But when I returned after changing clothes, the others seemed open to an extra body who'd even the sides.

One of them stepped up and extended a hand. "LaRon Vaughn." He was a big, rangy kid with an open smile. He ran through the nicknames of the others. "This here's 'Squint' (a guy with glasses), 'Porker' (a skinny fellow)," and so on.

"But then, we all looks alike anyhow. Ain' that right, Doc?"

"Sure thing, Jamal. Just like us honkers are all born with doctorates. Hey, I'm glad to meet you. My name's Matt Bradshaw. New dean of students. Call me 'Matt.' Actually, I used to play some ball here, but I'm a little out of shape. So you guys take it easy on me, all right?"

A couple of the players traded glances.

Slowly, I joined the flow of the game, following the lead of the others. Not initiating anything, I passed the ball each time I touched it. Never shot it. In a few minutes, I knew the basic moves and capabilities of everybody on the court. It was the best lesson Jeb Collard had taught me: "Let the game come to you."

I found myself matched up against Jamal. The kid had a quick first step to the basket and a passable outside shot. But I saw that he went to his right every time he drove to the basket. I started taking that move away from him and heard him mutter in frustration.

Finally, I began to move on offense, draining jump shots and driving on Jamal. At first, I went to my right as he had, and he cut me off. But then I put another move on him. Dribbling down with my right hand, I stepped back with my left foot and slapped the ball across my body. Then I picked up the dribble with my left hand, and drove by him in a flash for an easy layup.

There was a murmur from the others. The crossover dribble was a move they may have seen only on television.

Next time Jamal got the ball, he tried the same thing. But he neglected to step back. As he darted left, I slapped the ball aside and stole it, fed Porker in the low post and he slammed it.

Now a sharp, clapping sound rang across the gym floor—the applause of a single spectator. I noticed the kids had let the rap music run out. Jeb Collard walked up. "You guys see that play?" he asked.

"Not just stealing the ball, but passing up the shot. Looking for your teammates. Around here, we call that 'court sense.' You wanta play for me, you'll learn that."

Then he continued: "Jamal, did you see how Matt—uh, the dean, here—put that move on you?"

He nodded slightly, glanced at me with a glimmer of respect.

"Hey, Coach, I'll bet he can pick up that move in no time," I exclaimed. "Man's got an explosive first step. Say, Jamal, why don't we work on that crossover dribble sometime? Get that down, and I believe you could be dangerous."

He smiled faintly as he opened one palm, and I slapped it.

"Matt, I hate to pull you out of here, but we need to talk some," said Collard. "I've been hunting you down ever since our meeting ended over at Hazel's, from your house to your office. Figured I might find you here."

"Give me a minute to shower, and I'll smell better."

The players nodded as I headed for the locker room. Whatever Category they'd been assigned, I understood one thing. For the first time since I'd been back here, I felt somewhat connected.

Jeb Collard's office was bare and Spartan as a public bathroom. The room was done up in nondescript tiles, sort of khaki with a touch of dun. About the same shade as the campus.

The tiles enveloped all four walls, floor to ceiling, and curled up over the window ledge where a couple of spindly potted plants clung to life in the vain hope that Collard would remember to water them. It was the office of a man who didn't care to spend time there, and it offered few amenities.

But there was a coffee maker on the gray metal cabinet that sat beneath a blackboard where Jeb drew up his basketball plays. The coach waved at it as I walked in, and I poured myself a cup in a cracked black mug. The mug read, Hopewell College: NAIA champs, 1990. I took a seat in his folding chair for visitors.

He was rocking back and forth in a creaking swivel chair, staring out the window. As he half turned in my direction, he reached back to a gray metal credenza and produced a small box of cream-filled pastries.

"Clam?" he offered. "Left over from the meeting."

I shook my head.

That was all that was said for the next five minutes. I sat, taking time to collect my own thoughts rather than rushing into new ones.

A door slammed down the hall and a half dozen ballplayers spilled out of the gym. They laughed and scratched over some in-house joke as they trudged back to the dorm to mess around till lunchtime. Athletes have a talent for wasting time. Then it was quiet again. Finally, Jeb broke the silence.

"Not getting any easier around here. Know that, Matt?"

I said I supposed it was not and told him how I'd first met Jamal.

"Heard about it," he chuckled. "The more of these kids I get, the more I see they're just pushing at the world, lookin' for some limits. Along with a little attention, maybe. Most of 'em aren't bad kids. But they scare the be-Jesus out of the suits downtown, along with half the faculty."

"Why do they call them, Category Three?" I asked.

He snorted. "Started last year when the Trustees hired these candy-ass consultants to try an' shore up Julian, poor bastard. Enrollment was down, and he had no clue what to do. Knew how to handle a low turnout for Easter, but that was about the extent of it. This running-a-college stuff was way over his head.

"So they brought in this outfit called themselves 'The Gray Group.' Said they could turn Hopewell right around. Already done it with other colleges. Said they specialized in 'institutional advancement, enrollment management.' That sort of thing. 'Planned giving.'"

I told him it sounded like the kind of rhetoric I'd heard at Eastbourne.

"Well, they told us to think in terms of three kinds of students: Categories One, Two, and Three."

"Meaning what?" I took out the printout and handed it to him. He unfolded it.

"Well, okay. See, your Category One here is some kinda hotshot. Say a star athlete, or a top student. Kinda kid every college professor figures he's going to spend his life with when he goes into teaching. Right?"

"And Category Two?"

"Just your average schmo who's not dead set against picking up a book, if it's got a nice cover. Most of 'em can graduate, one way or another."

"Like Rollie Cleaver."

He nodded.

"Take you and Sarah Lyle. Category One kids. Say, you know she always asked about you. Guess you knew she married Wagstaff. Runs the local cable TV operation. He's your basic Two. Moved back once he graduated and got cut by the Kansas City Chiefs, more or less in that order. Yep, she always asked about you."

He leaned back in his swivel chair and perused me a while. Offered me some more coffee.

"Well, Category Three. That's what you came about. High-risk hombres. Tha's what they mean. Likely to bomb out, based on their high school grades and test scores. Sometimes police files. Just hope they don't tear the place down on their way outta here. Course, this is the kinda kid they want us recruiting. Category Threes."

I sat back. "Hold on a minute—recruiting! Jeb, why the hell would you go out looking...?" Then I answered my question. "Okay, jocks. I guess they'd be eligible to play ball fall term even if they couldn't find the library. Then after they flunk out first semester, they can close out the season on academic probation. Right?"

Collard stared out the window. "You always were a fast learner. But there's more to it, see..."

The phone rang, and as he picked it up his eyes swelled. Way across the desk, I could hear the high-pitched caterwauling. "Yes, Emily. Of course I know it's dinner time. And, yes, I remembered your sister and her husband are... Now just... hold on. I was just... I'll be there before you know it."

He shook his head. "Gotta make this fast. Where was I? Yeah: see, for every high-risk kid you bring in from some minority whatnot, you can pick up some big-time federal bucks. Ancillary funding. Maybe enough to buy you a computer lab, even put up a building... Well, anyway, pretty soon you start scoutin' those Category Three kids: build 'em right into the budget."

He unplugged the coffee pot, started turning off lights.

"So that's how Julian saved the school. And the creditors supported him."

"That's pretty much the story." He was at the door. "Not that I'm any kind of authority. They treat faculty like mushrooms—keep us in the dark, feed us bullshit."

"And the Gray Group?" I shut the door and followed him out. "How do they enter into this? And who in hell are they?"

"First I heard of 'em, they got Reid to can ol' Gus Sandstrom, the admissions director. 'Time to outsource,' he said. 'Gotta bring in some top consultants—enrollment management. 'Course you know where he picked up that kinda talk."

"From the same people who sold him their services." Now we were halfway across the parking lot. "Jeb, but what about the meeting? The presidency. Did you all decide what to do?"

"Huh! Guess that's what I set out to tell you," he muttered as he climbed into his car. "But it's a long story." He turned the key, glanced at his watch and winced. With a wave in my direction, he was gone.

Cynthia was upstairs in her office, printing off reams of email, when I got home. "Can't you take a break?" I asked.

"I suppose so, but then I've got to spend five more hours surfing the frigging Internet for new data sources. I don't know what's going on back at Intelcor, but something's heating up."

"What is it you're working on?"

She paused and looked away. "Actually, Matt, it's proprietary stuff."

"Yeah, well, whatever. But come on, Cyn. It's six o'clock: dinner time in Kansas. Down home cooking—fried chicken, mashed potatoes, cream gravy."

She looked up from her computer, aghast.

I pulled her to her feet. "Let's go see the Colonel."

We carried our sacks of fast food out to the back yard and I laid out a picnic blanket. Between drumsticks and swigs of beer, we fought off the flies of late summer with an arsenal of Handi-wipe towelettes. After a crowning course of carrot cake, Cynthia gave a mock sigh and stretched out on the blanket, her head on my knee. For a time I thought she'd fallen asleep.

Then she spoke up, "Hazel came by."

"Did she have anything to say about the meeting?" I described my confab with Jeb Collard, before he'd run off.

"The yes-ma'am/yes man. Talk about henpecked! That dude has some serious issues with women. Well, it seems he also figured in the great presidential debate."

Hazel had said they all agreed there was only one person at the college who could challenge Roger Squire. Or anyone else the Congo Church might designate.

"And that was?" I felt my stomach wrinkle.

"Jeb Collard: Local yokel. Ath-a-le-tic man of the year."

"Okay, Cyn, cut the guy some slack. But what are you saying? Jeb? As president of the college? You're joking."

"Hey, I don't make the news around here. I just report it. But to hear Hazel, that was pretty much Jeb's reaction."

"What'd he say when they suggested he be president?"

"'Not a damn thing. He went into one of his trademark trances. Just sat and stared out the window. That's when the others came to their senses.'"

"So they withdrew the nomination?"

"It seems Collard came out of his stupor and spoke up at the end. He admitted he was basically a basketball coach."

"So they're going along with Squire?"

"Hazel said, 'I guess that's all we can do for the moment.'"

I gave out with a groan. Then began telling her what I'd learned about the Gray Group and their recruiting strategies. Categorizing the students. And about my job and all my questions. I guess I'd been carrying on that way for some time when I became aware once again that Cynthia had fallen silent.

I looked down to see if she was asleep, but her eyes were open. They seemed a bit red, as though she'd been too long at the computer screen. Still, it was time to get back to work, she said. She stood up and stretched tall, toward the rising moon. As she pulled down her tee shirt, her nipples unfolded like flowers.

I sprang to my knees and grabbed for the cuff of her jeans. But she was already headed back to the job. Crossing the yard in quick strides, she swung open the screen door and vanished.

I cleaned up from our picnic. Tossed out the trash, folded the blanket. Then I stood up and looked back toward the house. Had she been crying?

8

"Con-vo-ca-tion!"

President Roger Squire stood before the student body in full regalia, his scarlet hood for theology draped over the same black robe he wore for preaching. "Con-vo-ca-tion!" He entoned the word in his big, resonant baritone. Then he paused for effect as the syllables echoed around the college auditorium.

"We are all familiar with the term, aren't we. We've seen it printed in the college calendar. In fact, that's how most of us found our way here this morning."

He chuckled at the modest joke. "But have you ever considered just what the word 'convocation' means?"

Squire stopped again and surveyed the cavernous auditorium. The place was about half filled, with upper classmen on the main floor and freshmen in the balcony. The faculty sat behind Squire on stage, also robed and hooded. I found myself in the front row.

Behind us, a huge black and gold replica of the Hopewell College seal hung from two thick ropes, like a backdrop for the evening news. "*Pro Christo et Kansas*," it read. Looking out on the assembled students, I wondered how many might be moved by the cause of Christ and Kansas, if they could make out the motto. While some seemed as bright-eyed and eager as the classmates I remembered, others appeared to be asleep outright.

Even for a professional speaker such as Squire, this looked to be a tough gig.

"Well, now, the word 'convocation' can be subdivided into two component parts," the president continued. "There is the prefix 'con,' which means 'with' in Latin; and the root, 'vocare,' to speak. A convocation is just a time to get together and talk, to talk with one another."

I began to hear a lot of one-liners from the faculty behind me. "Smart fella," sneered one prof, *sotto voce*.

"Yeah, next he'll be demonstrating his math skills. Let's see if he can count how many bodies we're short this fall."

"You got that right; this drought has really hit us."

"Say, speaking of favorite words, there's one I'm always saying to my wife." This was a raspy, good-hearted voice. It sounded vaguely familiar, from my college days.

"What's that, Harley?"

"Sensuous. Since-you-was up, will ya get me another beer?"

Oh, sure. Harley Applequist. Professor of special education, campus clown. Offered courses that no one I knew ever enrolled in.

If Squire heard this undercurrent, he gave no sign. He seemed intent on his address. I could see that he'd had his text typed on just the top five or six lines of each page. Evidently a trick of the trade, to maintain eye contact with the audience.

"Now, here is what I'd like to talk about with you this morning. It's a sign I saw on a billboard at the edge of town, when I first drove into Mayflower last summer. Have you ever noticed that sign? Do you remember what it says?"

From the row behind me, "Abandon hope, all ye who enter..."

"Shh!"

Squire continued, "'A Good Place to Grow.' That's what the sign says." He paused and surveyed the students, slouching in their seats. "Well, isn't that a fine motto for all of us here at Hopewell, as we begin a new academic year? A Good Place to Grow!"

Behind me, a colleague with halitosis wheezed in my ear, "Stand up and tell your story, Bradshaw. What was it, six inches in six months? Hell, you grew as much as anybody around here."

I shook my head as Squire ran on. He launched into some inspiring stories about people who had learned lessons that had changed their lives.

"In my case," he confided, "I found myself at a challenging juncture. Here I was, a successful broadcaster, anchoring the six o'clock news on the NBC TV affiliate in Schenectady. The top-rated news team in that market, I might add. But in time, I found myself asking, 'Is there nothing more to life? What does all of this signify?'" He told how he'd decided to enroll in seminary.

"So, how long does this go on?" hissed another professor. "I'm halfway to a midlife crisis, and it isn't even lunchtime."

I glanced at the podium. Thank God, he was down to his final page. "And so, my friends, welcome to Hopewell College. As we mark the beginning of a new academic year, let us all take time to dream. For dreams hold the seeds of achievement. May we remember the words of that great African American statesman and clergyman, Jesse Jackson: 'If you can conceive it, you can believe it. If you can believe it, you can achieve it!'"

I scanned some clusters of black students—there were more here than I'd anticipated—and saw a few yawns and grimaces.

"And so, welcome to Hopewell," Squire concluded, his right hand raised hospitably in the air. "Welcome to a good place to grow!" He gave a Nixon-like wave from the podium, as though awaiting an ovation. But there was only mild applause.

"Say, speaking of time: did you hear what the one frog said to the other?"

"What's that, Harley?"

"Time's fun when you're having flies!"

The faculty rose with a chorus of groans.

Harley Applequist turned out to be my closest colleague for the next couple of days. Nowadays, he ran something called the Office of Academic Support Services on the second floor of the Learning Resource Center, which is what they now called the library. What they'd done was clear out the venerable old reading room—a place that had been redolent with racks of musty journals and shelves of books for browsing. Now the big varnished tables and wooden chairs had been hauled away, along with half the stock of books. As I mounted the stairs the next morning, I felt a pang of nostalgia. I missed my old library.

In its place, the college had set up a crosshatch of study carrels under strata of fluorescent lights. It looked like the typing pool in a high-rise office. Some of the desks had computers and others just flat surfaces for testing. It seemed that was to be my job for the next few days: testing incoming freshmen.

"Didn't they used to give these tests before the freshmen enrolled?" I asked Applequist. We were sitting in his office having coffee and clams before the students arrived. "Seems a bit late in the game to be finding out if they can read and write, after we've already admitted them."

Harley glanced my way and I looked aside. How well prepared had I been when they let me in here?

"Well, that's a bona fide question, Matt. Solve that one and you get a second clam." He held out the box, and I shook my head. I hated the idea that I was getting used to these 600-calorie time bombs once again. Now my head didn't really start humming till the third one.

"But, you know, it's like they tell us. This is a new era here at Hopewell College. That's what our consultants say. Time to reinvent ourselves." He took the last clam for himself.

"And what does that mean?" It must have been the 475th time I'd asked that question in the past few days.

Harley thought a moment as he settled into his chair. It was an undertaking that took awhile, for the man was immense. At five-foot-eight and maybe 280, Harley was a coronary-occlusion-in-waiting. Yet, on him the pounds didn't look so bad. For Harley was not so much obese as rotund. From his round jowls to the sagging belt that cradled his underbelly, he had a certain symmetry about him. Harley was a perfect sphere.

Instead of answering my question, he pulled some materials from his desk and showed me how to administer the Miller Analogy along with a couple of other tests of English and math skills.

Then he looked at his watch and hoisted himself from his desk chair. "Time to get ready. I can hear 'em outside: barbarians at the gate. Say, speaking of vocabulary: what's a technical term for two physicians?"

He began rustling around his office, picking up cups and cleaning up wrappers from the pastries. It was about as fast as I'd seen Harley navigate, and he was winded from the exertion.

"Harley, I give up—no contest."

"A par-a-dox!"

"Okay," I groaned, "Now, here's a serious question. How the hell do you all decide if a kid is Category One, Two, or Three?"

"Category assessment? Say, now you're in my department," he wheezed. "That's my leading product line these days. Whole new, expanding market for special education." His housekeeping accomplished, he fell back in his chair.

"Look, I've shown you one approach: these standardized tests you'll be administering. Got a whole battery here and we don't even have to score 'em. Just ship 'em to the Gray Group: Fed-Ex, overnight. They'll run 'em through the scanners and zap back the results by modem. This time tomorrow, we'll know what kind of courses we'll need."

I peered at him, somewhat bug-eyed.

"You mean you make them up on the spot?"

"Well, not exactly. Modify the courses is more like it. It's just like special ed. See, you've got your basic curriculum, but you learn to pitch it to different levels. Depends on whether you have educable or trainable clients, say. Here it's more a matter of social class. Don't really need these upscale exams. I just give 'em the Northwestern Test."

"The what?"

The clock tower on the science building chimed nine.

"Whoop, time to get rolling." He roused himself to two feet and trundled toward the door.

"I'll leave my door open. Listen in when you get a chance. I'll be administering the Northwestern Test. See if you can tell who's a Three."

The students hadn't been given a schedule for testing, so half of them turned up at once. They were milling around the lawn outside the library and up the staircase from the main floor. But Harley seemed nonplused. He admitted the first thirty and told the rest to hold their places in line. Said he'd reappear on the hour and take them in as space allowed.

The freshmen were still pretty docile, newly arrived, but I could hear some outright grumbling out on the stairwell. I wondered if doing up a schedule had been my job.

I got the first group started on a set of exams, set the timer, and settled down by a big window, looking out across the campus. It was a rerun from my freshman year: the same worn paths, the hillocks, and the elm trees. In the distance, the same red barn and silo. This had been the reading room of the library.

A Saturday morning in the early spring, just after basketball season. Almost everyone I knew was still in bed, sleeping off a Friday night at the roadhouse, but I'd stayed in at the dorm. On crutches for the next six months. They told me it was the only thing they could do to ease the discomfort of my growth spurt. Constant pain in my ligaments. And an early end to my basketball season.

I clumped on over to the library, more or less to pass the time. Had a paper due for history class, so I checked out a book from the reading list. It was something about the "enclosure movement," back in the seventeenth century. I remember sitting there in the silence of the library, digging through a book about the Diggers. It seemed these guys had climbed over a stone wall to protest the landowners kicking the peasants off the common ground. Got themselves arrested, digging a symbolic garden.

"The earth should be made a common treasury of livelihood to whole mankind..." That's what one of their leaders said. Cool sentiment, but I wasn't up for all this reading. If I could only get up and get out and do something. Damn these crutches!

I found myself gazing out the window at that barn and silo. Not much else to ponder. The campus was a morgue. I hobbled over to a rack of newspapers and picked up the Wichita Eagle for the sports page. But then a headline on the front page caught my eye.

FARM FORECLOSURES AT ALL-TIME HIGH:
Record Round of Auctions Slated for Saturday.

I was halfway into some heavy-duty quotes from people who'd lost their farms when I glanced outside again—as the sun broke through the morning clouds and lit up that red barn and silo. The sunbeams glistened on the spring green wheat field that surrounded it.

And suddenly, for some reason, I saw a connection. The earth as a treasure, the loss of a farm. Nothing had changed, had it? It was the same tragic story, three centuries later. I turned back to the Diggers and when I looked up again it was lunchtime. I got an A on the paper, but that was a footnote.

It was the day I learned to shift gears and look at things in slow motion. When I got back on the court the next season, Jeb Collard was impressed—and not just at the fact I was now six-foot-seven. "My God, Matt, you just spotted the open man! Seems like you saw the whole court. It's what I've been harpin' on since you were thirteen. Slow down so you can see the game. And, by God, you just saw it."

⚜

My career started here, I reflected. In this room, at this window. And as I gazed over the campus, the sun broke through the clouds.

But something broke my séance. It was an odd smell—a whiff of exotic perfume. I looked up to see a tall blonde standing before me. She was wearing a loose, floppy sweatshirt and faded blue jeans, but there was a certain tailored air about her. Something vaguely familiar. Was it the dark cast of her eyes?

She had her tests in hand.

"Are you finished so soon? Did you do all three?"

She gave a vague smile and looked aside. Then she turned back to me with an eerie stare. For a moment she just stood there, twisting her long, flaxen hair. I looked at her curiously, took her exams, and told her to go out and enjoy the day.

Soon another coed came forward with her own tests completed. And another, and another after that. Maybe a dozen, and all with the same East Coast aura. More like Eastbourne students than anyone I'd ever known at Hopewell. As the other kids labored on—some still grappling with the first exam—I sifted through the tests of the fast workers and made up a list of their names. I wished I'd brought my printout. Hey, what about Harley's?

I found a copy on his desk and brought it back to my station. Sure enough, these girls were all from the East. Home addresses in Pennsylvania, Connecticut, New Jersey. And East Coast names: Rachael, Tracy, Bronwyn. If we were back at Eastbourne, they could have been my students. Among a cast of thousands.

I surveyed the columns. They were transfer students, every one.

And every one was Category One. But what the printout couldn't explain was why on earth they would turn up in Mayflower, Kansas. In a little school like Hopewell.

I took the printout back to Harley, but he was busy. I started to leave, then hung around to observe. He had a black kid in with him. A white guy in work boots and a denim jacket that read "Future Farmers of America" sat waiting.

"Now, son, I know you must be getting tired of taking tests. But this'll be a quick one," he assured the black student, a big, thick-muscled, football kid.

"I'm testing your knowledge of intercollegiate athletics," Harley continued in his wheezing voice. "What is the name of a large, private university in the north shore suburbs of Chicago."

The young guy looked blank.

"All right, I'll give you a bit more information. Their teams are called the Wildcats and last year they represented the Big Ten in the Rose Bowl."

The kid grinned and sat up straight. "Norfwestern," he said.

"That's very good. Thank you. Have a good day." Harley recorded a score. Then he called in the white kid in the future farmer's jacket. "Wildcats" and "Rose Bowl," Harley repeated.

Once again, he eventually got a response. "Nort'western," said the farm kid. And again, it seemed that Harley had got what he needed.

It was five o'clock by the time Harley and I finished testing, and he asked if I had time for a beer. "There's something I need to tell you," he said, with an air of secrecy.

"As long as they have bar food, Harley. I can't remember my last meal that wasn't a clam."

I called Cynthia, but all I got was a recording. "You've reached Cynthia Bradshaw of Intelcor: Midwest Field Representative. Dean Bradshaw and I aren't home now, so please leave a message at the beep. Or you can reach me on the Internet." She gave an email address filled with dots and @ signs.

So was that a new title? It had been a few days since I'd had time to really talk with Cyn—since that picnic in the back yard. Now, something about her voice in that message sounded different. More formal.

I left her a see-ya-when-I-see-ya voice mail, and drove out to meet Harley at the Hoof'n Horn. As I walked in, Happy Hour was hummin'. The juke box was pumping out a slow line dance, and the floor was swirling with a dozen couples who looked like they'd been practicing.

I saw Harley at the bar, but held up at the dance floor. Something about this place was captivating. It was like the old roadhouses out in the county. Those muted, colored spotlights. The pungent smell of sawdust on a pine-tar varnished floor. The shuffling sound of Western boots: sliding and stomping, shaking the rafters to the rhythm of a Fender bass guitar.

"Are you comin', or are you dancin'?" a raspy voice called out from the bar.

"Grab me a bar stool, Harley. I'll be right along."

For a half second I thought I'd caught sight of someone, out there in the line dance. I waited for the dancers to come around again. And then I saw her clearly, for certain. She was paired with a little skinny guy. That wasn't Walt Wagstaff!

But I watched them all change partners, and there was Walt, coupled with a big girl, down the line. As Sarah swung around, she saw me and her eyes grew wide. She flashed a smile, and I quivered. She looked every bit the girl I'd known before, on many a dance floor like this one. A far cry from the black-clad liturgist at the Congregational Church, Sunday-Sarah.

She was wearing a denim skirt and a rose-colored blouse, open collar. The red glow set her dark hair shining. She was rocking to the music in a subtly erotic motion: chest high, hips churning yet restrained. Tensile as a steel spring. This was Saturday-night-Sarah.

For a moment, I stood there and simply stared at her.

Then she mouthed two words: "See you?"

I gave her a wink, and nodded.

She mimed, "Where?"

I gestured back toward Harley.

It was the most sustained communication the two of us had had in five years. But it felt like a conversation resumed.

———————

"It's about time," carped Harley. "Thought you might have joined the line dance." He'd set a longneck Coors at my place. I noticed he was drinking Coors Light. A diet?

I looked closer at Harley. He seemed a little bit out of character, staring solemnly down at the bar as though he had business to take up.

"So, how'd the testing go?" he muttered, finally.

"Pretty well, except we had no schedule. If that was my responsibility, I apologize, Harley. Nobody told me. But I guess that's about par for the course."

"Don't worry, I'd say you handled it fine. And it's a good thing." He took a long draft of his beer and sat silent. Rehearsing his next one-liner?

I studied his bottle, waiting him out. How do people stomach that Coors Light? Sixty calories, and a flavor like mineral water.

Finally, I spoke up. "So I guess I'll be doing more of it."

He nodded. More silence.

"Hey, Harley, I believe I figured out that Northwestern Test of yours. It's a shibboleth, right?"

He looked blank.

I explained it was ancient Hebrew for a password, from the Book of Judges. The Gileadites had used a shibboleth to identify the Ephraimites who were trying to escape in battle, even though the two tribes looked alike.

"The thing was, Ephraimites had no 'sh' sound in their dialect. So they couldn't say 'shibboleth.' I guess that's the same principle with your Category Three kids, am I right? If they're not middle class, they can't pronounce 'Northwestern.'"

He chuckled appreciatively, but once again turned stone silent. I found myself gazing past him through a haze of cigarette smoke, out toward the dance floor. When would Sarah be coming? And would she bring that dead head husband with her? Well, I guessed this was one way to kill time and find out.

Finally, Harley stirred to life. He knocked back a slug of beer, then looked all around the bar. He lowered his voice. "This isn't generally known. But this afternoon I got a call from the new president. While you were testing. No time to tell you."

"Tell me what?"

"Well, it seems I got a new job. About four hours ago."

He paused to sip his beer. Then he set the bottle down and slowly turned to me. "Well, this is strictly confidential. But you should know. The president has..."

WHAP!!

Someone slapped a wet towel on the bar, right between us.

"Doc Harley, I jess heard the news. Congra-cha-lations!"

Rollie Cleaver swung a hand the size of a Hormel ham and clapped him on the back, stoppling his esophagus. Harley gagged and grabbed for the bar towel as his beer came back up in his sinuses. He sat rocking on his bar stool, red-faced, wheezing.

Rollie swiveled around and found Hazel with a tray of water glasses. He grabbed one. Harley took a sip and slowly recovered.

Rollie Cleaver carried on. "Matt, Hazel! did you hear the news? Tell 'em! Tell 'em what happened, Doc Harley."

"Just about to," gasped Harley. "New president... just made me... dean... of instruction!"

Hazel gave a jolt and looked down at the floor. Then she set her tray of glasses on the bar and leaned back on it. "Harley?" Her question caught in a curl of smoke, hung suspended. Then, "Harley! Why, Harley, congratulations. But I thought we already had a dean. What happened to Pemberton Todd?"

"Gittin' a certificate," advised Rollie. "You know, like all the others. See, I was there with the Alumni Council when the president announced it—how we need fresh talent, what with re-engineering the college and all that."

"That's about what he told me," confirmed Harley. "He said they wanted someone who could work closely with the Gray Group. Like this category assessment program I've come up with. I was about to tell Matt, here, that he'll have to take over testing tomorrow. Seems I'll be in meetings all day with the president."

"Evidently he didn't hear your routine during his talk at Convocation," sniffed Hazel.

Harley drew himself up tall on his barstool. "What the hell, Hazel, people can change." He took a sip of his Coors Light. "However, that reminds me—did you all hear the one about ... "

She flew off, and even Rollie allowed as how he had to get back to his duties. He picked up his bar towel and gave Harley a firm handshake.

"You know, he really has a lot of respect for you," I commented.

Harley was silent for a moment. "Guess that's a side benefit of special education," he said, dead serious again. "These marginal kids, you test their disabilities. Help 'em isolate their problems. They start seeing they *have* a problem rather than *are* one. Help 'em make it through here, they never forget you. And some of 'em surprise you: score a few successes. Not that it means a whole lot to those stuffed shirts on the faculty."

"Didn't Dean Pemberton Todd put Rollie on academic probation a time or two, back when I was in school?" I asked.

Harley fell silent.

I signaled for another round of beers.

With a fresh Coors Light, he brightened up. Suddenly he spun around on his bar stool with a flash of inspiration. "I'd forgot you had a doctorate in history. That reminds me of something else the president said." (I noticed he no longer referred to the man as "Squire.")

"Seems they've been having a tough time finding somebody to teach this new course the Gray Group has been piloting. Sort of a history course—been taught by a guy they had to send packing."

"Julian said something about that. Well, it depends. What's the title?"

"It's pretty weird—wrote it down." He fumbled through a stack of note cards in his shirt pocket. "Got it here, somewhere. Seems a bunch of real bright transfer students have come in from the East, just to take it. Where the hell—here it is. 'Sacred Sex and Primal Prayer.' Now, how's that for a course title?"

I blinked. "Does it have a syllabus?"

Harley ducked down and hauled up a tattered leather briefcase. He set it on the bar and began burrowing deep in the bowels of it. I watched in wonderment. This guy should be a marvel at keeping academic records.

Something caught my eye, over his shoulder. A patch of rose red, past the darkness of the bar. Sarah was leaving the dance floor, walking swiftly toward the front door. I watched Walt Wagstaff, her hulking husband, follow. Well, so much for the old class reunion.

"I must have left it at the office," Harley mumbled at last.

I clapped him on the shoulder, left ten dollars on the bar. "Hey, no problem, Your Deanship. I was just leaving."

There was a note on the kitchen table.

> Matt—Hey, dig that moon. I'm out by the river. Do full moons turn on deans? When I return, I aim to see! C.

By the river. With her sketch pad I imagine. But she hadn't been home since late afternoon. That's a long time to be out drawing anything. Even a moon. Well, I might as well hold off on supper. There was a stack of stuff I'd set aside to read, and an hour's worth of daylight. I took it out front to the porch swing on the veranda.

AGENDA

HOPEWELL COLLEGE

BOARD OF TRUSTEES

I riffled the pages, wondering why anyone would send me a document like this. Old Business. New Business. Reports from Standing Committees. It looked about as exciting as a home appliance manual. Someone had scribbled some notes in the margins. Trying to stay awake, no doubt.

I was skimming the report when one item brought me up short.

> "The public accounting firm of Nielson and Withers has completed a preliminary audit of Hopewell College financial records. At this time, it appears the budget deficit for the current year is five times greater than projected in the president's report last fall. More information will be forthcoming prior to the next meeting of the faculty."

Oh shit, that's tomorrow—8:00 a.m. I flipped to the end. There was an appendix of a half dozen pages. On each page, a photocopy of a certificate. "For distinguished service pro Christus et Kansas." That kind of thing. I saw what Rollie meant. They'd been passing out these kiss-of-death certificates like bug spray at a nudist camp. I recognized a few of the recipients: professors who probably hadn't planned on a premature retirement.

Julian Reid had signed each one, along with Gus Lindholm for the board of trustees. Just above the Hopewell College seal: suitable for framing. I sat back with a shudder, remembering my displaced egghead colleague, Channing Coe. God, I wondered what happened to him.

Then something else snagged me. It was the president's signature—so shaky I could scarcely make out his name. A couple of times, he'd had to cross out his first attempt at a "J" and start over. I went back over the notes in the margins. Same unsettled script. So the notes were Julian's. There were drawings interspersed. Something like a park, filled with trees. And surrounded by a fence. Or maybe a campus.

It took me a while to decipher what he'd written, and even then it didn't make much sense. There were some strange words and phrases—*yashah*, was that Hebrew? "The Counter Columbian Syndrome," whatever the hell that meant." And a pair of numbers, 12:1, maybe every other page, over and over again. A mathematical formula? A Bible verse?

It was getting hard to read. I put the report in my satchel and thought some about Julian, as darkness fell. About the dark, anguished side of him.

In the twilight, the cicadas were out in force, like a drove of droning oboes. Across Winthrop Boulevard, through the elm trees in the park, a perfectly round, golden moon was rising like a stage curtain. I closed my eyes and listened to the cars pass by on Winthrop. Whoosh, along the weathered bricks. Whoosh, whoosh...

I guess I'd dozed off on the porch swing when Cynthia came home. Thank God, she'd brought a pizza.

"Hey, what's this?" she asked as she came up the stairs.

"What's what?"

"This package, down here at your feet."

I picked it up and brought it inside, as Cynthia domestically cracked a couple of beers and set out the pizza on the kitchen table.

It was a big, bulky envelope with my name printed on it, once again in big, block letters. Inside was a spiral notebook filled with script. It seemed to be some sort of journal.

I picked it up and stuffed it in my satchel, alongside the minutes from the board meeting. I already could tell what it was—from the same, quavering handwriting.

It was the journal of Julian Reid.

9

G us Lindholm lumbered into the science lecture hall as the campus clock tolled eight. The big clock sat in a cupola on the roof of the old science hall, and it shook the building to its foundations every time it rang. Some said they thought the reverberations were getting stronger.

"Good morning!" Gus rumbled, on about the same frequency as the bell. "That is, if I may use that term loosely."

He was a big, burly man with the somber air of having lived long enough to have watched a lot of life pass by. His ominous greeting sent a ripple of whispers through the faculty. We were seated in tiers—three dozen professors and administrators stacked in rows like students at a lecture. Some had taken out note pads and swiveled up their arm rests for a writing surface. Others simply sat and stared straight ahead.

"When the trustees met the other night, we set to thinking about the best way to start off this first faculty meeting of the year," Lindholm continued. "And we decided it didn't seem fair to lead off with our new president Squire and have him tell you the news.

"So we decided to give ourselves the job of giving you the plain facts: what we know about the condition of the college, which pretty much comes down to the finances. Then, after that, we'll call on the new president to tell you what he believes he can do about it."

Lindholm half nodded at Squire, who was seated in the front row. Next to him was a wizened little fellow with the kind of rimless glasses only old people wore, before they came back in style. Like Lindholm and Squire, this guy was dressed up in a business suit with a crisply starched white shirt and a black and gold bow tie. The faculty looked as rumpled as a summer vacation.

Lindholm introduced the granny glasses guy as Calvin Withers and said he was an alum from back East and an auditor by trade. Said they'd brought him in to straighten out the college's financial records, now that there'd been a change in administration.

"Calvin, I can't tell you how much we appreciate your volunteering to come out and resolve these questions for us," Lindholm concluded. Then he sat down in the front row next to Squire as Withers rose to a trickle of applause.

The little man took a stance behind a big laboratory table that dominated the science lecture hall. The table had a sunken sink and a tall, shiny, chromium spigot that thrust up a foot in the air, then curved back downward toward the drain. The big, black table dwarfed him, and Withers seemed to cringe a bit behind it.

As he took out his notes and peered over his glasses, the clock chimed once for the quarter hour. For an instant, on the wall behind him I thought I saw a picture sway. But I blinked and it hung straight again.

I was having trouble focusing this morning, after the night that had just passed. But I had a day of testing ahead, and fought to keep my eyes open.

Calvin Withers passed out copies of his financial report and began piping out his figures in a singsong voice like a junior high school book report or a Sunday school lesson. As he rattled on, I peered at the blurring numbers, but they seemed to be swimming all over the page. The only thing I could clearly make out was that a number of the columns ended in parentheses. I knew what that spelled: DEFICIT.

I also noted the projected deficit for the new fiscal year. It was about $200,000— from a shortfall of a dozen students.

Two rows ahead of me, Hazel Gottschalk sat shaking her head. Not a good sign. She must really have a handle on this financial stuff. From what I heard, Hazel ran bar tabs in her head.

As the auditor droned on, my eyelids sagged and I found myself on cruise drive, half dozing. I began losing touch with every sensation save one. I felt a certain stirring in my crotch.

I blinked and looked closely at Withers. He was making a funny gesture. The auditor had formed a tight, little ring of his thumb and index finger and was stroking the tip of the spigot on the lab table. Some weird nervous mannerism. He rubbed it back and forth again and again as though trying to make it come.

I had a fleeting temptation to step up and give the faucet a good twist. A couple of other, younger members of the faculty traded sidelong glances as Withers worked the spout. "Now as to my projections," he squeaked.

I drifted off, back into the night. Cynthia and I had experienced one of our less adept sexual encounters. For all the fine physical features of my wife, only one of us had been aroused, and it wasn't me. What had been the matter? But I knew that was the wrong question. Not *what*, but w*ho*? Whose deep eyes, dark hair, upturned breasts? Whose whispered, no's? Then, oh's?

I shook my head, picked up on the scattered applause as Withers took his seat and Roger Squire stepped to the front of the lecture hall. And heard the rumble of the big clock on the rooftop, tolling twice for the half-hour.

As the chimes faded, Squire took a deep breath and set one hand firmly on the lab table as he raised a fist of resolve in the air with the other. I could tell we were in for a real stem-winder.

A ringing voice stopped him cold, in mid-gesture. "President Squire, before you begin, I have a question on the auditor's report."

As Hazel Gottschalk rose to speak, Roger Squire glanced at her warily. "Well, we have limited time. Is it something we might take up later?" Somebody must have tipped him off about Hazel.

"I'm afraid not," she went on. "But I believe it's a quick question. Perhaps just an error in calculation. You see, it's the figures in the column headed 'Endowment.' They don't add up. Could we have some clarification?"

Squire shrugged his shoulders as Calvin Withers ventured back to the podium. He held his report in one hand, scanning the top page. With the other hand, he reached for the spigot.

"It's a matter of restrictions on the endowment," the auditor responded. "Perhaps we might have made that point more clear. You see, while the college still has two million dollars remaining in endowment, after covering last year's operating deficit, three-quarters of those funds are restricted. They were given for specific purposes, such as to endow a chair in Latin.

"Actually, that happened to be my major here," he noted testily. "Although I see that you no longer offer..."

Gus Lindholm rose to his feet and faced the faculty. "That's a pretty good example of the problems we're facing. Here we've got $100,000 sitting in the endowment fund that can only be used for scholarships to baseball players. But we haven't had a baseball team for five or six years. And why's that? Why, it'd cost us $300,000 to field one."

Hazel sat down, sadly shaking her head, as Squire launched into his prepared remarks. As he picked up his notes, the clock tolled three times for the quarter hour, and I was sure I saw a few flecks of plaster fall on the dark desk in front of him.

"Of course, it's all a matter of facts and figures," he began. "But is it only that? Oh, there's no denying the challenges we're up against at Hopewell College. But beneath all those data in the auditor's report, there lies a big question mark. Can you see it there? Look hard now." (He squinted for effect.) "I believe it's the most important item on that page of figures. For, you see, it's a question of spirit!"

At that, Squire let loose a spew of sound bites on the general themes of teaming up and sucking up your gut. "Do you remember how we conjugate the verb 'can,' my friends?

"There is 'I can,' 'you can,' 'he can,' 'she can,' 'they can.' But there is one other form of the verb, and it is vital. 'We can,' all together . . . .

"What it comes down to is simply this. We must work together, all together, as a team," Squire enjoined. "Remembering that each member has a vital position. And recalling, of course, that there is no 'I' in team!"

He looked up with a sly smile, pleased with his verbal gymnastry. What a toad. Then I noticed him glance at his watch.

"For my part, I have been asked by the trustees to serve you as president on a part-time basis, while continuing to fulfill my responsibilities as minister of Mayflower Congregational Church."

A chorus of muffled exclamation.

"The reason I can do so is twofold. First, and on this point I have absolutely no doubt, I have been summoned here to serve you. To serve in this community, and in this—in these—two institutions. I was called to give up the success and security of my career and venture into the wilderness." That last line drew a rustle and a grumble from the faculty of Kansans. Was I imagining something, or had he slowed his pace? Was he timing what he had to say? He went on about his midlife journey.

I slumped down and pulled out Julian's journal. Whatever he'd had to say, it couldn't be more butt-numbing than this. I thumbed through the pages.

> People running, running, in search of themselves. And, oh, the cases we see in west Kansas! Like Coronado and his Seven Cities of Gold. Why is it they all come out this way? The seekers are always heading west.

> The Counter Columbian Syndrome. That's what I called it (preaching to KC the other night). Columbus thought he'd been around the world, when in fact he'd seen only half of it. While we've come full circle. Experienced all the earth can afford. And still we can't believe there is not more.

> "The truth is, we're short on diversions." That's how KC put it, as I passed him the jug. He snickered. "Out in these parts, whatever life you see is pretty much the life you'll get."

> That's the difference between a pilgrim and a fugitive, I told him. The pilgrim is one who can stop running, settle down.

The Counter Columbian Syndrome. Hmm. I reached in my briefcase and pulled out the minutes of the trustees' meeting. Compared the handwriting once again. Sure enough, they matched. It was Julian Reid, all right. But not the one I'd known.

Squire was still carrying on about his career transition: how God had directed him here and there. It seemed his car broke down in Mayflower on his way to a pastorate in California. Another unmistakable sign of direct divine intervention. I flipped back to the journal.

> "A chance for you to change direction." That's how Gus Lindholm put it. As though I had a choice. More or less

directed to take over the college. I suppose it was all the com-
plaints about my demeanor in the pulpit. What did they
expect me to do: glare at them? And the fact I seemed to go
off on excursions. So, maybe I did digress a bit.

But this "promotion." With no idea what the job entails,
much less how to go about it. So I smile in my adversity. A
reflex, like the rictus of death. And now I'm to assume the
position of president? As some of the students might put it,
basically that means to bend over.

I broke out in a snort, and drew a dark look from Squire. He
glanced back at his watch, then seemed to pick up the pace. "And
now, my friends, as to the other reason I shall serve you as president
part-time and not relinquish my pastorate. The trustees have decided
to use a portion of the president's salary to engage a full-time consultant from the Gray Group as Provost of Hopewell College. That
individual should be on duty very shortly."

A buzz among the faculty.

"In the meantime, I have been asked to share this memorandum
from the enrollment management people at the Gray Group."

Squire produced a page of email. "It is our urgent recommenda-
tion that Hopewell College take immediate steps to accept an additional twelve candidates from the contingent list, for admission in the
current term."

Now the buzz became a rumble. "Not more Category Threes!"

"Please let me finish," Squire insisted. "In view of the college's
debts, the mounting deficit, diminished endowment, and the deferred
maintenance on campus, the Gray Group advises . . . "

The muttering mounted. "Not on your life!" "Remember last
year!" "More Category Threes?"

Squire set his email message down until he could resume.
" . . . the deferred maintenance on campus," he began, but he couldn't
continue.

For the murmuring swelled, and melded with the tolling of the
bell, up on the rooftop. Ten o'clock. "Bong-Bong-Bong," the science
hall reverberated as the big bell sounded. The building seemed to

shake and I clearly saw a picture sway. Then another sound in the echo of the bell. It was a "POP" like a pistol shot or a small explosion. The sharp sound came from above, as the bell continued its sonorous tolling: five chimes, six, seven…

And suddenly the chiming turned to clanging and chaos. The bell was rolling down the roof! As it came tumbling down in a torrent of sound—BONG, BONG, BOOM—the clamor shook the building to its core. I spun around to the east, toward the clanging. And as I looked out the window, all the boards and bricks of the cupola came flying past in a tumult of dust, and the big clock and the campus bell came crashing to the ground.

In an instant, the room grew dark as a cloud of dust puffed up and blocked out the sunlight. Everyone sat back, stunned. Then they began squirming, staring up at the ceiling. I glanced up at Squire and was surprised to see he seemed assured. He raised his arms in a sort of benedictory gesture.

"Everyone stay seated," in his best soothing pastoral voice, his baritone like a mantra. "Let's all be calm. We'll determine what has happened. For the moment, please remain in your seats."

And for a moment, everybody did, as the dust began to settle and the room returned to light. Squire went on, "Now just one point before we adjourn. To complete the point I was making. As to deferred maintenance, it surely must be clear by now that…"

From somewhere outside, I thought I heard a moan and another faint sound like a wail. I jumped up, vaulting a row of seats, and ran for the door.

"Now, that's exactly what we don't need here. Dr. Bradshaw, didn't you hear what I just said? I asked everyone to remain in their seats for a moment, until I…"

As I spun back from the doorway, something snapped. "Until you what? Till you finish your fucking sermon?"

"Doc-tor Bradshaw!"

"Someone's hurt out there! Can't you hear?"

I saw Jeb Collard get up, peering out the window.

"Jeb, come give me a hand! Harley, get an ambulance and call the cops. I heard something explode before that bell came down."

"Dean Bradshaw: as your president, I am directing you…"

"Oh yes, and Squire, here's something you can do. You can take your speech, and shove it!"

Jeb flashed a grin and shook his head as he raced by and we took off running down the hall. As we hit the exit bars on the fire door, I heard a burst of applause from the lecture hall.

Outside, the building seemed to be intact, except for a gaping cavity at the front of the roof where the cupola had been. But there was a huge pile of debris on the east side, between the science hall and a sidewalk. It looked like a bizarre bonfire for homecoming with painted wood and bricks and clock springs.

The dust was still settling, and it was hard to see clearly as I ran around the pile toward the sound of moaning. It was a low cry, and I strained to hear it. Was it growing softer? On the sidewalk, two young women were crying. One of them lay on her side, clutching her left leg that jutted out at an odd angle. The other girl was up on one knee, holding a handkerchief to her head as blood came streaming through her long blond hair from a cut at her temple. With her other hand, she was clutching at the rubble.

In a second, I saw it: a small foot in a sandal, a leg clad in blue jeans. I hollered "Jeb!" and he came scrambling around, grabbing boards and bricks, clockworks, and glass—anything we could get our hands on. Soon our hands were scuffed and bleeding.

But then there were other hands alongside us, burrowing into the pile. Hazel, her nails in red polish, muttering whenever she split one. And two pairs of dark, mahogany hands darting at the bricks and mortar. Jamal and LaRon. Still, were there enough of us? I could hear nothing beneath the debris.

There was a tromping of heavy footsteps, labored breathing behind me. "Ambulance should be here any minute, Matt. And the grounds crew. I told 'em to bring some picks and shovels."

"I don't think that'll help much, Harley," I said, wiping blood from my knuckles on my shirt. "We need more bare hands—a whole ring of people around this pile. There's a student under there, and I can't hear her any longer."

I turned to see Collard wrestling with one end of a four-foot board, and I bent down to grab the other. As we jerked it free and flung it to the ground, I looked back to see Harley, leaning on his knees, red-faced, gasping from the exertion of his errand. Behind him stood another half dozen members of the faculty. They were hobnobbing, hands in their pockets. Pondering the meaning of the crisis.

"Hey, will you motha..." I turned on them, when a firm hand took my elbow and pulled me back around.

"Keep your head. You're not just passing through town, like some people."

"But, how the hell can they just..."

"I know, I know." He draped an arm around my shoulder, then we both dropped back down to the pile.

It was then I heard the siren, and the ambulance came racing up the sidewalk toward the science building. There was a second, deeper siren as a fire engine pulled up. The fire truck had a big hose with a suction device, and in thirty seconds they'd unearthed the coed in jeans and sandals.

She was a small girl in a bulky black and gold Hopewell sweatshirt. Long hair. Silver earrings. I remembered her from the day of testing. One of the half dozen East coast coeds. Eastern name: Annabeth, or Bronwyn. Something odd in these parts.

Especially now. She was ashen, and looked to be asleep. In a blanket of dust. The paramedics pulled an oxygen tank from the ambulance. They strapped a mask to her mouth and lifted her onto a stretcher. As they carried her into the van, I heard the wail of a second ambulance, racing up Winthrop for the other injured students.

Those two were lying where they'd fallen. On the sidewalk close together, softly crying. Two East Coast girls in earrings. Incongruous out here, in pain. I walked over and knelt down over them. Held a hand on each of them, until the medics came.

10

"Jeb, what the hell are we doing here? I don't have a lot of time, you know. Gotta find the names of those girls, notify their parents. And Harley's expecting me to monitor the testing, even though I don't know the first thing about it. Testing starts in an hour. Whole damn day was full, and then this...So, what are we doing in the coffee shop?"

"Keep your jock on. I had to get you off campus. Just get us a booth. Coffee's black, right? One clam or two?"

I gave him a peace sign and stumbled down the aisle of the Corner Cafe to an open booth. It was nearly the end of the morning coffee hour, and the regulars were starting to vacate.

"Better get outta here 'fore they start chargin' us rent," one muttered as he scraped back his chair. His tablemates chuckled as though they hadn't heard that line before.

Some were retirees in plaid shirts and suspenders who came here early and stayed late. Others were store owners who might as well have been retired, for all the business they did in a weekday morning on Main Street. They'd just hang a one-word sign on the door— Java—so customers would know where to find them.

I drew a few friendly nods as I made my way down the aisle, along with some puzzled glances. No wonder. I took a gander at my torn shirt and grimy pants. Scuffed-up hands. I looked like a resident ax murderer.

I shut my eyes and took a few deep breaths, trying to shift into slow gear. I grabbed some napkins and cleaned off the table top. Flakes of frosting, puddles of spilled coffee. It wadded into a good-sized ball and I shot it twenty feet across the room, nothing but net, right into the trash container. The regulars applauded.

Where was Collard? I spotted him up at the cash register, balancing a tray full of clams and coffee.

As he came down the aisle, the regulars were ragging him. "Hey, Jeb, you look about as bad as your phenom over there. What are you coachin' these days—basketball or mud wrestling?"

He chuckled as he set the tray down. I grabbed a cup of coffee and took a long draft. "Ow! Damn, this stuff's hot."

"I believe that's the basic idea, Matt. Here, have a clam. Stir some cream in your coffee. Just sit an' get your ass on straight."

I cooled my coffee with the cream and took a sip. Took a knife and sliced a clam in half. I looked out on the intersection of Winthrop and Main Street, the heart of the business district.

It was nearly deserted in the heat of mid-September, the height of the drought. One of the storekeepers was out on the sidewalk cranking out a green awning. Others had yellowed, celluloid shades in their windows shielding their merchandise from the sun. I noticed a phalanx of new signs in the windows of the furniture store across from the cafe. Two-foot high red letters:

HARVEST SALE

(IF YOU CALL THAT A HARVEST)

OUR LOSS, YOUR GAIN!

In the next block, a couple of old men sat in the shade of the veranda on the front porch of the retirement hotel. They smiled and nodded, and raised a hand in silent greeting to every passer-by. Across the street, some townspeople were bunched on the steps of the big, tan, sandstone post office: hobnobbing over the morning mail.

I wondered if the folks of Mayflower had heard about the catastrophe at the college. If so, it didn't seem to have spoiled their day. Then I wondered if this weren't the life I'd come back for. Not this hassle with the college, but just to settle down and be a part of the town.

Finally, I looked up at Collard. He was staring into space.

I shook my head. "So, what do you think?"

"About?"

"Well, do you think I lost my job? How's that for starters?"

He chomped off half a clam, took a long draw of coffee. "Pretty hard to know till we can see. You remember the first rule of coaching, don't you?"

"Yeah, Coach, I remember. I guess I heard it often enough."

"So?"

"Knowing when to call time out."

He smiled in satisfaction.

I sat back to wait him out, as we both stared out the window. My breath was back to normal, but I still felt shaky.

Finally I spoke up. "Look, Jeb. I lost it back there. I know that. Swearing at Squire, putting him down in front of the faculty. But he's a real rear end, all right? He has no right to be president of this or any other college." Now I was panting again.

More silence.

"And you're the only one who understands that. Am I right?"

"Well, shit, I don't know. But this is serious. I mean, I really think I heard an explosion. And there was something eerie about what he was saying: that stuff about deferred maintenance, maybe timing his delivery. I just have a feeling…somebody's gotta get him outta there."

"Hmm…So, is there any chance he might take himself out? Play himself right outta the game?"

Now I fell silent.

I understood the reference. It was a game in the quarter finals of the state tournament, back in high school when I was still playing point guard. The team we were playing had put a pressing defense on us—half-court trap the whole game—and one of their guards had been hacking me. For three quarters, that went on. We were drawing fouls all the while, so I just took it.

And then on the fifth foul, as he was out of the game, he gave me an elbow to the solar plexus, and I just lost it. Grabbed his jersey with one hand and hit him in the face with the other. Blood all over. Of course they threw me out along with him. With a quarter to go. And of course we lost the game. Knocked us out of the tournament. I could still feel the anguish.

"Ya know, young Matt, you're a disciplined guy. Kinda kid a coach can always count on. Real patient and steady, up to a point. But when you pass that point, you don't show it. Nobody knows you're displeased, till they're swingin' in their jock strap from the ceiling."

"'No bark and all bite.' That's what you called me. Right?"

He nodded and silently chuckled.

Then he glanced up the aisle. "Oh, God. Hide the clams ... Hello, Harley. Sit down." He slid over. "We can always use another dean around here."

Harley sat down tentatively at the edge of the booth. He was breathing hard, cantilevered on one enormous buttock.

"Coffee?" I offered.

"Naw, not now. Can't stay but a minute. Testing, you know." He sat back and caught his breath, beet red and wheezing. Took a knife and cut himself a sector of my last clam.

"Had to find you. Thought you might have gone off campus. Jesus, Matt! You look like the south end of a horse going north."

"That's okay. I've got time to wash up. But, I've got the testing covered. I told you I'd take it over."

He polished off the clam, wiped his mouth with my napkin. Then he looked away.

"What is it, Harley?" I asked. "Looks like you have something to say. Oh, no. Oh, shit. Is it about my job?"

He slowly shook his head. "No, it's mine. I came down here to tell you—forget the testing. I've been doing it for a few decades now. And, here. I found this stuff in the files."

He handed me a big, bulky manila envelope and I pulled it open. It was a thick course syllabus and a video tape, each with the same inscription: "Sacred Sex and Primal Prayer. Pilot Module. Copyright: The Gray Group. All Rights Reserved."

I glanced at Harley and he looked aside. "So does this mean you're still interested in me as an instructor? That's great, but don't jeopardize your position. Remember, you're academic dean."

Jeb chimed in, "Matt's right. You gotta watch your step, Applequist. Think like a politician. Stick a finger in the wind."

Harley gave a jolt at that. He spun around and slid into the booth, full girth, slamming Collard against the back wall, an imprint in the wood paneling.

"That's nuckin' futs," he muttered. "And it's why I resigned. I guess it was what Matt did, in spite of the consequences."

"Uh oh. You must have talked to Squire."

"It was when I went in to quit. That deanship wouldn't have

amounted to anything anyway if they're bringing in a provost. That's a powerful position. I told him I'd go back to special ed. And that's when he told me to tell you..."

He looked away. "Two o'clock this afternoon. He wants to see you in his office."

I told Jeb to drive back up to campus without me. It was only a few blocks up the hill to my house from the Corner Cafe, and I needed to burn off some stress. Maybe I'd still have time to head out to the hospital before my last dance with Squire.

The streets were peaceful. A block before my house at the top of the hill, the enormous American flag stood steady as a sentinel in the median of Winthrop Boulevard. As I watched, it gave a flutter from a passing breeze. Then it flopped back on its pole, in the doldrums of midday.

I trudged up the walk and threw myself through the front door into the cool, dark parlor. The screen door slammed.

"Who's there?" called Cynthia. She was in her study on the second floor.

"It's me."

"Oh, Matt, I'm glad you're here!" Cynthia came bounding down the stairs, barefoot but swathed in a deep blue business suit. Her face was shining as she ran across the room. "Matt, you'll never guess. I tried to call you. Hey, Dude, the coolest news..."

She stopped short. "Holy shit. What happened? Were you in a fight?"

"Well, sort of."

I half collapsed as she led me to the couch, supportive but keeping me clear of her dress clothes.

"Here, sit back. I'll get a washcloth. And, somewhere around here, we must have a first aid kit." Cyn was back in an instant, sponging my face and dabbing my hands with alcohol Handi-wipes from Kentucky Fried Chicken. It was a new sensation, being nurtured, and I lay back in her arms.

I told her all about the explosion and the calamity, from the beginning. Then I paused. "There's one other thing, Cyn. Squire wants to see me. I think I may have lost my job."

Cynthia sat quietly as I rested on the couch. When I looked up, she was gazing off in space with a strange expression. Beatific. Almost smiling.

I glanced at my watch: half past noon. "Whoa! I've gotta get up to the hospital, check on those girls. Call their parents, once I find their names. I think one of 'em's 'Bronwyn.'"

"Not Bronwyn Chiles!"

"Why, Cyn, do you know her?"

Suddenly she looked intent, almost graven. "Here, Babe, let me make you a sandwich. You go take a shower."

It didn't take me long to feel lots better. I called out to Cynthia as I tucked in my shirt, rounding the corner into the hallway from the bathroom. "Hey, Cyn, you said you had some good news... And don't worry about this. Okay? Hell, you've had mixed feelings about this place. We can always... Cynthia?"

My sandwich was there in the kitchen, along with a cold Coke, but that was all. I looked out front. Her car was gone. Then I saw the syllabus and video tape for the sacred sex class, lying on the floor. She must have dropped them as she headed out the door.

I settled for phoning the hospital. There was too much on my mind to rush up there. The admissions clerk was a friendly lady who told me there'd been three students admitted, but two had already been discharged. The other was comatose, in critical condition. And that was Bronwyn Chiles. I took down the names of the other two— Rachael Cartwright and Annabeth Stowe.

"That was a terrible tragedy," the woman said. "But it's so nice to see how concerned you all are about your students at the college. You know, your president was in here just a few minutes ago, checking on Bronwyn. Along with a photographer. I think he's still outside, with some TV news people from Wichita."

I shuddered as I hung up the phone.

I drove up to campus and headed upstairs to the president's office. It was past 1:30, but I was glad to have a few minutes to spare. It's always bad form to show up late for your execution.

Mavis Lindholm smiled wanly as I slunk into the waiting room of the president's office. She slowly shook her head when I asked if Squire had returned.

"Well, I guess I'll just take a seat here, till I can find out where I stand."

Mavis gave a maternal sigh.

There was a clatter on the staircase, and Squire came striding through the door. Hot as it was outside, he had his dark suit coat on and his hair looked freshly pomaded. He gave Mavis a perfunctory smile and nodded in my direction.

"Dr. Bradshaw, I shall be with you shortly."

I headed back to my visitor's chair, too fretful to continue the conversation with Mavis. As I picked up the printout from her desk, I saw there was a letter beside it. Neatly typed, with my name at the end. Evidently ready for my signature. I stood there for a moment and scanned it. "This is a letter of resignation..."

"Come in, Bradshaw." He walked over and picked up the letter.

I followed him into the verdant office where I'd last met Julian. Although still sheltered by the elm trees, the place now seemed gelid. Instead of the soft watercolors that Reid had put up, the walls were plastered with photographs of Roger Squire in the company of celebrities he'd met on the evening news.

I took a seat across from his desk as he closed the door. He sat down, reviewing the letter. Then he looked up and fixed me with a dark stare. He still hadn't taken off his suit jacket.

"Well, Dr. Bradshaw..."

I glanced at him, then at the photos on the far wall. I shook my head. "I heard you got a film crew to the hospital. Think you'll make the evening news?"

He stiffened, then composed himself. "See here, Bradshaw. I realize you lack the media sense to recognize a photo opportunity. Unfortunately, that seems typical—such a lack of sophistication around here. How do you think we're going to draw attention to this backwater? Keep this college afloat, if no one's ever heard of it? Have you even thought of that?"

He caught himself. "But all of that's beside the point. See here, Bradshaw: there are two ways we can resolve the matter of your employment. You're here on an administrative appointment. I consulted with our attorney. No problem with tenure or anything like that. I can dismiss you on the spot, and I'm prepared to. Or, if you want to save face and try to salvage your career, you can simply sign..."

The buzzer on his phone rang, but he ignored it.

"... sign this letter of resignation which I've saved you the trouble of composing." He shoved it across his desk. But the buzzer rang again, three blasts.

Squire set the letter down and picked up the phone. "Mavis, please hold all my calls. I'll be free in a moment. I thought I had mentioned...

"Oh, well, yes. I see. The Gray Group... Of course, I'll be right out. You know, I didn't expect our new provost so soon. Please have him take a seat and offer him... Oh, her?"

He got up so quickly, he appeared to have forgotten about me and our meeting. Then he returned to shut the door, giving me a good glower in the process.

He was gone a long time.

I took the letter of resignation and made a paper airplane of it. To pass the time, I gave it a few test flights, pausing to modify my construction after each sortie. I was considering adding a paper clip to the nose and firing a shot off his forehead, when the door opened and Squire returned.

But he didn't come in. He just stood in the doorway of his office, as though hesitant to enter. I could see he was perspiring. Slowly, he drew off his coat and rolled up his shirt sleeves. As he turned in my direction, he looked somewhat pale. I watched his face contort in a grimace, like a nightly-news smile.

Finally, he cleared his throat. "Isn't it silly? The things we do on impulse? Why, Matt, it's too foolish even to bother with an apology. I mean, if there's one thing this college needs, surely it's all us as a team—all pulling together."

He tossed his suit coat on his desk and leaned over, offering his hand. "What do you say we put it all behind us? Fresh start! Now, then, let's have that letter back!"

I sat and stared at him for a second in bewilderment. Then I took my letter of resignation and shot it through the open door.

"Hey, watch that!" cried a voice that sounded familiar. And then Cynthia sauntered through the door.

"Dean Bradshaw," Squire continued, with a cough to clear his throat. "I believe you know our new provost."

11

*F*or a moment, I stood there, slack jawed. Then I shook my head and gathered my senses and headed for the door. Brushing by her, I muttered something that might have passed for "Congratulations." But I stuck my head back in the president's office. "Look, Cyn, I'm going to the hospital to check on that student. Then you and I need to have a good, long talk. I'll meet you at the Hoof'n Horn—say, seven."

Squire glanced at Cynthia who looked at her watch and nodded. I could tell who was in the driver's seat in that roadster.

Jesus, why hadn't she told me what she was doing? As far as I knew, Cynthia had been nothing more than a run-of-the-mill Net Head. Hammering away on that computer in her home office, surfing Web sites for Intelcor with her modem. And now she was provost? Hell, that meant she'd run the school.

I mulled it all over on the way to the hospital. So the Gray Group was Intelcor, in academic guise. I thought of Harold Alabaster, who'd sent me out this way. What was it they called him? "The Great Gray Hope."

"The Gray Group." Ah, come off it! Don't be paranoid...

The hospital was a low, tan, cinderblock building at the far end of town. Set in a neighborhood of bungalows about the same height, it might easily have been missed, but for the big sign that blared EMERGENCY in red letters from one corner. Red as the vermillion of the afternoon sky. An arrow on the sign pointed to a back entrance. I parked my car in front and went in.

"Bronwyn Chiles," I told the gray-haired lady at the front desk. She smiled and pointed to a door marked "Intensive Care."

"Is it all right to go back there? I'm Matt Bradshaw, dean of students at the college."

She smiled again. "We know who you are."

The charge nurse was a big woman in a white pantsuit who looked like she might have spent some time on the offensive line of the Green Bay Packers. Not so much fat as stocky. And definitely in charge. "Who you wanta see?" she rumbled.

I told her, and introduced myself. She led me down the hall to the room of Bronwyn Chiles. It was one of those stark, sterile environments where efficiency had triumphed over aesthetics. All tile and shiny linoleum. Not even a photo calendar on the wall.

Bronwyn lay motionless in the center of a steel frame bed. She looked small there. Her head was slightly elevated and the right side of it was encased in a fresh, white bandage. She wore an off-white gown that matched her complexion. Both were the color of a cloudy day.

I couldn't tell anything about her condition other than that it seemed pretty serious, yet possibly stable. At least her breathing was regular, if that counted for anything. She was certainly a pale vestige of the girl who'd raced through all her tests yesterday morning, then run outside to enjoy the day.

I swung around to ask the nurse what else she could tell me, but bumped into her behind me. She'd followed me in. Her name was BEV, according to the plastic tag on her massive chest. Below the name, the tag read "R.N.," in smaller letters. I felt a bit encouraged. Registered Nurses generally know what they're doing.

"So how does it look, Bev? Does it seem like she's going to … " I felt a hammerlock on my left arm as she steered me out the door. All the way down the hall to the nurses' station.

"One thing we always tell our visitors," she spoke in a tone that brooked no nonsense. "When a patient's in a coma, you don't say anything in front of 'em you don't want 'em to know. A lot of these people can hear, you know.

"Sometimes I go in there and folks are speculating how much longer their uncle's gonna last. But I've had patients come out of comas and tell me everything everybody's said. You know, hearing's about the last sense to go, even when people can't feel pain. I remember one fella, couple years ago. Came to, called for his lawyer. Re-did his will. Been listening in on his relatives."

"Okay, thanks. But my student. How's she..."

"Seen 'em snap out of comas in a matter of minutes, especially the younger ones. First you might see an eyelid flicker. Next thing you know, they're sittin' up in bed and asking what's for supper. And two hours after that, they can be dead—keel right over on you."

She looked down at her chart with a frown. "As a matter of fact, we don't have a relative listed here... Say, you're dean of students. Maybe we should just put you down. Be someone to call."

I gave her a card with my office and home numbers. Then I got a phone book and jotted down the number for the Hoof'n Horn. I said, "I'm heading up there now."

She took the card and clipped it to her chart. Then she stepped up close, still frowning, though her eyes had softened.

"You asked how she's doing? She's not so bad. Semi-comatose, fades in and out. For all intents and purposes, she's just sleeping. But you know, I get a feeling you care about this kid. Not like that tinhorn president, mugging for the TV cameras. So, how'd this happen, anyway?"

"Bev, I have no clue. But I've got a feeling I'm going to find out a lot of things before all this is over."

The sky was a bonfire as I drove out in the prairie north of town. Deep red, with a metallic tinge: about the color of molten lava. Spectacular, and all in motion. A furious wind was tossing cumulus clouds around like blood-stained balls of cotton.

I parked the car and leaned back against the hood. Peering up in the clouds, I thought I saw something dark and gritty, and I knew I'd seen it before: topsoil. A west Kansas dirt storm. The last, deadly symptom of a drought season.

Inside, the Hoof'n Horn looked as ruddy as the ominous sky. But in here it was a warm glow from the spotlights, fuchsia with a dash of blue and amber. I don't know who Rollie Cleaver had hired for a decorator, but it was someone who knew Kansans, who understood how people found comfort out here. The walls were planks of unstained pine, rough and radiant. The booths had been stained a dark mahogany that set off the bright glow of neon beer signs. Coors and Old Style. Leinenkugel.

Rollie's roadhouse dance floor was manicured like an NBA arena, varnished slick and shiny, with a layer of sawdust to scoot your boots on. I remembered many a night in places like this, out with Sarah. The juke box was playing the same slow line dance.

I was bouncing to the beat as I made my way past the bar, and half felt like turning back to check out who was on the dance floor. But instead I headed down to the dark booths at the far end of the barroom. Cynthia and I needed a quiet place for a serious conversation. As I rounded the end of the bar, a couple got up from the last booth, and I grabbed it.

Before long, Hazel appeared with placemats and silverware.

"How many, Matt?"

"Two, at least in a while. I'm waiting for Cynthia."

"Coors draw?"

"Yes, please, and a tall one."

"No doubt." She straightened the place mat, leaned over and kneaded my shoulder.

I chugged the Coors and let myself luxuriate in all the sights and sounds of Rollie's place. Even the smells felt like a homecoming. Fresh beer and stagnant cigarette smoke. Chicken wings and onion rings from the complimentary boo-fay. Now and then, the sweaty smell of a couple just back from the dance floor. And the odd, pungent whiff of shit from the feed lot whenever the front door opened.

I'd closed my eyes, savoring all the sensations, when a fist the size of a football slammed my shoulder like an all-out blitz. "Hey, you noddin' off back here? Must've been one hell of a day."

"Hey, sit down, Walt. Yeah, it's been a day. I'm just waiting for my wife. You know, I really haven't seen you since I've been back. Although I've run across Sarah a time or two."

"So I hear." He eyed me as he slid into the booth. Walt Wagstaff was a square-cut, corn-fed sort of guy with the thickset frame that comes from growing up on farm chores. Perfect body for football, if the game didn't call for mobility. Even in his prime, Walt Wagstaff had the foot speed of a lawn ornament.

Now the torso looked a little lumpy under his dress shirt. My old rival was getting plump around the edges.

"So, Bradshaw, I hear you've picked up pretty much where you left off up at the college. Grad school and all. Do we call you 'Doc' now?"

"That's not recommended." I wasn't smiling. "How about you, Walt? From what I can see, you and Sarah are doing all right."

"Whaddaya mean?"

I took a draw on my beer and studied him. "Well, I guess just what I said. It seems she's teaching, active in the church. And I hear you're big in cable TV."

He settled back into his seat.

"I mean I wasn't referring to your marriage or anything." I don't know why I said that.

He sat bolt upright, flashed a shadowed look. "Yeah, well, cable's big in a place like this: forty-three channels, and we're lookin' at a whole bunch of spinoff services."

"Such as?"

"Home security, stuff like that. Once you've got folks wired, there's a whole lot you can sell 'em."

"Home security? In a town like this?" But I remembered the motion sensors we'd come across in Ellsworth: the small town with the big, barbed wire prison.

"Crime's a comin'. Don't matter where you live. Growth industry—that's what our consultants say. We got some good consultants." He told me he'd come out for line dance practice but now he had a meeting across town. As he was sliding out of the booth, I heard: "Matt! Telephone." It was Hazel, up at the bar.

Walking to the phone, I tried to envision Walt Wagstaff on a line dance team. He was about as nimble as a construction crane.

"Hello?"

"Matt, it's me. I'm running late. Be another hour."

"Well, I can always have another beer or two. But, look—come out as soon as you can, okay? You know we need to talk."

"Hey, lighten up, Dude! I just saved your ass back there, remember?" Then her tone softened. "Matt, take a minute and go look outside. There is just the coolest sunset!"

That triggered something. "Cynthia, what you're looking at is topsoil. A dust storm! The life of this community blowing halfway to Nebraska. Can't you … Ah, I'm sorry. Look, I'll wait for you."

Slowly, I hung up the phone.

"Another beer, Matt? You look like you could use one."

I carried my Coors toward the back booth, but Hazel stopped me.

"Hey, you can't sit moping back there in that booth all night." She whipped off her apron. "Come on, I've got a break coming. They're starting up a line dance!"

I muttered something about not remembering the steps, but she took me in tow and out to the dance floor. "She's Comin' Down the Line!" some clodhopper hollered. "Getcha a partner, even your spouse. Be swappin' partners in a minute, anyways!"

A cheer went up as the song came on—a Di-Di-Di-Boom-Boom drum roll.

"You say you're feelin' down,
So tired of searching 'round.
But look up, don't be cryin'
She's comin' down the line!"

I recognized the singer's twang, and it took me only a couple of rounds to pick up the dance step. It was a simple, country shuffle, and I knew it in my bones. All they'd added was a little turnout spin at the end of each stanza. Step by step, side by side, with an arm about Hazel's shoulder, I fell into a beat that felt as natural as breathing. But then came the kicker.

"You're looking for a sign,
Then she comes down the line.
Hey, can this really be?
Just look at who came free!"

At the last line, all the fellows spun 'round and everybody raised their hands and yelped. Then we hooked up with our new partners and settled back into the shuffle. Some of the verses proved shorter than others, and next time the chorus kicked in, I was a little late to twist and turn and change partners. I was still stumbling as I spun around.

And felt my knees give way.

She was gazing up at me with those warm, wide, brown eyes and a big, shy smile. There were beads of perspiration beneath her dark hair and a rivulet ran toward her peasant blouse, the cleft of her breasts. She was breathing hard. As we clasped hands, we clicked into a rhythm born of many nights like this. I held her shoulder tight, and she squeezed my hand. Then, as she twirled outside, she gave a little stomp the way we used to.

When the final chorus came on for one last "She's comin' down the line…" we spun out of line, still dancing. Adding subtle steps to the shuffle. Ricocheting in and out of spins. Scattering sawdust with a stomp across the shiny floor. Then another upbeat song came on, and we started again. Some of the other dancers had clustered around the floor to watch us. Then a slow ballad, and we kept dancing.

At the end of the song, I looked down at Sarah and she looked up at me, and we both saw the position of our bodies. She gave a shudder and took a step back. And I began to search the roadhouse for my wife.

As I limped back toward the bar, I found Cynthia sitting at the far end, sipping a glass of Chablis. "Hope that's the good house wine," I remarked as I mounted the barstool beside her. "Rollie's renowned for the quality of his cellar."

Cynthia appeared to be staring at a row of whiskey bottles.

"Coors draw, tall," I told the bartender, "And my friend here might be ready for another glass of Gallo. What say, Cyn?"

She shook her head and said nothing. I concentrated on my beer, and on getting my wind back.

"All right, Cyn, what's up? I thought we were coming out here to talk. You know, I've been waiting for an hour."

"But not in solitude, I'd say…Who was that chick you were glued to on the dance floor? Isn't that the same one I saw conducting the funeral service?"

"Her name's 'Sarah.' She's someone I knew in college."

"I have no doubt. Somehow I sensed you two were acquainted.

That choreographed dancing. Where'd you hook up, on the chorus line with the Rockettes?"

"All right, we dated. But she's married now, to some guy who runs the local cable TV station. And, as a matter of fact, last I knew you and I were married also. Even though it turns out I'm not much of an authority on what all you've been doing for a living. And, Cynthia, please don't say you can't tell me."

"Yeah, and be sure you don't say anything like, 'Nice going,' or that you're proud of me. Even though I just got one hell of a phat promotion, all right?"

I noticed that the bar had become very quiet. "Look, Cyn, let's go back to the booth. We can both use something to eat." I grabbed my beer. Cynthia got another glass of wine and followed.

She sat quietly for a few minutes as we sipped our drinks. Hazel came by and took our orders for supper. And then Cynthia began to speak in that new tone of voice that I heard now and then. It was a lower voice, almost older.

"Okay, Matt. I guess it's time. Opening question..."

"Sure. Who the hell is the Gray Group, and what are you..."

"No, it's my question. I was to ask you. Are you online?"

"What?"

"One question." She smiled a little. "Are you with us? Are you online?"

I drained my beer and got up to leave.

Cynthia put a hand on my shoulder. "Okay, I know it's too soon to ask that. But I was supposed to. You're right, it's time you knew something." She glanced at the dance floor. "Maybe past time... All right, they call it 'The Heartland File.'"

I sat down again.

"'Data warehousing.' Does that mean anything to you?"

I shook my head.

Then she started in. She described a company that had grown up at Eastbourne, ten years before, using computers for market research. With huge data banks, built up over time. One for every region of the country.

"Out here, it's The Heartland File. We track trends. Local news content in small town papers. Categories in the Yellow Pages: Security Services, Cable TV. Somebody has to keep feeding these data bases and it helps to have somebody local. 'Data hounds.' That was my job when I first came out here."

"Okay, Cyn, that's a start. But who's 'they'? The Gray Group? Intelcor? And what does this have to do with the college?"

She gave a smile and shook her head. "Hey, I can only handle six questions at a time."

Hazel came by with our barbecue burgers and Cynthia began chewing hers meditatively. Finally, she went on. "All right. When they started, they were doing stuff like franchise siting. Where to put the Boston Chickens—that kind of thing. Then they began getting calls from colleges.

"It was back when Generation X hit college age. A real birth dearth for the schools. Suddenly there weren't many kids of college age. And it really affected the places mostly known for their parties. These schools were running low."

"So, what did they do with the computers?"

"Here's another concept for you: 'database marketing.' Basically, it's how grocery stores use scanners. Intelcor came up with ways to identify certain kids who'd take to certain kinds of courses."

"Such as?"

"Remediation. 'Applied life studies.' It's big in junior colleges. Also four-year schools, for their ath-a-le-tic programs. Get these jocks who can't walk and chew gum at the same time, you can maybe teach 'em to say their names."

"You mean, like what Harley does?"

"Exactly. The 'Northwestern Test.' Actually, Harley's pretty famous. But there are courses in other fields. Lots of 'em. Plug-and-play modules. You can teach 'em anywhere, as long as the demographics match."

"Such as 'Sacred Sex and Primal Prayer.'"

She reached for the ketchup, started in on her French fries.

"I can see you're getting interested. Okay, Matt. The really cool stuff is enrollment management. Finding the good students good colleges miss. Kids who don't do well in high school 'cause they're so turned off by it. High IQ, low grade point average."

"So, how do they find them?"

"I can't get into ... don't glare at me. This is intellectual property, all right? It's how people like me make a living. Besides, I didn't invent this stuff. I only know what they tell me."

From where I sat, she knew a hell of a lot. I couldn't believe that a year ago, Cynthia was sitting in my classroom, taking notes.

I ordered another round of drinks, and in a minute she went on. It seemed they were tapping records at video rental stores. Say, who checked out "Above the Rim," "Blue Chip," and "Hoop Dreams," if they were tracking basketball fanatics.

I told her I thought there were laws against electronic spying. She said there also were ways to get around them. They kept track of high school kids who rented highbrow movies but carried low grade point averages. Foreign films. Or movies that appeal to special interests.

I thought of a cult film on teenage witchcraft: "The Craft."

So you could fill a college with bright kids top-line schools would ignore. I was following her, but I thought of a problem: all these alienated freshmen. Wouldn't a lot of them split? What was it? Half of all freshmen transfer out of their first colleges. I remembered something like that from my stint on the enrollment management committee back at Eastbourne. Now I wished I hadn't spent so much time nodding off in their meetings.

And then I remembered Bronwyn, and some of the other Eastern girls, and had a flash.

"What's up, Matt? You're bug-eyed. You got an inspiration, or is it stomach gas?"

"I'll bet you're into aftermarkets. Tracking misfits in their freshman year. That's why some of those girls looked familiar. I might have seen one or two at Eastbourne. Isn't that right, Cynthia? You're catching the runoff from Eastern schools, and funneling 'em out to places like this."

She stared at her fries. "I've told you enough."

"But why would any of those kids want to come here? And what about this college? You've got a velvet Elvis for a president, and you've never been a provost. So, who'll be calling the shots? How does the Gray Group plan to salvage this place?"

She considered the last bite of her burger. "You ask a lot of questions, Matt. You're good at that. But you still haven't answered mine."

She took a long sip of wine and I felt a knee beneath the table, nudging mine. "So whaddaya say? Are you online?"

I sat and pondered the Leinenkugel neon beer sign.

"Matt, telephone! Someone from the hospital."

"Thanks, Hazel."

Cynthia addressed the last of her burger, consuming it in smidgens. Deep in thought. She was watching as I walked up to the bar.

"Matt Bradshaw."

"Yeah, Dean. Bev here at the hospital. Well, I'm sorry to be calling you. But it's about that student. We just lost her..."

"You lost her ... oh, I see."

I hung up the phone and walked slowly back to the booth. "Cynthia, it's the girl I was telling you about. The one hit by the bell. She's gone."

I saw Cynthia's shoulders tremble as I got that far. She covered her mouth with her napkin, then raised it to her tears. "Oh, Bronwyn! Not that way. No! God, Bron."

She knew her? How? As we gathered up our things, I decided to have a secret of my own. Bronwyn hadn't died. She was just gone.

12

The police station of Mayflower, Kansas, sat two blocks off Main Street, just behind the post office. For all the times I'd been by, I'd never had occasion to go in. And I might not have noticed the small brick building at all, except for the color of its sloping roof. The roof was purple. Not the garish, preternatural purple they drape half the NBA teams in. This was a subdued, collegiate shade: a subtle plum, not unlike the colors of Kansas State University. But still an odd choice for a public building.

As I walked in, I found the lobby was done up in the same decor: purple Naugahyde waiting chairs, purple trim along the edge of the reception counter. A mousy little woman in an olive drab uniform stood behind the counter, disinterestedly filling out a form of some kind. She glanced up and asked what I wanted.

"I'd like to see the chief of police. I'm Matt Bradshaw, dean of students up at the college."

She flashed a civil servant smile and disappeared into the back of the station. In a few minutes she returned, along with a tall, angular, gray-haired man. I remembered sitting next to him at breakfast out at the Hoof'n Horn, the morning Julian Reid's body was found. He'd been called away so quickly, we'd not had much chance to talk. Now I noticed his age. The chief looked old enough to be my grandfather.

"Don't cops retire?" I wondered, following him back to his office. As we walked in and he shut the door, I gave a start. The whole room was furnished in purple just like the lobby, from the lampshades to the executive desk chair to the Venetian blinds.

There was a good-sized computer on a credenza behind his desk. A septuagenarian computer jock?

On the far wall, across from the windows, hung a three-foot swath of fabric. As I looked closer, I saw it was an old basketball jersey. Purple with white numerals: 55. There was a name above the numbers: CLODFELTER. And below, in larger letters: KSU.

"Kyle Clodfelter," he pronounced in a big, gravely voice. "We've met. What can I do for you this morning? Siddown, Dean."

I did, with a nod at the jersey. "Looks like you're a loyal alum. I should have guessed it from the color of the roof."

He snorted. "Stay in one job long enough, guess they gotta humor you. I been here in this department thirty years, ya know."

"You played forward for the Wildcats?"

"Nope, center. Weren't that many dudes stood 6-5 back then."

I blinked at the "dudes." For my benefit?

"So what brings you?" He rocked back in his swivel chair.

"You know, I'm not sure I've ever sought out the police before," I started slowly.

"Say, 'cops,' if it feels better." His purple chair squeaked with his rumbling chuckle.

"No, that's okay. Well, it's two matters, really. In fact, maybe more. Right now, it's hard to tell."

He shrugged. "Most things seem to be more'n one-sided."

"Well, okay. First of all, I just got back from the hospital. This student who was injured at the college. She disappeared from the hospital last night. I'm sure you got a report."

He made no response. I went on, told him what little I knew about Bronwyn, then the calamity at the science hall. How I wasn't sure it was an accident. That odd noise, like a "POP," just before the clock tower came crashing down.

He looked down and shook his head. "Sure wish you'd come by sooner. By now, I expect the grounds crew's cleaned up the debris. Sounded like a pistol shot, would you say?"

"That, or a dud firecracker. I'm not sure … But what's really got me bothered is that girl who was injured. She's somebody's daughter, and I have no idea whose. She declared financial independence—they can do that, you know—and the college has no record of her family. Can you do something?"

He looked down again. "There's a procedure, for what it's worth. Run a search on the NCIC." He spun his chair around and gestured toward the computer. "The National Crime Information Center: FBI operation.

"Somebody comes up missing, we can fill out a missing persons report. Then enter the information in this big data base."

"So, have you done that?"

He was silent for a minute. "You got one major problem, when it comes to missing persons, and it's a problem these computers can't solve."

"What's that?"

"Problem is, nine out o' ten of your 'missing persons' are gone of their own accord. Take your girl. Sounds like she had some help getting outta that hospital.

"People get fed up with their lives, I always give 'em twenty-four hours to think it over and head back home, or else get a running start. Cross the state line, the FBI can get involved. That's when we can try to use the computer. But, like I say, if a person wants to be disappeared ... "

"All right, but she was in a hospital. Suppose someone just took her."

He leaned back in his big chair with a sympathetic smile. "I know where you're comin' from. Gonna save her, right? Rescue fantasy. I tell you, it's one of the first delusions you grow out of, in this line of work."

I got up. "So there's nothing you can do. I guess I should have expected that."

He gave me a hard look. Then he chuckled. "You come around any time, Dean. Maybe talk some 'basketbull,' ya know? Hey, I can sling it with the best of 'em ...

"Or even ... " He turned solemn. "Even if you should come up with some other kinda half-baked theory, or maybe even wanta hear a few o' mine. Ya know, sometimes I get these old, unresolved cases all tangled up in the back of my mind. Helps to get my thoughts out on the table, know what I mean? Used to do that with your old prexy. Say, did you know Julian at all?"

"A little, as a student and then as my boss for a few weeks. But, you know, I thought about coming up here to see you, and filing a report. But there was no point. It's just that I saw him the night he died."

"Where 'bouts?"

I told him about the muffled sound from the fourth floor of the admin building late that night. How I looked up and saw him. "And—this is the weird part—he seemed to be crying. That was the sound he made, sort of a sobbing."

"And that struck you as strange?" He took a seat.

"Well, you know … " I sat down, found myself opening up again. "It was the way he was always smiling. 'Big Tooth.' I guess that sounds disrespectful now. But that's what the students called him. Who'd ever envision him crying?"

"I reckon only someone who'd seen him do it." The chief turned sideways in his swivel chair and swung his feet up on the corner of his desk. Then he slowly lifted an index finger and pressed a button on the end of his armrest. The woman at the front desk came on the intercom.

"Agnes, bring me in a couple coffees. Black?" he asked me, and I nodded.

He started in on a long and circuitous story, with deep breaths and long pauses. It was about his youngest daughter, the baby of the family, who'd come along when his wife thought she was past the change of life. Melissa had been eighteen, a freshman at the college, and was out with some guy he wished she hadn't been. Some boozehound upper-classman, according to him. About midnight, coming back from God knows what, he said, the fellow rolled his car off the bluff by the river.

"You know the spot, I'm sure. People been losing their innocence up there for generations."

There was a knock at the door and Agnes carried in two black coffees and a sack of clams. With a smile like a grimace, she exited without comment.

"Politically incorrect as all hell, sending a professional staff member out to get coffee. Am I right? But, like I say, you stay in one spot long enough … "

He slowly removed the lid from his coffee, passing me a napkin and a clam roll. Buying time?

"Anyway, I'm on duty that night, so I get the call about the accident." His voice was husky. "And who do I find when I flash my light in the passenger side of that crumpled-up car, but my own little..." He slowly shook his head.

"So, those days, the wife and I belonged to the Mayflower Congregational Church and Julian Reid had just come in as minister. I'm back at the house that evening, having broken the news to my wife. Both of us sitting there numb as rocks when there's a knock on the door, and it's Julian."

"He'd heard the news and come to call."

"Worst time to find yourself a cop or a preacher. You're the first one folks look for right after a tragedy, and the last one they wanta see. So—and I'll never forget it—he takes a seat there in the parlor. Asks what he and the church can do, and would we like him to say a prayer. And, all the while, he's grinning!

"I didn't know the new Reverend too well at the time, but I'm fixin' to ask how the hell he can be smiling like that, when I stop and have a look. 'Why, you're sittin' there with a big grin, but I can see your eyes and you're crying.'

"And, you know, he took my hand and told me he was so sorry. Said it was a nervous habit. The more anxious he felt, the more it seems he smiled. Went on to say he knew he wasn't all that great at what he was trying to do. But said he was there to serve us best he could, same as Jesus would've."

The chief dabbed a napkin to the corner of his eyes. He described how he and Julian Reid had maintained a friendship over many years. How they'd sit out on the back porch after supper, passing a jug back and forth, their wives back in the kitchen. The preacher and the police chief, pondering the meaning of things.

"Once, he told me he'd been keeping a journal. Made up titles, outlined sermons he never could give, especially after he lost his pulpit. But after he died, you know, we never found it."

He sat silent for a moment, and I started to come forward. But I held back, remembering how I'd received the journal. In an unsigned envelope. Was there a reason?

Suddenly, he swung around and yanked on a file drawer in his credenza. He pulled out a purple folder. "Could be there's some clue in there—to the puzzle I keep pokin' at."

"Puzzle?"

"Yup, the unsolved part of Julian's death."

"And what's that? I thought he left a note."

The Chief sat for a moment with his hand on the file folder. Then he reached inside and pulled out a single, crinkled sheet of yellow paper from a legal pad. He held it out over the desk so that I could read it, without handing it over.

I craned my neck and saw the sheet contained nothing but a set of those same numbers—12:1. I was still puzzled. Was it a formula of some sort, or a citation from the Bible?

"That was his suicide note?"

The Chief nodded gravely as he refiled the folder. "Thirty years in this business, I never saw a note like that one. Wadded up in the waste can, that's where we found it."

I thought about what to say, then turned toward the door.

He walked me all the way outside, and handed me a business card. "Call me up any time, Dean. Or come by. Any time you got a question. Or a clue."

I stopped home on my way back to campus, but Cynthia wasn't there. As my footsteps echoed in the empty house, it occurred to me that I'd come by here to talk with her. About what? Maybe why I hadn't told the police chief that I had Julian Reid's journal. Or why I'd allowed her to believe that Bronwyn was dead.

In the kitchen, I found a note on the table.

Matt:

Moving day! I'm setting up shop in the dean's office. Third floor, Cleaver Hall. Stop by if you're in the 'hood.

Also, I've got a team of techs here from Intelcor. Came in last night. They're networking the key administrators on campus.

That includes you, Babe, so check your email. My address: CBradshaw@hopewell.edu. You're: MBradshaw.

See ya. C.

P.S. Don't you think it's time we moved out of this hovel?

Oh, fine. Now it's intimacy by email. "Time we move out of here?" I gave a shudder, grabbed my gym bag, and bolted for the door.

In ten minutes, I was out on the floor of my old gym, firing up frenetic jump shots at a basketball rim that was not responding. Just one brick after another. Finally, I stopped and took a deep breath. Then bounced the ball a couple of times and settled into an old layup drill: trotting to the rhythm of my breathing. I centered on the ball as it slapped on the floor just as, years ago, Jeb had taught me.

Slowly, my tensions subsided as I finished shooting layups and found the rhythm of my jump shot once again. Now the shots were falling, swishing through the net.

Suddenly, the silence of the gym exploded. "Motha fucka! Call youself a coach? What the fuck you mean, they took away my scholarship?"

"Hey, cool it, bro! Let the man outta his office."

"No way! You gonna let this jive ass motha fucka do us..."

I came up to the clot of them who stood glowering at Collard. There were a half dozen in all: tall, lanky, black kids. Most of them bedizened in garish, NBA warm-up jackets. I recognized a few from the pickup game a few days ago. Not a highly gifted group. Warm-up jackets were as close as they'd get to the NBA.

"So, what's going on?" I inquired in a steady tone of voice, as I stationed myself between Collard and the kid who'd been hollering the loudest. Sure enough, it was Jamal—the one I'd already run into. "So, what is this, some kind of insurrection? Don't you like your role in the offense, Jamal?"

The kid was quivering with rage, and for the first time I could recall, I saw that Collard also seemed shaken.

"It's this notice we got. You must've seen it." The fellow who came forward was older and a bit less riled than the rest. I remembered him from the pickup game: LaRon.

He handed me a memo with the Hopewell College seal. I scanned down to the bottom. It was signed by Squire.

The college regrets to inform you that, due to an unforeseen demand for athletic scholarship funds, the grant which had been tentatively assigned to you has been withdrawn. Effective immediately, your financial aid has been converted to a campus custodial position. Please report to...

I turned to Jeb Collard, and he slowly shook his head. Then he just stared at the ceiling, the others muttering.

Finally, he spoke. "I told them I didn't have a damn thing to do with this. And I can understand why they're upset."

"Sure," I agreed, "But this is no way to handle it." I gestured to LaRon. "Come on, let's go sit down in the bleachers."

Begrudgingly, the group trooped out from the hallway outside Collard's office. "So, what can you tell us about this, Coach?" I turned to Jeb.

He stood in front of the bleachers, hands on hips. I could see he looked more settled, but he gave a deep sigh. "Got a call from the Gray Group, this bunch that's running the affairs of the college. What they said was, 'We've got the dozen students you need at Hopewell.' I guess you guys know that's what we gotta have to balance the budget, basically to keep this place alive.

"Anyway, they tell me, 'The good news is, they're prime time athletes and they've played together. At some place called Lone Tree—must be a community college—down in Texas. Since they're coming in late, you can deal with 'em as a group. Put 'em all in the same classes: applied life studies curriculum.

"'However,' he says, 'You're gonna have to redistribute some scholarships; the new guys'll need 'em. But, Coach, remember this,' he says. 'You just got yourself one hell of a team.'"

"Except you already have a fuckin' basketball team!" one of the players objected. "What kinda shit is this? Man, you jivin' us same as ... "

"Hang on, fellas," I intervened. "This man wouldn't do that. I've known Coach Collard since I was thirteen. Look, I'll take responsibility for finding out what's going on. But I need a couple of days. And I'd like one of you to help me."

I scanned the group, and settled on the fellow who seemed a bit more settled than the rest. "LaRon, can you give me a hand?"

He nodded slightly.

"Tomorrow, we'll meet back here. Same place, same time. Okay? I'm asking you to trust me that far."

The players sat in stony silence. Then, one by one, they all got up from the bleachers and shuffled toward the door.

After the other players had left, I asked LaRon to stop by my office. I looked for Collard, but only caught sight of his backside. Jeb didn't even say goodbye. He just trudged back toward his office, his shoulders slumping like a rumpled suit.

As we hiked across the barren campus, the afternoon sun shone wanly through a veil of gritty dust. The sun cast stick shadows on the sere ground, through spindly trees that seemed to be losing their very life along with their leaves this season.

"My wife complains…" I started to say when a car came barreling by on the gravel road that ran through campus. It kicked up a billow of dust.

"Jesus Christ!" I muttered, coughing and wheezing.

I saw the kid flinch and bow his head.

"My wife… maintains this… isn't really autumn," I gasped. "Says fall is designed to be spectacular, whereas this campus is toast. But I tell her this year's unusual. Ordinarily, we have some kind of color. Of course, she's from back East where… Say, where are you from, LaRon?"

"New York. And I know just what she means."

"New York City?"

"Upstate. Catskills. Small town on the Hudson."

"Huh. So, what brought you way out here to Hopewell?"

"I'm pre-seminary," he said. "Congregationalist. Grew up in this denomination. President Reid came East once and spoke at our church. Plus, I thought maybe I could play some ball out here."

"Gonna be a minister, huh? I guess I should watch my language around you."

He grinned. "I'm probably looking for people to look up to."

"You're here on an athletic scholarship?"

"Nope, and maybe that's why you don't see me creeped out like the other guys. I'm that rare breed. Just your basic, black student athlete with limited moves, and an interest in an education."

Again, he smiled. We walked down the stairs to my office.

"Well, that's not altogether unheard of. Grant Hill at Duke. Dikembe Mutombo at Georgetown: came over from Zaire on an academic scholarship... But look, let's figure out what to do about these other ballplayers. For starters, since I find I'm married to the provost, I think I'll get us an appointment with my wife."

I had to look up the extension for the provost's office in the campus directory. The phone rang four or five times, and I was about to hang up when the timbre of the tone changed and a recording came on. I recognized the voice of Mavis Lindholm:

"You have reached the office of Cynthia Lothamer Bradshaw, Provost of Hopewell College. Ms. Bradshaw is not available to take your call. But if you will select one of the following options, someone will respond to you shortly. You may press a key or speak your selection at any time during this recording."

For a moment, I could only shake my head as the message droned on. Cynthia Lothamer Bradshaw? I hadn't heard her use that name since we'd been married. And the maze of voice mail options. Was this what I was going to have to go through, just to talk with my wife?

"Shit!" I muttered, glancing up at LaRon apologetically.

"Thank you," the recording responded. "You have selected option six, our direct line to the admissions office. For information on the new degree program in applied life studies, please press one. For information..."

I slammed the receiver. "Come on, LaRon. Let's just hike on up and ask for an audience in person."

I looked at LaRon, sitting slouched in the waiting chair, his nose buried in a book. How much like me, not so many years ago. But how unlike me, as anyone of another race would always be until by chance I got to know them. I glanced sidelong at his broad nose, hair like steel wool, skin the color of a Brazil nut. I remembered a quote from Jean Paul Sartre:

"…there are men who die without—save for brief and terrifying flashes of illumination—ever having suspected what the Other is."

Where the hell was Cynthia?

My mind went back to Eastbourne, one night at Blotto's. I'd been deep in bar talk with a grad student in the sciences. Both of us bleary-eyed, over a pitcher of Genesee. Somehow, we'd gone from debating pro football to the subject of affirmative action.

"So, you think we can get along without racial quotas?" he'd challenged. "Well, think about it. Who gets trained to be the next chemist? Why, the person who looks just like I did when I walked through that door. That's what we think, you know: the system must work, because I made it."

I glanced at LaRon. The Other. A kid across a chasm. And an ally?

The door across the anteroom swung open and Cynthia strode out, swishing her hair. For a moment, I was struck dumb by the sight of her. She wore a deep blue sweater that sculpted her body and played against the glowing chestnut of her flowing hair. My God, the woman looked fine. And how long had it been since I told her?

"Matt: glad to see you, but I've got wall-to-wall meetings. Bronwyn, for one thing." She gave me a dark look. "Plus, trying to get this telecomm system installed. Do you know how long it's going to take to get a T-line in this town?"

"So, what's going on? Is this one of your students? Oh, of course. Our new players from that school down in Texas. What was it: 'Last Train'?"

"Lone Tree," I reported. "Lone Tree Community College in Deep Spring, Texas. That's what Jeb Collard was told. And he also was informed that the entire team he's currently coaching is losing their athletic scholarships. Can that be true?"

A voice rang out behind me, from the president's office, resonant and rounded. "Well, they'll not lose their academic standing in this institution. That's what I've been assured of!"

Roger Squire must have overheard our conversation, "WEL-come," he went on, marching up to LaRon. "WEL-come to Hopewell. I understand that you and the other new student athletes are quite some ballplayers. In contrast to the current team, I might add.

"That's what the Gray Group scouting report had to say. And, don't worry about your courses. We have a splendid new program, just coming online: applied life studies. 'We'll meet you wherever you're ready to learn.' That's the motto. Ah, I see you already have a book in hand. What a wonderful start."

"Ah, President Squire, Madame Provost," I intervened. "May I introduce LaRon Vaughn. As it happens, he is not here from Texas. This young man hails from upstate New York. And, as a matter of fact, he's a returning student. Pre-seminary: Congregationalist. President Squire, you'll be interested in that. But he *is* a ballplayer. Or was. Tell them about that, would you, LaRon?"

Cynthia glanced at her watch as LaRon recounted the meeting with Jeb Collard. "It doesn't affect me. I'm here on an academic scholarship. But the other guys on the team: hey, it's serious."

Cynthia thought a moment. "Can't they just compete against the new players? Maybe hold an intrasquad game." It seemed the issue had caught her interest, but she shuffled her feet and jerked her head nervously toward the receptionist's desk whenever the telephone rang.

"Say, I know what we can do for a start!" Squire declared. "Let's just get a list of all the minority students on campus, and review their financial needs. Then we'll all have a meeting.

"Oh, Mavis," he called, "Would you run a printout of all the applied life studies degree candidates? You know, the Category Threes. Including the new boys from Texas."

LaRon flinched and his brow furrowed. He picked up his books and started for the door.

"President Squire," I said. "If I may add one observation. Not all of the ethnic minority students are at academic risk. They're not all Category Threes."

Squire looked flustered and gave me a glare, but I went on. LaRon came back to listen.

"I suggest we just call up the records of the current players on the team. Then we ought to tag those who are on athletic scholarship and determine their financial needs. And we need to act soon. I told the players we'd meet again tomorrow."

The president stood there flummoxed, as we waited for his reply. Had this guy ever made an administrative decision?

Cynthia stepped in. She asked Mavis to run the printout. Then she wheeled around toward her office.

"Just a sec, Cynthia." I followed her in and shut the door.

"Matt, I can't talk now. My email light's flashing. Could be from Intelcor."

"Listen, Cyn, I'm afraid that you and shit-for-brains Squire could be lit up a lot worse than that if you let him run around loose much longer. Just whose idea was it to replace the basketball team, then leave poor Jeb Collard to break the news? Who in hell's setting policy for this place?"

She took a deep breath. "I said I can't talk now, and damnit I meant it!" She scooted into a high-back, executive chair and swiveled around toward her computer. Grabbing a mouse, she clicked on an icon: one of twenty on a multicolored screen. Immediately, the screen turned gold. "WELCOME TO THE WEB SITE OF THE GRAY GROUP," in big, black letters. "YOU HAVE MAIL!"

Cynthia paused, and slowly turned around. "Look, Matt, I'm afraid this message is confidential." Then she slowly stood and tilted her head to the side just a little. She came toward me with a conciliatory smile. "Tonight, Babe, okay? Look, I was going to make this a surprise, but ..."

"What the hell is this: a cellular phone?"

"Better'n that. It's a PCS: Personal Communication Service. Latest thing. Digital. Caller ID, voice mailbox, call waiting: the works. Only for the inner circle! Oh, and one other thing."

She held out a small, black device with a clip on the back.

"Let me guess. A pager?"

"You got it. Latest model: the Rampager. Ten-message memory. Set it for tone or vibration. The manual's inside. Look, that'll keep you entertained till I get home tonight, all right?"

"What time?"

"Babe, I wish I knew. Look, I'll call you when I'm ready to leave—maybe even page you." Brushing my cheek with a feathery touch, she steered me to the door.

13

I t took two beers and forty-five minutes to figure out all the settings of my cellular phone, plus another quarter hour for the pager. But still no sign of Cynthia. It was getting dark now.

I settled down in my easy chair with another beer. Fortunately I'd stocked up, although the best I could find at the Main Street liquor store was Coors. According to news reports, there now were fifty microbreweries in Colorado. But not in these parts, here in Kansas. Nothing but bland, boring Budweiser and its pale imitators.

Well, down to work. There was a pile of reading matter next to the chair, and I took the first item from the top. "Sacred Sex and Primal Prayer. Pilot Course Module." Oh, God! Had I really agreed to teach this? One glance at the reading list, and my stomach knotted. *Dreaming the Dark, Black and White Magic, Womanspirit Rising.* Where'd they find this blather, on a newsstand?

And there I was, listed as instructor. I tossed the syllabus and dug into my campus mail, which had piled up since the clock tower crisis. There was an envelope on top with an address on River Road, down by the Bottoms.

Dean Bradshaw,

Please plan to attend an organizational meeting of the Sacred Sex and Primal Prayer class at 10:00 p.m., September 14, in the first floor lounge of Elwood Hall. You will be met at the front door.

The Sisters of Aradia

A class organized by the students? Meeting at ten o'clock at night? No way was I signing up for this cruise. They could take their pop chart reading list and... Hell, I'd just call 'em up and resign. That's what I determined, en route to the kitchen for another beer. Except I realized I didn't have a phone number. And then I had another revelation: September 14 was tomorrow night.

Sometimes the only way out is through. Who'd said that—Oliver Cromwell or Jeb Collard? It was all starting to congeal. I fumbled in my satchel and found the pad where I sometimes made course notes. Then I sat down at the kitchen table and tried to piece together whatever I knew about witchcraft. I cracked another beer.

Surprisingly, I quickly filled a few pages, although I couldn't read my notes well as the room was revolving. But I'd been through this material for my doctoral exams on the seventeenth century. The witchcraft trials had been in full sway back then. Also, the last reported sightings of fairies—in Scotland, I believe. That was toward the end of that century.

The Sisters of Aradia. A sorority? And who the hell was Aradia? There were twelve names on the class list. And twelve members to a coven. That was something else I recalled. Like a board of deacons. The Puritan Cotton Mather had observed that witches organized themselves like a Congregational Church. Plus the leaders: The Goddess, The Grand Master. I'd read something about a Grand Rite, where those two ... "

Where was Cynthia?

I made a few more notes. There were a couple of good books on the aboriginal nature religion of pre-Christian Europe, which was what Wicca, the witchcraft tradition, basically represented. Both books were by anthropologists early in this century: *The God of the Witches*, and *From Ritual to Romance*. And both authors were women! That should score some points with the Sisterhood.

Murray was an anthropologist at Cambridge who believed in fairies. She thought they had been an ancient Neolithic race who were relatively small because they had a poorer diet than the tribes that had conquered them. The fairies had lived deep in the woods, from whence they'd staged attacks through a kind of guerilla action, mysteriously appearing and disappearing back into the forest.

Hey, this course might not be so bad if I could renegotiate the reading list. I glanced at the class list again, and opened another beer. Why was I doing this? I leaned back against the counter, thinking and drinking.

The address. Did these girls all live together? I looked at the roster to see if I might have run across any of them. Then I slowly set my beer down. I blinked and read the final name again. Bronwyn Chiles!

There was a video that had come with the syllabus, and I set out for the living room to pop it in the VCR. But it wouldn't go in—upside down. It was going to be hard to view this, the way the whole damn room seemed to be fogging. Must be the dew off the river... Then the phone rang!

I lurched across the living room and took the phone from the wall.

"Hullo? Tha' you, Cyn-sia?"

But it wasn't my wife. It was my coach, instead.

"Matt, you all right? You sound sort of funny."

I mumbled that I thought I wasn't sure.

"Well, listen up. I just got word from Roger the Dodger. You know, your buddy: President Squire. How any pack o' trustees in their right minds could pick a blatant fool like that... look, Matt, I got the word. The whole lot of these new stu'nathletes, The Dirty Dozen. They're scheduled to arrive sometime next week by Greyhound, straight from Lone Tree Community College, Tax-us."

"'The whole gang,' as it were," I managed to wisecrack, and he gave a sad laugh.

"Some time, and it had better be before long, I need to tell you what I think we're in for. Are you in any shape to talk now?"

I mumbled that I didn't think so.

"Aw right, try this. Tomorrow afternoon, four o'clock, we're havin' a confab over at Hazel's. Just a few of us from the faculty—and one of the trustees. Lotta rumors in the air, and we oughta get an update. Think you can make it?" I told him I had a meeting later that night, but I'd try.

"Well, one more thing. Lemme give you the new phone number here at home."

He repeated it three times, and I got it written down.

"Some damn fool calls we been getting," Jeb went on. "Middle of the night. Sometimes nothing at all on the other end. Nothing but silence. Other times, some weird sounds, sorta like drumming.

"Ya know, I never thought I'd need an unlisted number in a place like Mayflower, but I sure as hell got one now. Well, call me in the morning, after you sleep off whatever it is you got."

It was after ten when I woke up in my easy chair. The TV screen was blank and blue. A red light on the VCR was flashing. The tape must have run out. I got up and pulled out the cassette, and headed to bed. Guess Cynthia didn't make it back for supper.

As I was dozing off in bed, I vaguely recalled a couple of scenes from the Sacred Sex and Primal Prayer video, although it was dark. Must have been filmed in moonlight. There'd been a kind of line dance in the round, spiraling in and out. And the sound of drumming. I remembered that the dancers all were naked.

The women wore long hair that wafted in the waves of motion. There was a tall, slender blonde. And another dancer with swaying breasts and dark red hair that glowed in the firelight.

And someone else. A bearded guy who seemed to be in charge. The Grand Master? Whoever he was, he managed to look a bit prim while prancing about bare-ass naked. Somehow, I was almost sure I knew him.

Later, I heard the front door open and close and in a minute Cynthia slipped into bed beside me. Half conscious, I reached around to cradle her hips, nestling into the soft contours of her. When I sprang up with a jolt—a shot to the crotch. A buzzer! I came awake in the grip of an erection.

Cynthia was snickering. "Just a service call, Dean Bradshaw. Had to test your vibration mode. Hey, call us any time you wanta check your Rampager."

It was barely light when I cocked one eye and ventured a gander at the new day. My head was pounding and my stomach felt like a septic tank. As I struggled to set two feet on the floor, a couple of details slowly dawned on me. Cynthia was missing (so, what else was new?) and the pounding wasn't just in my cranium. Somebody was at the front door.

I drew on a pair of jeans and stumbled out through the living room. "Hang on, friend," I hollered, as the hammering went on.

I opened the door, and took a step back.

He was probably the scruffiest young guy I'd ever laid eyes on. Tangled hair, filthy sweatshirt, food-spotted jeans. Horn-rimmed glasses, taped at the hinges. Head to toe, I took in the full apparition. And in the next breath, I caught an awful whiff of him.

"Dean Bradshaw?" he inquired, in a high nasal whine.

I nodded.

"I'm Damon. Tech support: Intelcor. Looks like I caught you at a bad time. But I'm wingin' it out of Wichita in a few hours. Told your wife I'd stop by and give you a hand."

Cautiously, I invited him in. The young gent smelled like a dumpster. I commented that I'd just got out of bed.

"Hey, no problem-o. I'm just here to get you wired, Man."

"Huh?"

"You know, networked. Hooked up to the system. The wife said she brought you home a new laptop last night. She asked if I'd come by and get ya set up. Got all of twenty minutes to do it."

I told him I knew nothing about a new computer. But back in the kitchen, there it was. A flat-black laptop in a canvas case. I switched the thing on, and it booted up in a couple of seconds. Color screen, with a dozen bright icons.

"Can I offer you some coffee?"

Damon shook his head. "Naw, I really gotta get movin'. Don't wanta miss my plane and get stuck all day in Wichita. Jesus, they musta settled this state before God invented grass and trees … Cynthia said you got a new cell phone and a pager, too. Right?"

I produced the other devices and excused myself to take a shower. On my way out, I cracked the kitchen window a full inch for ventilation. The air outside was cold, but deodorizing.

It was no more than fifteen minutes before I reappeared—showered, dressed and shaved. But in that time, Damon had done his duty. He showed me how the pager and the cell phone were tied in to the computer.

"Had some problems with your modem; gotta get you an upgrade. But keep that pager on your belt—you'll probably want to set it on vibration so you don't go beepin' at odd times—and you'll know whenever you've got an incoming."

He rustled up his tools and checked his watch as he started for the door. Then he spun around, just as he was leaving.

"Oh, almost forgot. They didn't mention this, but—hey, you're a dean, right? An administrator. I spose they want you hooked into the Heartland File. Here, it'll just take a minute."

He switched the computer on again and clicked on an icon labeled, NETWORK. Then he entered, PASSWORD INFORMATION.

"I'm sure you dig how this goes. They've got various levels of security in their data banks and all. Full access on down. So, we'll get ya set up once we identify your level." He glanced at his watch. "Shit, running late… Look, I'll just skip all this bullshit protocol—cut to the core code. What's your mother's maiden name?"

I busied myself with the coffee maker. "Hilliard," I replied.

He entered the name. "That got it. You're in the loop." Then he gave a low whistle. "Jesus, that password must've triggered something. They've got you in for access to damn near the whole fucking file. You must be some kinda … well, whatever. Hey, gotta boogie."

I stood at the front door and watched Damon dash down the sidewalk and dive into his rented Ford Taurus. He peeled down Winthrop, off to Wichita. And I was left to ponder what I'd just done.

Hilliard was not my mother's maiden name. It was the maiden name of Cynthia's mother instead.

The sun was starting to call it a day as I locked up my office and headed over to Hazel Gottschalk's house on Gothic Avenue. The day was bright and I enjoyed the stroll across campus, down into the residential neighborhood across Winthrop. Hazel lived on an elm-lined street of red brick bungalows. She had a one-story, restored Victorian with a small porch framed by a big picture window, and an air of small town elegance about it.

I heard voices inside and let myself in. Hazel was hollering out in the kitchen. "Harley, put that rib down! I knew you didn't come back here to help me."

Her house smelled warm and welcoming, redolent of sizzling ribs. Herbs, and spices, and animal fat. On the dining room table sat a big ceramic bowl stocked with ice cubes and cold Coors. I grabbed a longneck and wandered into the front parlor. Jeb Collard was sitting alone on the divan, gazing out the window.

"Great view," I said as I took a seat beside him.

"Great town," he mumbled. "Or, it used to be."

I noticed how gray he looked in the shadows of the late afternoon. Not just his hair, but his pallor.

Harley Applequist came bounding in with a Coors in each fist, followed by Hazel who was doffing her apron with one hand as she unscrewed the cap of her beer bottle with the other. The three of us clinked bottles: "Cheers!" Jeb just sat there.

"Anyone else coming?" I asked.

"Only a member of the board of trustees," Hazel replied. "Mystery member. Said she'd be late. Say, can you stay for supper?"

I stepped out in the alcove and dialed up Cynthia's office on my cell phone. Got nothing but the recording with its litany of options. On a whim, I called home and this time, I scored; there was a message: "Hey, Matt, better zap something in the microwave for supper. I've got a conference call that's going late and a meeting after that. See ya..."

When I came back in the parlor, everyone else had left for the dining room. I started to join them, but something stopped me. Maybe the glow of the waning sun. For a moment, I stood at the window, watching it play on the trees, and I may have been breathing a prayer of thanksgiving when I heard a rustling sound.

She was standing in the doorway, shedding her coat. Trim and tailored in the skirt and blouse and cardigan sweater of a classroom teacher. With the same, dark, shining hair and eyes like deep brown caverns. I don't know how long she'd been watching me.

"Sarah."

"Hello, Matt."

"So, are you the mystery trustee? How are you?"

She came to the window. "To the second question," she responded, wrinkling her nose, "I'm kinda okay. In fact, I'd say I'm better than a short while ago. I wasn't sure you'd be here.

"Say," she brightened. "Have you ever tried to stage South Pacific with a baritone who's six inches shorter than the female lead? I mean, the kid has a super voice—you ought to hear him sing "Some

Enchanted Evening"—but set him next to Nellie Forbush and it looks like he's romancing his babysitter."

We laughed, then she turned somber. "You had another question: I dunno about the 'mystery' part, but I guess I'm a trustee, all right. For as long as we have a college ... Do you think we should get something to eat?"

"In a second," I said. "Just look at that sunlight." On impulse, I put an arm around her.

But she made a pivot that would have done credit to a point guard with a crossover dribble, and I caught nothing but air. Except for a hand she left trailing. I clasped it, and she led me to dinner.

"Well then," Hazel sighed, as she polished off her last rib. "So, where to begin?"

"With the budget, I guess," muttered Jeb. "That always seems to be the bottom line around here. You're on the faculty finance committee. Why don't you lead off, Hazel."

"Well, Sarah's the trustee and all. That's one reason I asked her to join us." She stressed the *one* and glanced my way.

"But here's what I calculate. This month, we started the fall term with zero endowment and a deficit of twelve students—thirteen if that poor girl who was struck down has to withdraw."

Jeb shook his head and sighed. "Jesus God Almighty ... "

Hazel asked, "Anyone heard how she's doing?"

I told her the girl had disappeared from the hospital, and that I assumed there'd be a police investigation.

Jeb erupted, "By Kyle Clodfelter? That old codger couldn't find a hooker in a whore house!"

Sarah said, blushing, "I may as well tell you about another bill that's outstanding. For poor Reverend Reid. We still have his medical expenses."

"Poor Reverend Reid!" scoffed Jeb Collard. "Why if he'd known the first damn thing about running ... "

Hazel wheeled on him. "Jeb, the man was Sarah's childhood minister. I'd tell you to shut up if it didn't make me sound just like your wife."

"Hey, Hazel, any time you wanta join the harem!"

I was glad at least to see him lighten up.

"It was last fall," Sarah continued, slowly. "Mid-September, about this time of year. Reverend Reid—I still call him that, force of habit—Julian left town for a couple of weeks right in the middle of the fall term."

"I remember," said Hazel. "His wife called in and told Mavis Lindholm to cancel his appointments. She said he needed a break. Not that we couldn't get along without him. (Now I'm doing it. Sorry, Sarah.) But what about the medical bills?"

"They arrived last month, with a form from the insurance company. The form read: 'Claim Denied. Condition Not Covered. Cosmetic Procedure.'"

"Excuse me?" said Hazel.

"We asked for more information and they sent us a photo taken after they'd treated him. A hospital down in Wichita," Sarah said.

"So, what'd it show?" I wondered.

She gulped. "A perforation, all down the front of him." Sarah stood up and shrugged back her cardigan. She traced a line straight down her torso. "All the way from here at his sternum, past his pelvis."

There was general silence, and a group cringe.

"It stopped at the base of his, um … you know."

"Sarah, I believe the word you're searching for is 'penis.'"

She wrinkled her nose at me. "Not all of us have been to graduate school. Well, it seems he'd been tattooed. There was a faint design, a line of blue corn stalks. Strange. But then he'd developed an infection. It must not have been done right."

"Now, why on earth would a man like that want a tattoo?"

"I know, Hazel. That was our question. They recommended that we request … "

"An investigation by Kyle Clodfelter!" the others chorused.

"Couldn't find his ass … " Jeb started.

Hazel hit him with the butt end of her beer bottle. "Well, moving right along, the big picture is basically this. If we want to keep the doors open, we need to have another dozen students."

"Which we will," muttered Jeb. "I'm here to tell you. Got the call this afternoon. They're arriving next Monday, God help us. I've seen their records. And you can forget about Category Three. These guys are Fours, full grown!"

The others gave a sigh.

Jeb went on. "Any of you heard of a 'pipeline college'?"

No one had, so he launched into a short course on academics and college athletics. He explained how some of the most notorious bad actors in the NBA ever made it into college.

"Take Nick Van Exel with the Lakers. Isaiah Rider, currently with the Portland Trail Blazers, who's been on half the teams in the league, when he hasn't been in jail. Latrell Sprewell, damn near strangled his coach. Now, how'd they get in college?"

"Never thought much about it," admitted Harley as he took a swig of his second after-dinner beer. I noticed it was regular Coors. Ever since he'd abandoned the deanship, he'd given up dieting on Coors Light. "But, you know, you see so many others who can't make the NCAA academic requirements. Like that young kid, Kevin Garnett. Went straight from high school into the NBA."

Jeb explained that the NCAA has an escape clause. A player can enroll in a two-year college and, as long as he earns eleven credits per term, he's eligible to play ball there. Plus, once he gets an AA degree from the junior college, he can be admitted to a major college program. Forget about your qualifying exams.

"So, I'll bet there are certain JCs that'll take anybody who can walk, and chew gum, and can the occasional jump shot," I said. "And I'll bet passing courses at these places is not a problem."

"So, where are we getting our new stu'nathletes?'" Hazel consulted her notes. "Lone Tree College? Never heard of it."

"But you will," Jeb avowed. "And you can bet Intelcor has."

"If I understand all this, we're about to get slam-dunked with a dozen dumb jocks who might be carrying criminal records," I reflected. "But if I remember correctly, they're also carrying federal grant dollars for at-risk students. Isn't that it, Jeb?"

He stared out the window.

"Hey, you think things can't get worse—did you hear about the custodians? Next week, the janitors are going out on strike!"

We eyed Harley, cautiously.

"That's right. They're demanding sweeping reforms!"

"Sarah, do you have anything to add?" asked Hazel.

She shook her head. "Same discussion the trustees had this morning. Nobody's looking forward to this. But, you know, it's not just the medical bills. The college has debts all over town.

"And then the outside creditors. If those debts are called in and the college defaults, it's the trustees who are liable. And we already owe Intelcor a ton for consulting services."

"For what!" I cried. "Recruiting services? Coming up with a president like Roger Squire?" I saw several pairs of eyes swing toward me, but no one said a word about the provost.

"Actually, Matt, the sad news is we're dependent on Intelcor," Hazel sighed. "They're our pipeline to warm bodies. We've been living this way for the past several years. Intelcor tracks 'em down. We get the tuition, Intelcor gets the atrisk funding."

"And I get the pleasure of trying to keep these jokers off the streets and outta jail," Jeb groused. "One rumble in some bar down on Main Street, the townies'll shut this place tighter'n a nun's—sorry, Sarah. That part about the townies."

She flashed him a smile to melt ice, but it faded as she turned to each of us. "There's one other thing I have to report. And I'm afraid I've been postponing it, just enjoying all of us here together."

"At the next meeting of the trustees—that's two weeks from today, the first of October. We've just received word. Intelcor is planning to offer the trustees a way out."

"A way out?" There was a murmur around the living room, then silence. And a thud as Harley let his beer slip.

Sarah went on almost inaudibly, "It seems they have a prospective buyer for the campus."

The silence was like death.

"Well, it's like they always say," muttered Harley at last. "Bad news is always good information."

It was about 9:30 when I left Hazel's place for my meeting with the class. I had more than enough to mull over. The conundrum of the college, the sense of Sarah. I took my time strolling over to the dormitory.

Elwood Hall was one of those plain-vanilla dorms that went up in droves back in the 1960s, when colleges fantasized the Baby Boom would go on forever. It was from the architectural school of square-and-brick-and-fast.

Walking up to the entrance of "E-Hall," as the students knew it, the building seemed so nondescript that one might have been on any campus in the country. Still, I could recall an enchanted evening or two at a certain southeast corner of the third floor.

For a moment, I stopped and stared up at Sarah's old dorm room. I felt the same tug I'd experienced a few hours ago, back in Hazel's parlor. And the same, recurrent question: will she or won't she? It seemed some things never changed much with Sarah.

I looked at my watch. It was quarter to ten; I was early. On an impulse, in the pain of my nostalgia, I did something strange. Instead of walking in the front door of Elwood Hall and taking a chair in the lobby, waiting, I took a hard right and started circling the dormitory. There was a door in the back of the building that the kitchen help generally left unlocked. A dorm door you could enter, at whatever hour you chose to come calling.

Sure enough, the door was open. I stepped inside and took a minute to reorient myself. I was at the head of a long, bland, institutional corridor with cinderblock walls. I knew it well. The hall was empty as I started down. Revisiting, remembering. Nothing much had changed. Here and there, some hot-blooded, dorm-worn soul had taped up a poster:

~ SLIPPERY WHEN WET ~

~ A HARD MAN IS GOOD TO FIND ~

For an instant, I had an impulse to follow an old path up the stairs to the third floor, but instead I headed farther down the hall. The lights were off in this section. Was this ever stupid! What if I were caught?

Aw, screw it. I'm the dean.

There was a lounge at the far end of the corridor, and the door stood slightly ajar. I could see a dim light flickering. Drawing closer, I heard sounds inside and saw a sign on the door: RESERVED: THE SISTERS OF ARADIA.

It was not quite your typical dorm lounge. While there were ordinary furnishings—couches and carpets and floor lamps—all the chairs had all been drawn into a circle. There was a table in the center with a solitary candle. The windows all were covered, draped in black.

As my eyes grew accustomed to the dim light, I could tell they were all coeds, and thought one or two looked familiar from the placement testing. They were sitting still, in silence.

From the shadows of the doorway, I stood and watched. After three or four minutes of silence, one of the girls gave an audible gasp. Then she and the others dropped to their knees, as their hair fell in a rustling susurration.

They took a breath in unison: "Whooshhh." And then, "Perfect love and perfect trust!" They all chanted, kneeling for a moment. But at the signal of another gasp, they began to rise. First to one knee, and then standing in a circle with their arms uplifted.

Once again they chanted: "Perfect love and perfect trust. Ekeh, Ekeh, Aradia!" With that, they took a short step forward. Bowing heads, clasping shoulders. I could feel a surge of energy, even from where I stood. I also could hear my heart pounding. Then the women let go as quickly as they had embraced. They took their seats in silence. One rose to extinguish the candle, as another turned on some table lamps.

I glanced at my watch: two minutes to ten. With a quick turn, I made a beeline down the corridor to the door where I'd come in. Loping around, I gave the building a wide berth, took a minute to catch my breath, and came strolling up the walk to the front entrance.

"Dean Bradshaw, good evening. Welcome to Elwood Hall. I am Gwendolyn Davenport." My hostess was a plump girl in a basic black Hopewell College sweatshirt and blue jeans. She looked about as ordinary as the dorm except for her long, dark hair. But she spoke with a certain air of refinement. There was a sort of East Coast aura about her.

Gwendolyn said nothing more as she led me up the same corridor I'd just darted down, and I followed her into the lounge. She nodded at a chair at the head of the circle. I sat down and took stock of the group. I thought I recognized a couple of the girls, but opted not to greet them. They all seemed preoccupied, if not vaguely haunted. A tall blonde sat cross-legged at the far end of the circle, methodically twisting her hair. She gave me a furtive glance. In all, they looked about as friendly as a cornered snake.

I noticed that all of them were dressed in black Hopewell sweat-shirts. And they all wore their hair long and flowing.

I was still up when Cyn came home, poring over a couple of books on Wicca that I'd pulled out of a box in storage. I was into this. The students had agreed to my revision of the reading list and even talked about adding a book. How many profs have taught a course where the students increased the requirements?

Cynthia had tousled my hair as she came by, and then headed straight for the sack. When I stuck my head in a few minutes later, she was fast asleep.

"Must be tough," I thought as I put my notes away. "I should be more supportive. If the rest of us are uptight, think of what it must be like as provost—with a colleague like Squire."

I thought of joining her in bed, but my brain was still abuzz. So old Jules had been tight with Sarah. I guess I'd known that. The Congo Church had always been a big part of her life.

I could guess who had slipped me his journal, under cover of night. As I drew it from my satchel, that much seemed clear. I turned to the very beginning: the secret life of Julian Reid.

The Devil is in the distractions. That thought just came to me. Perhaps it's a fragment of a sermon I'll never deliver, now that I've "changed career direction," as they say. Or the first entry in the journal of a ruminant, a budding aphorist.

Is that who I am now, a preacher no more? All I know is that these odd thoughts keep popping up and there's no more pulpit. Unsignaled, at times: when I ought to be paying atten-tion to something practical, such as the calamitous budget. Or the prattle of a prospective donor.

Talking with one the other day, grinning graciously, I had this thought as he nattered on: everything he hoped to do for Hopewell and humanity.

"My friend, there was a time in your life when you couldn't explain what you believed about the world, even if you had to. You couldn't frame it in concepts, but it didn't matter. For you believed what you saw; you and your senses were one.

"But that was before you set out to get someplace in the world. And that's when you lost the power to see it. Of course, in the process, you lost yourself as well.

"So, I understand why we're tacking up this sign with your name on this building. And I know why the biggest donors need the largest signs of all. They are trying to remember who they are."

14

*H*arley had a way with clams. From the first coffee break, I'd seen the man was serious about his pastries. I noted how he went about dissecting his clams, and with his personal cutlery. Harley always brought a steak knife down to the Corner Cafe, Home of the Bottomless Coffee Pot (with purchase of two clams). He carried it in his satchel, next to his ballpoint pens. The knife looked suspiciously like the silverware at the Hoof'n Horn.

This morning, he arranged a couple of clams on his napkin, bulging with vanilla frosting. Then he drew his steak knife from his satchel and proceeded to puncture the first, round pastry in the center. He took care not to press so hard that the filling in the middle could ooze out the sides, but sliced it precisely both ways to the edge. Then he consumed the clam by halves, with the flat side up to keep his nose clear of the cream frosting.

For a moment, I sat in rapt admiration. Then I remembered our agenda. "Harley, it was the most hostile bunch I've come across, since the time we went up against the reform school in the state high school playoffs. I mean, these women were pissed—for whatever reason. It was like I'd walked into a den of she-wolves."

He licked a dollop of frosting off his finger and surveyed his next clam.

"You know, there's something else I haven't told you." I went on to describe the ritual I'd seen, although I left out the part about sneaking into the dorm in order to see it.

Harley ingested all of this information without neglecting a crumb of his clam.

"Of course they seemed enthused about the course—even added a book to the reading list. But I gave 'em an assignment they probably didn't appreciate."

"What was that?"

"I told them to turn in a one-page account of what they hoped to get out of this course, and how they proposed to learn that."

"Well," he pronounced as he began to get up, "Seems to me the battle's half won."

I watched him extricate himself from the booth that fit him like a tight sweater. He trundled across the dining room to get us more coffee. When he returned, he had a stack of paper napkins and began inscribing four large letters on the top one: D-O-T-E.

"An acronym?

He lowered his voice. "Intelcor thinks it has potential." Then he turned the napkin over and printed out four words:

- DIAGNOSIS
- OBJECTIVES
- TREATMENT
- EVALUATION

I pondered the latest creation of the applied life studies program. "So, 'T' is for 'Treatment.' Don't you mean 'Teaching?'"

"Not anymore. The future is all about special populations."

He went on to give me a short course in how to assess the "learning readiness" of one's students, and then pitch whatever one hoped to teach them to a level and a learning style they could handle.

"A lot of this you already know, Matt. You made a comment about that class, a while ago. You called 'em 'distinctive.'"

"Yeah, but here's what I meant. You know how, in a really good college, every student seems to have some special ability? One can sing, one can dance. Well, from what I could judge last night, every one of those girls has a special disability."

I described the tall, leggy girl back in the shadows. An honest ten on any ten-point scale. "But she just sat there in full lotus, staring off in space. Never said a damn thing. And twirling her blond hair round and round. On the other hand, that Gwendolyn who met me at the door. She was well spoken. But a bit of a porker, somewhere between dumpy and obese."

I immediately wanted to swallow that statement, but Harley didn't seem offended. He said I was well underway with that first assignment. Now all I had to do was find out how those students best expressed themselves—in writing or giving oral reports. Maybe even a film project. And to be clear about how I'd evaluate them. What merits an A, and all that.

E was for Evaluation.

By the time we'd drained the bottomless coffee pot, I was feeling more confident about the class, if not the future of Hopewell College. Harley intimated that Intelcor had approached him again about serving as dean of instruction.

"Just stay focused on your objectives," he advised as we stepped outside. "You know, that's where the last fellow had his problems. Hopeless egghead. Intelcor ships him out here from back East. Down-sized, I guess. Then he gets into this cult stuff."

He chuckled. "Course, it might have done him some good."

"Was that the guy I saw chasing around buck naked in the video?"

He sniggered. "They like to say, 'sky clad.' You know, he had a real promising course. Good module. Intelcor had more students in the pipeline. Problem was, he lost sight of his objectives—all those rites of nature. Channing got too close to his students. There was some talk he was grading 'em in bed."

"You wouldn't catch me in the sack with that outfit. Not with a cast-iron condom... What'd you say his name was?"

"Coe. Dr. Channing Coe. Came out here all the way from East-bourne. Say, isn't that where you went to grad school?"

I left Harley and took off up the hill to see Cynthia. She'd be sure to remember Chan from Eastbourne! Maybe even had a course from him. What a saga: Channing Coe and a cult at Hopewell College. My pedantic, bookworm buddy. Chasing bare-ass with the Sisters of Aradia. Talk about your midlife transitions...

But in the first half block up Winthrop, I came to my senses. Cynthia wouldn't be working at home. And it was unlikely she'd even answer a phone call. The best I could do was leave a message. Trudging along, I found myself wondering if my life had changed any less than Channing's. I was feeling somewhat downcast as I crested the hill at the big town flag and caught sight of our little home. And suddenly my sadness flared into rage.

There was a sign in the front yard: FOR RENT.

I took the last block at a gallop and raced up the steps to the front door. Whipping out my ring of keys, I jammed one in the door. It didn't fit. I held it up and examined it. It was the key to the front door, all right. I tried it again: same result. Then I looked at the lock. It was a new lock, bright and shiny.

I rummaged around in my satchel for my cellular phone and dialed up Cynthia's number. It rang a half dozen times, and then Mavis Lindholm's recording came on with its smorgasbord of options. I punched O for operator, but Mavis was not at her desk.

The robotic menu started over again: "For President Roger Squire, press one; for Provost Cynthia Lothamer Bradshaw, press … " I made to heave my satchel across the porch floor in frustration, when I remembered my laptop computer was in it.

I sat down on the porch steps. It was all I could do: the chairs were gone from the veranda. With the phone to my ear, I sat gazing at the park past Winthrop Avenue. All along the brick-paved boulevard, the tall trees cast comforting shadows.

But the very idea of giving up my home here only stoked my anger. I recalled Cynthia's note about "this hovel." But we'd never really talked about moving.

I tried the phone again and finally reached the point in the script where I was permitted to leave a message. By this time, I was steaming. "Cynthia—what the hell! Did you actually cancel our lease? And changed the locks?"

I was striding up and down the porch by now. "So where am I supposed to sleep, or do you even give a flying fuck? You owe me a phone call, Madam Provost!"

As I punched off the power to the cell phone, I was too riled up to relax. I flopped back down on the veranda and dialed up the police station.

"Clodfelter."

"Hello, Chief?" I told him what I'd found on Bronwyn Chiles. "Her name was on the roster of a class I met with last night. It's a class on Wicca. You know: witchcraft. The students seem to have formed a cult of some kind. Call themselves 'The Sisters of Aradia.' I thought you might want to question them, although I'll warn you they're not so warm and fuzzy."

"Jesus, whatever happened to the Pi Phis? Don't they have sock hops anymore? Yeah, sure, I'll have somebody look into it."

"And Chief, did you find out anything about the bell tower?"

"Oh, I said I'd look into that, too, didn't I? Got it right here, written down . . . So, what's on the docket for you today?"

I told him about my new computer, that I wanted to get into data base searching—maybe scan the Internet. Look into scholarships for some disenfranchised basketball players.

"It's easy enough. Just your basic Boolean logic," the chief assured me.

"What?"

He chuckled. "Sometime, bring your computer by. I can help you get the hang of it."

No sooner had I hung up than my buttock buzzed. I picked up the phone: it was Cynthia.

"What is this message I have here from you? I am just about to go into a conference call with corporate, and I get this? How the hell do you think I can function in this godforsaken place if the dude who trucked me out here phones me up and talks to me like that?"

"Well, about the same way I can if I don't have a bed to call my own. What the hell do you mean, Cynthia, canceling our lease? Changing the locks on me!"

She took a deep breath and let it out, hissing in my ear.

"Matt, the realtor did that. You know, they have to show the property. Besides, we're all moved out. It wasn't my decision. Corporate got the word from Damon, that tech consultant. He said we seemed to have a pretty modest house for a provost. They called up the realtor, got us moved into the old Armbruster place on Grant Street."

"How'd they come up with that house?"

"How do you think? The browser scanned all the realtors' data bases. The computer said it was the best available property. Didn't you get the message I left you this morning? Don't you check your mailbox regularly for messages?"

Her tone softened. "Look, Matt. I know this high-wire stuff is a new phase for you. I'm going to have Damon add a couple of cool features to your cell phone. From now on, you'll be able to review a message before you send it. And also—Babe, this is just for us—you can mark any message you send me as urgent."

I told her I was ecstatic.

"Lighten up, Matt. Look, don't you have that meeting with the old team this afternoon? Let's hook up about six—at our new place. We'll figure out what to do for dinner."

She was kind enough to give me the address.

The locker room echoed as the door creaked open. The place was dark and deserted. I stepped inside and glanced at the clock to be sure I had the time right. I'd expected the team would be out in the gym with Jeb, at practice. I switched on the lights.

And there they were: a clutch of lanky black kids hunched over on the benches in front of their lockers. No rap songs this afternoon, no sound at all. They sat in abject silence, sad as a band of molting crows.

"Hey, fellas. What's up?"

LaRon looked up in my direction, but he was the only one. I scanned the others for signs of life, and my eye settled on Jamal. The kid looked seriously subdued, and somehow different.

It was his clothes. He had on a high-fashion pullover in a kind of forest green and russet combo. Nothing like gang colors. More like Gentleman's Quarterly. I looked at the inscription on the front of his sweatshirt. "Polo by Ralph Lauren."

I set down my satchel and sat down.

"Where's Coach Collard?"

They shook their heads. I left them and walked down the corridor that led to his office. There was an envelope taped to the frosted window of his door, and it had my name on it.

Matt—

I suppose I ought to leave you a phone message on this newfangled system, but I hate those things. Change in plans. The Dirty Dozen arrive next Monday, instead of today. Had a couple of messages from Intelcor, by way of your wife.

The punch line is, I'm outta here. Retired at age fifty-five. Turns out they're bringing in a coach of their own. Seems I've been offered what they call a "buyout." Early retirement package, equal to my salary for the rest of the year if I were to stick around which I suspect they don't want me to.

Well, good luck with your meeting. Guess I'd be a fifth wheel with those kids. What would I tell them? Hell, what'll I tell Em, for that matter?

Jeb

Slowly, I took the long walk back to the locker room. The door creaked as I opened it with a sad, sepulchral sound.

"Coach Collard's been let go," I sighed as I sat back down. They made a sound like air escaping from a punctured tire.

"Along with the rest of us," Jamal muttered. Then silence. "Guess maybe I shouldn't o' been so hard on the dude."

Finally, I spoke. "I'm afraid I don't have much to offer… The only thing I can think of is to do a database search for other scholarships, once I get the hang of it. And I guess we can check out the data we already have on you guys. Here, let's see."

I took out the student body printout I carried in my briefcase and slowly unfurled the pale green pages, scanning them as they cascaded toward the floor.

"So, what else is going on?" I was listening with one ear as I looked over the data.

"Started on our campus jobs," LaRon reported. "And it's sort of ironic… Hey, Jamal, tell the dean what you were saying."

"Same job as my granddad. Tha's all I said. I'm a de-activated ballplayer, and designated janitor. Same as granddaddy."

Something about that pronouncement caught my ear. Maybe the alliteration. Or that he delivered it in standard English. Wasn't this the kid who was always playing gangster rap, screaming scatology? I took another look at Jamal, then flicked to his page on the printout.

"Wait a second. Is that your ACT score?" I pointed to a two-digit column. He glanced at the green sheet then peered at the floor, half nodding. He shuffled his feet.

"Why, you could have got in Northwestern with that! So, why'd you come out … Oh, I see. Your high school grades. They look a lot like mine.

"But you say your grandfather was a janitor? If you don't mind my asking, what do your parents do?"

Jamal scuffed his feet and studied the floor. "School teachers," he muttered. I heard a few snickers.

I turned to the other players' records. "Why, every one of you has the same kind of stats. High scores on your college entrance exams and high school grades in the crapper."

LaRon bowed his head and gave a shudder.

"Okay, guys. Your secret's safe with me. I can see what Coach Collard's been doing these past few years. Going out after players with the same kind of profile I had. High academic potential, low achievers."

"And don't forget one other thing—good actors," LaRon added. "Dudes who learned how to tie a do-rag from a Spike Lee movie. Ain' that right, Jamal?"

Jamal jumped up in a flash and turned on him.

LaRon stepped up in his face. "Don't like that much, do you, J-Man! Hey, why don't you go ahead—air it out. Tell the dean where you grew up. Where you went to high school, all that. Tell him!"

Jamal's eyes became slits and his nostrils flared in anger. Then he slowly turned back toward his locker, smoldering. He mumbled, almost inaudibly, "Winnetka, Illinois. New Trier High School. Muthafuckin' north shore suburb of Chicago."

A couple of other players high-fived and chortled, until I asked where they were from. I recognized the names of most of the suburbs. No wonder not a one had a respectable crossover dribble.

"Okay," I announced, "so, I guess I'm on to your game plan. Some of you guys have figured out the formula. How to scare the be-Jesus out of this Snow White faculty. Come out here with a two-dollar blue bandana and make like a Crip. But why give it up now? What's with the Polo shirt, Jamal?"

The group fell silent for a long spell. Finally, LaRon spoke up. "You haven't heard about the new guys?"

I shook my head, but remembered receiving a supplemental printout. I dug around and found it in my satchel.

"Word's out," said LaRon. "You know, we've still got networks. There's a code out there, and we can read it."

He took me through the indicators. Midnight basketball leagues. The pipeline college in Texas.

"We know who they get to go play out there. Kinds of grants they give 'em. You know all about that, too, don't you, Dean?"

"Not much, LaRon. You've got to remember I've been in grad school."

He flashed a smile that quickly faded and pointed to a set of initials in the last column of my printout. "'GD.' You know what they mean by that?"

"Goddamn? No, you wouldn't use language like that, LaRon. And, incidentally, I notice you don't bow your head and turn all different colors when anybody swears but me."

He shrugged. "GD: Gang Deterrence. Or 'Gangster Disciples.' Chapters in thirty-five states: 30,000 members. Now they says it stands for 'Growth and Development.' Take your pick. It's all code for the bros from the gang diversion projects. And that's who they're bringing in: bona fide gang bangers."

"Only thing we still don't know," Jamal muttered, "And tha's why the fuck they doin' it."

We agreed to meet again in a week while I looked some more for scholarships. And then I had another thought. "Tell you what. For the time being, maybe you keep practicing."

"Be cool if we had a coach," Jamal said to the floor. Then he raised his head and cocked one eye, perhaps in my direction.

By the time I left the gym, it was past six. I drove by the new house, through a neighborhood of towering elm trees. I found the address. I saw the house had a long porch all along the front and a gazebo out back. But I saw no sign of Cynthia.

I parked the car out front and hiked up to the front door. It was locked. I peered through the door panel and saw our furniture in there, but no other signs of life. As I sat down on the porch swing in resignation, my butt buzzed. The pager blinked: phone message.

"Matt, we have a big-time, online conference call. Just came up, last minute. I'll be an hour or more. Look, the key to the front door is under the flower pot on the north ledge of the porch. Let yourself in and see how you like it.

"And, oh, you know one item on our agenda? One of the Intelcor analysts thinks he has a line on some scholarships for the old team. I'll tell you what I can when I see you. Let's make it the Hoof'n Horn at 7:30. No, 7:45. No later than 8:00! And, hey, are you online? I have a feeling they're gonna ask me."

I shut off the phone and tracked down a flower pot. Actually, there were three. I found a key under the middle one and tried it in the front door. It didn't fit. I circled the house to look for other doors. The key clicked in at the back entrance.

It took me an hour to load up the car with my clothes and books. I left her the food and furniture and thought about leaving a note as well. But, hey, we had a date at the Hoof'n Horn...

With a U-turn past the provost's mansion, I headed back to Winthrop, south toward Main. As I drove along, it seemed I picked up speed. Hmm. This was the route to the highway, all right. So, why not? Where to? Further west, for damn sure. Denver?

I felt a surge of liberation, a sense of release. The life in this town—it was far more than I'd bargained for. Who needs it?

But there was something in the whirring of the weathered bricks on Winthrop. It sounded like home. I slowed down. A block north of the big flag, I pulled up in front of a familiar bungalow with a rental sign. I got out of the car and took out my phone.

"I'm calling about the house with the rental sign, on Winthrop. Still vacant? Well, you can come by for the sign. You've got yourself a renter."

The realtor was there within a few minutes, with keys to the new locks and a lease to sign. He was a pleasant, paunchy fellow. Seemed pleased to make my acquaintance. ("Anything we can do...") If he knew anything about my circumstances, he gave no sign. But I was sure I'd be a hot topic at the Corner.

By the time I was unpacked, it was 7:30. I hoofed it out to the steak house and found a vacant bar stool. Hazel was on duty and she drew me a Coors. "Be back around," she promised. "Had anything to eat?" I told her I hadn't; I might wait for Cynthia. She tossed me a package of beer nuts.

As I diddled with my beer, my thoughts swirled around Cynthia. Maybe Sarah. But the rest of me felt numb. Tapping my foot to the juke box, I drained my glass and glanced at my watch. Five minutes to eight. I climbed off the bar stool. Then I heard the door open and peered around the corner, prepared to intercept her. We could have our tete-a-tete out in the parking lot.

But it wasn't my wife. It was Walt Wagstaff and his wife, instead. I turned back to the bar and ducked my head. It occurred to me that I'd never been with Walt and Sarah since I'd been back in town. For that matter, I wasn't sure I'd even seen the two of them together. This wasn't a time for any of that.

Not long afterward, I looked up through the miasma of the smoke-filled barroom, just in time to see Sarah give a start and bolt from Walt. She turned my way, but I stayed out of sight.

I was struck by her eyes. They were always bright and sparkling, warm as sunlight. But tonight they were turbid. As Sarah wrenched away from Walt, she looked worn and maybe frightened. I could see that she'd been crying.

I climbed down off my barstool and took a step in her direction through the dark haze of the barroom. She still didn't see me. I saw that Wagstaff had stopped to greet some cohort, clapping shoulders with a horse laugh. Ah, yes. It was our host at the Hoof, Rollie Cleaver. And it was hard not to overhear their conversation.

"Okay, Rollie. Ya got me," growled Wagstaff with a mirthless laugh. "So what is the difference between a clitoris and a golf ball?"

Cleaver set down a tray of beer mugs and surveyed the bar. He had everyone's attention. "Well, I'll spend twenty minutes lookin' for a golf ball!"

Walt guffawed as he reached out to reclaim his wife. He took her arm like a fish on a hook, but she jerked away again. Now the two of them tensed up in a half crouch, faced off like a pair of Greco Roman wrestlers.

I moved closer, still out of sight. They were talking in muted tones. Suddenly, Sarah looked up and for a second I thought she saw me. She gave a half smile and her eyes softened. But then she slowly shook her head and turned toward the dining room, Walt Wagstaff trailing after her. Evidently they'd arrived at a consensus. It seemed they were staying for Rib Night.

I picked up my briefcase and turned toward the door, perhaps to face my own marital Waterloo out in the parking lot. But just as I was leaving, I felt a grip on my shoulder. It was Hazel. Her face was flushed.

"Matt, Emily just called, and she's frantic. She can't find Jeb—been waiting to hear from him all day. She says he's been gone for a very long time. Since supper last evening."

15

There was a dark blue pane of smoked glass in the center of the Collards' front door, and I watched Emily take shape there as she came up to answer the bell. Through the translucence, I could see she was walking at a brisk pace: head up, resolute. But when she opened the door her eyes were puffy, rimmed in red. Her close-cropped, gray hair stuck out here and there in spikes, like a character on LA Law.

She looked up with an expectancy that faded as she peered past my shoulder. Jeb wasn't there.

"Oh, Matt!" She grasped my arm with one hand and half tried to tidy her hair with the other. Emily looked a good deal older than the last time I'd seen her, only a few weeks ago.

"Come on in, Matt. If you're looking for Jeb, why, so am I! I have his dinner warming here in the oven, and I just can't imagine... Have you eaten? No? Why, come sit down. Always plenty... I'll fix up a platter."

She led me by the elbow back to the kitchen, and plunked me down on a bench in the dinette. As she bustled about, mining troves of roast beef, potatoes, and gravy from the oven, she carried on a running monologue, scarcely pausing for breath.

"Thirty years of married life, he's never once done anything like this. Course he's been late now and then: practices, road games, all those reporters coming 'round when you were playing."

In the middle of the kitchen, she came to a halt, a steaming plate of supper in hand. She gazed at the clock—it was 8:30. "You know, those were just about the best of all our years here. Especially compared to what Jeb's been through the last year or two. Those long, long, losing seasons. Now this business with the scholarships. What on earth are they thinking?

"Oh, look at me standing here with your dinner in my hand." She set it down in front of me. "Now, what'll you have to drink?"

I told her a glass of milk sounded fine. "Emily, I wanted to talk with you. You know, I was out at the Hoof, and Hazel said you'd called. I came right over. Can you sit down a minute?"

She came by with a tall glass, clinking with ice cubes. "Ice tea, you said?" Then she circled back to the kitchen where she untied her apron and hung it on a hook next to the oven. She took time to straighten it, smoothing the folds. Finally, she made her way to the dinette. As one might enter a dentist's chair, she reluctantly sat down.

"Emily, I think you should see this."

I handed her Jeb's handwritten note, and she perused it. Then she folded her hands in her lap. I sat there for several minutes, listening to the humming of the clock on the wall. As I finished my supper, mopping up the last dab of cream gravy with a thick slice of homemade bread, I finally broke the silence.

"Emily, I believe that was the best meal I've had since the last time I ate here!"

She blinked, and remembered I was there across the table. "Dessert, Matt? Got a big rhubarb pie in the fridge. Kind you always liked. Jeb, too." Her voice broke as she got up and started back to the refrigerator. She returned with a big slab of pie. Then she reached for my glass to go back and refill it.

I laid a hand on her arm. "Emily, you know I think we should talk now. Look, Jeb didn't show up for a meeting with the team this afternoon. That note of his was taped to the door. Do you have any idea where he might have gone?"

For a long time, she simply sat with her hands in her lap and said nothing.

"You told me he'd never done this before. But do you have any idea where he might run off to if he were feeling depressed?"

More silence. Then she mumbled, "Last I knew, he was accustomed to comin' back here." She looked up at me with a glint of anger. "And he's not one to just 'run off.' Don't you think his tail's been draggin' around here for a long while now?"

I met her stare. "Emily, of course I know that. Ever since I've been back here, Jeb's seemed more and more morose. But nothing like this! And no wonder. I mean, the man's just lost his job. I think we should..."

There was a vibration in my back pocket. I pulled out the pager and read the screen. It was a number I didn't recognize.

"Emily, excuse me. This could be something about Jeb." (If not the latest, captivating chapter in my domestic saga.) I dialed up the number on the cell phone.

Someone picked up the phone in a den of cacophony. Clinking glasses, amplified guitars, and waves of roaring laughter. It was Hazel in the din.

"Just a minute. Let me get this phone around the corner into the coat closet…. Can you hear me all right, Matt? Did you talk to Emily?"

"I'm with her now. You haven't had any word from Jeb? Listen, Hazel, he left me a note. He was offered a buyout from Intelcor, and he took it. I'm worried about him. I was about to ask Emily if we should call the police."

As I said that, I saw her body spring bolt upright across the dinette table. Emily gave me a harsh, frightened look.

Hazel thought for a moment. "If I know this town, I'm not sure she'll be ready for that. You tell anything to Kyle, it's like taking out an ad in the newspaper. Let me make a few calls next time I get a break."

She fell silent again.

"Say, Matt, there's one other reason I called. I'm not sure I should get into this, but Cynthia came by about fifteen minutes ago. She asked if I knew where you were. Said she was supposed to meet you. And then she told me how you'd moved out on her."

I gave a bitter laugh. "Hazel, it's more like I never moved in. It seems Intelcor's got her a new house. Guess the other wasn't fitting for a provost… Moved out, huh? Well, if I can ever get an appointment with the woman, maybe we can coordinate our stories. Did she have anything else to say?"

"I believe she said you'd just made a 'career decision.'"

Emily settled down as I was leaving, apologized for acting impolite. As I was walking out the door, I paused for a second. "Emily, has there been anything else unusual going on here? Anything at all. I mean, one time Jeb mentioned some harassing phone calls."

She looked aside. "That's one word for it, I'd guess. Well, you know, coaches get phone calls. Especially after losing a game. But he was getting calls where nobody said a thing. Sometimes he'd pass me the phone and I could hear these weird sounds. Like somebody pounding on a hollow log. That's what J-Jeb called it." And then she started to cry.

I asked her to call me if he turned up—whenever, night or day—and wrote down my pager number. "If we don't hear from him by morning, we're going to have to tell the police."

She shuddered, but didn't object.

I drove back to my once and future home on Winthrop Avenue, thinking I'd call it a night and try to sleep. But as I walked in the front door, a chill came over me. What would it be like here without Cyn? Should I call her? Or maybe just go over to the new place? But, for some reason, I couldn't do either. Some kind of chasm had come between us. Not a new fissure, but newly defined.

Finally, I went out and grabbed a sleeping bag from the car. Tomorrow, I'd call up one of those rental stores they have in college towns and get myself some furniture. On my way back inside, I noticed something on the porch—a pile of student papers. I glanced at the top page. It was the assignment I'd given the cult class. Seemed they'd submitted it as a group, a day ahead of the deadline.

I tossed the papers on the living room floor. I was in no mood for dealing with the Sisters of Aradia, nor any of this hog shit. Not tonight. But I wondered if I'd be able to sleep. So I headed back to the car one more time and brought in the journal of Julian Reid, along with a flashlight.

As I stuffed myself into the sleeping bag, I rewound the reel of the last few hours of a disastrous, decisive day. That one brief, footloose moment: heading south on Winthrop with an option to turn west. One last chance at liberation. Jesus, had I blown it? I wrestled with the sleeping bag, twisting and turning. Thank God, at least the floor was carpeted...

I must have drifted off, for I sensed I'd been dreaming. It was a ritual of some kind. Women chanting as they danced around a tall, dark object. An obelisk. Maybe the bell tower from the science building. Trees around it, in a kind of glen. Women chanting, dancing. A lead dancer with swaying breasts and flowing hair. I stared at her face, but she turned aside. Dancing to the sound of drums. Staccato sounds, like rain. Then, THOOM—like a kettle drum. THOOM! THOOM! And CRACK like the sound of an explosion!

I sat up, scrambling to untangle from the sleeping bag, and as I shook my head awake I recognized the sound. It was a thunderstorm. Full bore, right above me. The drought had broken! I listened to the staccato of the pounding rain. With a sigh of relief, I lay back down. But now I couldn't sleep.

> *Yasha.* The ancient Hebrew word meant something like "free space." Then the Bible translators came along and called it "salvation." But I'd say they missed the point. It might be all we need to be "saved" is nothing more than a sense of space inside us. Some room to roam the soul.

> What was it Jesus meant in Luke? "Seek ye first the kingdom ... " Better to seek than to find? Does he ask not for believers, but seekers?

I got up and stretched. Sometimes Julian's philosophizing was like a snow cone in a blizzard; a little went a long way. And it wasn't easy, reading by the flashlight. Yet, I found myself responding to something in his journal. Maybe the tone of probing honesty. So, was I starting to take soundings from a guy like Julian Reid? Incredible. I opened it again.

> Sometimes I wonder if the only valid purpose of religion is to help us ask good questions. And then, in the absence of answers, to take action.

> Which brings me to the question of the college, and my calling. Is the voice of need the voice of God? And is the need the call?

I wandered outside to the porch and turned to the end of the journal.

My fears are mounting. And it's not just the condition of the college that I find unnerving. It's some data I came across the other day, based on the last census. All about the ratio of growth, between prisons and colleges. It seems that for every new student in the U.S., there are twelve new prison inmates. That's the ratio, 12:1!

And I'm to save this school, in times like these? I'd say the odds are worse than 12:1.

I thought back to the minutes from the board of trustees meeting. Julian's doodling in the margins, over and over, "12:1." The man must have been obsessed.

But was he so despondent over a scrap of census data that he'd have done himself in? I turned back to the journal.

And now this Celtic, cultic business. Drumming by the river, chanting in the dead of night. The phone rings: no one's there. And the invitation to that ceremony. Trying to please them. The humiliation of that ridiculous rite.

Will we ever learn to love the limits of our lives? Or even tolerate the mere fact that we're mortal? Out here on the plains, there are no apparent bounds: no limits to what one can imagine. But still the human fact remains. The infinite will undo you.

I can see the limits of my life these days. The reality of bankruptcy, my time here almost done. I find I'm seeking answers to just two questions. How? and Now?

I shut off the flashlight and sat in the dark. My eyes were tired and it seemed my head was pounding. Kind of a thrumming sound. I shook my head. But when I stopped, it came again: same cadence.

No, it wasn't in my mind. In the night, behind the rain, there was the rhythm of drums.

All around the house it was pitch black. I stepped off the porch and walked out on the lawn. For a moment, I stood out there with arms widespread, drinking in the rain. I grabbed the sweatshirt I'd slept in and pulled it up over my head. Out in the downpour, I had a strange sense that I might wash myself clean, slough off all the residue that clung like scum, the decisions dangling there.

In time, I walked back in the house and lay down in my bedroll. As I nodded off to sleep, in the back of my mind I began to hear a conversation.

❦

"Have you been crying?"

She shrugged. "Shit, I've just been lying here, thinking about the times when things felt right. And all the places we've been. Do you still remember that afternoon I wandered up to your office? For a while, I had you back, Matt."

"Dunno you've ever lost me. But I have no idea how to deal with the rest of your life. Never have. I just can't fathom it."

She fell silent.

"There's a lot I can't control, Babe. Can't even talk about. Not if you won't even make this move, go online … Look, I know these next few months could be tough. But it doesn't mean you and I can't go on. Matt, we've come so far."

I lay there for a long time.

"Did you go back to sleep?"

"Naw, but I wish I could. Maybe wake up two years down the road, mash the replay button. Catch up on what transpired."

"And you can't even answer me, can you? Fuck! I think there's something else going on with you out here. Something—someone—more than me."

There was a CLAP of thunder, and I steeled myself. Tried to think of what to say. "Some old, odd feelings … "

I lay there, waiting for the outburst. But, strangely, it never came.

"Okay, I know," was all she said. "I think I do. And if I'd known..."

And that was how we left it. As the sky began to blanch, I thought I saw Cynthia walk slowly to the door. Then it seemed she turned back toward me. She wrapped me in a hard hug, her head softly bobbing on my shoulder. And brushed my lips with a fleeting kiss that might have meant good-bye.

I got up and sat out on the porch for a long time, watching the sunrise, pondering the night. Till finally I got up and slogged over to the gym for a hot shower.

The place was dark and vacant, as usual this hour. I made my way down the long corridor to the locker room, toward Jeb Collard's empty office. I saw something taped to the door. A note from Jeb? I ran to look. It was a crudely lettered sign: LAPS AT 3:30, PRACTICE AT 4:00—LRV.

LaRon Vaughn. My man! My spirits slowly lifted as I stripped off my sweat suit and jumped in the shower—luxuriating in the soap, and the steam, and the pulsating jets of hot water. Maybe I'd come by and watch them for a while.

When I'd toweled off and dressed again, I started to call Emily from the locker room phone. Was she ready to talk to the police? But I stopped and dropped the receiver. There was too much going on to take my cues from her. Instead, I called the police station, and got an appointment with Chief Clodfelter in a couple of hours.

I drove by the U-rental store and ordered four rooms-full of their finest scratch-and-dent-ware. I left them a key to the house, then went shopping for some sheets and towels and kitchen utensils.

Main Street was teeming with traffic, windshield wipers whacking. People were darting from their cars and vans and pickups into stores and cafes to join the ubiquitous conversation.

"So, how long you think this'll go on? Floodin' bad, out by your place? Weather bureau'n Omaha says it'll last all week. Two months late to save the corn, hey? To say nothin' of the farm."

The rain ran down off the roof in rivulets, and left a glistening sheen. On this morning, the police station of Mayflower, Milo County, Kansas, looked like a purple polyester umbrella. I trotted in from the parking lot about ten o'clock.

Agnes, the clerk, was at her station on the front counter, diligently filling out some sort of form. I saw it was the morning crossword puzzle from the Omaha Herald.

"I'm here to see Chief Clodfelter. Remember me? Matt Bradshaw, from the college."

She half-lifted an eyelid. "Go on back. He's on the phone, but I guess he's expecting you. Huh... 'a cereal grass used for hay in the United States, for food in other countries.' Four-letter word, starts with 'M.'"

"Agnes, here's a hint: the name on the county courthouse."

She stared at me vacantly as I came around the counter.

"You know, 'Milo.' As in 'Milo County.'"

She nodded thoughtfully, moistening her pencil as she filled in the puzzle.

"Yes, I do understand." The chief's voice boomed all along the back corridor. "Of course you're concerned. He gets outta control. But unless you're willing to come in and file a complaint, there's not a whole hell of a lot I can do to help you."

There was a pause. "'Then everyone will know!' he said in a mocking tone. "And how many times this week have I heard that."

I stopped ten feet short of the door, uncertain whether to go in. But he hung up the phone. I walked up and knocked on the door jamb. "Good morning, Chief. Are you ready for me?"

Clodfelter was sitting slumped in his plum-colored Naugahyde chair, his chin on his fist. He looked up with a worn smile. "Come on in, if you'll towel off at the door. Still comin' down pretty heavy out there, huh?"

He swung around and looked up at me. "Jesus, you look like the latter end of a misspent life. Rough night, huh? Well, let me tell you, it's no picnic around here, either.

"Worst part of it's the ambivalence of people, when it comes to the truth of their lives. Folks may need you to know a secret or two, just to save 'em from themselves. Who gets mean when they're drinking? Whose key fits whose back door? But they don't want you to know, all the same."

"I guess you've picked up a lot of data, all these years."

He sat and stared at the far wall, his old basketball jersey. I glanced at his diplomas. A Bachelor of Arts in Anthropology from Kansas State University, Magna Cum Laude. A certificate in "Law Enforcement Information Technology" from Bell and Howell.

"But, listen, Chief, there are a few things I came by to go over. That incident with the bell tower—you were going to look through the debris. Did you ever come up with anything?"

He shook his head as he took a little notepad from his desk, wrote something, and put the pad down. He looked up, bleakly.

"They say the largest part of living in a small town is looking past things. You've heard that. But I can't look at anybody around here and see just what they wanta show me. Julian was the same. He knew a whole lot. But he'd just grin at everybody. Tried to make 'em think he thought the best of 'em."

I reached for my briefcase, Julian's journal. He'd reminded me of an entry I'd read. But, no. I stayed on course.

"Then there's Bronwyn Chiles, Chief. The girl who was injured. She vanished from the hospital. In fact, I've heard it was you who went up and settled her bill. Word is she's been convalescing out at your place—staying with you and your wife."

He rocked back in his swivel chair and shut his eyes for a moment. Then I saw him push the button on his armrest. Agnes came on the intercom and he placed an order for refreshments. Finally, he swung back around and smiled at me. "Don't we have a whole lot we could talk about! But let me guess why you're really here: Jeb Collard, right? Been gone three days. I know about that."

I blinked, then took out the note I'd found on the door of Collard's office. The chief read it slowly and turned it several ways, holding the stationery and the envelope up to the light.

He shook his head. "Another enigmatic message from a middle-aged male. Ol' Jules and then ol' Jebster. Seems to be a run of 'em."

He sat there, no longer reading the note. Just holding it.

"So, can you do something, Chief?"

He looked up, slowly. "I'll call Emily in good time. But I'm not about to file a report on the NCIC, at least not right away. You remember what I told you: if a full-grown adult … "

I nodded.

"Later on, I might post a notice."

"Although maybe it's a bit redundant, right? I mean, her laundry's already hanging out all over town."

He gave me a hard look and curled his lip. "Just what I was sayin'. A place like this, you can forget about your private affairs. Take you and your wife. 'Splitsville,' the way I hear it. Hey, do they still say that?"

My jaw dropped and for a moment I sat there speechless. This old codger must have a tape recorder up everybody's ass. Was that why they kept him in office?

There was a knock on the door and Agnes came in. She had a cardboard tray of clams and coffee, and a suspicious dab of frosting on her chin. Once again, she left without comment. The chief passed me a clam and a black coffee.

"So, what else have you been up to?"

I took a deep breath and tried to come up with reasonably safe subject. I told him about the course I'd taken on at the College: Sacred Sex and Primal Prayer.

He snickered. "No telling what they'll come up with to keep that place alive. Back in my day, even if you could play some ball, they thought it'd be nice if you also declared an academic major. I tell you, there's not a week goes by, I don't draw on that degree in anthropology. Taught me to probe the unknown. Sure glad I went to Kansas State. Got me a good education."

That cleared my head. "You know, I've heard a few cases of that happening at Hopewell College."

He passed me another clam and a napkin. If he was aware of my irritation, he didn't show it. "See that other diploma up over there on the wall? Certificate from Bell and Howell. Hey, I'll bet you haven't met too many computer jocks like me."

"You mean … "

He chuckled. "At my age? That's what you're thinkin'. But in the law enforcement biz, you will. Lot of wireheads."

He took off on another tangent. All about the Omnibus Crime Bill, back in the sixties. It seems the government created something called the Law Enforcement Assistance Administration, the LEAA. The budget grew like grassfire—from $63 million in 1968 to $900 mil in '75. And, he said, a lot of it went for training the fuzz in electronic surveillance.

I told him I'd heard of the program, and he grinned. Then I told him why. "It was the Karen Silkwood case. There were charges the pigs in Oklahoma had been spying on her, electronically. Did I get that right?"

I watched him flinch at the "pigs," but he grinned and nodded. "Lotta suspicion about this technology. But, like as not, they didn't care about Silkwood. Those cops were just bored. They just needed somebody to try out their high-tech surveillance on. For the most part, you know, we can't use it. Lotta legal restraints."

"Well, that's a damn shame," I said. I got up and picked up my satchel.

"But that don't mean we can't look into things," he said quickly. "Say, for instance, we were curious about who in town might take an interest in this crazy course of yours. 'Sacred Screwing an' ...'"

"Primal Prayer. Sacred Sex and Primal Prayer. You know, I didn't name it."

"Right. Someone who might be a member of some like-minded group. Bearing in mind, of course, that what you're lookin' for is basically an organization of self-professed witches.

"Now, say we located such a group. I think I came across one once. What'd they call themselves? Somethin' about goddesses. 'The Council of the Goddess.' By the way, here's something I read one time. You know the prime occupation among American witches? What the largest number do for a living?"

I didn't.

"Computer programmers. Got one life by day. Full moon, it's a different story. But, anyway, suppose we try to find their home page, see what kinda firewall they got rigged up, to protect their data."

He turned on his computer, and it croaked, "Good Afternoon." Jesus, was it already after twelve?

I watched him type in something at the search prompt and in an instant a technicolor Web site flooded the screen. "COGWEB," it read. "The Latest Word on Wicca."

He tried several passwords to get in, but nothing clicked. "Hmm. That COG's a slick acronym. Uh uh. Maybe COGMODE. Nope. How 'bout COGBAUD?"

The screen went blank, and then a menu flashed up:

Council of the Goddess: Active Members.
List by state.
List by Zip Code.
List by municipality.
List by member category.

"Now look at that," he marveled. Then suddenly he slapped his desk. "Aw, shoot! Completely slipped my mind." He jumped up. "Forgot to go over something with Agnes. She'll be taking off for lunch. Be back in a jiffy."

I sat there for a minute and studied the menu. Then I slid into his chair and entered "*Mayflower, Kansas*" under "Municipality." For "Member Category," I typed in: "*Student.*" The screen went blank and then a list of names sprang up. I recognized the roster of my cult class.

On a whim, I went back to Member Category and typed in: "*Chapter Advisors.*" This time only one name appeared: CHANNING COE.

He had an address down in the Bottoms.

16

"Emily, you know I had to tell him."

I was slumped down on a sagging Naugahyde couch, one elbow propped on a quavering end table. The telephone was a half foot from my ear, but it didn't help. Emily was steaming.

"Yes, yes, I know," I stammered. "I said I'd speak to you before going to Chief Clodfelter. But, the point is, he already knew Jeb was missing."

That didn't seem to assuage her. She explained, leather-lunged, that everyone in Mayflower lived under the assumption Kyle Clodfelter knew all of their affairs. But the unwritten rule was that if you told him what he already knew, that gave him license to tell others.

As I waited for Emily to wind down, I cast a dubious eye on the furnishings I'd picked up, courtesy of U-rental. Two fuchsia side chairs faced the Naugahyde couch where I sat. The couch was orange. Across from me stood a bronze lamp with a lime green shade, and beside that a burgundy settee.

The folks at U-rental must have scrounged up every random stick of leftovers they had in the store. Then they'd raked over Goodwill Industries and the Salvation Army for rejects.

"Jesus, how'd I get myself into this!" I wondered, and I didn't mean just the furniture.

Finally, she paused for breath and I went on the offensive. "Look, Emily, I don't know a lot about criminal investigation, but I'm coming to understand Chief Clodfelter. The guy's loath to look into anything around this town. It's how he keeps his job. But that's not good enough, in this case."

I told her something I'd read on the psychology of serious crime. In the case of foul play, your best chance of finding the perpetrator is within the first twenty-four hours. After that, people's defenses set in and they distance themselves from what they have done. It's a theory that makes sense of people like O.J. Simpson. Here he has a gun to his head in the first twenty-four hours following the crime, but he's grinning on the golf course not long after.

"Now, Emily, here's what I want you to do. You call up Clodfelter and ask him to come by this afternoon. I want you to give him all the data you can find on Jeb. A recent picture, credit card numbers, that sort of thing. Tell him to post a notice that Jeb's missing on something called the NCIC. That's right, N-C-I-C. It's a computer file. And one other thing…"

It was a test of sorts. I asked her to give him the address of a certain house down on the Bottoms. "Ask him if he's ever heard of the place. And then I'd like you to call me back—leave a message if you have to—but tell me how he reacts."

She gave another blast of protest in a voice as shrill as a referee's whistle. But in the end she agreed to do what I'd said.

I called up U-rental—told them to retrofit the place in basic brown and black—then beat it out the door before I threw up. I headed for my office to prepare for my evening cult class.

I settled into my desk chair and began shuffling through the campus mail that lay scattered on the floor behind the mail slot. Not much there but notices of meetings.

SPECIAL FACULTY MEETING

That was one announcement, from Provost Cynthia Lothamer Bradshaw and President Roger Squire (listed in that order). The gathering was scheduled for Saturday, 10:00 a.m. at the Congregational Church. No word of an agenda. The other notice was headed:

CONSULTATION ON THE FUTURE OF HOPEWELL COLLEGE

This one was unsigned. The meeting was slated for 6:00 this evening, "back booth of the barroom at the Hoof'n Horn." I suppose that'd be the same bunch that had met at Hazel's. Minus Jeb.

I shelved the mail and settled down with the students' proposals. That was one great, hidden benefit in the life of a college prof. You always had a good excuse to tune the world out.

I was pleased to see that the proposals, on the whole, were not half bad. Sure, there was the usual schlock that some kid would always try to palm off for academic credit. Self-help books with half-assed titles—*Goddess Aglow*, in this case—but, hey, what else was new?

If there was one part of teaching I seemed to understand, it was the obligation to challenge preconceptions. I tried to do this in a probing but gentle way. Helping students view the world from new angles, so they didn't stay stuck inside their skins.

I wrote comments on the papers and set the stack aside. Then something caught my eye. It was the book they wanted added to the reading list, on the ritual death of the aging king. I remembered reading it years ago. *He Who Must Die.*

I scanned the other books on the reading list and made a few notes for class. Then I put the course material back in my satchel and wrote out a few headings on a legal pad. They were concepts I'd come up with a few years ago in a book on methods of historical research. Soon my mind was churning over everything I'd seen.

KNOWN   UNCLEAR   PRESUMED

Did I understand anything more of what was occurring in Mayflower, Kansas? Under KNOWN I wrote, "Kyle Clodfelter." I had a bit of a fix on that old fox. But of what else could I be sure? I sat there for a long time and stared at the columns.

Under KNOWN, I wrote, "Hopewell College—for sale to the highest bidder." But that felt so onerous I moved it to PRESUMED.

Back to KNOWN. "Cynthia gone. Marriage done." And that felt bad as well. But I had no reason to mark it PRESUMED or UNCLEAR.

I was descending into a deep funk when my phone rang—saved by the bell. It was Emily. She reported that she'd met with the chief and had given him the information on Jeb. He agreed to post the notice on the NCIC, just as planned.

"How'd he seem?" I asked her.

"Well, sorta kindly, if I had to say. I got to thinking this wasn't such a bad idea to call him in. And I'm sorry I lit into you, Matt. But since Jeb's gone … I mean, just who else … " She started to cry.

I tried to soothe her, but also get her back on track. The address down on the Bottoms. How did the chief react?

"Well, now, that was odd, all right. I wrote out that address and gave it to him, like you said. And before I could ask him, why, he gave a grunt and shoved it in his pocket. Then he walked right out the door. Not even a good-bye."

I thanked her and turned back to my notes—drew a line through "Kyle Clodfelter" where I had him under KNOWN. I moved him to UNCLEAR.

And then I sat and stared at my columns until the words began to swirl and my mind went blank. Just what in hell was going on? Was there some strand that tied Jeb's disappearance, the cult class and Channing, Cynthia and Channing, the incoming basketball squad, the buyer for the campus? Some sort of logic to it all?

Well, enough of that. I slammed my pad shut. Somehow, I needed to focus on just one facet of this scene. Intelcor? It was a gut cinch I'd not get any more intelligence from Cynthia.

I took out my computer and clicked on the Internet browser that tech consultant Damon had left me, then tried to follow the instructions. A window: SEARCH. I typed in THE HEARTLAND FILE. A message flashed PASSWORD REQUIRED.

Oh, terrific. I tried "Bradshaw." ACCESS DENIED. So what else? What's a password? What was it these guys usually used? I know— your mother's maiden name. That's what that dweeb Damon had asked me for. I tried it: "Addison." Uh uh. ACCESS DENIED.

Hey, wait. I'd put in *Cynthia's* mother's maiden name.

I typed in "Hilliard" and the hard drive started humming. The arrow on my screen became an hourglass as zillions of numbers flashed along the bottom: 25 percent of 450K files. All that.

And then slowly, v-e-r-y slowly, the screen began to etch out a Web site. A big, saffron sunflower looming up from fields of green at the far end of a russet road. With a deep, cerulean sky in the background. Beautiful, but the pace was agonizing.

T--H--E

H--E--A--R--T--L--A--N--D

F--I--L--E

At this rate, if I had the Book of Life online, I'd be a corpse before I could peruse it. But now I remembered what Damon had said: he'd fix me up with a faster modem. Although that was back when I had Cynthia on my side. Before my career decision.

At last I got into a Table of Contents: Levels of Access. I clicked on Senior Management, and was admitted. Then: Market Opportunities: Higher Education. There were half a dozen titles, and I clicked on the first one: Faltering Colleges.

I quickly scanned document. As professional marketers, it seemed that Intelcor saw a green field in colleges, ripe for the picking. And so they concluded:

It appears we have two market niches. (1) We can use our demographic research tools to recruit students who have opted out of other schools (provided we can overcome their alienation and come up with appealing courses). That is the modest course.

(2) Or, in extreme cases, we can help no-hope colleges to reinvent themselves as alternative institutions. That is the radical course of action. And one that, in the year ahead, we may have an opportunity to pursue.

So, where were they heading with this analysis? Suppose Intelcor had designs on this college. What did they want the campus for? And then one larger question: even if I knew, what in hell could I do about it? My head began spinning like the wheels of a pickup, high-centered on a muddy road. Oh, Jesus: the paralysis of analysis! I'm getting just like Julian. Head in my hands, I fell to my desk...

When the phone rang.

"Hey, Coach—you comin' by?"

I sat up straight and shook my head. "How's that?"

"Time for practice. Four o'clock. You comin'?"

I felt a shiver down the cord of my spine. ("Coach"?)

But I snapped back. "Sure thing, LaRon. Just give me a minute. Got my gym bag right here in my office."

I glanced at my watch and out the window. The sun was out.

The rain had stopped. I shut down the computer and snapped the lid shut.

The phone rang again, as I was reaching for my gym bag.

"Dean Bradshaw?" I recognized the cultured tone.

"Sure, Gwendolyn, I finished the proposals and I'll be... Say, what time are you meeting? No, not just for class. Don't you have an organization meeting of some sort beforehand?"

I asked them to switch the schedule. I'd meet them for class at 9:00. They could have their meeting after that.

And then, before anyone else could find me, I lit out for the gym.

"Shee-it, LaRon. Quit jivin'! What you talkin' about?"

"I'm just tellin' you what we learned in class, Jamal. If you'd show up once in a while it might not come as such a shock."

I listened from the hallway outside the gym.

"Yeah, well what's the point? I mean, what we doin' out here, anyway? This cow-shit college. I had me a call last night—one o' my home boys..."

"Jamal, will you ease up on all that candy-ass street talk? And throw out that jive bandana. Everybody knows the only home boys you got are cruisin' in them BMWs up in Winnetka."

"Whoo! Candy-ASS!" An appreciative murmur from the others. "LaRon, tha's almost profanity!"

I walked up. "All right, Jamal, so what'd your friend say?"

"These dudes comin' up here from Texas on Saturday. There's twelve of 'em, and one's maybe seven foot. Said he's a monster!"

"So, I guess we've got our work cut out for us, fellas." I walked over to the clutch of kids, huddled under the far basket. "LaRon, what was it you picked up in class?"

He glanced warily at Jamal and the others. "It was Doc Harley's course on special education. He drew up this diagram."

"Oh yeah? What was it? Here." I handed him a clipboard.

LaRon knelt down and scribbled out four lines of text. Then he held up the clipboard. The guys were still gathered around. It was the kind of "teachable moment" that faculty would kill for.

- UNCONSCIOUS INCOMPETENCE
- CONSCIOUS INCOMPETENCE
- CONSCIOUS COMPETENCE
- UNCONSCIOUS COMPETENCE

"So wha's that about?" questioned Jamal, now somewhat interested. LaRon went through the series in rapid fire with quick, succinct examples applied to basketball—how we can progress from a state of not knowing that we lack a skill, to knowing that we don't, to using a skill only if we take time to think about it, to the highest stage where we can use the skill unconsciously.

The kid was a natural teacher.

I told him that I couldn't have presented that material any better myself. "But I'm sorta surprised. Do you guys often do this—go over your notes from class?"

They sat in silence.

I chuckled. "Maybe we oughta put LaRon here on the faculty. Hey, I'll break out my printing press. Do you up a doctorate."

No one else laughing. Then LaRon slowly turned. He eyed me up and down. "Ya know, we've only got each other."

I looked at him askance. "What are you saying?"

He didn't answer. But Jamal spoke up. "Whaddaya think it's like, Man, us livin' out here? The times we not playing ball, the one or two hours they like to see us. Rest the time, they look past us. What the fuck you think it's like, the other twenty-two … "

I looked back toward LaRon. "Jesus Christ, I know… "

"No you don't!" he snapped, and stared at the floor. I stood there for a time. Then, finally, I shook my head and walked away.

"Hey, Coach."

I stopped and looked back. It was Jamal.

"Remember what the man said? 'Conscious incompetence.' Be a hell of a start. You knowin' what you don't know about us."

We stood there for a moment, and stared across the chasm.

Then, one by one, they reached out into no-man's land and I put out my hand. We clasped hands, then swooped down toward the floor and up again. "One, two, three—HOPE!" We all knew the ritual. It was what Hopewell teams did in the huddle.

"Let's go, fellas. Get loose. Layup drill, five minutes." As the team instinctively split into two rows—one shooting, one rebounding—I stood and listened to the litany of the game. The slap of the ball, the guttural grunts, raucous shouts that rattled around the gymnasium. For a moment, it seemed I could feel Collard there with us. Not saying much. Maybe just clapping.

Then I did hear someone quietly applauding. I looked high in the stands and there she was, sitting where she'd always sat. I grinned and waved and she pumped a fist somewhat decorously—it had been a sign between us. I felt a warm rush as I turned back to the floor. But the next time I looked up, Sarah was gone.

It seemed these guys had pretty solid skills, however unspectacular. As I watched them whip the ball around, setting screens and defending, I had an idea. It was something Jeb Collard had said, one time when we'd faced an overwhelming opponent: "If we can't match up against them, maybe we can make it harder for them to match up against us."

You know, these guys were all pretty close to the same size. Jamal, the "center," was a skinny six-foot-seven. But the smallest guard was a good six-four. I remembered a maneuver Jeb had used, "the Drake Shuffle." Suppose I worked them all out in both back court and front court positions, posting up and also out on the perimeter. We might be able to trap the Texans in mismatches.

I tried it and it seemed to work. They all had decent ball-handling skills and they all knew how to rebound. Maybe that's the benefit of not being a phenom: you don't specialize too soon.

Every fifteen minutes, they'd rotate in and out of the post, and back out to the perimeter. I was surprised to see Jamal can a couple of three-pointers. The kid had a decent outside shot. We spent another half-hour running through some basic offensive sets when LaRon muttered, wheezing, catching his breath, "One time, Coach Collard showed us a tape of the Utah Jazz—John Stockton and Karl Malone, running picks like this."

"Look, LaRon, you know where the film library is in Coach Collard's the office, don't you? Tomorrow, I'll get you an extra key. Use the films, anything you find in there. "

Then I turned to the others. "You're not bad ballplayers," I told them. "Not at all. Most of you've put in a couple of years with Jeb Collard, who's the best coach I know. And, best of all, you understand team basketball..."

"Fat, fuckin' lotta good it do us. Dudes they shippin' in!"

"I know, Jamal, but you haven't seen these guys. How do you know they can play as a team? And just because one guy's a seven-footer doesn't mean a thing. He may have small hands and short arms—moves like an armadillo."

"Texas road kill!" A couple of guys hooted.

"That's it! Now, look, we've got a week to prepare, and I just had an idea. When those guys get here, I'm gonna find a way to challenge them to a game—winner take all for the scholarships. And one other thing. I'd like to LaRon to run drills as player-coach, the times when I'm not here."

"Not here!"

"That's right, Jamal. You know, I was hired here as dean of students. And, on top of that, a friend of mine is missing."

I pulled up to the Hoof'n Horn about quarter to six, plenty early for the meeting. There was a RESERVED sign on the back booth, but nobody was in it. I settled down in the booth to relax and there I sat for a long while, savoring the melding smells of sawdust, brewers' yeast, and smoldering tobacco. There was a hot number on the juke box.

My toes were tapping and my pelvis pumping—maybe I should go see who was out on the dance floor. But, no, I had class in a couple of hours. Better settle down from basketball. Take time for some quiet reflection.

I took out Julian's journal and riffled the pages, but then I clamped it shut. I signaled for a beer, and the barkeep who waved back was none other than Rollie Cleaver. As he hoisted a schooner, he rubbed his gut. "Long one?" he mimed.

I grinned and mouthed, "Why not?" suddenly relishing the sight of him. Thank God some people were beyond analysis.

I took out my legal pad and began to doodle some notes, maybe for courses I'd teach if anyone ever let me. As I started to write, the words began flowing. For the first time, they weren't gleanings from grad school—aphorisms from historians and the like. They seemed to be quotes for a course on the teachings of Jeb Collard.

- Play your game plan, not the opposition. Don't just take what they give you. There's only one reason they're giving it to you: they think you can't do it.

- Concentrate on the things you can control. Take your shot as it presents itself. Let the game come to you.

I wasn't sure what all of that meant in the broad scheme of things, but right now it felt mobilizing. Whatever Intelcor had in mind, I'd take my shots and play my game plan—not the opposition.

As I shoved the legal pad in my satchel, a colleague of Rollie's came ambling down the aisle. She slid a schooner of Coors to a spot just between my nostrils, undid her apron, and sat down.

"Hi, Hazel. Are you here for the meeting?"

"What meeting?"

I showed her the notice as I took a gulp of Coors.

She giggled. "First I've heard of it. But I can bet I know who called it. A quorum of two. And I'll wager she has an agenda."

She caught me in mid-swallow. "H-hold on," I spewed.

Hazel handed me a terry cloth bar towel. "Sorry, Matt. But, you have to realize, we all know it all. That's the first premise in a town ... "

She looked up. "Oh, hi, Sarah."

Hazel gripped her in a quick hug as Sarah sat down. Then she picked up her towel and flicked a last dab of suds from the front of my shirt. She took orders for beers and barbecue, began heading back up the aisle.

But not so fast. "Hazel, is there a second premise?"

She turned around and flashed a smile. "Maybe it's not just that we know. It's that we care, as well."

Sarah shook her head in puzzlement. Then she took a deep breath, all business. "Matt, do you know where your wife is?"

I made a quizzical frown.

"No, I don't mean where she's living. Of course I know that. I mean where she is today, on business. Look at this."

She handed me a thick, gray brochure.

"Walt must have forgot this. He left it on the kitchen table this morning."

I fingered it and felt the quality of inlaid type on heavy stock. It was the kind of brochure you see in major cities, not hamlets like Mayflower. It was an announcement of a two-day conference sponsored by two innovative outfits: "Intelcell," a corrections company, and "Intelsell," a telemarketing firm.

The conference was in Wichita, today and tomorrow.

REBUILDING YOUR ECONOMY
A SEMINAR FOR COMMUNITY LEADERS:
Growing Industries on the Great Plains

I scanned the program. According to the sponsors, there were several local industries slated for growth:

+Meat Processing ("Beyond the Labor Shortage: The New Immigrant Workforce")
+Telemarketing ("Selling in the Dialect Americans Trust— Cashing in on Midwestern Accents")
+Corrections Careers in Rural America ("Retraining Farmers as Prison Personnel")
+Hazardous Waste Depositories ("Big Business on the Wide Open Spaces")

There were other seminars on "Captive Audiences: Inmate-Oriented Cable TV," and "Crime in the Heartland: New Markets for Home Security." Right up Wagstaff's alley.

"At first, he wouldn't tell me where he was going, just packed up his suitcase. Finally he said he had business in Wichita, overnight. And then I saw them out the window when they came by for him. Cynthia in the driver's seat, and Roger Squire."

Hazel came by with two platters of barbecue and a couple of more beers. She also handed me a flier. "Matt, did you get one of these? It showed up in campus mail, addressed to the faculty."

The flier was in Hopewell College colors, black and gold.

CAREER OPPORTUNITY

Educational Consultants Needed! One of America's fastest-growing telecommunications companies needs consultants in this area. Personal freedom and the chance to motivate others. Flexible hours. Call IntelSell today.

There was a local phone number.

"What do you make of that?" asked Sarah, as she reached for the barbecue sauce.

"Calling people up to sell 'em siding? Sounds like a shit job with a coat of frosting."

Sarah grimaced.

"Oh, sorry. I remember. You never were much for profanity."

We said nothing for a time but I could see her relaxing. The same song came back on the juke box. A kicker. I watched her shoulder start to shake in time.

"So, we're the meeting, right?"

She colored just a little.

"I saw you in the bleachers, at the gym."

Her color deepened as she looked up with a shy smile.

"Well, I'm glad to see you smile again."

And then we started talking, and I opened up as I always had. Told her just about everything. My second thoughts about Clodfelter. How he wouldn't check out the house on the Bottoms.

"So, what's that about? Can't he get around anymore?"

She shook her head, and frowned. "Don't you know the story of his daughter? That car wreck down at the foot of the bluff?"

"Holy shit. Of course!"

She looked down with a frown.

"Sorry."

I considered what I was about to say next.

"Look, Sarah. It's feels so great just to sit here, I guess I've been putting off telling you some things. Out here the other night, you and Walt. I know you didn't see me, but ... "

The rib clanged on her plate as it slipped from her hand. Then her head lowered, and she covered her face. She shivered as though someone had thrust her in Rollie's beer cooler. "You think I didn't see you?" She began crying softly.

Hazel came by and set down a stack of napkins. I sat there in silence, passed one to Sarah when she reached for her purse. Turning aside as she'd been taught, she blew her nose. And then she just sat and stared at the wall.

Finally, she took a sip of beer. "I had this soiree all scripted." She shook her head with a sad laugh. "The other night, it just came over me. I had a sense that you were leaving town."

She took another swig of beer. Rocking subtly, the juke box thumping. Now her head was bobbing and she smiled. "Wanta dance, Matt?" I knew the look well. It was Saturday-night-Sarah.

I sat there for a minute. "I don't think so," I said.

She returned to her ribs for a time before she spoke again.

"Oh, I'm sorry to be so morose, Matt. I've been that way a lot. But you know, some night we'll be out here changing partners in a line dance. And then you and I will look up, and hook up ... "

She looked up and smiled.

"And we'll get to have our little fling. Is that it?"

"That's it—cut loose the way we used to. Oh, Matt, you'll see. We'll take what they give us. And there'll be good times. I just know it!"

I sat and considered that scenario. Then I lifted up my beer mug and slammed it on the table. "Sure, Sarah. There must be a lot of adulterous fantasies set loose in line dancing. It's all in the script. And you guys have your parts down, don't you!"

"Matt, stop it. Those people at the bar. They can hear you."

"And they've cast you as a Dresden china doll. Sunday-Sarah. We'll all look past you on a Saturday night. For you're the only one in town here without a fucking blemish!"

She gave a jolt as though I'd struck her, and then slowly set her napkin down and snapped open her purse. She laid a ten dollar bill on the table. She got up and put on her coat.

"All right, good exit, Sarah. I'd sit and applaud except I've got a scene of my own to deal with: witch class in half an hour. In your old dorm lounge, in fact. And after that I'll have to figure out how in hell to track down Jeb, since the guy you've assigned the role of police chief can't seem to function. And you know the irony? For just a while there, I had a thought that you might help me."

She winced, but in an instant she was up the aisle and gone.

For a minute I sat there and fumed. The old birds on the bar stools turned back to their beers. As I gathered my books to get up from the booth, I noticed Harley at the bar, sitting alone at the far end. I thought I'd ask if he'd enjoyed the theatrics. But I saw Hazel coming around the bar behind him. I sat and watched. She must have been getting off work, untying her apron and fluffing her hair. As she came up to Harley, I thought she'd tap him on the shoulder or slap him on the back, they were such buddies.

But she did neither. Hazel paused and shot a quick glance up and down the bar. Then she put out a finger and touched him just behind his ear. She drew the finger slowly down his spine, all the way to the small of his back. At that, Harley glanced along the bar, as well. Then he reached back and rubbed her thigh.

I sat there, dumbstruck. Didn't Harley have a wife? But he did seem to turn up a lot with Hazel. "We all know it all." That's what she'd said. What was it Clodfelter had told me? "In a small town, you learn to look past things."

I watched Harley follow Hazel out the door.

17

Elwood Hall was ringing with rock music and raucous laughter. A good omen. Perhaps no one would be transferring, at least overnight.

Gwendolyn met me at the door and tonight she smiled a little. She asked how I was. Hey, maybe I'd got higher marks from the cult class than I'd imagined. But I was past caring. I had my own game plan with the Sisters of Aradia.

Walking down the hall, I asked where she was from. "Darien," she said. "It's a town in Connecticut." I knew the place, a half-hour up the Merritt Parkway from Greenwich, Cynthia's home town.

"You must be on medication for culture shock," I thought.

As I walked in, a few of the Sisters looked up and almost smiled. They sat in an informal circle this evening, more like an ordinary college class. I saw they weren't all in uniform—only a couple were draped in those sable Hopewell College sweatshirts.

One of them was the tall blonde I'd noticed before. She sat cross-legged at the far side of the circle tugging at her hair, with the same abstracted gaze. But tonight her hair looked different. It appeared she might have washed it.

"Good evening, group. I have your proposals to hand back, and we'll do that before the end of the hour. But, first, I'd like to talk about one theme in our readings—the autochthonous religion of Europe, the vegetation rite." (I watched for a reaction to "autochthonous," but no one batted an eye.)

"Let's start with a passage from Jessie Weston's book, *From Ritual to Romance*. I'd like to have your thoughts on this point."

This was a time-honored technique for involving students in a discussion of material you weren't sure they'd read. But I had another purpose, as well. So I'd read a selection and offer some comments. Then I'd just sit tight and invite them to respond.

"Mysteries such as divinity are entrusted to speech, not to writing. Setting such things down in writing is already almost profanation."

"Here's an anonymous quote on the same point. 'The highest cannot be spoken, only done.' So, what would you say to that?"

They sat in silence, watching me.

I watched them in return, let the silence take hold. Then I went on. "Aren't there others who maintain that, when it comes to religion, written creeds and sacred texts are nothing but an extraneous distraction. They'd say that any sort of scripture is so much patent bullshit. Ritual is at the heart of spirituality."

More silence; I waited them out. Then, softly, from the back of the lounge, came my first response: "Coo-wal."

"Well, all right, that's a good start. Now, what'd I say that sounded so inspiring?"

"Nothing new, but it pretty much concurs with our beliefs. We're not into scriptures and creeds. We believe in Gaea, the life of the earth, and in the Craft—the infinite power of rites we can feel. That's why we're out here, to study that."

She was a rail-thin girl with long, straight hair and wire-rimmed glasses. Her voice was thin and reedy, but there was no mistaking her fervor.

"That certainly was very well said. May I ask your name?"

"Penelope Hobhouse."

"Well, Penelope, what does the word 'autochthonous' mean?"

"It refers to the earliest inhabitants of a region. Similar to 'aboriginal' or 'indigenous.'"

"Say, that's not bad! Anyone else familiar with the term?"

More than half the hands went up.

"I see. Say, Penelope, where'd you go to school last year?"

"Mount Holyoke."

"Uh, thanks…" (As I paused to consider the proposition that anyone in her right mind would transfer from Holyoke to a place like Hopewell College, I was gazing off in space toward the hallway. And I thought I saw a shadow cross the open door.)

"All right, let's move on. What do you think of when I say the word 'Wasteland?'"

Silence. "Waste-land," I repeated.

From the back of the room: "A synonym for 'Kansas?'" There was a chorus of snorts and snickers.

"I hear you," I chuckled. "But in the history of Western civilization? 'The Wasteland.'"

"A poem by T. S. Eliot," another student chimed in.

Then Penelope commented, "There's something else I came across. In a legend of some kind."

"That's right. It's the legend of the Grail. Now, here's a point I want to make tonight. I believe that at the heart of every religion there's a single concern. The crux of it is what to do in the face of desolation. How to cure the Wasteland. How to recover life, revive it when it dies.

"We've had a touch of that sort of thing out here this fall, haven't we—that devastating drought." (I saw one or two trade glances.) "Now, in the religion that preceded Christianity in ancient Europe, the way to cure the loss of life was ... what? Does anybody have a sense of that?"

More silence, and again I waited them out, gazing in space. Again, I thought I saw a flickering shadow. Was someone listening out in the hall? Must be a new wrinkle in auditing classes.

"No response? Well, let's see if any of this seems familiar. In the vegetation rite—the original fertility religion—the way to cure the Wasteland was ... to kill the ruler of the land!"

I saw a bit of squirming.

"Maybe not actually waste him, as we say, but subject him to the same kind of ordeal the land is under. Wound him in some way. Maybe in a literal sense, maybe only figuratively. How might one do that? Any ideas?"

I waited. "Well, for example, a ritual tattoo ... Now then, it seems the time for such a rite is just about upon us. What's the next festival on the calendar of Wicca? What do you call it?"

"Hallowmas," someone muttered.

"Of course. Well, thanks. And, here's the rest of my spiel."

I saw I had their attention, even the blonde in the back. She fixed me with a riveting stare.

"At some time between the flourishing of the fertility cult that evolved into Wicca, and before Christianity got a hammerlock on Europe, we believe there was another faith waiting in the wings. Sort of a cross between Celtic and Christian concepts.

"It was a nature rite—still out to cure the Wasteland—but it had a different mindset. It was the religion of the legend of the Grail. And in this tradition, there also is an aging king. He's called the Fisher King—we're not sure why—and he reigns over a Wasteland.

"But in the legend of the Grail, there's a different way to revive the Wasteland, to end the drought. It's not to kill the Fisher King... but what? Is anyone aware?"

Unbroken silence.

"Why, it was to heal the king. To cure him of his illness."

I sat there for a moment; no one moved. Then something stirred at the far end of the circle. The blonde had begun to twist her hair. I picked up my books and set out the papers.

"Well, please get started on your projects. You'll find my comments on your proposals. And give me a call if you have any questions on the notes I've written—or any concerns at all." I sat for a moment and surveyed them, one by one. "Good night."

My footsteps echoed as I walked out in the hall. The lounge was still dead silence. But I heard a rustling in the shadows of the doorway, and a warm arm came wriggling 'round my waist.

"Oh, Matt, I just thank God you're back."

She didn't say much more as we walked out of her old dorm to my car. We settled into an old, easy silence as I turned south on Winthrop. Past my house then west on Main Street toward the river. No sound but the whirring of the wheels on brick pavement.

"Say, where are we going? Don't tell me you're taking me back up there on that bluff!"

"Hey, you said you'd been feeling uptight... No, my love, actually we're going to look up that address I told you Clodfelter got off the Internet. Down on the Bottoms."

She was silent for a minute.

"Do you really believe there's some connection between Jeb's disappearance and the girls in that class? Is that what you were getting at with them?"

"I have nothing to go on but the spirit of the moment. That's what I'm going to have to trust... Say, would you take a look in the glove compartment?"

"Hold on—I know what you used to keep in there."

"Ease up, it's just a flashlight. I think I might have an old one... Hey, am I ever glad to hear you laugh."

She rummaged around and found it, then shut the glove box and laid her head back on the seat, her hand around the headrest. I remembered that. Soon we lapsed into a silence, familiar and deep. I turned off Main Street onto River Road.

"Sarah, you were right. The other night, when I was moving my stuff out of Cynthia's. I damn near kept on going."

She was silent. Then, "I guess I'd better grow up fast."

I laid an arm around her shoulders. She didn't move away.

"Matt, you called me 'love.' Do you know that?"

We said nothing more for several blocks.

"Let's not push it, Matt, okay? You resolve your marriage and I'll take care of mine. I know I have to do that. Quit papering everything over, playing Prom Queen. But... but then, when all of this is over, why... Oh, Matt, I can't say it. There's so much inside. And I'm so afraid there's no time. The college will fold and you'll be... "

I squeezed her shoulder, and we rode some more in silence.

River Road was an upscale address, as far as the city limits went. One of the original residential boulevards, it was lined with elms and paved with old red brick, so you heard the road hum and felt it as you drove along, just like Winthrop. A half dozen marvelous, musty mansions sat high up on the road at the edge of the bluff, where it peered down over the valley and encircled the southeast end of town like an antique necklace.

But at the very edge of town, River Road dropped like a rock down the length of the bluff to the flatlands by the river. And so did property values. There were houses down on the Bottoms (before the river changed course, there'd been more) but they never held value on the flood plain. The houses that remained were obscured from the road—roofs peeling, lawns gone to thistle. Engulfed in groves of cottonwoods.

It was dark down at the far end of River Road, past the streetlights. Only a waxing yellow moon, half full and low on the horizon. The last cicadas of late fall were chirping faintly from the bare branches of the cottonwoods. I drove slowly, pulling off to the side of the road every twenty yards or so, as Sarah shined a flashlight on the mailboxes.

She had the address for Channing Coe that I'd got from the COGWEB, but it was hard to read the mailboxes. The flashlight had a cracked lens and the batteries were low, the light bulb flickering and fading. But three or four miles down the road, she gave a soft whistle. She'd spotted it.

There was a road alongside the mailbox, leading down toward the river. All I could see of it were two ruts and a thousand tangled branches. I started to leave the car in the path, but pulled it back out of sight, in the bushes.

"Geez, Sarah, I'm glad you thought to put on jeans and tennis shoes."

"We small town girls have our virtues."

"Tell me about it!"

She clipped me in the ribs.

Sarah took the flashlight and, as an afterthought, I grabbed the cell phone from my satchel and stuck it in my back pocket.

"Matt, do you have any idea what's back here?"

We were thirty yards down the road, and I couldn't see five feet in front of me.

"I've heard some tales, but I don't know I've ever…YOW!" I caught a tree limb in the forehead.

"Look, Sarah, we'd better slow down. And let's turn off that flashlight—we may need the batteries. Plus, if anyone's down there, there's no point in announcing our arrival."

We stopped talking, but it was as though we didn't need to. Now and then we'd touch hands in the dark. In tandem, in synch, I was thinking. Then, WHAP! Another overhanging branch. I'd better pay attention to my surroundings. I peered into the darkness, in the dim light of the moon.

As we rounded a corner, I thought I saw something—a light far down the road. It disappeared behind a thicket, but then I saw it again. A candle or maybe a kerosene lamp, glowing faintly behind a window. And I saw a face in the flickering light.

I reached back for Sarah's hand and she came up beside me. "Shh. See that clearing, on the far side of the window? Let's go up the road that far and cut across to where we can see inside. But stay at the edge of the brush—we may need to take cover."

It was a big house, I could see that. Two stories tall, with an attic, and a gabled roof. A side porch. Somehow, I'd assumed there was nothing but shacks down here. But this place looked like it had housed some prosperous merchant, back when people did business on the river from the Bottoms. I'd heard there had been a levee and a street full of stores, till the hundred-year flood when the river had decided to join the neighborhood.

We crept on another thirty feet toward the clearing. Now I could see inside. Tattered curtains, and a candle at the center of a table. But there was no one in sight. I kept moving closer, peering in the shadows of the lambent light. And then, suddenly, the figure came back in view, the face flush up against the pane.

"Sarah, I've seen that woman!" I was at the edge of the road. "Down at the police..." was as far as I got. As I took a step forward, the road bank gave way and I tumbled into a ditch filled with rocks and mud and brambles. My ankle snagged a root, and it twisted like a corkscrew.

"yow!" I screamed, in spite of myself.

As I peered up from the ditch, the light went out.

"Matt, are you okay?"

I felt my ankle. It was sore, but I could put weight on it. "And now, for my next number..."

She pushed me back. "Stay down, they might see us. Look, you started to say something—in the middle of your swan dive. Who'd you see? Who was it?"

As I started to answer, the candle reappeared, although it was back in the room; the light was dimmer. And then slowly it receded until the room returned to darkness.

"It was that Agnes," I hissed. "You know who I mean. From the cop shop. Works for Clodfelter, gets him his coffee. That little rodent of a woman at the front desk."

"I think I know … Shh, I thought I saw the light again. Around the far side of the house. Matt, get your head down!"

"No way, Jose. This ditch water's freezing. Come on, let's make a break for the bushes."

We scrambled up the far side of the ditch, away from the road, and dived into the foliage. But before we could find cover, a bright light glared around the corner of the house. No candle this time. It was a foot-long, high-powered flashlight, the kind cops shine on suspects. Agnes was wielding the light with her left hand. In her right hand, she held a revolver.

The flashlight made a sweeping arc as it bore across the clearing, closer and closer to where we crouched behind a veil of branches. One swipe of the torch, and we were sure to be seen. If a twig snapped, she'd hear us.

Now the light was ten feet away, stabbing at the edge of the under-brush. Sarah laid her head on the back of my shoulder, and I could feel her tremble. But I couldn't think of what else to do.

And then, far down the road, we heard voices.

Agnes must have heard them, too. For she froze stock still, the light at our feet. Then she did something odd. She turned off the flashlight and set it on the ground. And with both hands on her pistol, aimed downward like a divining rod, she stalked across the clearing and started down the road.

In a moment, the night was quiet again. Only the intermittent murmuring of cicadas.

"Matt, she has a gun! We need to get out of here."

"Yeah, and it looked like a police revolver. So, tell me again why you think Chief Clodfelter can't make it down here."

"I don't know what to think. Except that we need to get … "

"Wait. Did you hear that?" At first I thought it might be down the road. Women's voices, at least two of them, coming this way. It sounded as though they were arguing, growing louder.

But, no, it was another sound. It was coming from the house. A sort of moaning.

"Listen, Sarah. Do you hear it? Upstairs, from that window... Here, I'm going in that house to see who's there." I pulled the cell phone from my jeans and pressed it into her hand, told her to slip back in the bushes. "If worst comes to worst, you can call somebody—assuming you can figure out who. Till a minute ago, I might have suggested Kyle Clodfelter."

I scooped up the flashlight Agnes had abandoned as I ran across the clearing. It had the weight of a night stick, a serious flare. In a few steps, I was on the porch to the back door.

The door gave a squeal, but there was no other sound. I shut it and stood immobile till my eyes could take the dark. No point advertising my presence with the flashlight.

I seemed to be in a long hall with a window at the far end, shuttered tight. Thin, milky, moonlight sifted through the slats. I could see a closed door on my right and a staircase ahead, to the left of the window. I crept slowly, stopping to listen for any sound beyond my footsteps. And then, as I reached the railing at the foot of the stairs, I heard the sound again. It was unmistakable this time, that groaning.

The stairs creaked loud, but I paid no attention. If anyone else were lurking in the house, they'd have heard me by now. There! The moaning sound. As I cleared the top stair, I could make out a door on either side of me. I hugged the wall and stood stock still until I heard the sound again. It was coming from the room on my left. The door was ajar.

As I stepped across the threshold, I flicked on the flashlight and cast it around. The room had the dimensions of a master bedroom. It was long and wide, with a window at the far end. In the center was a huge, four-poster, canopied bed—the kind they charge a hundred bucks a night for in bed and breakfast inns.

But the guest they had in this place wasn't paying. He was red-faced, thrashing feverishly—straining at two broad leather straps that had him pinned down, a pillowcase knotted in his mouth to muzzle him. His shirt had come loose from his trousers, pulled up high above his stomach and I could see strips of bandage on his belly. Dark, encrusted blood between them. In two strides I was across the room, unraveling the straps and the gag.

He appeared to be trying to talk, but he couldn't—either drugged or in delirium. There was a stench like rancid buttermilk. I felt his forehead; he had a fever.

"Oh, Jesus, Jeb! What've they done to you? Can you hear me?"

I told him I was going for help, although I didn't want to leave him. "I left my cell phone with Sarah. I'll be right back. Hang in there now, okay?"

But as I stood up to leave, he became even more agitated and his eyes grew wider. He seemed to be flailing his head toward the door. I glanced back, but saw nothing. I ran to the window that looked down on the clearing. And I was about to shout to Sarah, "I found him!" when I saw the light just down the road.

There they were, around the bend. Three of them, with Agnes out front. The other two were following single file, about six feet apart. They appeared to be carrying something between them. As they came nearer, I saw it was a stretcher. What were they doing? Coming for Jeb? One thing was certain: whatever their mission, they weren't in accord. The two at the rear were yelling at Agnes, chewing her out. I leaned out farther, trying to hear.

And then I heard another sound, behind me. A faint squeak on the stairs, and a rush of footsteps through the doorway. I ducked down and pulled my head in, just in time to glimpse the figure racing round the foot of the bed. Before I could straighten up, I was grabbed by the hair, my head snapped back. And then a thick, bristly rope scraped round my neck.

I struggled to get free, but the attacker was on my back, legs wrapping my thighs. I fought for breath as the rope twisted tighter. My chest was burning. Gasping, I grabbed the rope and tried to pry it. I couldn't. I knew I didn't have much time.

Slowly I let myself go limp, sagging to my knees, and for an instant I felt my assailant relax. That was all I needed. As I fell to the floor, I groped for the flashlight—and found it! There was a point at one end to tie a lanyard. I got a good grip on the shaft as I struggled to one knee. And with my last, strangled breath, I sucked up all my strength and rammed it backward.

There was a whoosh of breath and a male squeal, as the rope slacked for a second—time enough to free my neck and collapse against the wall. I was panting for air, my vision blotted, but I could make out my opponent.

He wore some sort of hood, and seemed to be clumsily shifting the eye slots as he got up from the floor. Pretty good-sized guy, but poorly coordinated. I pushed off from the wall, sucking wind as I circled him, brandishing the flashlight like a hatchet.

"Have a good ... gander, you asshole," I gasped. "Just as ... soon's I get ... my breath ... I'm gonna stick this ... up ... "

Now I saw him peering through his eye slits. And as he craned his neck for a closer look, the sight of me seemed to undo him. His elbows flapped as he threw down the rope. And with a half skip and a pirouette, he lit out for the door.

"Come back, you fucking coward!" I took off across the bedroom, but was three steps behind him and still groggy. I knew I had but one chance. As he came around the railing at the top of the stairs, I dived straight across it and lunged for his head.

He ducked, but not quite fast enough. And I missed him, but not entirely. As he clambered down the stairs and out the door, I chased him as far as the back stoop.

I stood there, scanning the clearing, the flashlight in one hand. His long, black hooded cape was in the other.

18

"Whaddaya mean, you suspected I was in on it! You don't talk like that to an officer of the law!"

"Bullshit, Clodfelter. I'm sick of this. Here, I just got attacked in that house down in the Bottoms, that place you won't even visit. Look at these rope burns on my neck! And then we end up hiding in the bushes—scratched up, no telling if we picked up poison oak or ivy—and who do suppose is after us but fucking Agnes."

"Matt!"

"Sorry, Sarah ... That Agnes, who's a member of your staff. What the hell do you expect me to think?"

The chief picked up the black sackcloth hood I'd tossed in his lap and held it to the light. He propped it open and peered inside. Then he let it fall on the desktop and transferred his gaze to Sarah and me.

He tipped back in his big purple chair and rotated slowly toward the wall. I saw the chair begin to shake, his shoulders heaving. Finally, he turned himself around and took to rummaging through his desk for a Kleenex. When he looked up again, there were tears of laughter streaming down his face.

"Oh, it's not (sniff) humorous ... I know that. Nothin' funny about it. I mean, locking up my secretary in a holding cell. Carting poor Collard off to the hospital, intensive care. Nothin' (snort) to laugh at ... But if you could have seen your face just then ... Beet-red, bug-eyed." He doubled up, helplessly rocking.

Sarah and I glanced at one another, then back at Clodfelter. And we started snickering. It was totally absurd, but a break in the action—a respite from the stresses of the night.

None of us had been to bed at all and, till the sun had come up, I'd had no sense of the hour. The chief switched on a tape recorder, and we began to tell our story. After seeing his kaleidoscope of emotions, I found I trusted him again.

212

I told him how I'd stumbled around in the clearing until I'd heard Sarah call from the bushes. There was no way I'd have found her back there.

Then we'd heard the others coming up the road. "Did you call Clodfelter?" I'd asked Sarah, after a very long hug that I neglected to mention.

"I tried, but I can't get this phone to work. Here, look."

"Well, all you do is punch in the numbers. And hit Send."

"Oh, 'Send.' So that's it."

"Chief, I guess she'd never used a cell phone."

Clodfelter slapped down his pen and started giggling again. We all had a bad case of delirium. Then he turned dead serious. "All right, let's cut to the chase. You call me up and we send down the squad car and ambulance. You're right. I still can't go down there, not after what happened to my daughter. And it's a good thing those gals hauled down that stretcher. We'd never have got the ambulance down that road."

"Well," I continued, "After we overheard their conversation in the clearing, we knew why they were there. They'd come for Jeb. Those two girls had relented."

Sarah interjected, "You know why they changed their minds, Chief? You should have heard Matt's lecture in their cult class."

He raised his eyebrows and nodded. "But, why'd they take him off in the first place? Then try to do that foolish tattoo. With an athame. That's what they call it."

Clodfelter pulled a small black dagger from his desk drawer and tossed it on the hood. "Picked this up once in an anthro course. Guess I've got me the rudiments of an occult collection."

"Chief, from what we overheard, it was what I'd suspected, from the reading I've been doing for that class. It's an ancient rite per-formed at autumn—takes on more importance in the presence of drought. A ritual sacrifice of an aging leader—an attempt to purge the land. They tried to enact it with a tattoo."

He stared at me intently. "So, do you think they meant to kill Jeb Collard?"

"I doubt they did, nor Julian either. It **was** the same rite someone tried on him. But they would have—in fact, may yet have done him in—the way they left those wounds to fester."

"Then there's Agnes," he said sadly. "Hey, I knew she was moon-lighting some as a security guard, but as to her whereabouts? I had no idea. Nor who was employing her. I guess I'm just gonna have to interrogate her, 'bout all that. I hate interrogations."

"I'd say she was more than a hired guard," Sarah commented. "Wasn't that your impression, Matt? I think she was trying to join up with this, this..."

"Sisters of Aradia."

"Right. To get in this cult as a kind of novice. She kept arguing with the two who showed up with the litter."

"Gwendolyn and Penelope."

"Those two. She kept going on about how she had her instruc-tions from the Goddess. She said the Goddess was unavailable, but that she still expected Agnes to follow her orders."

"While the others claimed she could still call on the Grand Master," I added. "They said he was still around."

"Except [she was snickering again], except he'd just come hot-footing it down the road, hollering that Matt was after him."

"I meant to ask you about that, Sarah," I said. "Did you get a look at the guy? Something about him seemed familiar back there when he was trying to play horsey."

"He was sort of a pedant, I guess you'd say. I didn't get a good look, he came tearing across the clearing so fast. But he had on granny glasses and an odd haircut, parted in the middle. Kind of bookish. Like your stereotype of a college professor."

"That's about how he fought... Did they call him by name?"

"Something like 'Shannon.'"

"Oh, wow. Channing. Of course. My late, great colleague—turned Grand Master. Of course, I should have known. That was Channing Coe!"

Clodfelter looked preoccupied, almost pensive. He glanced at the clock on the wall, then down at the hood and dagger lying on his desktop. Finally, he leaned across his desk to shut off the tape recorder.

"Well, I expect we'll learn a lot more from those two young women in your class, before we're through. But I need to get up to the hospital, see if there's any change in Collard."

He sat back and eyed the two of us again. "Jeb owes a lot to you both, going down in there. Much longer with that infection, and they said we'd have lost him for sure."

Sarah and I parted at the purple police station, although not as I'd planned. As we stepped out to the street, she tugged at my sleeve and drew me back inside the door, into the alcove. She set her arms around my waist, and raised her lips for a kiss. I reached down with both hands and cupped her, pulled her to me.

She drew back. "What on earth are you doing?"

"Just warming up, I hope. Look, let's go grab some breakfast and we can crash at my place. Get some sleep, and … whatever."

She stared at me, wide-eyed. "Matt, we're both married. You know we can't do that."

"Why not?"

"Don't you remember what I said last night?"

"About attending to our lives? I agree. Sure, you bet. But you don't have to always go by the script. For what we've been through, Sarah, what the hell—we've earned a little R & R."

She lowered her head and looked aside. "You know, I don't believe I even heard that. Is, is that all it means to you to make … " When she looked up again, she was crying.

"Oh, shit, Sarah. Come off it! And, no, I won't apologize for cussing. I'm getting tired of that. I mean it! Look, this feels entirely too familiar. It was one thing to go through this fucking contest— and I mean that quite literally, Sarah—that vying for your virginity, back in school days."

"Matt, stop it! You're being crude, and cruel."

"Yes, you're right, but I won't stop. See, I don't play that game. Not anymore. As a matter of fact, I don't think it's played much outside Kansas. Oh, Christ, Sarah. I mean, I really didn't know it until right this minute, but I am still so furious … "

As she flew out the door, my rage dissolved to sorrow. I collapsed against the door jamb and wept big, bulbous tears of exhaustion and self-pity. Two lovers lost in the past 48 hours.

In time, I got up and gathered myself. Made to leave. But then a shadow through the glass door to the station caught my eye. I saw a figure standing behind the counter, in uniform. I wondered how long Kyle Clodfelter had been watching.

Squire had called the faculty meeting for nine o'clock Saturday morning. An ambitious time to roust academic types from their weekend lairs. Especially today. It was a raw, gray, dismal morning. I'd slept all afternoon and right through the night.

As I slogged up the hill toward campus, I saw Tyler Ware, a professor in the English Department, stumble out of his house and head up the sidewalk. Then Wellington Withers in history, who lived across the street, called out to Ty and caught up with him. I watched them trudge along from a couple of blocks back—briefcases swaying like pendulums, shaking their heads in commiseration over some sort of mutual, academic complaint.

I was shocked when they turned east at the corner, not north toward campus. Then I recalled. The meeting was at the Congregational Church. The lecture hall in the science building was still boarded up, a shambles from the last faculty meeting and the debacle of the bell tower. Maybe that was the first item on Roger Squire's agenda. I supposed he'd targeted a rich alum who'd pony up for the repairs, in exchange for a brass plaque with his name on it.

I rounded the corner, toward the gray stone Congregational Church. The church had a two-story bell tower of its own and a marquee that listed the following Sunday's sermon. I squinted at the sign from a block off, wondering what Squire might have come up with for tomorrow. He'd surely have a knack for sermon titles—sound bite theology.

Oh, shit. Sure enough. The sign came into focus:

Mayflower Congregational Church
Rev. Roger Squire, Minister
IF YOU'RE LOOKING
FOR A SIGN FROM GOD,
THIS IS IT!

The sanctuary was a downer—sparsely filled and tenebrous on the cloudy day. But the altar was all laid out for the service tomorrow. Brass candles on white linen. Trays of communion cups. A novel setting for a faculty meeting. I peered across the pews and spotted Harley and Hazel in the last filled row. I slid in behind them.

"So, what's on the agenda, guys?"

Hazel shrugged her shoulders and shot me a smile. "No idea. But look who's up there behind the lectern."

It was Cynthia. She seemed taken up with some notes on her lap. But then she stood up and shuffled some papers on the stand. She looked sleek and appealing in a dark blue pantsuit, in the way a new car in a showroom is attractive. Glancing at her watch, she sat back down. If she took any notice of the faculty, scattered among the pews, she didn't acknowledge them.

"What's going on? I'm the last one to ask," Harley hissed in a full-throated whisper. "But, I am something of an authority on biology. Say, Matt, you have any idea how to tell the difference between a green toad and a horny toad?"

Hazel poked him in the ribs: "Harley!"

"Why, the green toad says 'rib-it, rib-it.' The horny toad goes 'rub-it, rub-it!'"

I saw Cynthia cringe up there in the chancel. The acoustics must be better than I'd thought. Now she started scanning the faculty, then turning back to something on her lap. I knew what she was doing—sketching some of us. It was a way of distancing herself, objectifying the crowd. I looked at my watch; it was well past time for the meeting to start.

Just then, Roger Squire came striding into the sanctuary, his head cocked forward and his elbows pumping like pistons. He looked like the business end of a locomotive. The presidential pastor wore a somber, black business suit that echoed the shadows under his eyes. For a moment, I felt sympathetic. I guess his dual career was catching up with him. The guy looked fried.

As he climbed the stairs to the chancel, Squire turned to take his accustomed place in a great oak chair behind the pulpit. He leaned down on one arm of it, his head in an open hand as in meditation. But then he sat up with a start, and blinked as he perused his audience. Not a parishioner in sight, never mind a true believer. Nothing but a disheveled bunch of disaffected faculty. It was about then he remembered what he was there for.

Squire got up and, with a glance in Cynthia's direction, stepped up to the pulpit. He seemed not only tired but hesitant this morning. Maybe he hadn't rehearsed this scene before summoning the faculty to the inner sanctum. For a moment, he stood and fiddled with his notes. The place was deathly quiet.

He began: "Friends of the faculty, welcome to this gathering of…"

I heard a door creak and shuffling feet behind me. It sounded like a whole troop of latecomers, clambering into the back pews. Squire stood silent, his brow furrowing as he watched them.

"Friends of the family, welcome to this faculty of Hopewell…" Something didn't jibe, but Squire didn't miss a beat. "You know, my friends, a thought occurred to me on the way over here this morning. Why, a human being is like a bicycle, and so is every human institution. To make progress, we must go forward. The moment we stop—why, we fall and we fail."

There was a buzz on my backside, and I pulled out my pager. I recognized the number on the green liquid screen. It was the college gym. Oh my God! Could they be relaying news of Collard?

I whipped my cell phone from my briefcase and sped back to the vestibule. En route, I got a glimpse of a long, dark delegation in the last row. There must have been a dozen. Another man sat alone, across the aisle from the others. Something struck me as odd. It was his hair, round and flouncy, like an Afro from the 1970s. As I passed by, he looked up. It seemed he gave a start.

I shut the door to the sanctuary and dialed up the number to the gym.

"'Lo?"

"Matt Bradshaw, here. Did somebody call?"

"Yo. Hey, Coach, we been trackin' you. Thought you was comin' by last night, 'fo' practice."

"Hey, I'm sorry, Jamal. I was zonked. But did you hear the news?" I told him about Jeb Collard.

"Now do some work on that crossover dribble, okay? I should be over by noon, and I'll want a demonstration when I get there."

As I stepped back in the sanctuary, Squire's spiel was still in process. I wondered what priceless pearls I'd missed.

"So, let us remember, friends, that the game of life is a contest in which the outcome is ever in doubt. Like a football game where the ball can always take that odd bounce. Even late in the fourth quarter!"

There was a restless rustling in the pews. Across the chancel, Cynthia got up and stood behind the lectern. But Squire didn't see her. He rambled on for a few more balls and bounces. Maybe if she'd give her chest a jiggle ... Finally, he glimpsed her from the corner of his eye.

"Yes, uh, well ... we could go on with that theme. But, I see that our provost is ready to get to the meat of the meeting, and we do have a full agenda. As the first order of business, it is my personal pleasure to introduce a group of young men whom we've been eagerly awaiting. Members of the faculty, please welcome the new men's varsity basketball squad of Hopewell College!"

There was a smattering of applause as a dozen young black men unbent from the back pew and began making their way down the center aisle. They strode in a subtle sort of order. Not quite in unison, but swinging their left arms in rhythm, somewhat ominously. They were clad in black Hopewell College sweatshirts and black knit watch caps pulled halfway down their ears and to their eyebrows. A sort of neo-Neanderthal look, a la MTV.

These guys were big, all right. That was clear enough as they came looming out of the shadows to the front of the church. But the last one in line dwarfed them all. He was maybe seven feet tall, and wide as the center aisle across his shoulders. It appeared he might have stuffed a coat rack under his sweatshirt.

As they came forward, they faced the chancel. Then, at a silent signal, they swung around to face the faculty as one. And at that, the applause evaporated. From the back of the church, where I was standing, I heard a muffled gasp. The twelve players stared down at the faculty and staff and more or less glowered.

For a full minute, Squire himself stood immobile in apparent awe of the kind of clientele Intelcor had seen fit to ship him.

Then he gathered himself, master of ceremonies again. "And now, one final introduction," he exclaimed. "Together with the new team, our colleagues at the Gray Group have assigned us a new coach. I'm told that he's a nationally recognized authority, and not just on the game of basketball. It seems he is the author of two widely regarded books in the emerging disciplines of multicultural consciousness and diversity studies."

The solitary figure who had sat across from the team rose slowly to his feet. As he made his own procession down the aisle, he half turned toward me and I got a closer look at him. He was a tall man, about my height, with a complexion the shade of stained mahogany and an Afro like a big black ram.

In the instant before he turned back, our eyes met and I felt a shock of recognition. Even with the wig and all the applications of Man Tan, I'd have known him in a crowd.

"Ladies and gentlemen," Squire announced, "I give you our new head basketball coach and Distinguished Professor in the new Department of Multicultural Studies: Dr. Harold Alabaster!"

To a more spirited but still perfunctory round of applause, the noted scholar/jock marched down the aisle and took his place before the team. As he turned to face the faculty, my jaw fell. I stared at this apparition. Tried to imagine why Harold Alabaster, the Great Gray Hope—dean at Eastbourne University, when last observed—would turn up here at Hopewell.

I'm sure my eyes were wide and my mouth agape as I stumbled back down the aisle to my place behind Harley and Hazel. As I leaned forward to whisper what I knew about this dude, I caught sight of Cynthia. She was standing at the lectern with a wry smile, an eerie fire in her eye. As she stared my way, her lips rounded slowly into two daunting words: WATCH IT.

I took another look at Alabaster and my mind cleared. I returned her smile, and mouthed two words: STUFF IT.

Squire spoke up as the smattering of applause died down. "Dr. Alabaster, it has just occurred to me that you might like to come up here in the pulpit and say a few words to your new colleagues." (I could guess when that idea "occurred" to him. About the time Cynthia handed him his script.)

Alabaster spun on his heel and, bounding up the several steps to the chancel, barged into the pulpit. Squire barely beat a retreat to his big oak chair to avoid being flattened. The squad remained at the front of the church, hands clasped behind them at an ominous parade rest. They stared across the sanctuary toward the great window where stained-glass Jesus gazed back in return.

"My friends," Alabaster began in his booming voice. "My new friends of Hopewell College. My brand new friends … I bring you greetings from your friends and colleagues at Intelcor. To date, I believe, you have met only two of us—your charming provost, Cynthia Lothamer, uh, Bradshaw, and myself.

"And, I must say that, try as you may, you won't be gettin' us confused. Am I right about that, now, Cynthia? You know, no one has ever accused me of being charming!"

Cynthia smiled to an echo of nervous laughter from the pews.

"In a moment or two—an' you know, I ain' a-gonna be up here long—in a minute, your president, the Reverend Squire, who has filled in here so admirably … why, he'll be fillin' you in on our brand new department of multicultural studies."

I shot a look at Squire, and wondered if he'd picked up on the "filled in." And the title "Reverend"—not "President"—Squire.

And then, that fast, Alabaster dropped his street talk for academic argot. He reported some results of Intelcor's research into the demographics of higher education.

(After striking bottom in 1994, the ranks of traditional college age students will climb steadily until the year 2008. Since 1983, tuition revenue has grown at twice the rate of inflation.) "Boom times a-comin'!" he rumbled in his big Afro basso.

"Still, we must recognize that the higher education market is changing. It is becoming differentiated, an industry of niche markets. Colleges will be required to learn the subtleties of sophisticated marketing strategies. Not merely if they are to achieve maximum preferred enrollment, but if they're to survive!"

There was a sepulchral silence among the faculty. Now he had their full attention.

"So, what is called for, my friends, is fresh thinking about new techniques to identify and serve new markets. And, in addition, a new commitment to excellence in enrollment management."

I saw some gray heads turn with bewildered expressions, as the profs tried to figure out what the hell this big black fellow was saying. By this time, they'd surely concluded that Alabaster was no ordinary basketball coach. But what was he doing out here? That's what I wondered, too.

"In short, my friends, we need to be alert to innovative market opportunities—even new institutions, if we're to keep pace with these changing times.

"And that brings me to a message that has been stirring in my heart and in my mind from the moment I awoke this morning, my first day here in Kansas. It is our corporate mission statement at Intelcor. A testament—a creed—that I knew I had to share—was called to share—with each of you this morning."

He bowed his head and breathed deep as he laid an open palm on a railing of the pulpit. The big, beefy hand started slapping in time, as Alabaster raised his eyes to the heavens. The squad of ballplayers below him began to shuffle, bobbing heads in cadence. At last, he drew a great breath and thundered:

"FORGET THE PAST."

"Forget the past!" the players echoed.

"THINK FAST."

"Think fast!"

"WHAT'S NEXT?"

"What's next? What's next? What's next?" The squad gave an antiphonal chant, four by four, all down the line. Now they were bopping in a shuffling shag dance.

"All together, now. Let's us all join in." Alabaster shook his big Afro like a sheepdog with fleas. "Every-body! All family! You profs, you brothas on the team!" The players began clapping in rhythm, bouncing on the balls of their feet.

"FORGET THE PAST."

"Forget the past . . . "

Behind the lectern, even Cynthia began to step it out. She swayed as she waved her arms, working the crowd like a Big Ten cheerleader. It was a side of her I'd never seen, and the effect was intoxicating. I watched some of the younger profs jump up from their pews and join in. Soon, Squire leapt from his oaken chair, dancing and chanting, his fate for the moment forgotten.

"FORGET THE PAST."

"THINK FAST."

"WHAT'S NEXT?" ("What's next? What's next? What's next?")

The chant went on for a good five minutes, until Alabaster pulled a white handkerchief from his vest pocket and waved it in the air, as the participants applauded. Maybe a fourth of the faculty had been moved to join the celebration. Even Harley had been up in the aisle, his belly bouncing to the primal beat, although Hazel hadn't budged from her pew.

As he stepped down from the pulpit, Alabaster wiped his brow and a pink-gray streak appeared on his forehead. I wondered if anyone else had noticed.

Cynthia took over the meeting as Alabaster marched back up the aisle and out of the sanctuary with a broad smile, waving his handkerchief, his retinue of jocks striding behind him.

"Well, now that we're relaxed and can put our minds to work again, I want to share some wonderful news," she announced. "For some time, we have all been concerned—not only about Coach Collard, certainly, but about the teams here during the past few years. Clearly, the record has been less than all of us had hoped for. Our colleagues at Intelcor have shared this concern. And they concluded that a new coach and a new team were in order."

There was squirming in the pews, and a round of muttering. For my part, I could only stare at Cynthia. Her poise and competence, not to mention the cheerleading. My mind went back to the first time I'd noticed her in class. That time she ran out of my office. And the day she'd turned up in my life again and asked me out to brunch. Same week I got the job notice from Hopewell.

Had I ever really known her at all?

"Our concern, of course, was what to do about the scholarships that had been awarded to the original team," she continued. "And, I'm happy to announce that this problem has been resolved. We have just received word that, as a first step toward our upcoming major in criminal justice—that's another item on our agenda—Hopewell

College has been awarded twelve full scholarships in the new federal Police Corps Program."

"Oh, yes, the Peace Corps!" exclaimed a graying professor from the front pew.

"No, no, the Police Corps," Cynthia repeated. "This is a very now program, very nineties. You see, the Police Corps offers scholarships of $7500 a year to students who agree to serve four years as law enforcement officers upon graduation. Any course of study. And of course, minorities are especially encouraged..."

That did it.

"Madam Provost," I began as I rose from my pew and moved to the aisle. "If I may offer a comment..." I started up the stairs to the chancel.

"Dean Bradshaw!" Squire stepped up. "If there is time for discussion, you may be assured..."

We met at the altar, by the brass cross and candelabra. As we crossed paths, before the embroidered cloths and the communion trays, I took him by the collar. There was a throttled sound as I twisted the knot in his necktie, his face florid, eyes bulging.

"It's over, Squire," I told him. "All over. It's gone far enough. Forget the past! Think fast! This is what comes next."

I was still groggy from the night before last and God knows what I might have done to him. But as I hoisted him off the chancel floor, I heard a familiar voice from behind the lectern.

"Go for it, Babe. You know he's got it coming!"

I shot a glance at Cynthia, and shuddered. Of course, that was just what they wanted. And then I heard the echo of another voice, in memory: "Matt, I just thank God you're back!"

I looked at Squire and let him go. And I stepped up in the pulpit.

19

I t was two or three hours before the adrenaline flushed and I stopped rushing around. After dashing out of the faculty meeting, following an impromptu sermonette from the pulpit, I raced over to the gym to deliver the news. Alabaster and his minions had agreed to a winner-take-all-the-scholarships game.

That was the good news. The sobering news was that the game was slated for tomorrow night.

I put the team through an hour of defensive sets, then ran through some set-screens on offense. We worked a lot on "hedging," where a defender feints which way he'll go around a screen. "It's the nemesis of point guards. Who knows what that guy's gonna do? But there's one cardinal rule: Keep an eye on the hedge man, but make your own move. Don't ever take your cues from a hedge man."

It was the same theme I'd addressed from the pulpit.

When I left practice, LaRon had plans for a half-hour shoot-around and then running some laps after that.

"That's enough then, fellas," I'd told them. "No more ball till tomorrow night. I want you to show up rested and relaxed. So go do whatever works to get yourselves in that condition, okay?

"And that could include some studying!"

I was still on a tear as I sped into the hospital parking lot, brakes squealing in a streak of black rubber. But as I was slamming the car door, something stopped me.

It was the setting sun. The hospital lay bathed in the last, lambent rays of late October—its cinderblock walls alive with light, transfigured from tan to terra cotta. The building was simply glowing. As I stood there in wonderment, a couple waved from across the street. They were bundled up in chamois shirts, sweeping leaves into smoldering piles. I just savored the scent, the sense of home.

Inside, the redolence of roasting leaves gave way to the acrid scent of an antiseptic hospital. Wherever you were, they all smelled the same. The place was ominously quiet.

"So, how's he doing, Bev?"

She looked up from the nurses' station and gave me a grimace that I took for a smile. "About the same as this morning, which is somewhat better'n when they trucked him in last night."

Bev dropped her deep voice lower. "But he'd be doin' a whole lot better if that wife of his'd go on home. Been yammerin' on that telephone all day from his bedside. Can't boot her out."

I said I'd try to persuade her, that I'd take over if they'd let me stay past visiting hours.

"Hey, Dean, you'll never catch me kickin' you outta here." She gave me a genuine grin. "You're a guy that cares, and people feel that. Even in a coma. Maybe especially then."

Emily greeted me with a gripping hug. I could tell she knew my part in rescuing Jeb, but she just swept up her things and headed for the door. I said I'd stay, and that I'd call her if there were a change in his condition.

After she'd gone, I stood and studied Jeb. Reached over and kneaded his shoulder. Then I walked back out to the nurses' station. Bev was posting a sign—VISITING HOURS ARE OVER—in the middle of the hallway. I caught her arm.

"Bev, is this the same kind of coma we saw with Bronwyn?"

"Whaddaya mean?"

"I don't know. It just seems a bit different. His breathing, for one thing. It's more rhythmic, maybe."

"Well, you're right. We think he's been given some kinda narcotic, but we can't identify it. Doc sent a blood sample down to the lab in Wichita. Should get word back in the morning. Between that and the infection—those damn fools. If they're gonna try and tattoo a guy, why don't they at least have the sense to sterilize ... Say, I'm going up to Pizza Hut. You want anything?"

I gave her some money and wandered back to Jeb's room. Now he was snoring. His color looked more normal, his face less florid, but he still seemed worn and frail. There was a plastic clip on his upper lip with tubes running into his nostrils. I pulled up a chair to the side of his bed. And before long, I found myself in a one-way conversation.

"It wasn't much of a sermon, Jeb. After I tossed Squire back in his chair and got up in the pulpit. And I'm afraid I started railing at that faculty. I said I knew there was a plan at work—Intelcor had designs on Hopewell College—but I wasn't sure what for. And the worst thing we could do was sit around and speculate.

"We have to act, not react. That was what I told 'em. I went on about defense in basketball—splitting the screen, how you don't take your cues from the hedge man. Well, they had no clue. But I saw some of 'em taking notes. And that really got me.

"Look, I told them. Here you go again, reacting. You're setting yourselves up to be the audience at your own execution. And these goons are gonna be selling you tickets! At that point, I guess I turned around and pointed at Squire.

"And just then it came to me. Why, we'll have a fund-raiser to rebuild the clock tower. Winner-take-all-the-scholarships, and we'll sell tickets to the game!"

That was when Ty Ware had come forward. The English professor. He couldn't tell a ball game from a bungee jump. But he stood up and asked when I wanted to play. Tomorrow night, I told him, and he took off down the street after Alabaster and his goon squad. A few minutes later, he came running back, panting. Alabaster had agreed. Seven o'clock in the gym, tomorrow night.

"Well, that's most of it, Jeb. At the end, I went back to the point about hedging. You can't spend your life taking cues from somebody else's game plan. I offered 'em an alternative as a course of action, and this ball game was the one way I knew how."

I flopped back in the visitor's chair, uncertain how Jeb had taken to my oration. Well, at least he hadn't got up and walked out. I recalled how the faculty had reacted. Some of them applauded, some people I hadn't expected. And Harley had stuck his hand out in the aisle for a low-five as I walked out.

I took out my notepad and began sketching out a few plays for the game.

"Hey, Dean," came a guttural voice. "Did you set up shop in here? We're gonna have to start charging rent."

The pizza smelled fabulous. Bev gave me some change and told me she'd leave us guys alone for a while. What a teammate. I listened to her steps slap down the hall. Put a set of cleats on Bev, and you've got yourself an NFL lineman. Shoulders like a hod carrier. And a heart just as broad.

As I turned to the pizza—pepperoni and black olive—my pocket buzzed. I took out my pager and scanned the screen. It was a number I'd learned by heart. I dialed up the Hoof'n Horn.

Hazel picked up the phone at the bar: "So, how is he?"

I glanced at Jeb. "About the same, although his color's better." I told her about the drug analysis. "I've brought along some work and sent Emily home. Guess I'm here for a spell."

"Well, you might have company. That's why I called. But, say, that was some performance you put on this morning. What are you doing, practicing to be the next King Kong?"

I told her I wasn't proud. "But something's about to happen here and it's past time to cut out all the bullshit. Intelcor's ready to make a move."

"Matt, I agree. I don't know if you saw them, but there was a crew out surveying the campus this morning. Now why would they be doing that? Somewhere, these people must have their plan in writing. Maybe a computer file..."

"That's it! Of course." I'd told her I'd spend some time back in the Heartland File. If I could get the hang of it, and if the computer would cooperate. "At least, it'll keep me awake."

"Well, I don't think your problem will be boredom. Here's why I called you. I have to get back to work, but let me tell you this..."

As I put down the phone, I stepped out in the hall and stared down toward the lobby. The only light came from a side alcove, the nurses station. But there was no sound. The no-visitors sign was a dim shape in the hall. I moved my visitor's chair so that my back was to the wall. Then I took out my laptop and booted it up. INTERNET. SEARCH. THE HEARTLAND FILE. PASSWORD REQUIRED.

I typed in HILLIARD and the hard drive started whirring.

I thought I heard another noise, far down the hall. And then CLANG. Somebody knocked over the no-visitors sign. I set down the computer and walked to the door, just as it swung open.

"Well, Walt. You're out late. Come by to check on Jeb?"

He stepped through the door and shoved it shut. I saw his face was flushed, from liquor and from rage, in some ratio. I also noticed that Walter filled the doorway like a dray horse. I'd forgot how enormous this guy was. He had arms like thighs.

He shot a glance at Collard. "He gonna make it?"

"We don't discuss that in here, Walt. People in comas can hear, you know. You wanta talk about Jeb, we'll go outside." I moved toward the door, but he blocked me.

I didn't budge. "So, what else is on your mind?" As if I couldn't conjecture.

He walked by me to the nightstand and glanced at my computer, shook his head in disdain. I looked at the screen. There was the outline of what appeared to be a flower slowly forming, about as fast as a mudslide of molasses.

"Spend a lot of time on the Internet, Walt?"

"Not like that," he snorted. "Laptop computers—for shit."

"I didn't know you were such a Web master. Lotta kid porn on there these days, am I right?"

He wheeled around.

"All right, Wagstaff. You're in an intensive care room in a hospital and it's past visiting hours. You must have some reason for being here. Why don't you say what for and clear out."

He turned his back. "You oughta know, asshole. Rollie told me he saw you two out at the bar. I go outta town overnight an' ... Had some trouble at the Horn," he muttered.

"So I heard from Hazel. Said you shoved Sarah against a wall and she ran out. She also heard you hollering about coming for me. Well, you've found me. Listen, Wagstaff, and I mean this. Whatever you and Sarah do about your marriage is ... "

I remember thinking that I didn't mean that. That I knew full well what I wanted to see happen to that marriage. And I half remember watching his weight shift. So I might have seen ...

He wheeled around with a fist like a ham hock, his face the color of sirloin, and he caught me square in the solar plexus. I went down in a pile, and in the same motion he was on me. Clawing at me, stabbing at my head. "Get up, you fucking bookworm. Honors grad-u-ate. Game-winning, jump-shooting hotshot!" Every ancient indignation his addled brain could muster.

I shook my head clear and gave him a shot to the gut, so I could get to one knee. As I raised up, I saw he was just watching me. So I took a stab at his nose. It was a lucky punch. I heard something crunch and he staggered back, his hands up to his face. Now he was screaming—bloody, berserk. As he lowered his hands, his eyes were wide with rage.

I maneuvered myself between Wagstaff and the bed. "Get out, you imbecilic jock. Get outta here!"

I knew I had no chance in close quarters, but all I could do was stand my ground. Now he was grinning insanely and wheezing. Spitting blood. Flexing his fists as he reared back to charge me. But as he stepped back, the door swung open.

It was a stolid figure, in a nimbus of dim light. Carrying a vinyl clipboard, clad in white. She gave a roar as the clipboard came down in an arc. It caught Wagstaff just behind his right ear, and he toppled to the floor like a sack of hog nuts.

I fell back in the bedside chair to catch my breath, and took a quick inventory of my body parts. No damage done. At the end of round one, I appeared to be in better shape than Wagstaff. But I was just as glad there were no more fisticuffs to follow.

"Well, Bev…" I panted. "I believe the lesson here is to respect…your visiting hours. Walter must have not have read the sign."

She flashed a grin. But that faded as she flipped him on his back to check his vital signs. "Oh, my God, I know who this is. Mr. Wagstaff! Big cable TV fella. Donor to the hospital. As a matter of fact, I think he's on our board!"

"Well, he wasn't such a solid citizen just a minute ago. In fact, he was drunk out of his gourd. So, what'll we do with him?"

Bev propped a beefy arm against the door jamb. "Can't say this has ever come up before… But I'm the charge nurse, so I better take charge, think of something."

"Want to call the cops? I'll sure as hell file a complaint."

She stood there transfixed, staring at Wagstaff.

"Whaddaya mean, Bev? This dork just tried to dismember me,

and in a hospital room where my coach is supposedly your patient—but you haven't even checked his vital signs. Come on, let's pick up this sack of shit and throw his ass in jail. Then you can go back to running a hospital."

She frowned. "It ain't that easy. Not in a town like..."

Another figure came through the doorway. This time a trim figure. "I understand. You're right, it isn't easy. I know that for a fact." She gave Bev's arm a squeeze as she slipped by and stooped over Wagstaff.

"Sarah! Geez, I'm glad you're all right. Hazel said you guys had a tussle out at the steakhouse."

"He threw me against a barnwood wall."

"Well, I guess that's what I meant to say. Although I didn't want to."

"Nor did I. Not for the past few years that all of this has been going on. I didn't want the people at church to know. Or the parents of my kids at school."

She stood up and took a deep breath as she turned around, her eyes watering. "You see, I didn't want them to suspect..." She took the neck of her windbreaker and pulled the zipper down. Shrugging off the jacket, she let it fall. She pulled her turtleneck jersey from her jeans. She took hold of the hem cross-handed, paused, and in one sweeping motion drew it over her head.

As she stood there in the dim light, I could see the blotches—dark bruises of blue flesh, to the edge of her brassiere. With a sigh, she reached back and undid it. She dropped the bra on her pile of clothes and turned round in the dim light.

I remembered her breasts—pear like, upturned nipples. Now they were ravaged. "Oh, God, Sarah," I sputtered. "Oh, Jesus!" There were clouded, purple blots across her breasts, and a grotesque red welt at the edge of one nipple.

Even Bev gave a gasp. I found myself choking.

"So, Matt... you see, it's not just that we're provincial out here. Sometimes there's more than meets the light." And she began getting dressed. "What do we do, Bev? Have you decided?"

Bev gave a labored sigh. "Awright, a couple of options. One of you can call the cops and file charges. Or, I could put him in another room and let him sleep it off a while. He's gonna need a Tylenol or two. The way his nose is bent, it could be broken."

I felt a shameful sense of satisfaction.

We decided to admit him—it was less complicated for all concerned—and Sarah filled out the forms. That included an authorization for restraints. Finally, Bev got around to checking Jeb. No change; he was holding his own. We hoisted Walt Wagstaff up on a gurney and hauled him down the hall. He still hadn't stirred, which was fine with me. Comatose was how I liked him.

When the two of us were back in Jeb's room, I touched Sarah on the shoulder. As she turned around, I took her gently in my arms. "You know we've got to get you out of that house. Come on, let's go on over right now. I'll help … "

"Whoa. Steady, boy. Easy, big fella." She laughed, eyes bright for a moment. Then she looked at me in earnest. "I want you to listen to what I am trying to learn. The person who has to take care of … "

"You is you. Of course, I know. But you've got to get yourself out of there, Sarah. Now, let's go get your stuff."

Sarah backed away and turned to Jeb. "I'd say he looks a bit better than when I first walked in, wouldn't you, Matt?" She moved to the head of the bed, leaned over and laid her cheek on Collard's grizzled jaw. "Just hang in, Jeb," she murmured. "I think I can feel the wind shift."

I felt my heart swell with love. And guilt. I said, "Sarah, there's something I need to tell you." I started to recount the faculty meeting.

"You think I haven't heard that? Especially your maneuver with our minister in front of the altar."

"It's a time-honored sacrament: 'the laying on of hands.' Seems to be making a comeback." She slugged me.

I went over to the tray table to check the computer.

Sarah followed. "What's that?"

I showed her the image laboriously forming as the file and bit data dribbled across the bottom of the screen.

"You know, Matt, I can't say I'm any kind of expert on these things, but I don't believe that's working right."

"Yeah, I got into the file, but that's all. Damn modem is too slow. Walt was scoffing. And at this rate ... "

"Wait."

"Where are you going?"

She came back from the car with a long, black keyboard and a couple of cords.

"Walt brought this back from that conference. Left it lying on his desk along with this manual. I thought it might be something you could use, and so I ... Well, I stole it."

We scanned the manual and plugged in the contraption, one end to the computer and the other to the television set in Jeb's room. It took a while to figure out the settings, but the instant I turned it on—ZAP! The faltering graphic on the computer screen flashed up in full color on the TV: THE HEARTLAND FILE.

I remembered the colors. That big, full, yellow sunflower at the far end of a russet road. Engulfed in fields of green, with a deep cerulean sky as backdrop. Talk about a Web site!

A gray box popped up to obliterate the scenery.

ACCESS LEVELS 1—6
Checking Password ...

For a second, the screen went black. Then:

PASSWORD APPROVED FOR LEVEL 6,
FULL CLEARANCE
Proceed with search ...

I clicked on Human Resources, and entered my own name.

BRADSHAW, MATTHEW. B.A. Hopewell College, 1990. M.A., 1992; Ph.D., 1995, Eastbourne University; Current Position: Dean of Students. Performance Rating: Promotable, 6. Retainable, 1. Status: Not Online. Under Review.

"What's that mean, Matt?"

"Maybe that I'd best not apply for any long-term mortgages in Mayflower. Might be they're getting ready to give me the ax."

Then I called up Cynthia's personnel records. In an instant, her chart popped up and filled the screen. I scrolled down to:

Performance Rating: Promotable, 6. Retainable, 6. Online. Status Upgraded as of 10/95.

"Well, that suggests who's hot and who's not. I wonder if we're looking at the next president of Hopewell College."

"Wait, Matt, I saw something else. Scroll back up a minute. Wasn't Cynthia a student of yours at Eastbourne?"

"That's how we met. She had to take a required course in … Oh, no!" I blinked and stared at the computer screen.

CYNTHIA LOTHAMER (BRADSHAW). B.A., Sociology (High Honors), Minor in Art, 1990, Wellesley College.

"But she took your intro class at Eastbourne?"

"Required course, lower level," I muttered.

"Matt, that wouldn't appear to make sense."

"Unless…" I fell silent as a flood of images came over me. The morning I'd caught sight of Cynthia in class. In the front row, sketching. That tattered sweater, strategic hole at the edge of one breast. The billow of brilliant chestnut hair. Provocative questions, erotic drawings. That clumsy assignation in my office.

And, suddenly, the weight of the keyboard was more than I could bear. It clattered to the floor as I cradled my head on Jeb's nightstand—pounding my fist on it.

"Oh, Matt…" Sarah put a hand on my shoulder and then she sat back with a long sigh. "You guys. The hopes you all invest in women. The trust, the expectations. Then, the rage.

"You know, that's what I really fear. Underneath, I'm afraid you're really all the same."

20

We spent a couple of more hours on the Internet—scanning the Heartland File, perusing the parts that might pertain to Hopewell College. "Sarah, look! Here's some stuff on those two side businesses. You know, from the conference in Wichita."

+ Update—INTELSELL. Mayflower Telemarketing Center opens November 6 in renovated furniture store on Main Street. Recruitment goal: thirty telephone solicitors. Prospective employee pool: former faculty and staff of Hopewell College. Flier distributed October 30. Job Fair follows closing of the College.

"The what? Oh, my Lord, Matt! Can you believe that?" But there was more.

+ Update—INTELCELL. Plans nearing completion for acquisition of Hopewell College campus. Balloon payment on outstanding loan due October 31, with campus as collateral. Site currently under survey for retrofit as correctional facility.

Transfer of first twelve inmates (aka Hopewell College basketball team) now underway via work release from Deep Spring, Texas correctional facility. Additional contingent of skinheads awaiting reassignment from Limon, Colorado federal prison.

Appointment: Dr. Harold Alabaster, Vice President of Intelcor, named director of Camp Mayflower, contract pending with the U.S. Bureau of Prisons.

For a time, we just sat and stared at the screen.
"So that's why they wanted those guys in a separate dorm."

"Matt, I knew something had gone really wrong. For a long time, I saw it in Julian. I wondered why he suffered such a sense of guilt. That must be why he let that cultic bunch tattoo him."

"Well, I guess he was the one who put his John Hancock to that loan. That balloon payment. With the campus as collateral!"

"What can we do?"

I wasn't sure, but I did know enough to take on only one challenge at a time. In eighteen hours, there was a ball game.

Jeb was snoring lustily, although now and then his body gave a quiver as though he were traversing a dream. In a perverse way, I almost envied him. Weren't there times when all of us could use a good coma?

Now it was midnight. I was burned out on the computer, and I knew we were both ready to crash. So I shut it down, inhaled deeply, and turned to Sarah. And returned to my favorite theme.

"Listen, I'll go with you. We'll pick up your stuff, then we'll drive over to my place. And you can move in..."

"With you, my friend?"

"That's it, exactly."

She was silent.

"And make passionate..."

"Love? No doubt. You bet. But not in bed."

"What? Whoa, am I hearing this right?" She put a palm to my head. "Where's that Bev? She must have a thermometer. Is this the same Matt Bradshaw we all know, and most of us have loved?"

"No, I'm serious. I want you to heal and feel secure. No sex until it's right for you. And damn it, I mean that, Sarah."

She took a step back and surveyed me. "Move in with you... That could cost me next year's teaching contract."

"Not to mention your standing as a Deaconess."

"Move in. And maybe pick up where we..."

"Left off? You bet. Now, come on. Are you ready? We'll go by the house and get your things."

"They're out in the car."

We stood for a moment, eyeing each other, and then we just broke up laughing. For a second, I almost thought I heard someone else join in. I looked around the room—no one there, of course. Then I glanced in Jeb's direction. It was hard to see in the dim light, but an eyelid might have flickered. And I thought I caught a faint trace of a smile.

Outside the room, I heard something more: a lowing groan from down the hall. Then, "Ow, Goddamn it. Leave my nose alone!"

In a growl almost as low, "There, at least we got it set. I can see that's not the first time you had your nose broke. Football, am I right? Now, let me just adjust these bed tethers."

Sarah and I slinked down in the direction of the voices.

"Lemme up, nurse, Goddamn it! Get me the fuck outta here. All the dough I've coughed up for this place, you'd think..."

"Now, there, Mr. Wagstaff. You know I have my orders. Mrs. Wagstaff signed you in herself, till Monday morning. Of course, that's a long time to be lyin' there, hands tethered down like that. But a nice shot of Nembutal oughta settle you. Right hip, okay? I'll just lift up your gown, and ... oh, my. Say, that big thing 'bout poked me in the eye!"

We angled for a better view.

"Ya know, some guys just don't realize—what they need's a woman 'bout their size. Full-bodied kind, to keep 'em in line." Now there were sounds of nuzzling and unzipping. "Hold on there a second, Walt. Just lemme get the door."

I lay awake a long time, and not because I wasn't fatigued. Not after the day I'd put in. Nor was it from sexual frustration. Sure, Sarah was in the house. But I'd made her a pallet up in Cynthia's old office, and I was bound to my resolution. Shit...

About two in the morning, I gave it up and walked outside. The night was magical, the yard luminescent in the glow of a near-full harvest moon. The Sisters of Aradia would be pumped, all right—in anticipation of whatever the hell it was they were to do this time of year. At the moment, I was past caring.

And so the ball game was tomorrow night. I guess that's what had me sleepless. Our last chance to rally the townsfolk, and the odds did not look favorable. What if we lost? What would the future hold? And what more could I do? I was flat out of inspiration.

"Chirrup." From the trellis behind me.

And, "Chirrup." An echo from across the yard.

It was the last of the cicadas. Survivors of that full-fledged chorus that had buzzed around town throughout August. Now there were just two, in their last night in Kansas. But there they were, still at it, resonating with the rest of creation.

I walked back to the kitchen and picked up Julian's journal. Flipped back toward the beginning, before his hope had clouded.

If a college did nothing more than give us back our senses: a lens or two to see the world—receive it—what a gift to God's creation that would be.

So, how is it that I find myself in this life, here today? Surely it's a wonder. Not just the processes of life—the fluids and the flesh—but the odd fact that life has gathered here in me. Isn't that the mystery in every existence? The miracle of coherence. The life in this creature. Here and now. Today.

I turned off the light and headed for bed, more settled now and certain I could sleep. But as I lifted the covers, I came upon a miracle of my own. For I was no longer alone. She raised up and drew me down in a long, warm, lingering embrace. And slowly, with care, her body above, she gathered me inside her.

We pulled up to the gravel parking lot behind the gym an hour before game time, but the lot was already full. Cars were circling the side streets, in search of open spaces. What a mob.

"Sarah, I'd better drop you off here. You've got the programs, right? Do you have enough?"

"I don't think so. But there's the Lindholms' car. Mavis'll help me run off some more."

"On the copier in Cynthia's office? I wouldn't count on it."

"Hey, don't forget I'm still a trustee. For as long as we've got a college." She leaned across and gave me a kiss.

"Sarah, not to scare you or anything like that … but I love you."

She quivered in my shoulder as she burrowed her head. "Sometimes the good things take time," she said.

I had a four-block walk back to the gym from the street where I finally found parking. It gave me time to try turning my head around, from Sarah to the game. How could we appeal to the townspeople, get them to look beyond the ball game to the fate of the college? I could scarcely call time out and tell 'em what I'd read in the Heartland File, much less in Julian's journal. But I'd turned up some great stuff for the public address announcer.

A block from the gym, I began to feel the game. "Programs, get your programs!" Students out hawking. Bright lights outside, sparkling in the sunset. Hell, if we could generate this kind of energy every week, we wouldn't need Intelcor. How about a game of the week? Take bets at a casino in the parking lot! Naw…

I was hiking briskly—almost at a trot—when I thought I heard someone hiss my name. Not my nickname, but my full, given moniker—"MATTHEW." The voice came from the shadows of a big frame house. Now I noticed where I was. This was Cynthia's new place. I peered into the shadows underneath the veranda.

"MATTHEW!" There it was again. I stared into the penumbra of the shrubbery. But part of me already knew. There were only two people who'd ever called me by my given name. My mother was one, and the other was…

"Channing Coe—where the hell are you? I can't see you back in those bushes. What are you gonna do—jump me again?"

No reply. Then sniffling. "You know I wouldn't (snort) have done it on my own. It was simply the role they assigned me."

"When they made you Grand Master? Jesus—how long have you been out here? And where are you staying? Chan, I've got a lot of things to take up with you—about Jeb and all. But I've got a game. Where will you be later on?"

"In the morning, before sunrise. Park your car on River Road. By that mailbox, same place. Take the trail to the top of the bluff… And, I didn't harm Jeb Collard!" Then he was gone.

The gym was humming. A half-hour before the start of the game, a thousand students and storekeepers and farmers filled every cranny.

Not just the bleachers, but the aisles and even the exit ways. They were packed in like a Third World soccer stadium.

I strolled over to the coach's bench as the team broke into their two-line layup drill. The noise was deafening, although I couldn't tell who the crowd was for. Alabaster's squad was already firing up jump shots at the other end of the floor. It was unsettling to note that most of them were going in.

Someone had thoughtfully left me a coach's clipboard in the locker room, and I carried it under one arm, mostly for effect. There wasn't much clipped to it but a few outlines of basic sets on offense and defense—plays that Jeb Collard had drummed into me. And, fortunately, into my team as well.

I walked over to the officials' table and shook hands with the refs. Then on to greet Kyle Clodfelter. He was a fixture as P.A. announcer at the college games, and I'd remembered that.

"Got some background on the new team, Chief." I handed him a roster that Sarah and I had made up. It had your typical info—name, uniform number, height, and weight for each of the players—plus another column on the far right hand side.

"What're these numbers? I'm to read all that?"

"Why not? It's fresh off the Internet. I think it'll be meaningful to these fellows. And one other thing. How are you at tracking assists? Not just who scored but who fed him the ball?"

"Whaddaya mean? Can I keep track of assists! I played this game, remember?"

"Then, look, Chief, every time our team makes a bucket—I don't care if you announce the guy who scored. But I'd sure like you to give the name of the player who fed him the ball."

Clodfelter looked at me quizzically, but he didn't object.

I hadn't said much to the team. But as the warm-up ended ten minutes before game time, I called them together in the locker room. Instead of standing up and talking down, I took a seat on the bench beside them.

"Fellas, I spent a lot of time last night with the man who taught us all to play this game. It's too soon to know if he's gonna be all right. But I have a pretty fair idea of what he'd say to you and me if he were with us right now. And I'll bet you all know, too." Then I settled into silence.

They sat staring at the floor. Then LaRon spoke up. "Three things. Play hard and fast. Play together. And play with a plan."

"That's what I remember. Anything else?"

More silence. Then someone else: "Can't say it exactly, but 'A concentrated team will always beat a bunch of individuals.'"

"Yeah," another added. "He'd go on about how basketball is a game for a team, not a showcase for hotshots."

"All right, you get As. Now, here's what I want to add..."

"Hey, hold up a minute, Co-itch."

"Jamal?"

"This rhetoric, lessons for living an' shit. Who you jivin'? I mean, I'm inspired, but shee-it! You dig the size of them brothas? That one huge mothafucka..."

"Jamal!"

"Fuck that shit, LaRon. We ain' gathered for no worship service. We 'bout to get our asses kicked. No two ways about it."

I saw that most of the guys were staring at their shoes, and just let them sit for a moment. Five minutes now to game time.

Finally, I said, "Well, you and I both know that if you go out there in that spirit, you're dead meat. You might as well shower up right now. Now, look. I'd rather not say this, but if I could suit up one more time, I would. You know? I'd go out there with you. And I believe you know what we'd do to these guys."

Someone muttered, "I seen the films; we'd torch 'em."

"That's right," I went on. "But I've used up my four years of eligibility, and I also damn near killed myself last time I tried to jam. What I can do is keep us in our game plan. So, I want you to forget about the outcome, and about the opposition. Let me worry about that stuff. Just go out and play your game.

"And one other thing. Coach Collard would have told you, too, if he could've brought himself to say it. I'm proud of you all, the way you've hung together. And, guys, I gotta tell you this—I love you!"

They rose in a slow but fluid motion, twelve dusky guys in midnight black suits trimmed with gold. Twelve hands swooped and pumped and slapped as a couple of gangly arms reached around and hauled me in the circle. Now all of us joined hands, as my eyes filled and I flashed back five or six years—"One, two, three, HOPE!"

"Shee-it," Jamal muttered, as we trotted to the door. "Shee-it! Let's get 'em!"

I stepped out to center court. The referees were there, and so was Alabaster. We went through the rules—mostly timeouts and how to call them. Alabaster stared blankly as he extended his hand. I looked him in the eye. "What a privilege. The Great Gray Hope!" He turned on his heel. I went back to the sideline.

As the pep band bleated out the national anthem, I stood beside my team and kept an eye on Alabaster. He hadn't had a lot to say to his squad. Now he was staring my way with a look of some uncertainty. I wondered if he knew any more about coaching than I.

"Ladies and gentlemen! Welcome to this historic intrasquad game at Hopewell College." Kyle Clodfelter's big voice boomed across the bleachers and rattled the rafters. I looked around for Sarah—couldn't find her. But I saw Cynthia in the first row, just back of Alabaster's bench. She caught my eye and cracked a grin, nodding at my team then at the new one. She slowly shook her head. I merely smiled and shrugged.

"And now, the starting lineups for tonight's contest. For the incoming squad, from the federal facility at Deep Spring, Texas—at one guard, six feet four inches tall, hailing from South Chicago, Illinois, number 14, as well as number 502-718-93, LeRoy Robinson!"

There was a round of applause, but I saw a lot of puzzled faces in the crowd. Two sets of numbers?

I shot a glance at Alabaster, saw him scramble to the scorers table. He was livid—grabbed at Clodfelter's mike. But the big chief shoved him backward with an index finger to the sternum and ran through the rest of the roster. The new team blanched, their faces almost pale. Those were their inmate numbers.

The game began much as I'd feared, and it was all I could do to sit there on the bench—not take a hand in it. It was clear that Alabaster's team had played together before, and they were indeed damn good.

It seemed they could do everything but pass, although it wasn't clear that they needed to.

LeRoy Robinson was a gunner—a classic veteran of the play-grounds who shot first and looked for teammates later. First time down the court, he fired up a thirty-footer from the top of the key and canned it. Altogether, it had taken his team eight seconds to score.

Our guys used up most of the thirty-five-second shot clock running a pick and roll off the high post. Two points as Jamal got free for a back door layup. It was going to be a long night if we had to score like that!

Clodfelter followed my instructions. "That basket by Jamal Simpkins, ASSIST LaRon Vaughn."

Then back came Robinson. Three or four strides past midcourt, he fired up another rainbow jumper. Nothing but net. Then another, next time down. And again.

The score was 12-4 when I called time out.

"LaRon, I'm beginning to believe this guy can shoot. Now I want you to try playing up on him, soon as he crosses the half-court line. Let's see if he can drive to the basket."

In the very next possession, we established that he could. Robinson put the ball on the floor and spun around LaRon like he was a traffic signal.

Time out again. Now it was 16-8. "Catch your breath, guys. It's okay…" (Although I knew full well it wasn't. So, what the hell would Jeb do?)

"All right, this guy's gotta have a weakness. Maybe he's got bad breath…look, let's throw a half-court trap on him. See if he can pass out of a double team."

At last, a strategy that worked. LeRoy couldn't pass worth hog fodder. Perhaps he'd never tried it. Our guys draped him like a do-rag. We created a couple of turnovers, and converted.

"Vaughn scores on the fast break, ASSIST to Simpkins," Clodfelter boomed.

By half time, it was a game again. They were up by four, but we were in it. The crowd was buzzing from the action, but I still couldn't sense a favorite. A troupe of cheerleaders in black and gold sweat suits came running out on the floor during time outs. They led cheers for both sides.

As I walked off the court, I heard Sarah's voice over the P.A. "What a night! What a game! And—to all of us in Mayflower—what's a college worth? Tonight, we have an exceptional opportunity to show our support…"

There wasn't much said in the locker room. It was pretty clear that our guys were giving it their all, but it wasn't quite enough. I couldn't think of much else to do strategically. And if Alabaster were any kind of coach, he'd have another weapon up his sleeve. What would he come up with next?

As the second half opened, I didn't have long to speculate. My worst fears were realized. They started looking for the behemoth in the middle. Jamal was guarding the seven-footer. He was our tallest guy—maybe six-seven—a college center in name only. First time they threw the ball down to the low post, the big guy dunked in his face. Second, third, and fourth times down, it was the same story. Now we were down by twelve, ten minutes to go.

I called time. "Guys, get your wind. Just let me think."

Jamal sank to a seat, and looked at me askance. "Lemme know what you come up with. You got a growth hormone?"

Someone else muttered, "Or a ladder?"

I tried emulating Collard, and stood staring off in space. But no revelation was forthcoming. The truth was, we were flat outmatched. "All right, guys. Let's try double-teaming the center. See if he can pass out of double coverage."

Within two minutes, he showed that he could. As soon as the ball came down into the low post, he fired it out to the back court and Robinson buried another couple of jumpers. Now we were down fourteen with less than eight minutes left. I was about to call another time out—possibly for prayer—when my pocket buzzed.

Shit, I'd forgot to leave this contraption in the locker room! I pulled the phone from my pocket to toss it aside when something stopped me. It could be the hospital calling!

And it was—Bev's number at the nurses' station glowed on the cell phone screen. I signaled for a time out, our last. The team came back and collapsed. "Guys, just gather yourselves and get your breath.

You won't believe this, but I've gotta take a phone call. I'm pretty sure it's news of Coach Collard."

Bev's voice came on the line. "Awright, Dean, I know this is weird. But we been listening to the game on the radio. And I got a guy here who says he wants to offer some advice..."

There was silence, and the rustle of the phone being passed.

"Matt, Matt...gotta tell you somethin'."

The voice was weak and raspy, but I recognized it.

"Jeb! My God, can that be you?"

"Short o' breath, but not much time. Feed 'em to the flocks, Matt. Tell Jamal I said that—feed 'em to the flocks, every time down..."

"You get that, Matt?" Bev came back on the line.

"I guess so, but look, is he really coming out of it? Is he gonna be all right?"

"Doc just came by. I paged him at the game. Says he's gonna be laid up. But he's comin' through it. Says he's gonna be fine!"

I clamped the phone shut and ran over to the bench. As I told the team, they sprang to their feet, whooping and hollering. The crowd went stone silent. These guys are down fourteen in the fourth quarter, and they're celebrating? I saw Alabaster frown—what the hell can they be up to? Behind him, Cynthia looked down and half-smiled. I thought I caught an expression of relief.

The horn sounded—the end of time out—but I kept my team on the bench. A ref came over. "Wanta technical, Coach?"

"Look, I know this is unconventional, but I need to make an announcement over the P.A. The news is that important." And I told him. He stepped over to confer with Alabaster who looked up at me and glowered, but he nodded.

I walked over to the scorers' table, and Clodfelter handed me the mike. I yanked the cord free and took it out to midcourt.

"Friends, this has been one hard-fought game and—take it from me—the outcome's still in doubt." A cheer went up, and some wag hollered, "Suit up, Bradshaw. Put yourself in the game!"

"Wish I could, but this is what I came out here to say. You see, whoever comes out on top tonight, why, all of us are winners here in Mayflower. Coach Collard has come out of his coma. I just talked to him on the phone. He's gonna be all right!"

Now the roar was thunder. I pumped my fist in the air and they shouted louder. I handed the microphone back to Clodfelter. I watched him wipe his brow, and could see it was no empty gesture. The old chief looked genuinely relieved, like Cynthia. I headed back to the bench.

"He had a message for us, guys," I told them as the horn sounded, the referee coming our way again. "It was for you, Jamal. But his voice was so weak, I couldn't understand it."

"What'd it sound like?"

"'Feed 'em to the flocks. Feed 'em to the flocks.' He said, 'Tell Jamal that.'"

They shook their heads, puzzled, as we formed our circle one last time. "One, two, three, HOPE!"

"Hold it, Coach!"

"What's that, LaRon?"

The ref pointed at me and blew his whistle. "Technical foul! Delay of game. Incoming squad, shooting one."

I ignored him, as one of their players walked to the line.

"LaRon, what is it?"

"'Beat him to the blocks.' That's what he's saying! Jamal, he wants you to hustle down on defense. Get down court ahead of that guy and set up in the high post. That way, he's gotta push you back and foul you, or else shoot from way out there."

"Of course," I cried. "Hey, Jamal, I told you that. Back in practice, remember?"

"Shee-it, but you spaced it. You forgot."

Jamal did not forget. He raced that seven-footer down the court and beat him every time, setting up out near the free throw line. If gonzo had been gifted with a turnaround jump shot, we'd have been toast. But he wasn't. All the guy knew how to do was dunk, and we'd taken that away. We left Jamal as his lone defender, and ran traps on the outside shooters.

As the clock wound down, we had the ball and a five-point lead. LaRon caught a cross court pass as the horn sounded and he gave the ball a spin. He tossed it to Jamal who flung it to the ceiling. I watched it soar, my fists raised high. Then I was scanning the bleachers for Sarah, when the team rushed back and my feet left the floor. They carried me off on their shoulders.

As we were leaving the gym for the locker room, I could hear Clodfelter rumble: "Drive careful goin' home, now." And then Sarah, in elation. "Our goal to rebuild the bell tower was $8000. Tonight, we took in $8500. Thank you, May-flow-er! Construction starts in the morning."

21

*F*or a while, the night was euphoric. The campus was lit up like Mardi Gras. Dorm lights blazing, rock music blaring. I was maybe more excited than I'd ever been, just wired with the wonder of winning that game. After a quick shower, I ran outside to wrap my arms around Sarah.

Walking to the car, we didn't talk about tomorrow—my rendezvous with Channing Coe first thing in the morning. And, in the afternoon, a trustees meeting on the fate of the college. A meeting that could be terminal. But, for now, we just needed to unwind.

So we got in the car and headed for the Hoof'n Horn. But halfway out of town, I heard a CLICK from the far side of the front seat. Some memories tingled as Sarah slipped out of her seatbelt. Then her head was on my shoulder, her hand on my thigh.

Hey, there was more than one way to wind down. I did a U-turn toward home.

On our way back to the bedroom, she stopped and took my hand. We stood there for a long time in the shadows of the moonlight. She was crying and she was beaming. "Matt, can you believe this?"

I simply shook my head.

It was five a.m. as I drove past the mansions at the crest of River Road and wound down the bluff into the Bottoms. I was steering with one hand, swilling my breakfast of black coffee with the other. And remembering my last words with Sarah.

Something had stirred me awake about three in the morning. It was a soft, moaning sound. As I turned, I saw her sitting on the far edge of the bed. She had my shirt on, and she was shaking.

"Sarah, what is it?"

"It was just a dream," she said. She squeezed my knee and lay back down. "You and I were in Denver, and we were teachers, I guess.

I know we had each other. But ... the college, and everything else was gone.

"We were down on that mall they have there in Denver, downtown. And there were people all around—maybe it was lunch time—thousands of people, all milling around. And I turned to speak to one man. But then I looked and saw he couldn't answer me. He had no face! There were thousands of people in the place where you and I lived, and none of them had faces!"

It was pitch black, not yet 5:30, but I found the mailbox all right. Fortunately, I'd thought to clock the distance from the bottom of the bluff on the odometer, last time we were down here. I pulled off the road behind the same clump of bushes.

I'd also remembered to bring a flashlight, and I clicked it on as I peered across the road for the trail up to the bluff top. But no sooner had I flicked the switch than a raspy voice hissed from the ditch at the far side of the road.

"MATTHEW. Snuff it!"

I crossed the road and he came clambering up beside me.

"Snuff it? Hey, Channing, that's quaint."

He held a branch aside to point out the trail at the base of the cliff. And then he started climbing. In a couple of steps, he turned around. I could just make out the wiry glasses, the slicked-down hair parted in the middle, splayed out like palm fronds.

"We'll talk up at the top. But, meanwhile, I have two words for you, Matthew. And I'd like you to consider them."

"Two words?"

"Health insurance."

The trail was no more than fifty yards long, but it was tough trekking; it felt more like an eroded gully. We scrambled up through rocks and sand, all kinds of detritus. I could still barely see Channing, but halfway up the hill I heard him let out a grunt as he fell on his face. He came sliding back beneath me.

"Chan, is this best way?" I helped him to his feet. "And, Christ, it's cold! You know, back in my day we used to drive up here—watch the submarine races. There used to be a road."

"There still is, but I don't want to run into the others. I've got a spot where we can look out—and not be discovered."

It was a little niche in the crags between a couple of large rocks, sheltered by a few saplings. As we burrowed in between the boulders, I could see that it offered a great vantage. We looked out on a clearing with what appeared to be a few small mounds in the center. There were logs around the edge and a cleft in the trees on the far side. That would be where the road came in.

The whole scene seemed vaguely familiar. This must have been the spot they'd filmed that video for the cult class.

Channing leaned back against a rock face and gave a weary sigh. He removed his glasses and wiped his eyes. "Well, where to begin? I've, uh, never been very good at this…but there are some things I need to tell you."

"How long do we have? And what the hell are we doing here? What're we waiting for, Chan?"

"We call it a 'sabbat.' It's a gathering of the covens in this region. This morning is a special occasion—Hallowmas. The Chief Warlock will be here."

"When?"

"I'd say we have twenty minutes. All right—Eastbourne, when we last spoke. That afternoon in the student union. How long ago was that?"

"Several years, I'd say."

"It all congeals, time collapses. Well, then, to begin … "

The story was familiar. There'd been cutbacks at the university, and he had lost his job. He had a year to find another, and he needed one. For the family's health insurance, he said. But there were no other jobs. No one else was hiring in religion.

"Then they came by with an offer. You see, they'd approached me before through a, uh, a student." He fiddled with his glasses.

"Who came to you? Intelcor?"

"We refer to them as 'corporate.' Yes, Intelcor. A high-tech marketing company, just getting into higher education. I imagine you know some of this. They were taking on contracts with other colleges. Places that were desperate for students."

"Such as Hopewell."

"Intelcor has all sorts of capabilities in market research—some of the most definitive work on DUBS. You know about DUBS? Consumers who will always covet the latest electronic product. Digital Upscale Believers. DUBS. But their real expertise became enrollment management."

"Come on, Chan, I've heard some of this and it explains a lot. But not why you and I are freezing our butts on this bluff, and it's 5:30 in the morning. Cut to the chase! Just how in the hell did you become the Grand Master of a witches' coven?"

"My actual title is Senior Fellow. I'm a research associate for Intelcor, you know. Matthew, do you have any idea of the number of cults in America? The scope and significance of this social trend? Why, you know, at last count ... "

"Channing, where are your wife and family?"

Haltingly, he told me more about his involvement in the world of neopaganism. How it began way back when, with a student who'd pretty much seduced him.

"At Eastbourne?"

"In my office. You know, my wife and I had been together since college. Young-old marrieds, you might say. I'd never been with anyone, but ... back to the essence of the story. Yes, of course.

"Well, you see, my inquiry into alternative forms of religious affiliation led me to ... Oh, Matthew, all these women—the variety."

"And you loved it."

"They passed me around like a rag doll. Until that one young lady. Her obsession with the aging king. The ritual humiliation. The depressed president. Botching the tattoos. It was barbarous!"

I studied him with one eye as he wrestled with his story. But I was also watching the first faint signs of sunrise on the horizon. And, slowly, I became aware of an incredible transformation. The mounds were taking on an almost mystical configuration. A harmonic pattern. The long, earthen oblong and the hillocks. I watched the shaping of those mounds, their geometric balance ...

There was that blonde. Beautiful, but vacuous eyes. Except when she became intent; then she'd bore right through you. With that strange habit of twisting her hair. It seemed she'd been intrigued by some rite they'd come across in their readings. More than fascinated,

in fact. She was obsessed with the notion of knocking off old patri-
archs. Purging the earth of aging kings. They'd approached it as a
symbolic rite, but she wasn't much into symbolism.

And the blonde had been smitten by Channing. He called it a
classic case of ABD.

"Sounds like an academic ailment. 'All But Dissertation'?"

"'Affectional Bonding Disorder.' When I tried to disengage and
become merely her professor once again, she couldn't cope."

"I think I know the student. And I don't have to speculate what
she did to Julian and Jeb. Patriarchal figures, a good way to get back
at Dad. But what the hell were you thinking, Chan? I mean, who was
in charge out here? Screwing your students?"

He put up a hand. It was nothing more than what goes on in
every American college, he said. At Eastbourne, it was de rigueur. But
in this case there were complications, and so ...

"Shh." Again, he raised his hand.

I listened. It was a deep, plangent sound, drifting up from the
river.

tha DUM tha dum tha dum tha dum,
tha DUM tha dum tha dum tha dum ...

A dark, rumbling resonance. I felt a chill. Now more drumming
and chanting. But I couldn't make out what they were saying.

"We don't have much time. My wife? Some time after I'd left,
I received word. She filed for divorce and remarried. Fellow with
tenure in microbiology. Meanwhile, of course, she'd retained our
health insurance. Intelcor saw to that."

"And you? You've not formed any other attachment?"

"Ah, well ... I already had. That first student—mine for a time.
Then Intelcor sent her off on another faculty recruitment assignment.
To 'hook up,' as they say, with a young chap in his office. As fate
would have it, she became emotionally involved. And they married.
She and I were merely friends and colleagues once again."

He took off his glasses and held them up to the faint light. Dug
in his pocket for a Kleenex.

tha DUM tha dum tha dum tha dum,
tha DUM tha dum tha dum tha dum...

Now I could hear snatches of rhyme in the drum beat through the branches. The lot of them, drumming and chanting.

As above, so below.
As the body, so the soul.
As without, so within.
Let the rites of light begin.
Let the rites of light begin ...

"It's what they call a 'shadow site,'" Channing explained. "Have you noticed how the mounds take form in the morning light? The pattern can be discerned only twice a day, at sunrise and sunset. A hierophany, a sacred site. You see, for the Quiviran Indians, descendants of the prehistoric Hopewell culture..."

"Chan, they're getting closer. Is there anything more?"

He examined his glasses. Put them on again. Rubbed his chin.

"She took me in after that unfortunate incident, the tattooing. Back in town, from the place I'd been staying down here in the Bottoms, watching over Collard. When I moved in, I assumed it was, uh, a professional relationship, as before. You see, she'd cared about that other fellow.

"But then, the other night, a rustling in the hall... Oh, you'll see her in a moment, following the warlock. Leading the procession. She's the Goddess who'll..."

"Channing!"

"Yes, well, all right. She slid her business card under my door. And I went to her, and... oh, isn't she beautiful, Matthew?"

I couldn't disagree. As the drums and chanting filled the glen, two figures emerged from the tree-shrouded road, ahead of the others. One was a tall man who strode with a slight limp but a fluid motion, like an aging athlete. He wore a black hood that looked a lot like the one I'd ripped off Channing.

Then a tall and slender woman in a dark cape and gown. Her

hood was black with white lining. Her hair billowed, cloudlike, all around her face. Glowing chestnut.

"The hood of lambskin lined with calfskin—the tradition," Channing sighed. "It's ageless!"

I watched the Goddess step to the center of the glen. And there, at the midmost, she set her hands to her chest, then drew them down across her breasts to the mound betwixt her thighs. Then she lifted her arms to the skies.

It occurred to me I'd seen fragments of this rite a time or two in the course of my habitation with the Goddess. But now I found myself merely shivering, from the ecstatic nature of the proceedings or because it was no more than forty degrees out here and I was fucking cold.

Cynthia knelt and took up a handful of soil. Then she circled the glen where the others were standing. Pausing at four points, she tossed it to the wind.

"Casting the circle," Channing sighed. "Oh my, what a rite! No wonder we neopagan theologians speak of 'The Christian Interlude.' The Wiccan Craft—it's so timeless, so primal."

"Chan, this may be an obvious question, and I'd do better if I could feel my feet. But if you're so into this, why aren't you out there? What are you doing back here in the cheap seats?"

"Shh! The spiral dance. It's just begun."

They'd formed a circle, surrounding the mounds, all facing outward. There were maybe twenty of them clad in black—mostly in Hopewell College sweat suits. Another four or five remained behind the ring of logs, flogging their drums.

tha DUM tha dum tha dum tha dum.

They were all holding hands as the circle drew tight, until Cynthia gave a nod and dropped her left hand free. But she held fast to the hand of the warlock on her right. She stepped inside the ring to the beat of throbbing drums. Drew the others to a second inner circle as the web wound tight. And then, just as they fronted, the tips of bodies touching, they began to snake the circle out again.

Some of them brushed kisses as they passed in the dance. But not the warlock. He seemed to hold himself aloof. And I noticed he was puffing. It appeared he might be fighting to keep up.

"Chan, why's he dancing so funny, holding that one leg up?"

"He's playing the lame God, wounded in one heel. It's part of the dance. Usually my part... But, no, I see what you mean. He's struggling to keep pace. It could be his age."

At last, the whole group unwound in a circle, and the drummers gave a flourish as the dancers flopped down on the logs. There were elbows to the ribs and wisecracks as they gasped for air. I was glad to see the Wiccans loose for once, more like raucous college kids. Not reborn Calvinists.

But suddenly everyone sat up straight as Cynthia strode to the center of the ring, along with the warlock. She stood silent behind the long, high mound that served as a kind of lectern. All was still in the clearing except for the wind that came whistling through the trees. The sky was light but leaden. Although we were only fifty yards from the road, with houses and a river beyond that, this place seemed ominous in its isolation.

Cynthia seemed somehow on edge. "It is," she began in her best provost's voice, "It is my pleasure to pleasure—uh, to present—a man whom we have long admired, but never chanced to meet. One whom we have known only by his Craft namè..."

She whipped out a note card. "'Lynx.' Hey, that's just another name for a wildcat, right?" She shot a sidelong glance at the warlock but he stood impassive, staring through the slits in his hood. Cynthia coughed nervously.

"Members of the coven in this hole... holy time of Samhein, I give you the Grand Warlock!"

There was a light round of applause and a rumbling of drums.

Cynthia retreated to a seat on the front log as the guest advanced to the oblong mound. He was so tall that he towered above it. For a moment, he stood and gazed out on the assemblage. Then he raised his arms to the slate-gray sky and reared back his head, his robe sleeves unfolding to a regal purple lining. "Rentum tormentum!" he roared. Perhaps a kind of invocation.

It was a huge, stentorian voice, the kind you don't readily forget. I saw Cynthia cringe and the whole group gave a start. Beside her, the blonde began twisting her hair.

"Now, I appreciate the chance to get together with you all. What we have here is a communal religion, and as the saying goes, you can't ... can't be a witch alone."

He gulped, as if trying to catch his breath. For a moment, he steadied himself on the large mound. Then he went on.

"But I have come here today in some sadness, for I'm afraid this roundup may have come too late. In fact, I have a lotta grief about the fate that has befallen the great Craft of Wicca—for it seems it's been dishonored in this place."

He took another deep breath, propped forward on the mound.

"You see, when the Kansas Craft heard that Hopewell College was aimin' to offer a credit course out here on Wicca, that a big corporation was drummin' up students, why we were mighty glad. For the Craft stands in need of trained leaders. And we all knew about Intelcor. Upscale outfit, corporate intelligence. All that."

He paused and seemed to shudder.

"So whadda they send us? Bunch of binary bozos. Some wirehead yuppie—a 'priestess of the Craft.' And a geek teaching witchcrap ... "

He began to sputter and his body quaked. A long, bony finger protruded from his robe. He pointed it at Cynthia, or the blonde, or maybe the two of them. They huddled together, shrinking into the log.

"Channing, what is it with this warlock?"

He sat slack jawed. "It—it's not what I supposed. I knew they weren't entirely pleased. They said we could expect some reorganization. But, say—is there something wrong with him?"

Indeed, the warlock had begun to gyrate. One hand on the mound, he swung a fist in the air as though he meant to deliver his diatribe with a tomahawk chop. But now it seemed he couldn't speak. He shoved the fist to his sternum, pressing his chest.

"He's having a heart attack!" I hollered as I leapt from the crevice, ducked under the saplings. I ran down into the clearing.

"Matthew, come back. This is a secret rite!" cried Channing, from his spot in the rocks. But then he was up and running after me. We got to the mound same time as Cynthia. The warlock was rocking at the waist, his fist in his chest, hood bobbing.

"Funky chicken!" some miscreant shouted.

I vaulted the mound, grabbed the hood and tore it off him. Then fell back on my heels. "Oh my God! Everybody get back—give him some air!"

His face was as gray as the morbid sky—just ashen. Sweat was pouring down his forehead and he was gasping. I knew that if we didn't get Kyle Clodfelter to a doctor soon, he was history.

"Cynthia, do you have your cell phone?"

She shook her head.

"Well, mine's in the car. In the bushes down at the foot of the path, across the road. Look, Chan and I can carry the chief—the warlock, whatever—carry Kyle to the head of the road. Run down and drive the car up, okay? And call the hospital, tell 'em we're bringing him in."

She seemed dazed—just stood there and stared at me.

"All right, Cyn? Madam Provost? Hey, how 'bout it, Goddess?"

Then a wink within the hood, a grin. I tossed her the car keys and she took off at a gallop, hiking up the hem of her gown.

"Chief, can you hear me?" I loosened his collar.

He nodded, peering up at me. There was a glaze in his eyes.

"I'm going to haul you over to the head of the road—along with Channing, here."

Clodfelter shot a glance at Chan. He scowled and shuddered.

"It'll be okay. Then we'll get you right to the hospital." I thought I saw him shrug beneath his robes.

We got him to a little knoll, right next to the road at the far edge of the clearing. Channing stayed back a few feet, still wary of the warlock.

I cradled Clodfelter. At first it seemed he couldn't speak, even though he was breathing a little better. His complexion was the color of bathwater.

I listened for the sound of my car. There it was—the low growl of the engine in first gear. It was a rough road, slow going. Then I heard another, guttural sound. I looked down at Clodfelter. His lips were moving. I put my ear down.

"Remember what I used to say? In a town like this…"

"'You look past things.' But you shouldn't be talking."

"Don't hardly matter…" He shut his eyes, his breathing fast and shallow. I looked toward the road. No sign of the car, but I could hear it coming.

"Dean…"

"Chief?"

"Don't lose sight of the oblique. That's what Julian used to tell me. Ya know, I'd send him up here—couldn't bear to come myself. Sent him up at sunset, sunrise so he could see the shadow site."

"Kyle, I can hear the car. It's getting closer."

"Forget it. Don't sweat it. Hey, do they still say that?"

"Sure they do. You always were hip to the latest…"

"Forget the latest. Full o' shit, those byte-sized bastards. Intelcor! This binary bullshit. One or zero. Yes or no. Naw, Matt, the truth is in the shadows."

The car was coming slowly round the bend.

"Kyle, I've got it. Don't lose sight of the oblique. I hear you guys. Now, save your strength…"

"Ol' Jules loved his shadows. Said to me, 'You be a seeker. Don't stick to their damn script.' And I heard that. But there's one more thing I just don't get. And now I guess it's too damn…"

Cynthia drove the car up in the clearing and turned it back downhill. I watched her open the front door and flip the passenger seat to a reclining position. She and Channing came over to where I sat with Clodfelter, and they bent over to lift him up.

"We're going into town now, Kyle. Gonna get some help."

"J-just one other thing." He craned his neck and peered at Cynthia. "So, tell me this. How in hell I could have let all this go on!" Then he gave a groan and fell back to the ground.

Once we'd crawled back down the bluff, we made it to the hospital in record time. I raced up to the emergency entrance. They were waiting for Clodfelter. I left the keys in the ignition as Bev came around to the passenger side along with the doctor on call. They hoisted Kyle up on the gurney and carted him inside. Cynthia and Channing didn't come in. But I followed the chief. This place was beginning to feel too much like home.

It must have been a good half-hour before they gave it up. Pumping on him, paddles to the chest. Bev and the doctor were exhausted. I walked out to the waiting room as they broke the news to his widow, and wondered what she thought of the ceremonial robes. Although I guess she must have known, same as Julian.

I glanced up at the clock and said my good-byes. I'd done what I could and there was one more tragedy on the docket: a meeting of the trustees in about an hour.

ended here

22

I t was always warm in the board room, any season. The sun would come streaming through the west windows of the admin building and stoke up the temperature like a sauna. Not that the heat was all that unpleasant. It broke down the resin in the furniture wax, spewing fumes of pine tar. Sometimes the board room smelled like a polymer pine forest.

Today was one hot day in the forest, if Gus Lindholm was any indication. The big, beefy chairman of the trustees sat hunched over the head of the conference table, beads of sweat trickling from beneath his gray crew cut. He was poring over a ledger and shaking his head. Calvin Withers, the squiggly little accountant, sat beside him. Now and then, Withers would point to a column and the two would mutter softly.

It was four o'clock as I walked in, and almost every chair was taken. There was a low rumble in the room—businessmen in shirt-sleeves trading news of the day. Mumbling references to "the poor chief" and "Kyle." Then Lindholm rapped for order.

"Well, welcome to a meeting that most of us would just as soon forego. But a lot of us went to school here—met our wives here—and we're obliged to see this through. So most of us are present, and I thank you. In fact, I see we're missing only one trustee. That's Sarah, uh, Wagstaff... you know, Sarah Lyle."

He gave a halting look in my direction and I caught a few covert glances from the other trustees. But I couldn't help them. When it came to Sarah's whereabouts, I had no clue.

Then Lindholm turned my way again, and this time he smiled. He introduced me as a special guest, not merely dean of students but triumphant basketball coach as well. There was a burst of applause and now everyone bestowed a big grin—on the noted jock, not the clandestine lover.

"Friends of Hopewell College," Gus Lindholm went on, "this is a sad day in more than one respect." He announced the death of Kyle Clodfelter, for the benefit of anyone who'd been in hibernation. Then he called for a few moments of silence.

As I sat there with the others, I thought back to the many sides of Kyle—and remembered his last words. We'd strapped him in the passenger seat, tilted back like a recliner, and he'd seemed comatose. Cyn and Channing were scrunched up on the driver's side of the back seat, right behind me. Now and then, I'd heard them whisper. Or it might have been the whiz from the brick-paved River Road, up by the mansions. But then I heard another sound. And it was not the whisk of the bricks nor the back seat conspirators.

"Cynthia, Channing. I think Kyle's trying to say something."

She leaned forward and put an ear to his lips. "I can't make it out. I know what it sounds like. But, naw, that couldn't be."

"What is it?"

"Something like 'Spam you, Intelcor, spam you!' Here, Chan-Babe, you listen. If you wanta get off this shit brick road, Matt, we might be able to hear better."

I turned off on Main Street. "'Damn you?'" Channing wondered. "Why no, you're right. My word. He's saying, 'Spam you.'"

Cynthia was silent. Then, "Spamming? Naw, he wouldn't … "

"What's that? Hurry up, Cynthia. We're almost there."

"Hurry up, Cynthia!" She mocked me. "What the fuck is this, another executive order? Just because you won one lousy ball … "

"Cyn, stop it! Please—just give me the information!"

More silence. "All right, 'Spamming.' Verb: transitive. It's a way to shut down a Web site. You input shitloads of data—say, mailing lists from a hundred organizations. You penetrate the inbound ports, pouring in raw data. Do it long enough and you overrun the firewalls. Muck up their data bases. Swamp the site. I saw it done once, and it pretty much killed the organization."

"So you think that's what he's threatening Intelcor with?"

"Beats the hell outta me. But that's what it sounds like."

"Except that an individual his age wouldn't have that much knowledge of computers," Channing speculated.

"Yeah, of course," agreed Cynthia. "You're right,"

"Well, here we are at the hospital." That was all I said.

Jesus, what a day! I found myself mopping my brow. It was hot in this conference room, all right. With a nod to Gus Lindholm, I stepped outside to see his wife.

"Mavis, can you spare a glass of water? You know, I've been hoofing it around all over town."

She gave me one of her big maternal smiles, got a tumbler from the shelf, and filled it at the gurgling water cooler. "Say, Matt, that's just a shame you lost your car."

"Oh, you know about that? And I guess you know who took it."

She gave a weary smile as I handed back the glass.

"Oh, and Mavis . . . " I took a floppy disk from my shirt pocket. "Would you mind printing out these files and running off some copies? It's just some administrivia I downloaded from a big data base called 'The Heartland File.' Nothing of much interest."

It was a guarantee she'd read it.

As I walked back to the conference room, I glanced at Cynthia's door—shut tight. Inside, the group had grown. Harley and Hazel had turned up. And there was Rollie Cleaver, decked out in his purple plaid suit.

I scanned the room for Sarah—no such luck.

But I did spot a dark, familiar figure down at the far end of the conference table. No Man Tan nor Afro wig on this afternoon. Harold Alabaster was coming to us in plain sepia, and decked out in a four-hundred-dollar black silk suit.

"And, finally, our newest member of the faculty and staff," Gus Lindholm was saying, "the uh, chair . . . (Lindholm probed his notes). Yes, well, Dr. Alabaster, maybe you could fill us in."

"I can, indeed," he stepped up. "As your new, on-site representative from Intelcor, I bring corporate greetings to you all."

"And could you tell us your title, sir?" asked Lindholm.

Alabaster shrugged. "How about 'CEO?' I assume you intend to inform this group of the latest developments at the college."

"Why, yes, sir. I was just about to." He held up a couple of letters. "From the Reverend Roger Squire, dated yesterday, October 30. This is a letter of resignation, effective at once. The Reverend Squire indicates that he intends to devote full time to his ministry at the Mayflower Congregational Church."

I fought hard to hold back my tears.

"And then this message. It arrived by email just this afternoon. A memo from the corporate offices of Intelcor. It seems that, also effective immediately, our provost, Cynthia Lothamer Bradshaw, has accepted reassignment ... "

"Thank you, Mr. Chairman," Alabaster broke in. "That will suffice. Given the stipulations of your agreement with Intelcor, you understand of course that I shall be directing administrative operations of the college, for the duration of its tenure."

To most of his new friends in Mayflower—his brand new friends, as he liked to say—Harold Alabaster must have been an unrecognizable sight. That black business suit, the nondescript complexion. He looked every inch the crosscultural, professional mulatto I remembered.

As he got to his feet, he surveyed the table with a self-assured smile that faded as he came to me. Several of the trustees squirmed. I saw some downcast heads and anxious glances. Gus Lindholm took a seat.

"Now, then. I have a few items pertinent to the new mission of Hopewell College—as a rehabilitative institution. Here are some data from the Heartland File." Alabaster picked up a notepad and strolled over to an easel.

He ticked off some figures that I found incredible, even though I'd just seen the same data. About why the corrections industry was booming. It seems in the past two decades, the number of prisoners in the United States had doubled. How more than 1.6 million people were incarcerated in this country. Highest rate of lockups in the world. Average cost—$54,000 per inmate per annum. About twice what it cost to keep a kid in college.

I sat there, benumbed, as he rattled on. It was going to be damn hard to argue with pulling the plug on a dying college, in favor of an industry that was coming on like gangbusters. I sure could use some moral support. And where the hell was Sarah?

There was a soft tap on the door, and I spun around. But it was Mavis. She slipped in and handed me an envelope with my name on it. As she tiptoed to the door, she flashed a dark glance at Alabaster. He had his head down in his notes. With a hand on the knob, she gave me an intent look of concern. And repeated the gesture, this time to her husband. Then she left the room.

I slit the envelope. Alabaster was still perusing his notes.

Matt -

One more thing I can do, but I need a little time. Keep the meeting going past 5:00. Make sure they haven't yet come to a decision. This might help, at least a little.

It's all I can do—as well as love you!

S

Alabaster looked up from his notes, and I glanced at the clock. It was only 4:35. Time to come up with a game plan.

Alabaster smiled broadly. "Now, then, my friends..."

"Isn't that supposed to read 'my new friends?'"

Harley snickered. Hazel jabbed him.

Alabaster gave me a baleful glare. "Do you all know what the leading growth industry is these days in rural America—the number one new business in the Heartland? Well, it's an inspiring industry. For it's based on the promising premise that human beings are capable of change."

Some trustees in rumpled suits sat up and took notice.

"Dr. Alabaster. Could you please repeat that last line? 'Promising premise?' I mean, I've heard some forced alliteration. But did you actually say that?"

He flashed a dark glance. "Mo-fo!" sotto voce.

Then, for the assemblage, "Whatever Dean Bradshaw may choose to believe, this is vital information. I am about to cite statistics from Intelcor's proprietary data base, the Heartland File. Now then, what is this business bent on human transformation?"

"It's bent all right. Bent out of shape."

Now Hazel frowned. I stood up and glanced around the table. "Friends—my old friends—I believe I know the answer, and I'd guess some of you do, too. Can we all spell 'prison?'"

"Matt—Dean Bradshaw!" Gus Lindholm sputtered. "I'm surprised at you. Dr. Alabaster has the floor. Please remember his position here, and yours."

"I know my position: bent over. About the same as yours."

Now there was a rustling among the trustees, hostile glances. But I saw Rollie Cleaver crack a grin. He always had a nose for barnyard humor. "Bent over. That's a good one. Huh-huh-huh!"

Which was all Harley needed. "Speaking of change. Do you all know how many psychiatrists it takes to change a light bulb?"

"Got me, Doc!" acknowledged Rollie, red in the face already.

"Only takes one. But the light bulb has to want to change."

Now the others were fidgeting. "Just whaddaya think you're doing?" a guy in a Wal-Mart suit admonished. "Don't you know what's going on here? Don't you realize the position we're in—the opportunity these people are givin' us?"

"Gee, maybe not," I admitted. "Tell us more."

Alabaster took his seat with a smug smile. "Yes, tell him."

"Now, I don't have all the particulars," the business man began, "and we'll have to ask our Intelcor man here for that. But most of us in town here know this college has been going downhill for some time. Look at some of them 'students' they been admittin'. Why you can get in here with an expired fishing license!"

Rollie belted out a big belly laugh, and stole a glance at Harley. But the special ed professor was not amused. He cocked an eyebrow and nodded at Cleaver, whom I suspect he had taught to read. Rollie frowned and looked down at the floor.

"Sure, we may hate to admit it," the vocal local carried on, "but maybe it's time we just pulled the plug on this place. What were those statistics on that there growth industry, Dr. Alabaster? You was tellin' me the other night before the ball game."

Alabaster rose as the suit sat down. "That's a good point to resume our narrative. You see, the ratio is twelve to one."

"Twelve what to one what?" demanded Hazel.

"Convicts to college students. That's what our market data tell us. For every new student who enrolls in an American college today, there are twelve new prison inmates. So for a community with an eye toward economic development..."

He was cut off by a clamor in the hall. A chorus of voices, alto through soprano. Then a pounding on the door.

"Mr. Chairman, perhaps you could go out and see … "

He didn't have to. The door swung open and a dozen stalwart, Midwestern women swept into the room. Some were in aprons, others dressed for the office. The trustees snapped to attention. To a man, they looked up, goggle-eyed.

"Whatever we were doing, I guess it can wait," Gus Lindholm mumbled as Mavis stepped to the fore.

"And so can your dinners," crowed one of the interlopers.

Mavis passed out a stack of stapled documents to the women, who took them to their husbands. "Read this," Mavis instructed, an unlikely Lysystrata with fire in her eye. "Seems to be some sort of master plan for Mayflower, Kansas—and for Hopewell College in the bargain."

I don't know how many of the townies had been privy to this material—Gus Lindholm didn't seem surprised—but there were some wagging heads as they completed the reading assignment.

"It's not that these statistics are wrong," Mavis began.

"No, no, not at all," said a woman in a blue business suit. "Down at the newspaper, I see studies like this all the time. But this is not our study. It comes from out of town."

"That's right," echoed another. "We didn't agree to this. Do we really want a prison on this campus? Or telemarketing jobs downtown? I saw what they've done to Foley's Furniture. They've got it gutted like a warehouse. A shelf all around the walls, desk level, a telephone every ten feet. We wanta work in there?"

"Just who are you, Intelcor, to be planning our town?"

Alabaster erupted. "Mr. Chairman, who invited these people? How'd they get this information? I'm not finished!"

There was silence. And then I heard Harley scrape back his chair. "Well, sir, I'd say you were. You're finished. An' so's Intelcor, at least around this town. We can stick a fork in you. You're done!"

Now the silence was so deep you could hear the water cooler gurgle, as every head at the table swung Harley's way. They all looked mystified. Then someone gave a snort and they all burst into laughter. Even Hazel. And soon Harley was laughing, too.

Alabaster stood there wide-eyed with his notepad, peering down at Harley. Then he gave a shrug and half smiled. What a tribe, such folkways ... He went on to the next page in his notes.

But I got up again. "You know, I've read those stats: 1.6 million prisoners. Highest rate of incarceration in the world. Now let me guess what follows. Prisons for profit. I've read about that business, growing 35 percent a year. But there's something else I've read. You know, I've seen your correspondence. You've been out marketing new prisons, and every major city has turned you down. That's why you're into small towns."

"Where the hell'd you get all that?"

"Where do you think?"

"Who gave you that kind of access to the Heartland File?"

Lindholm stood. "Dean Bradshaw, that's enough. If you can't cooperate, I must ask that you leave. It's ten minutes of five and we haven't begun to address the purpose of this ... "

"N-no, I think we have." Again, Harley scraped his chair back. He looked around the room. "Oh, I know how you see me—good ol' harmless Harley, town clown. But I can't sit here and take this in. Ever since he's been back, we've been sittin' by, watchin', lettin' Matt, here, fight our battles for us. You an' I know that's not the way we do things. It's not right."

"So, what do you propose?" Gus Lindholm asked him.

"A different kind of college. Like one I've seen."

A few heads turned.

"A kind of school where we take students who have special interests, special needs. But we'd look hard at their needs—say, whether they can read." He paused and looked at Rollie. "And we'd take an interest in the subjects that mean something to 'em. Even something weird as witchcraft.

"We'd look closely at these kids, not past 'em—passin' out bogus grades. All that hokum: Harvard of the High Plains. You know, I've seen it work here. A basketball team, in a cult class. I've seen kids grow 'cause someone cared about 'em. It's possible. That's all." He plopped back in his chair.

There was silence again, but no laughter. Hazel sniffled and shifted her chair a mite closer to Harley.

"He's right," I went on. "We could we make a go of this. Especially with the kind of market data Intelcor has. Sure, we'd have to reconstruct the faculty. Quit this jive business of job tenure. Stop teaching just what professors happen to know."

At that, I sat down. The trustees and their wives were looking up with interest. But Calvin Withers, the accountant, was shaking his head. He leaned over and whispered to Gus Lindholm.

"It's a noble thought, all right, but it's not enough," Lindholm said, sadly. "That doesn't solve the financial crisis."

"Just a minute." Alabaster put down his notepad and sat down with the group. "I agree with you on that score, Mr. Chairman. You have a balloon payment coming due in (he glanced at his watch) in thirty-six hours." Then he turned to Harley.

"But I need to say this. I don't believe I've ever heard our philosophy of education at Intelcor put quite so eloquently. And, sir, it sounded like you meant it!"

I heard a few grunts of concurrence.

"So why are you setting us up to shut the school down?" I demanded. "Look, do you all know what's gone on here? I can get you details from the famed Heartland File if you're interested."

Alabaster thrust his head across the table. "I don't know how you busted in that data base, but you got no right... "

"I have every right. Chill out. Sit down. Now, suppose we all try to level with one another. Who the hell came up with the idea of that loan, with the campus as collateral?"

There was deafening silence.

Alabaster sat scowling at me. But he settled back. "You know, you could be right. I've been thinking about what your friend said. Maybe there is a market for another kinda college."

"Then why in hell are you shutting us down?"

"Don't shout at me! Look, Bradshaw, you think I want to operate a prison? I'm an educator. You know that."

"And you're a honcho with Intelcor. So, rework the loan!"

More silence. "I can't."

"Well, it's getting late and looking dark," muttered Lindholm at last. "It's almost five o'clock... "

"And it's Rib Night! Hey, Gus, I believe we're gettin' someplace,"

Rollie exclaimed. "Let's take this meetin' down the road. It's all on the house—as long as you tip Hazel."

I saw her color rise, grinning and cringing. And then she rose slowly, and held up her hand. "Shh, you all! Shh. Listen."

It was the bell, back up on the science hall, tolling and tolling. I felt my eyes brim. I felt the resonance in my bones.

23

We hooked up at the Hoof'n Horn.

"Hey, Matt, Sarah, I got a booth for ya." Rollie grabbed a fistful of red plaid placemats, utensils, and napkins from the "boo-fay" where we'd stocked up on ribs. He nodded toward a cloister of dim-lit booths on the far side of the bar. The acrid pall of smoke lay thick as a dirt storm, but I always liked to sit back there in the barroom. You could see and not be seen. Watch the human drama evolving on the bar stools.

As he toweled off the table and set up the booth, he turned to help us with our plates. "Geez, Bradshaw!" He gaped at mine. "Is this a meal or a contest?"

Then he grinned and kneaded my shoulder. "Ya know, Matt, when you come back out here, I don't guess none of us knew what to expect—some kinda East Coast egghead, whatever. Didn't know, did we Sarah?"

She looked down with a demure smile.

"But hey, big guy, ya always were one to make things happen. An' I'm, I'm just glad…Ah, screw it!" He gave the table a slap with his bar towel and took off down the aisle.

"So, is that what they call 'male bonding'?" Sarah inquired. We ate in silence for a few minutes. Then she looked up at me with a sly smile. She pushed her plate back and gathered up her silverware, and moved around to sit beside me. Just the way we'd sat when we were dating.

"Do you think this is a good idea, Ms. Deaconess? I mean, it's sort of dark back here, but…"

She put down her fork and wrapped me in a very long embrace. Then, in a convincing tone: "People see what they agree to. I think you're learning that, Matt. I am, and we both need to. It's not that we

270

don't believe in other truths—half facts, back in the shadows. It's just that we haven't agreed to make them visible."

"Yeah, but you're a pillar of the church—shapely pillar—and a teacher in this town. All that, and a backstreet lover?"

"Who made a serious mistake. Everybody knew that. Now they can see that I'm letting that be seen."

"I wish they could give that kind of leeway to the college."

Hazel came by on her break. She stood aside, shedding her apron, as Harley came huffing up the aisle, then slid in the booth behind him. He was balancing a plate in each hand, with a longneck Coors clamped in his armpit.

After two beers and a dozen ribs, I was feeling mellow, back here in my home town with my friends. Hazel said she didn't have long to stay. Nor, I thought, did the rest of us at the college. But for now I just wanted to savor the moment.

"Sarah, that was ingenious," Hazel was saying. "How in the world did you get that bell tower repaired so fast!"

"It was the dad of a kid in my drama class, an alum. He put every-thing aside. Got a double crew out there. And there are lots of folks who'd do as much. If we just had some leadership—if they could see what we're trying to do up at the college."

There was a burst of laughter from the dining room, and we craned our heads around the booth. "I don't think I've ever seen Gus Lindholm really smile, much less laugh like that," I marveled. And then we were quiet.

"Thing is, I hate to see you get your hopes up, Matt," Hazel said. "I suspect this is a show for their wives. I heard them talking in the rib line—those town dads—and they weren't so jolly. And look at that little number cruncher, Calvin Withers."

I saw him. "You're right. He just keeps shaking his head. And I guess I've begun to understand why."

For the rest of Hazel's break, I recapped what I thought I under-stood. How ten years before, when the college almost went bankrupt, the biggest creditors were awarded seats on the board of trustees. They'd decided to call in Intelcor, hotshots in the business of enroll-ment management, to turn the place around.

That's when Julian Reid was brought in as president, since it was his parishioners who were carrying most of the debt. Not only God's anointed, he was Intelcor's man, as well, his major qualification being that he didn't know squat about running a school.

"Unconscious incompetence."

"No, I'd say it was more like 'conscious incompetence,' Harley. Julian Reid was a sensitive, intelligent man, to those who cared to look beneath that nervous grin. And he suffered for what he was told to do—signing away the campus on that loan."

I said Julian must have come to believe that all the problems were his doing. He saw himself in some crazy, cultic context as the obsolescent leader, old and over. The king who must die.

"And so he did," said Hazel. She blotted her eyes on her apron as she was getting up to put it on. Sarah was sniffling. Rollie blew his nose.

"And then," Hazel gripped her bar towel, "to succeed him, they came up with the most genuinely unconscious incompetent … "

"That's right, Hazel. Old News-Weather-and-Sports, Roger Squire, was to preside over the demise of the college, turning it over to Intelcor for a prison. It was easy enough to sell him as a candidate: just another minister on call.

"And it might yet work. These guys could recoup their bad loans and then some. If the college goes bankrupt, the prime creditors will have first dibs on the assets—the computers and all that.

"But, Hazel, before you take off—I've been thinking we still might have a slim chance. I mean, there was a lot of good energy back in that board room. Now, this may be a long shot at the buzzer. But here's what I'd like you to do … "

Sarah and I sat awhile in silence, after Hazel and Harley moved on. Diddling a bit beneath the table, if the truth be known. I was eyeing the bar, savoring these moments until the ax would fall. There was Harley on his favorite stool. He seemed to like that spot by the kitchen door, when Hazel was working. I watched her bustle through the swinging door. This time, as she went by, she gave him a rap on the rear with her bar towel.

Sarah was tracing a line along my knee with her left hand, sipping the dregs of a Coors draw with the other. "You know, Matt, you're right. There is a new energy. And that's something." But she slumped back. "Even if there's no hope for the college."

"Well, I guess we'll be finding out soon. You know, I wonder if Alabaster ever made it out here. The last time I saw him … "

My eye lit on a figure at the far end of the bar. A big guy with a sun-bronzed complexion. Sort of a Tex-Mex hue about him. He wore a tall black Stetson, unfaded blue jeans, and Western boots. The boots were bright tan, shiny. His plaid shirt had creases, fresh out of the box.

As I watched, he swung down from his bar stool and turned our way, a longneck Coors in hand. "Aw naw. It couldn't be … "

"Hey, y'all mind if I join you? You remember the old Groucho Marx gag, don't you? Your line is, 'Why, are we coming apart?'"

"Uh, Sarah, may I present my one-time dean in grad school. And, more recently, my adversary in the coaching ranks."

She stared at him in the dim light, eyes like saucers. "Not Harold Alabaster!" With a whimsical smile, he sat down.

"You know, Harold, Hal … what do your friends call you?"

Alabaster flashed a glance beneath the brim of his sombrero. "Call me 'Hope.'"

"Surely not for 'Hopewell!'" Sarah marveled.

"More like 'Great Gray Hope,'" I muttered. "You know, Hope, there's something I've been intending to tell you." I paused for a deep breath, a swig of beer. "Next to Cynthia—Alabaster, I believe you are the most enigmatic individual I've ever known."

He sat for a time. Took a draw of his beer, hunching toward me. He scrutinized me, slit-eyed. "I can be anything," he muttered. "And so can Intelcor. Could be you're catchin' on."

I pondered that statement. "But I still cannot fathom why you'd give up a position like you had at Eastbourne to come all the way out here."

"Huh. No, I guess you wouldn't. But you still say you know all about Intelcor, nosin' in them files. Shee-it! You know how many years I been a dean? How long you think a man can take that, signin' his name all day with a fountain pen, fencing with them fops on the faculty. You ever hear of burnout? That's why we started Intelcor.

Career administrators, bored out of our skulls. And why'm I out here for a spell? Put it this way, why are you?"

"Well, Hope," I glanced at Sarah. "In addition to some personal affinities, I happen to love this life out here. I mean … "

"And of course it's only you and your kind see that." Alabaster bristled, his voice rising as some wranglers turned our way from the bar. "Folks like me, we don't aspire to such as … "

Then he settled back with a dark laugh and lowered his hat brim. "Look here, shit-kicker. That might be all the revelation ya get outta me, now that we's in competition."

I crouched low, under his hat brim, catching his eyes. "And why is that?"

"Why's what?" asked Hazel as she leaned in over the table. "Meeting starts in ten minutes, back dining room. Gus asked me to come by and tell you. And, Matt, I did poll the trustees, serving their beers. In the presence of their wives, as you said.

"And you were right. They're all willing to write off those bad debts if we can just save the campus—get past that loan."

Alabaster slowly lifted his brim and peered at her in wonder. Not just at the news, but at the transformation of a math professor to a cocktail waitress. It was his turn to ponder an enigma.

"So, what were you two disputing? Do I know this fellow?"

"It's why we have to be competitors out here," I told her as I got up from the booth. I didn't introduce him.

I headed for the men's room, trailing Hazel and a couple of her townie friends.

"But if it comes to that or a prison in the heart of town," the lady was exclaiming, "I know which way I'm voting. And also my councilman-spouse!" She had him by the necktie.

As he broke free for the bathroom, the woman whispered to Hazel. "So, what do you think will happen? Here they were, these trustee fellas, laughing and ragging all during supper—having all kindsa good time. But their faces fell like my figure at forty, when it came time to reconvene the meeting."

"But what about jobs?" a townie demanded. In the pine-paneled dining room, the meeting was off to a heated start. There was a speaker's table where Gus Lindholm sat. I looked for Alabaster. He was sitting in the rear, with his hat on.

"You know, even if we save the school, you're talking about letting more faculty go," the vocal local continued. "Where are they going to find work?"

"Well, there's always that telemarketing center," Gus muttered, shaking his head.

Alabaster looked solemn, as well. He grabbed his cell phone from his brief case and gave it a poke.

"You know, that's the third time he's done that since he came in here," I told Sarah.

"Why does he keep stabbing at his telephone?"

"He's hitting a button—transferring his calls to his voice mail. Although I'll bet if it's some top honcho at Intelcor, they can buzz him, make him pick it up. We'll see."

"Yes, well, friends, we've had our fun," Gus Lindholm started. He paused and peered at the chandelier, then down at his shoes. He sorted his notes. "We've had … " he tried to speak, but turned away. Drew a handkerchief from his back pocket. He blew his nose. When he turned back around, his face was crimson.

"All right, this isn't easy, but sometimes some things must be done. So, now it's come upon us. Folks, it's time to close … "

I waited for a chorus of "Nos!" and "Whys?" "Not close the college!" But the atmosphere was like the aftermath of a hot air balloon race.

"You see, there's no getting around the loan that's due. In a matter of hours. How many hours, Dr. Alabaster, thirty-six?"

The Great Gray One glanced at his watch. "More like thirty-four," he said.

"But Gus," I stood up. "Can't we at least try to negotiate?"

He nodded at Alabaster, who stared back at him glumly.

Slowly, the Intelcor exec in Levi's got to his feet. "The reason is … " He shook his head and reached for his satchel. Seizing his cell phone, he poked it one more time. He said it was the sad reality of the modern corporation. They were beholden to their stockholders, and he said he didn't mean that in a personal sense.

"The investors are not people. They're mutual funds, pension funds, other corporations. No one owns stock as an individual anymore. So we've got computers constantly monitoring our performance. We're tied into a network of efficiency analysts. Again, not even people—data systems, just like the Heartland File."

"So, even if you wanted to ... "

"And I do, God damnit, Bradshaw. You mothafu ... "

"Don't interrupt him," Hazel hollered. "He's our next president, if we can figure out a way to save the college. Am I right about that, you trustees?"

There was a thunder of "Ayes."

I glanced at Sarah and she squeezed my arm.

"And Harley's dean," I added.

There were enough "Ayes" to carry. And then another sound in the background: BREEP, BREEP, BREEP, BREEP.

Like a fire alarm, but it wasn't from the ceiling. It was a piercing sound—people plugged their ears. BREEP, BREEP. It was Alabaster's cell phone. He lunged for his satchel.

It took a few seconds for him to punch in a code: online to Intelcor. I watched his eyebrows slowly furrow as his color turned from Tex-Mex to magenta.

"They've what? Overrun the firewalls ... you're calling me from a pay phone?"

Alabaster threw the phone down and spun around. "I don't know if anyone here has heard of 'Spamming.' It's a new telecom, terrorist practice and somebody's targeted Intelcor. We're in deep sh ... real trouble. Some bunch called 'The Covenant of the Goddess.' Chapters all over hell. They're flooding us with mailing lists, newsletters, phone numbers. Inundating our Intranet. Another twenty minutes, we'll be past tense. Out of business."

There was a murmur of amazement. This was like a crisis from another planet.

"What they want is the name of the individual who gave the order for the spamming. Then they'll shut it down. They say it's a prominent witch. Some senior neopagan. Somebody in this town. Now, can anyone come forward? Does anybody know the individual?"

I'd drafted a note by the time he got that far—an agreement to cancel the loan. I began scanning the room for a lawyer.

I said, "Ask them if you're authorized to take this action, Hope. They need to void the loan, forgive the debt. Give us back our campus. And then all of that will need to be verified."

I found the lawyer in the back row, asked her to come get on the phone. She talked for a minute, then turned to us, her hand over the receiver. "They're faxing us the authorization, from Kinko's. It seems their copiers are out of commission."

In five minutes, we had it all done. I asked Alabaster for his cell phone so I could give Intelcor the name of the Spammer, to call off the Covenant of the Goddess. He threw it at me.

I took the phone out to the feed lot, well out of earshot from the others. Not everybody needed to know the name of the Grand Warlock. In a town like this, you looked past things.

Di-Di-Di-Boom-Boom.

I'd no sooner got our draft beers and started for the back booth than the drum roll came thundering from the juke box. A dozen of us headed out to the dance floor.

> "You say you're feelin' down,
> So tired of searching 'round.
> But look up, don't be cryin'
> She's comin' down the line!"

There was a certain standard practice in a line dance. You spent the first verse and chorus with "the one that brung ya." And then you were off, changing partners.

I watched Sarah's moves, already regretting that I'd lose her to the line dance. Saturday-night-Sarah had a subtle force about her. Head down, shoulders steady. An offbeat stomp that shivered your spine—and triggered a mass reaction.

WHOMP! The floor shook as we took off in a turnout. I spun round and there was Hazel. Next verse, Mavis. Then a wisp of a woman in a business suit—the lawyer. By now I was kickin' it, even conversing. "Way to go, Matt! Hey, Pres, we're with ya, win or tie!"

About then, I encountered my next partner. She came reeling around the guy ahead and hit me with a body slam. "WHOOF! Oh, hi there, Bev! Say, who are you out with?"

She grinned and gave a nod to a fellow in the next row. I glanced over my shoulder, saw the nose encased in a plaster cast. "Hey, Walt. How ya feeling?" He only gave a half nod, but I can't say he looked unhappy. Bev had time to tell me Jeb was going home tomorrow, before barreling off to the next partner.

And that was how we spent the night: Dancing, drinking, ribbing.

"Hey, can this really be?
Just look at who came free!"

It was late in the evening, in a slow, soulful dance, when I looked down at Sarah. She smiled and nestled her head against my shoulder. Same as always.

But then she pulled away. "Oh, Matt, do you really believe we can do this?"

I was silent for a few bars. "Well, I guess it's like Jeb says. 'One hundred percent of the shots you don't take don't go in.'"

"And what about Intelcor? Do you think you can keep them in line? That Alabaster!"

"Sarah, they're marketing professionals, and that's what we need. But they're also our consultants, and we're in control. Hey, we'll draw up a contract. Just as long as we're clear about…"

I looked up just then, past the dance floor. Down the bar, back in the shadows. I saw his Stetson, then the woman who was with him. She was a tall blonde. Leaning into him. Listening intently. And slowly twisting her hair.

William Charland is a graduate of Yankton College, with a master's degree from Yale University and a doctorate from the Chicago Theological Seminary. He is the author of six non-fiction books and another novel, *Soundings*. Bill and his wife, Phoebe Lawrence, live in Silver City, New Mexico where he directs the Honors Program at Western New Mexico University.

Printed in the United States
202243BV00004B/7-24/P